"Honey," she said, looking straight into Alecia's eyes, "I can only take blood to live." She waited for the inevitable fear to creep into her baby girl's face, for Alecia to draw away in horror at what she was and how she had to live. Nothing happened. Alecia just looked at her with the same trusting expression she always had. *She's afraid of me*, she thought.

Oh, God. If Alecia bolted from her now she would have no protection from Nolan. *This is hard*, she thought. *I have to make her understand what I am without her being afraid of me.*

Were those tears on Alecia's face or was water dripping from her wet hair?

Oh, God. *What was she?*

Jeanine bowed her head. The shame of what she was now and how far she had fallen was just too much. Alecia's love for her had become the core of her life, her very existence. If she lost that, what would be the use in going on? Cold tears, like when Nolan beat her, started to drip down her cheeks. She felt so totally alone. Alecia reached her tiny hands for her. Her own little face had drawn up in tears. Tears for her, Jeanine thought.

"Don't cry," the little girl said.

Jeanine thought again of the little picture Alecia had drawn for her. The both of them together. Safe. Happy. Free from Nolan and the likes of the blood cult. Blood spurting from the sacrifices, she vividly remembered. Years upon years upon years of blood. People dying.

What was she?

DISCLAIMER:

This storyline deals with vampyric blood drinking people and includes scenes where the characters drink blood, hunt for blood, kill for blood, or shed blood. It is not our desire to promote fear yet it is human nature to have an adverse reaction to blood drinking. This is why we refer to these living people as having a vampyric medical condition. They are not undead nor occultic. While violence may be present, it is never glorified. These people survive as best they can under difficult and bitter conditions. Any that survive any length of time become efficient predators.

Rites of Passage

by

Douglas Robinson

Without Love
Nothing
Changes

TM

SILENTLY PUBLISHING
Birmingham Alabama

RITES OF PASSAGE

A SILENTLY SERIES NOVEL
BOOK TWO – MODERN DAY

Rites of Passage
Published by Silently Publishing

Cover Art © 2012 Sam Wall   www.samwall.com

Library of Congress Control Number: 2013907286

ISBN 978-1-62551-003-7
ISTC

TRADE PAPER EDITION: August 2013

Printed in the United States of America.

10 9 8 7 6 5 4 3 2 1

This is a work of fiction. Names, characters, places, and incidents either are the product of the author's imagination or are used fictitiously, and any resemblance to actual persons, living or dead, business establishments, events, or locales is entirely coincidental. The publisher does not have any control over and does not assume any responsibility for third-party websites or their content.

Silently Publishing
PO Box 11732
Birmingham AL   35202-1732
United States

ISNI 0000 0003 7313 132X Douglas Robinson
ISNI 0000 0003 7313 1290 Silently Publishing

www.silently-publishing.com

DEDICATION

For Alecia and sojourners everywhere

The SILENTLY Series Storyline

Modern Day

Silently Comes The Night
Rites of Passage
With Deadly Intent
Overkill

Eve of Delusion
Shadow-Wielders
D'mirri's Curse
Flight 7486

Sacrifices
Heaven's Gate
No Safe Haven
Beddia's Endgame

Historical

Majken's Story
Ester's Song
Scot's Lament
Lost Voyage of the St. Therese Marie

Prolog

The young man found himself running. Thomas Kline reached for a nearby tree to balance himself on the primordial path. Faint ribbons of bright moonlight sliced through the thick canopy above. He was overheated and panting, a sure sign of exhaustion, but he could not stop. Through the distance, a piercing howl reached his hearing. Mournful and desolate, the sound rattled his chest.

The hunters were coming for him.

He started downhill in the mossy, wet undergrowth. His ankle twisted sharply as he slipped on a protruding rock. He bit back a cry and kept moving. The path narrowed into a gully at the bottom of the hill. This was not good, he thought. He should have gone uphill. His thinking was clouded. He picked his way beyond the larger rocks and fallen limbs in his path. It was darker and harder to see here.

In his mind, *her* face appeared.

Sometimes her visage smiled at him, the girl he thought he loved. Mary Harris, or so he believed. Yet the girl he had fallen for was not the person he thought she was. Her long chestnut hair swayed in an invisible current, but her dark violet eyes always reached for him.

This time there was a touch of sadness along the creases of her eyes.

He thought he loved her, but his life suddenly when wrong. Horribly wrong.

The path beyond the gully was barely passable. He could almost see the tendrils of mist that drifted upwards from the bramble strewn embankment. Thomas pushed through the undergrowth with his hands, desperate to reach safety – safety somewhere. Another piercing howl reached him. Then joined by another hunter coming for him. Some primal instinct told him to find a large piece of wood to use as a club, find a steep rock face to hold his back so he only need defend the front, and make a stand for his life. The rocks in his path would be next to useless. He might be able to pry a few loose and throw them, but digging them out would take far too long. Time he did not have.

Beyond the thick undergrowth, the path again cleared and turned clockwise before him going uphill. He willed himself to run, to leap, to fly uphill. The painful stitch in his side below his ribcage told him he was spent. He could not say how long he had been running. With monumental effort, he pushed his body uphill again. Between gasps, his thoughts turned dark.

He did not know where he was going.

To stop and give up now would mean sure death. The wolves were nearer now, he could almost sense them. The skin on his arm prickled into goosebumps, but this was no fun scare – a rush of adrenaline, then a laugh with friends. This was the real thing.

He laughed to himself bitterly. The sound in his throat came as a death rattle, a cross between coughing up blood and a wracking heave of trying to vomit and nothing is there.

Little by little the canopy overhead was allowing more moonlight through. His heart was uplifted in the bright clearing ahead, although only briefly.

He found himself on the face of a cliff lined with sharp rocks. The scars on his hands and forearms were reminders of where he had been dashed again and again. The bright full moonlight a hand's breadth above the horizon flooded the forest landscape around him.

He was trapped and he knew it.

It was too late to go back the way he came.

There was nothing to fight with here. Nowhere to go. The muted wind rushed over the bare rock facing, dropping abruptly to the forest floor below. He did not know what was over that ledge, but he imagined jagged rocks like he had seen in pictures engulfed in sea foam and fury.

A nearby low growl chilled his blood.

Yellow-gold eyes glowed from the shadows.

The hunters had come for him.

He moved with exaggerated slowness.

As the wolves approached him, the leader was snarling and Thomas backed as close to the edge of the drop-off as he dared. He was too timid to throw himself to his doom, but he believed he could sidestep the attack and possibly escape.

Her faint laughter drifted on the wind screaming up the rock cliff to his back. He saw her again in his mind, the smiling friend he thought he had found at school. He remembered walking with her to her class, escorting her to her dorm, meeting her in the cafeteria or student lounge in the afternoon.

Then the image changed.

He saw her face awash with golden lamplight as she lay naked on top of him; his body covered in a thin sheen of sweat, her pale skin as cool as the night. They had just made love. He remembered her moving his arms above his head and tightening her grip until it became unbreakable iron.

In his mind he remembered. Her other free hand drifted over the edge of the table. Now he remembered the slight sound of ripping surgical tape. The small glint of the knife in the lamplight he saw out of the corner of his eye was insignificant compared to her smiling face close to his.

Yet, now her face held great sadness.

She whispered her real name. Majken.

What's this? he thought.

She said, *I must take something from you to survive.*

Then she cut his shoulder with the knife.

She held him fast as she started to lap the blood that pooled on his skin from the wound. He had learned too late that she was a real vampyr. Human, yet not human, forced to live by blood alone. She said she did not intend to attack him, but her recent association with a killer vampyr – a man he later learned was named John – had driven her blood needs much higher than they would have been normally.

She did not mean to hurt him, but she did indirectly when John kidnapped him to use him as bait to deal with her. She did try to save his life, but in fighting John, she was badly cut across her abdomen. Her blood must have seeped into his open wounds as they struggled to find shelter together.

The wolves charged toward him together and he screamed.

Thomas awoke in his own bed at his parent's home. He felt flushed with a cold sweat. Did he cry out this time? He found the bedsheet had twisted and coiled around his torso. He only slept with pajama bottoms now. His chest was bare.

His fingers seemed to tingle and his hands felt strangely numb. When he balanced himself in the middle of his bed, his left hand slid across something wet. Along his left arm, his own blood seeped into his bed clothes. His own left arm smarted below his elbow, like he had jabbed himself with a nail or something, in his sleep. Pink scar tissue was below his elbow.

The bright light of a nearly full moon made the floor of his bedroom glow through the gauzy curtains his mother insisted he have in his bedroom.

Thomas pushed himself to the edge of his bed and swung his feet to the cold wooden floor of his bedroom. His bedroom was on the second floor with his sister, two rooms down. His parents slept on the ground floor. The late August breeze through the slightly open window felt good to him. His senses opened to the night. He turned on the small lamp next to his bed. A single expletive escaped from his lips. His bed sheet was smeared with his own blood. Thomas quickly bundled the sheet, with his own pajama bottoms also stained with blood, and looked for a place to put them. He stuffed the sheet under his bed, for now, reached his dresser and pulled on fresh underwear. No sounds in the sleeping household meant that no one heard him. This time.

He walked to his small adjoining personal bathroom – one of the advantages of having a father who is an architect design your own home – and splashed cold water from the sink on his face. The mirror light glared brightly at him and he snapped it off.

Everything I told you about myself is regrettably true, she had said.

He washed the blood off his arm as best he could, then walked to his bedroom window to look out at the night sky. Outside, the gentle swaying of neighborhood elm and poplar whispered to him.

This was just a minor setback, he thought to himself. Everything will be all right. You will be okay. It's understandable you would have a case of the nerves after the brush with death you had as Majken battled John.

Thomas gripped the cheery white facing of his window sill. "You're going to be all right," he told no one but himself.

PART I

THE WOLF AT MORN

Chapter One

"Wake up, sleepy head!" Thomas heard his sister pound on his bedroom door twice before she skipped downstairs to family breakfast. Thomas was sitting in the camping chair next to his stripped mattress. He must have dozed off. Too bright sunlight, a glorious morning, shone outside his bedroom window.

It was actually a very good day.

Just three days past his twenty-fourth birthday, he slipped on the new fancy watch his parents had given him. It had dials for everything and it was supposed to be waterproof down to fifty feet underwater. He smiled when he thought of the festivities approaching the next holiday weekend and all. People in Sumter would be celebrating for Labor Day with cooking, football, and visiting relatives you only see twice a year anyway.

Somehow the thoughts of breakfast, and his mother's famous buttermilk and blueberry pancakes were not filling him with joy. He felt faintly sick. He pulled on a shirt, blue jeans, and sneakers, then tried to make himself presentable in his bathroom mirror.

Dark circles were under his eyes. His mouth was completely dry. He felt like something their beloved Golden Labrador Retriever Bud used to drag in – a ragged doll with most of the stuffing chewed out of it. Bud went to dog heaven his senior year in high school. Yet he remembered the dog fondly. Thomas splashed cold water on his face, raked his fingers through his ash brown hair, and tried to put on a presentable face for his mother and the pancake ordeal. She would expect him to eat at least six or more. Feeling presentable, he went downstairs.

Patricia Kline, his mother, was doing her Betty Crocker impression in the kitchen by serving steaming pancakes on the buffet. She was wearing a red and white checked apron. "Good morning," she said, as he came by and went to the refrigerator.

Donald Kline, his father, sat at the head of the table and his face was in the morning paper. Kim was eating her pancakes like there was no tomorrow. She was dressed in her carpentry clothes, her hair was in a pony tail and her tool belt was next to the door.

"Morning," Thomas said lowly.

He reached for the ice water pitcher and a glass in the cupboard above the sink and poured himself a glass of ice water. Without stopping to sit down first, he drank almost the entire glass of water, refilled the glass, then sat down at the family table.

Donald glanced at him by lowering his morning paper; his readers had slipped halfway down his nose. Balding prematurely in his early fifties, his blue eyes were lined with laughter and Thomas remembered business partners that had to adapt to his father's rather dry sense of humor. Momma said in her youth, The most risky thing Donald did was marry me.

"Going job hunting today?" he inquired.

Thomas nodded. Since he had come home from Trenton, finding a job or returning to school had been his father's new favorite topic.

Kim smirked at Thomas.

He made a face back at her. At least she was holding up the family honor by working so soon after her graduation from high school. Patricia smiled at her son as she placed the first plate of pancakes in front of him, with thick bacon like he liked and real maple syrup. He tried to hide the wave of nausea that caused his stomach to roll. She placed a glass of freshly squeezed orange juice in front of him. He smelled the tang of the orange rinds in the garbage disposal. His mother believed in fresh, not frozen. He took a sip of the orange juice, not a gulp, just to please his mother. "Where are you going today, dear?" Patricia asked him. He sat numbly for a moment. He was supposed to be job hunting and he had not given it even the first thought.

"Kimbrell's," he said without thinking.

His sister gawked at him. A retail store?

Patricia's brown eyes warmed and she took her place next to her husband. She curled her ash blonde hair, now turning gray, behind her ear.

What was he saying?

He pictured his mother thinking of the time she dressed him up in his "little man" suit and took him with her to sell Avon products. He had hated suits ever since and any kind of selling job. His mother calmly sipped her morning cappuccino. "Why don't I call Starla and put in a good word for you."

Donald glanced at his wife. "Good idea," he said, then went back to his paper.

"Uh," Thomas quickly said, "I'd rather get the job on my own merits. I don't want them to be pressured to hire me if business is slow right now."

Kim drank the last of her milk, then stood up abruptly from the table. "Mom, I've got to be there before eight!"

Patricia stood and took off her Betty Crocker apron. She retrieved her purse from the lowest kitchen cabinet and told Thomas, "Dear, just put your dishes in the sink. I'll cleanup when I get back." She picked her keys off the key rack in the vestibule leading to the back door.

"Kimberly, be safe," Donald called to her as she grabbed her tool belt and bounced out the back door behind her mother.

Donald lay down his paper and looked at Thomas. He motioned to Thomas and spoke in a low conspiratorial voice, "Are you really going to Kimbrell's for a job?"

"Not unless I can help it," Thomas replied.

"Didn't think so," he said. "I'll run interference with your mother."

Thomas grinned, actually relieved. He set his plate of pancakes, barely touched, on the kitchen counter. He retrieved the keys to his Honda off the key rack and checked his wallet.

"Hey, Dad. Can I borrow a ten? I think I need gas."

Donald humphed, and said, "What, borrow?" but produced his wallet and gave Thomas the money he asked for. He smiled at his father, waved, and strode out the back door. The small deck on the east side of the house was brightly lit by the morning sun. When Thomas stepped into the sunlight, the sun seemed excessively bright. He winced and shielded his eyes with his hand and went to his car parked in the shade to his right. The autumn air was crisp and cool to his senses. Somewhere, nearby, he guessed someone was burning leaves. Several miles away, on highway 521, Thomas passed a man in his yard raking burning leaves.

Thomas first stopped by a Fred's store and looked for cleaning products. A black lady who worked in the store came over to see if she could help him.

"I need something to take out blood stains," he said.

The woman looked up and down the aisle with him. "Blood stains," she repeated. She found a small applicator. "You rub this on the spot and soak in cold water."

"Don't you have anything bigger," he asked.

The saleslady stared at him. "Bigger? How much blood you thinkin' of cleaning up?"

Thomas instantly became wary.

"I cut myself pretty bad while helping my father outside a few days ago. I used one of my mother's favorite towels because it was handy. I'd hate for her to have to throw it away."

The woman seemed to notice the scars on his palms. Scars where he had caught himself on the sharp rocks where John had pushed him again and again. He closed his eyes for a moment respite. His lie came too glibly and too easily for his conscience.

"We don't have nothin' that can clean up a stain that size. You'd best take it to a professional cleaners and see what they'd do with it." Thomas bought a roll of plastic bags and left the store. Midweek traffic was sparse in town this time of day. Most everyone was working or going back to school after the summer.

A few old men sitting on a nearby bench in front of a convenience store were watching him. They seemed to be soaking up the sun.

Thomas left the parking lot, and stopped at the next gas station on his right. He filled his tank and paid his tab. He drove on the main boulevard until he found the Broad Street turn off to the VA clinic. The small squat brick building was surrounded on three sides by parking lots. Thomas chose a lot that appeared to be for patients, gathered his courage, and strode inside.

Two men were in the small waiting room. One man, a small man, had no limb below his right knee. The man next to him was on an oxygen tank. He could push the tank with a little stroller.

A huge black lady spoke from behind the window. "Can I help you?"

Thomas turned. He leaned down to speak through the little opening in the window. "I want to see a doctor. I'm not feeling well." The lady gave him a clipboard with sheaves of paper to fill out. A medical questionnaire. Confidentiality form. Employer and insurance information. He filled in all except the employer and insurance information part of the forms and gave them back to the receptionist. Another, stern looking woman had joined her at the counter.

After a while, the stern looking woman called him to the window. "Mr. Kline," she said. "You did not fill in the insurance information on your paperwork."

She started to hand the paperwork back to him. Thomas waved it back. "I don't want this on insurance." He checked himself. "I mean, I don't have insurance."

The woman seemed to stare at him. "The fee to see the doctor is one hundred and fifty dollars, plus the lab work fees." Thomas stammered, "All I have is a hundred."

"Your total should be about three-eighty counting lab work. Do you have a credit card?"

Thomas hesitated, then fished his wallet out of his pocket. His checking account at home was tied to his mother's account. While at school they had kept a student credit card for him for incidental expenses – but most of his living expenses, food, and so forth came from the account his father maintained.

Any large expense, like a doctor visit, or lab work, would stick out like a sore thumb. He sighed. He needed medical help – if he could even begin to explain what he thought was wrong with him. Maybe they would find something that could be reversed. He gave the attendant the credit card. She recorded the information on a credit card release slip and passed it through the window for him to sign.

In a little bit, the man with oxygen was called to the treatment rooms. Thomas watched the clock. About forty-five minutes later, the next man was called back. When he had been sitting there almost an hour, a nurse with a pleasant face and frosted blonde hair came to the outer door and called his name.

Thomas rose quickly and entered the door.

She escorted him to a seat to take his blood pressure and pulse, then asked him what his complaint was.

To say he was a little nauseated seemed too vague. To say he hardly wanted to even think about food was too abnormal. To say he was thirsty all the time seemed insignificant. "I don't feel well, like, in my stomach."

The nurse made a note of his comment, led him to an empty treatment room, placed his file in the door file holder, and closed the door. Thomas sat on a paper roll out sheet and crossed his legs at the ankles. The room was a little cool, but not freezing.

There was nothing to do in the little room except look at the pictures of sea gulls and a cut-away drawing of a person's heart, lungs, and upper torso. He heard a man's footsteps outside his door, he judged about two rooms down. The soles of his shoes were likely smooth leather, maybe designer shoes. He wasn't much of a shoe person anyway. There seemed to be a faint click to the man's steps. Maybe he had stepped on a tack somewhere and it was still embedded in his heel.

Thomas waited. More clicking. One door down. More waiting. Then Thomas heard a man approach, tap on the treatment room door, then come inside. A middle-aged man with short blonde hair and a stethoscope came inside. His name plate said, REYNOLDS.

"Mr. Kline?" the doctor said. He was looking at the paper Thomas had filled out. "My name is Dr. Reynolds." He extended his hand. "What is your birth date?"

"August 29th, 1969," he said.

"Well, Thomas. You've just had a birthday. What can I do for you?"

Thomas sighed inwardly, then pressed in. "I haven't felt well for the last three weeks. I'm nauseated sometimes. I don't think I'm sleeping very well either."

The doctor touched his throat, feeling of the glands in his neck, then checked his heart and breathing. He then asked Thomas to lie down and felt of his abdomen with cold hands. Nothing hurt, although the probing did tickle a little. He tried to keep a serious face. Dr. Reynolds made a note on the chart.

"I'm going to order some blood work, check CBCs, a basic profile."

Thomas at once wanted to ask a million questions, but he did not know how to begin. "When I was up north –" he began. In his mind, he finished the statement – faced a homicidal vampyr and was exposed to another vampyr's blood in the fight.

He rubbed at his eyes with his fingers.

"I guess I'm just tired, too."

The doctor seemed to just notice the scars on his palms and lower arms. "How'd you get these?" he asked.

"When I was up north, I had an accident. I fell out of my car on the expressway."

The doctor looked him in the eye.

"How does one fall out of their own car?"

My girlfriend pushed me, he thought.

"Some guys in my class and I were fooling around. My door just came open and I fell." Dr. Reynolds examined the scars in more detail.

"How fast where you going?"

About a hundred and twenty, he thought. "Forty."

"Well," Dr. Reynolds said, "you were very lucky."

Tell me about it.

The doctor made a few more notes on his file. "When did you have your last bowel movement?"

Three weeks ago, Thomas thought. "Two days."

"How is your sleeping?"

Barely. "I wake up a few times in the night."

Dr. Reynolds smiled.

"I'm sure we can find what's wrong with you. Just relax. An orderly will be here in a moment to collect a blood sample." With that, he left Thomas and closed the door. The promised orderly arrived in about five minutes. He was a young man. He had seen this man help the patient with oxygen into the treatment rooms. "What is your name?" he asked.

Thomas answered.

"What is your birth date?"

Thomas answered again.

"Would you roll up your sleeves, please?"

Thomas complied. The orderly placed his cart next to him and began poking at his veins at the bend in his elbow. Thomas examined the venipuncture cart. The cart he carried was blue, and filled with sterile tubes, and an assortment of things to stick you with. It looked kinda like the cart his mother used to do crafts and painting with.

Finally selecting Thomas' right arm, he placed a blue constricting band around his upper arm, asked him to make a fist, then prepared the needle to stick him.

He felt only a minor stick. The orderly filled three tubes full of blood. Thomas watched his own blood spurt into the little tubes. He'd had his blood drawn a few other times in his life, but it never really seemed to be this *interesting*.

With that, the orderly disposed of the needle, snapped the blue rubber band off his arm, and carried the little tubes of Thomas' blood with him. Thomas wondered what they do with three tubes of blood when maybe only one was needed.

Thomas heard the same clicking footfalls ten minutes, eleven seconds, and thirty milliseconds later. He knew precisely. He had used the stopwatch timer on his new watch.

Dr. Reynolds reappeared in the door. He carried Thomas' file. He wore a doctor smile. "Your blood workup was fine, except for a slightly elevated white blood cell count."

Thomas asked, "What does that mean?"

"You seem to have a mild infection," the doctor said. He flipped through a few sheaves of paper. "Nothing, really, to be concerned about. We should be able to treat this with a broad spectrum antibiotic." Dr. Reynolds scribbled something that looked remarkably like Kimberly's scrawling on a prescription pad and gave the little page to Thomas.

Just take two of these, and call me in the morning, Thomas thought. "Thank you, Dr. Reynolds."

Dr. Reynolds smiled and shook Thomas' hand. "Nice to meet you, Thomas. If you don't feel better in two weeks, call the office and make another appointment."

Thomas left the VA clinic with a foreboding impression. There was nothing anyone, any doctor or medical specialist, could do for him.

Kimberly nailed the fitted plywood in the corner section where she was working to the nearby scream of a ripping saw. All over the new little house the carpentry crew was busy measuring, fitting, nailing, sawing, and bringing the small frame house up.

"Your brother is a looney tune," her coworker shouted over the din. Her coworker, a rail thin young man named Peter, mopped at his face with a bandana and handed her the next finished piece to be nailed in place.

Kim took the piece of wood and laid it next to the piece she had just nailed.

"He is not," she asserted.

Peter put his gloves back on and held his palms up in his defense. "Hey," he said, "don't get steamed at me. I'm just telling you, since he came home from school he's not the same person he was before he left."

Kim aimed her hammer at the small finishing nail and whacked at it with great vengeance. It bent. She bit back a swear word she had learned on the job and turned the claw end of her hammer to pull the nail. Momma didn't like for her to sound like a sailor. So unlady like.

She turned with a sour expression on her face to Peter.

"Nothing's wrong with him," she said pointedly. "He just needed a break from his studies for a while. He said he was just burned out." Kimberly turned back to the piece she was working on and nailed it correctly.

"Yeah," Peter replied. "Then why does he spend his time staring out into space all the time." A loud thunk sounded behind them. In the noise, it barely registered. "I passed him in the mall last week and he was sitting in the dining area. I said, Hey, and he just sat there looking straight ahead. He didn't even respond."

Kimberly holstered her hammer in her tool belt and placed her hand on her hip. What Peter had said needled in her thinking. Thomas had come home suddenly. He was different in some way. She had noticed, where he was normally outgoing and friendly and generally talkative, her brother had become quiet and moody. "I guess he just has something on his mind," she admitted.

Peter said, "I didn't mean to make you mad. He's my friend, too. I graduated with him. Something's different about him now."

Kimberly glanced around Peter, looking for the master carpenter in charge of the job.

"Why don't you find out what's bothering him?" Peter asked. "Finding out things is what you do, isn't it?"

Referring to her dream of being a real journalist.

Kimberly brightened. "Yes," she said.

"We get off the job at three today," Peter added. "The sooner you find out what's bothering him, the sooner we can have our old Thomas back."

The sky had clouded somewhat before Kimberly called her mother to come pick her up. She was hot and sweaty and felt grungy, but also well satisfied. She had apparently inherited her father's love of angles and dimension and space and textures. Whether she was helping building a real house for someone, or helping by looking at the angles, dimensions, space, and textures of the events around her, she felt whole in a way that defied description.

She was doing what she was meant to do.

Momma pulled up in her new Trans Sport. The back had been crammed with groceries. Kimberly climbed in the passenger seat and immediately rolled down her window. She liked the wind blowing her hair. She pulled the hair tie out of her hair and shook her shoulder-length hair free.

She was eager to get started on finding what was bothering Thomas and Momma had always been her closest sounding board.

"Mom," she said.

"Yes, dear." Patricia glanced at her.

"What do you think's wrong with Thomas?"

Patricia slowed to change lanes. She had her turn signal on and was carefully moving over.

"Nothing's wrong with your brother," she said. "I think he was just burned out from school and needed to come home for a while."

Perhaps, Kim thought. Perhaps not.

Kim noticed she kept her turn signal on. She whispered, "Mom, the turn signal." Patricia turned the signal off.

Stymied for a moment, Kim kept thinking.

"What about that girl he was seeing? Mary – something." Kimberly remembered her talk with him on the telephone. Even his voice was smiling so much she thought his face would crack.

Patricia wanted to make a left hand turn from the right lane. Her mother waved a car behind her to pass, then moved slowly to the left. Kim silently prayed when she was riding with Momma sometimes.

How she wanted a car of her own!

"I remember her," she said. "Mary Harris." Her face darkened just a bit. "He just stopped talking about her."

"Why?" Kim asked. She looked expectantly at her mother, hoping she would say something insightful.

This was the first angle she could find. Before, when Thomas called, he went on and on about being with her, the places they went together, and he even took her camping. Momma and Dad had a conversation downstairs thinking this could be their future daughter-in-law. Then – nothing. A few weeks later, he called saying he had been in a minor accident and not to worry. He wanted to come home for a while.

Kimberly considered. The girl plus her brother meant happiness. Her brother without the girl meant gloom and moodiness. Didn't take a rocket scientist to see this one.

Patricia was approaching their turn off.

"Did he ever tell you what happened to her?" Kim asked.

"I didn't pry, sweetheart. Whatever happened between them, I know Thomas still thinks of her. I see it in his eyes when he's looking straight ahead." Patricia turned in their lot. Beautiful brick house on a hill at the end of the road. Kim glanced under the shade tree where Thomas had taken lately to park his car. He was not home yet.

Kimberly helped her mother unload the family minivan, then excused herself to get a shower and rest a bit before supper. In her room, she blew a kiss at her Bon Jovi poster before tossing her tool belt on her bed and dropping at the end of her bed to tug off her work boots.

What Peter had said to her rang in her mind. The sooner you find out what is bothering him the sooner we can get our old Thomas back.

Kimberly went to her bathroom and turned on her shower while she undressed, then stood under the hot spray still thinking about her brother. Time for some quality investigation work, she admitted to herself. Kim dried herself and dressed quickly in sweats. Thomas was not home yet, so far as she knew. It was time to get some answers about what had happened to her brother.

Barefoot, Kimberly tiptoed to the end of the upper story hallway to glance out of the window. No car yet. Then she sneaked past her room to Thomas' door. She tried his door. Unlocked, as she had hoped it would be.

She never locked her door either.

The late afternoon sun poured through his open window. Some of his clothes lay strewn on the floor. Socks and underwear were piled in a heap beside his old desk.

His mattress had nothing on it, not even a sheet.

Strange piqued her mind. What had he done with his bed coverings?

Kim checked his desk. Nothing. Kim looked in his closet and checked the pockets of his coats. Nothing. Kim lifted gently and examined the few books he had on his bookshelf. Nothing.

The bare mattress bothered her. Kim knelt at the head of his bed and swept her hand under his bed and found a sheet wadded up and stuffed near the headboard. She pulled the sheet out. When it unfurled, she saw the dark stain near the center. She knew this was blood. This was the sort of thing you only see in the movies.

She was actually dumbfounded for a few minutes.

How blood could have gotten on his bed sheet was an utter mystery to her. She stuffed the stained sheet back where she had found it.

On impulse, she swept her arm between his upper mattress and his lower mattress. Her fingers brushed what she believed to be a magazine hidden there. She lifted the mattress and found an old copy of Playboy. The date on it would have made it in his eleventh grade year of high school.

She said, "Hmmm," and looked through it.

The buxom model did not impress Kimberly much.

She was much more interested in the photograph of her brother that fell out. He was smiling and waving with his arm around a girl. She was smiling with him, too, and obviously close to him because it looked like a picture taken after a rugby game at school. This had to be the elusive Ms. Harris.

Kim stuffed the old magazine back where it was, but kept the picture. Glancing at his room, she made sure everything looked like it had before she broke into her brother's private life. Yes, it was a dirty thing to do, but someone had to get to the bottom of this!

Kimberly closed Thomas' bedroom door quietly and went to her bedroom. She sat cross-legged on her bed and turned on her reading light. She studied the photograph. Thomas was obviously happy. The girl with him, call her Mary, also seemed happy. They were both smiling and everything is rosy. Kim studied the girl. Long hair. Lithe figure, although shorter than Thomas by at least six inches. Pale complexion. But a pretty girl, she decided. She heard a muffled car door slam.

Thomas must have arrived home. No need postponing this long. She did not want him to discover his picture

missing and come hunting for her. She would take the
picture to him and ask him to explain what was bothering him. The direct approach.

Hey, some major criminals confessed when confronted
with overwhelming evidence this way.

The sky was bands of mauve, gold, red, and purple
as the sun descended over Lake Ponchartrain. A solitary
figure stood alone at the end of the dock overlooking the
water. She breathed deeply, locked in stillness. Majken
sighed. She was again in New Orleans with Stefan. At
least she had met Stefan's intended Michelle since she
had returned. She visited a few familiar places, but New
Orleans was only a temporary stopping place for now.

A discrete distance away, her driver stepped out of the
limousine and stood with his door open. She could hear
the blur of static as he spoke on the car telephone.

Josè Hispanic accent was thick as he said, "Yes, sir."
He paused. "No, sir. She's just standing there looking at
the water." He was quiet and listening for a few moments,
then she heard, "Yes, sir." Stefan checking up on her.

He worried, she supposed.

Since she had left Thomas in Trenton, she had learned
two things: Thomas had returned to his parent's home in
South Carolina, and, she believed, he was in The Change.
She could feel the voice of his blood, calling her, even
across the distance. Having just celebrated his twenty-
fourth birthday, she knew that his change would happen
very quickly. Typically, twenty-two was the maximum
upper age limit for a young person to survive The Change.
Reactive changes, such as his, were most often too quick
for a normal human body to survive. Majken bowed her
head and pulled her shawl tighter around her shoulders.
Her problem was – she was not ready to watch him die.

* * *

Kimberly slipped Thomas' picture in her jeans pocket and joined the family for a late supper. Thomas talked some when Dad tried to draw him into conversation, but mostly he just drank water and ate little. That left more green bean casserole for her, but Thomas had to eventually eat something.

He excused himself and went to the back porch. Facing east, bright moonlight spilled over the honey gold stained deck – making it appear ghostly white.

Kim volunteered to help Mom with the dishes because she wanted more time to decide how to confront Thomas.

The more she thought about it, the more convinced she became that Thomas was hiding something incredibly bad. This stiffened her resolve to see this through. She had to find out what was bothering him so she could begin to help him out of whatever it was. When she finished with the dishes, she excused herself and went outside also. Thomas had turned the porch light off and had settled in the hammock tied between two trees in the middle of the yard. He was in the dark, beneath the dappled elm leaves.

He seemed to be studying her as she approached. Although his manner seemed casual, she felt an edge as she walked up to him. He went from a gentle swaying with his left leg over the hammock touching the ground to absolute stillness.

Kimberly shivered, in spite of herself.

"Hi, big brother," she said lightly.

"Hi, brat," he returned. Brat, as in Army brat.

She entered the shade of the elm trees above. Funny, she thought, to think of shade in the middle of the night. The moon above was full tonight. Many voices whispered in the light breeze that stirred the leaves of the trees above them.

Thomas began rocking himself again.

He turned his gaze away from her, looking into the night, she suspected.

"How are you doing?" she asked. He looked back at her.

"Great," he said – no enthusiasm, no inflection.

Kimberly stuck her hand casually in her jeans pocket, ready to extract Thomas' photo. How to start this? she wondered.

"Peter said he saw you at the mall last week. He said, Hey, and you were sitting in the dining area – he said – and you didn't respond. He said you were just staring into space." *Like you are now*, she thought. "Made me wonder," she added, "that you might have something on your mind. That you might want to talk about it, just to get the load off."

Thomas almost smiled, and she thought she caught a glimpse of the big brother she remembered. Then his smile faded and he resumed staring into the night. "I'll be fine."

Kim caught that. I'll be fine – in that, I am not fine now. Her fingertip was on the picture, but now was not the right moment. "Mind if I just hang out?" she asked.

Thomas shrugged, which Kim took to mean, Okay.

She went around the tree the long way and found a folded lawn chair. The webbing was decayed, but she thought it would hold her long enough. The chair squeaked when she unfolded it. Thomas was able to look at her, and extend his gaze to the edge of the yard where the woods swallowed up the manicured grass their father so studiously maintained.

She paused for a moment to collect her courage, then jumped in. "You've changed," she said solemnly. She waited to see if he would have a reaction, or protest, or tell her she was all wet.

His silence seemed to indicate agreement.

"Many of your friends are concerned. I'm concerned. It's like you're pushing all of us away – Mom and Dad included. Whatever is bothering you," she leaned forward imploring, "we can handle it together." Thomas swung his left leg that was trailing the ground across the hammock and moved to a sitting position in front of her. She could not see his face clearly in the dark. She wished he had left the porch light on.

"Nothing's bothering me," he replied, "I'm just tired."

Kim paused to think about what he said.

It looked to her now like he was trying to do his best impression of a fence post. Hard and uncaring. Yet as she searched his deep brown eyes, she knew the look behind his eyes that meant pain.

At least two times before in his life she had seen that look: when his dog Bud died his senior year and when the girl he was with his senior year eventually married someone else. In fact, to get away from Julie and the dentist he enrolled in a school as far north as he could go. Each time was loss and a broken heart.

He was seriously hurting, she guessed, but it seemed to be more than the girl he was dating in Trenton. Well, she wouldn't know if she didn't ask.

"What happened between you and that girl, uh, Mary?"

Thomas sighed and lay back on the hammock. "I don't know where she is. I don't know where to even begin to find her."

He rubbed his face with his hands, then dropped his hands to his lap. To Kimberly it looked like the most hopeless gesture she had ever seen.

"When did you last see her?" Kimberly asked.

She was getting warmer. This was more than Thomas had said about his girlfriend since he came home. "The early morning of my, er, accident. She brought me to the hospital." Kim noticed that Thomas spoke with more vibrancy when he mentioned finding her. A clue!

"Maybe I can help you, put out a few inquiries –"

Thomas bolted up like he had been hit from behind by napalm. "No!" he shouted. "Under no condition are you to do anything to find her, or trace her, or anything like that!" Thomas was standing over her. The small aluminum frame of the lawn chair she had been sitting in collapsed and fell backwards. Now she was sitting on the ground looking up at him.

Forgot how tall and how big Thomas was.

Just because he's your brother – Kimberly's rear end and lower back smarted because she hit the ground on the rickety chair. He reached his hand down to pull her up. When she grasped his hand, he pulled her up so hard her shoulders ached. Whew! Kim caught her balance and her breath. This simple little interrogation was not going exactly as planned. But she had learned a few things.

Time for the ace card, now that he was off balance (sort of).

Kim slipped the photo from her pocket and held it before his eyes. "I found this in your room. Is this Mary?"

Thomas' eyes went wide and his mouth formed a silent "oh". He snatched for the photo. Kim was quicker. She flipped it just out of his reach. "You brat!" he exclaimed.

He looked like he wanted to jump down her throat. Her brother looked angrier than she had ever seen him, but he was also standing rigid and still. Like he was afraid of his own strength. "You had no right to go through my room like that," he said.

Beggars can't be choosers, she thought.

"I wouldn't have done it if I didn't think you needed help." *Or had something to hide.* She held the picture where he could reach it.

He plucked it from her fingers and smoothed it over his heart. The anger seemed to drain from him once he held the photo. Kimberly reflected. This had to be Mary. He would not be this passionate if this was anyone else. He held the photo in his palm and looked at it. His expression seemed to soften as he looked at the photo. The point in time that this snapshot represented was now only a shadow of the past, but what it meant to him was still very much alive inside of him.

"It's her," he said evenly.

Kim felt a pang of regret at her actions, but Thomas was no longer angry at her. In his mind, he appeared to have gone back in time to the photo – holding this young lady close to him again. The ache on his face was a tangible thing.

Thomas smoothed the photo again on his shirt and slipped it in his front jeans pocket.

In the full moonlight, Kimberly became aware of her brother's, uh, interest. He was obviously thinking of this girl as more than just a friend. Yet he also seemed resigned. As if Humpty-Dumpty had fallen and would not be put back together again. "I'm sorry I searched your room," she admitted.

Thomas smirked at his sister. "No, you're not."

Okay, Kim thought. I'm sorry I got caught.

"What's going on?" she asked. "What happened up there?"

Thomas' voice had the strained patience of a parent telling a stubborn two-year-old why she can't have a pony right now for the *millionth* time.

"Leave it alone, Kimberly Denise. There's more going on here than you could ever begin to understand." Kim was startled. Thomas never used her middle name unless he was deadly serious with her. Her impression that something *very* incredibly bad had happened to him again seeped into her consciousness. Yet, finding things out was what she did. She did not think it wise to mention the blood stained sheet under his bed right now.

"Okay," she said, resigned. Not meaning it. Whatever had happened was destroying the brother she loved. She intended to find the truth – one way or another.

Chapter Two

High thin tendrils of clouds were wisps across the full moon shining over the Montana mountain forest. Hidden in an impassible ravine, an ominous chant filled the night sky. Two robe cloaked people, a man and a young woman, stood over the sacrifice bound to the rock slab.

Blood would be offered tonight.

The man stood above the victim's head with the double sided jeweled knife that would slice the sacrifice's throat cleanly. Already their captive bled from smaller wounds inflicted under his arms and around his groin.

Jeanine stood at her place at the victim's feet. The rock slab had grooves that would collect the blood shed in two collection points at the head and the feet. Her body felt cold, although the temperature tonight was not below freezing. She hated this, but Nolan always made sure she watched. Although he spoke only in a hushed voice, she heard him enunciate clearly: *"quia anima carnis in sanguine est et ego dedi illum vobis ut super altare in eo expietis pro animabus vestris et sanguis pro animae piaculo sit."*

In her mind, she rehearsed, The life of the flesh is in the blood. The life of the flesh is in the blood. The life of the flesh is in the blood. Nolan's almost coal black eyes were staring directly into hers. She met his gaze and tried to harden herself to what was about to happen.

The poor young man on the slab pleaded with his eyes. His brown eyes were wide and frantic. He was securely bound by his wrists and feet, spread wide and helpless. The lone hiker she had lured off a forest trail two states away, his life was over the moment he turned to follow her.

Nolan made sure she watched.

Nolan always made sure she saw the moment of death, the shudder of the victim's body when blood loss is severe – how Jeanine hated it, hated it, hated it!

Yet she was just as bound as the poor young man before her. Nolan had paused to allow the high thin clouds to pass and allow the blue-white light of the full moon to shine on the secluded spot.

Her face became as a stone mask as the moment came. Oh, God, she thought. Oh God, oh God, oh God, oh God.

Nolan grabbed a handful of the young man's thick hair, pulled hard, and made sure the young man saw the knife poised over his throat. The blue-white moonlight made the blade shine. The ruby jewel in the haft shone blood red. Jeanine felt herself stop breathing.

Get it over with bastard! she felt herself think.

Nolan made a gesture as if to lay the knife down, but quickly and deeply cut the victim's carotid artery in his neck. A thick gush of blood sprayed over the young man's body.

The scent of blood filled the night.

Oh God, oh God, oh God, Jeanine repeated to herself.

She was ever wary of sounds in the forest around them. Wolves, forest predators, would be drawn by the scent of blood. Nolan kept his rifle close at hand for such protection.

The sacrifice's body began to convulse.

Such severe blood loss – the young man's eyes set in death. Rich blood, appearing black by the moon's light, pooled in gently carved cisterns at both ends of the sacrificial slab.

Blood seeped into a gold chalice.

Nolan lifted the chalice and Jeanine took her place to kneel at his feet. The robe she wore dropped to the ground. Nolan's eyes were feverish. By the effect of the moon and her need for blood, his eyes almost appeared bright red. Glowing blood red.

She lifted her face to his.

He did not dip the chalice for her to drink until she

looked at him. Until she adored him. Until she submitted her body and her soul to him. Oh God!

She drank the offering. By this time, she needed it so severely her body shuddered. She felt cold, always cold.

Jeanine drank the blood given to her.

She had been trapped now, as her mind drifted back, over twenty-four years. She appeared as a young winsome nineteen- year-old girl with honey blonde hair and a sweet face. Her eyes, a lovely hazel green, could entice or draw a male sacrifice so easily.

She needed the blood given to her.

She *needed* it.

Trapped, with years upon years upon years, Jeanine finally finished drinking the blood. The young vampyric girl's body began to absorb the blood she had consumed. Her face and body did not appear the forty-one years she actually was.

Nolan knew her secret. The other distant California members of the blood cult knew who she was and where she lived, literally. Nolan lay the chalice on the rock slab for a brief moment, slipped the robe he wore off, then lifted the chalice over his face to drink the sacrifice's blood also.

Rivulets of blood spilled over his chin, down his bare chest and body, dripping down his legs and pooling at his feet.

Wolves howled across the distant mountainscape. Desolation whispered in the wind. No escape, Jeanine thought. Members of blood cults never retire or leave.

Jeanine bowed her head to the rough stone between Nolan's feet. Blood dripped off his body into her hair. He again spoke in Latin: *"anima carnis in sanguine est."* Jeanine translated in her mind, the "life of the flesh is in the blood".

Nolan added, *"sacrificium primogentium."*

Sacrifice – what? Jeanine thought.

Nolan said the strange phrase three times, then reached for her. He pulled her to her feet and lifted her. He deliberately set her buttocks in the pooling blood cistern at the young man's head. Now she could avoid looking at their victim's glazed open eyes. She spread herself for Nolan.

Another part of the sacrifice.

Oh God, how she hated it, hated it, hated it!

Jeanine's entire body ached. It was always like this the morning after a sacrifice. She groggily tried to move, but only part of her body obeyed. Nolan had spread her face down on his bed, her left wrist and left leg were still secured. The pillow under her face had been drenched by cold tears and was wet on her cheek. Jeanine struggled to reach the clasp of the left manacle with her freed right hand. Nolan did this deliberately; he seemed to draw a perverse pleasure in watching her try to get free. Sometimes she could feel him watching, but now – she sensed – he was not in the cabin.

Gentle white morning light flooded the upper story bedroom loft. When she moved her butt hurt. Raw bleeding welts on her backside would hurt for a few days. She healed quickly, thankfully. She slid her entire body left and reached over her head. Almost there. The key to the manacle was under her pillow. This was where Nolan always left it. The lock on the left manacle wobbled from side to side, perversely, as she tried to get the key to fit by using her fingertips.

She let her hand rest for a moment.

Twittering birds outside made a sweet melody.

By her body's internal clock, she felt it to be about seven o'clock. Nolan never kept real clocks around. For some silly reason, clocks seemed to bother him.

Was today a school day? she wondered.

Frantic to escape, she lifted the key again and tried to open the left lock. She managed to twist the tumbler and the lock opened. Now she had to maneuver the opened lock hasp up and out of the manacle ring.

She grimaced. Almost.

With her sensitive hearing, she picked up an almost inaudible whirring sound.

"Fuck," she swore aloud.

Nolan was filming her again. He could be watching her now from the safety of his van, or he could replay the digital video over and over again. This was the benefit of owning your own security company. The best video and surveillance technology was yours to be had. Nolan was a respected small business man. Some of the firms he consulted for were high profile, high tech, high profit companies. Jeanine redoubled her efforts to get the manacle free and the lock came off. She jerked her left hand a few times until she pulled it out. Where was the fucking camera this time?

She felt her entire body turn flushed. Nolan had already seen and defiled everything she had. Still, when she knew he was filming her, her face burned hot with embarrassment. He could film in infrared also. Probably had everything he had done to her, all night long, on video. Her entire body ached and protested when she tried to roll to a sitting position. The formerly white bed sheet was smeared with her blood. She cried as the raw stripes on her buttocks slid on the bed. She gingerly picked her butt up and gently, oh so gently, twisted and bent to reach her left ankle manacle.

This was getting old, she thought.

At least, this year, Nolan would be at the end of his six year tenure. Every six years a new blood cult leader came from darkness and returned to darkness. She had first met Nolan when he was a twenty-two-year-old firebrand. Now, at twenty-eight, he only had a few more sacrifices before he would be moved – to a galaxy far, far away, she hoped.

Only to be replaced by someone twice as bad.

The strange phrase Nolan had said, "*sacrificium primogentium*," came to her mind. She reminded herself to look it up later.

Six years of Nolan almost over.

Alecia! Jeanine gasped. "Fuck," she swore as she winced and finally stood. Today *was* a school day and if she didn't hurry, she would be late getting Alecia to school.

Jeanine found her jeans in a drawer and cried as she pulled them on. Oh God, how she wished she had a loose fitting pair. But, Nolan purchased her clothing and knew the tight fitting jeans would hurt her now.

Labor Day weekend was coming up. Maybe she and Alecia could do something fun together. Jeanine dove into a bulky sweater, ran a brush through her tangled hair, slipped dark contacts over her sensitive eyes, found her sandals, and rushed out the door with her wallet. Her vintage '68 Mustang, now orange, gave a throaty growl as she raced away.

Twenty minutes later, Jeanine rolled into the small trailer park next to the restaurant outside Helena. Crisp mountain air and thick cloud cover promising rain greeted her. Dust billowed around her Mustang as she came to an abrupt stop.

Her trailer was in lot three. She hurried to the trailer beside her, lot two, and tapped on the door. Ms. Lillian Daugherty, the little park manager, had been with her for over twenty years. Now in her sixties, her hair was slate gray, but her dear face was filled with kind wrinkles. Lillian's cherubic face smiled as the door opened.

A little girl in a red dress rushed to her.

"Jennie!" the little girl called.

When the door opened, she was greeted with the biggest hug anyone could hope for. Momma Lillian's home always smelled of cinnamon and spice, everything nice for little girls. Jeanine knelt and Nolan's seven-year-old daughter hugged her for all she was worth. Oh, she relished that hug.

She hugged Alecia back then let her climb off her bent knees to the floor. She was ready for school, thank heaven. Momma Lillian's clock over the fake mantle gave her at least ten minutes to drive across town and get Alecia into the school on time.

Hopefully.

"Hello, dear," Lillian said. "How was your business trip?" The elderly woman seemed to live in a world all her own, but she was at least connected to the outside world enough to know when she and Nolan went hunting. They called it a "business trip."

Jeanine stifled the images racing through her mind. "Fine," she said absently. Alecia was getting her book pack. Such a big girl now. Jeanine smiled at Alecia. Here was life and everything good that Nolan was not. It amazed her that such a bastard as Nolan could have had any part in producing such a sweet and loving child as Alecia.

Alecia reached for her again and Jeanine bent for another quick hug before they had to run. "Thank you, Momma Lillian," Jeanine called. She led Alecia to her car.

She whispered to Alecia, "Wave, honey." Alecia waved at the elderly woman stooped in her doorway. Ms. Daugherty was already closing her door. Alecia reached both hands and tugged on the passenger-side door to Jeanine's Mustang.

Jeanine suspected that Alecia was a thrill seeker in

disguise. The little girl seemed to thrive on riding with Jeanine, actually, no matter how fast Jeanine drove.

Well, Jeanine thought, as she hopped into the moulded driver's seat – Alecia would get her thrill this morning because she had eight minutes to get Alecia to school. Alecia was already reaching for her seat belt as Jeanine whipped onto Euclid and headed due east, into the heart of Helena, racing for Smith Elementary.

The traffic on Fifth was backed up.

Alecia would only be a few minutes late.

Once Alecia was settled safely in her classroom, Jeanine began to unwind from the adrenaline rush that had been propelling her all night and into the morning.

She was soooooooo tired.

Jeanine turned onto the street that would eventually lead her back to her trailer. This time she drove at a leisurely pace. A county patrol car passed her going the other way.

She rubbed at her eyes, but she again saw the poor boy Nolan had just killed in the black swirls in her vision.

I killed him too, she thought to herself.

Nolan screwed her over the poor boy's body until his body grew cold to touch. Nolan would pummel her for hours at a sacrifice sometimes. She wondered how he could stay horny for so long. Maybe he took something.

She'd never seen him take anything.

The awful truth was Nolan was a sick, sick, sick bastard. Watching that poor boy die is what gave him his jollies. The power over a person's life was the turn on for him. And Nolan's control of her was just an extension of his power trip over the blood cult.

After this came the gruesome part.

Jeanine was required to do cleanup.

He would only step in when something changed or she was not doing it to his standard. She tried not to make mistakes. When she did it wrong, he would slap her hard.

Completely drain the body. Done.

Dismember the limbs at the joints. Done.

Quarter the torso. Done.

Spray a coagulant on the pieces. Done.

This funky blue stuff they had caused the blood to gel, harden, then crystallize in less than fifteen minutes. Once the sacrifice's blood crystallized, she could no longer smell it and this freaked her out big time.

Package the body into six bundles. Done.

Cleanup the sacrificial stone. Done.

Cover the stone altar with bramble, leaves, moss, and foliage to conceal it from the air. Done.

On cue, one by one, little cars appeared with a driver dressed in a sweatsuit hood, balaclava, gloves, and no distinctive clothing. They would arrive going the long way up the fire trail. The drivers, likely all males, would pick up their bundle and put it in the trunk, then drive away.

These drivers never spoke and never showed their faces.

Creepy.

Truth be told, these people scared her.

Six little cars would take the six little bundles to six different incinerators, maybe at a hospital, a mortuary that cremated, or some other sterile heat source. Wouldn't want the ashes identified as human, now would we.

When the altar was sanctified and secure, and the sacrifice disposed of, Nolan always took her to his cabin for additional "fun."

Jeanine turned into her trailer park and pulled into her lot. Each time she came home, her trailer gleaming white in the sunlight, her gaze lingered on the neat silver block letters inscribed on her dash with a soldering iron.

BB/JB ...
I'll be with you forever, rang in her mind.
Bobby's last words to her.
Bobby's last words to anyone.
She felt cold to the core of her being. And utterly alone.

Hours later, past lunch time for most people, Jeanine toured Prospect in front of the Wal-Mart shopping center. She considered for a moment stopping by the automotive department to see friends from her brief time of employment at this store. It was during her redhead days, about eight years ago.

Every four to eight years, she was told to go to a certain beauty shop in San Francisco. There, her hair color – and often, her Mustang color also – was changed. She had been a brunette. Hated it. She had been a redhead. Hated it. Now, at least she was back to her original honey gold hair color.

Her Mustang, formerly her boyfriend's car, was originally white, then bright yellow, then blue, and now racing orange. Nolan saw to it that her car was well maintained. The responsibility of her was part of the deal he inherited with the blood cult.

Jeanine passed by the Wal-Mart for now. Friends could wait. It was past one in the afternoon and traffic was getting heavy. At three she would go get Alecia from school. Before then, she had a pick-up.

She went down US Interstate 15 and took the exit that would bring her back to Smith Elementary, and more importantly, St. Peter Hospital. Jeanine took the back way, down California street that would take her to the back of the hospital complex.

This was the normal time for employees to be coming

and going. She changed from her sandals to white sneakers, took her empty lunch tote from the trunk and walked to the employee east side entrance. She took her vendor badge and swiped it in front of the scanning device embedded within the wall. She was very conscious of the ceiling-mounted camera above her head to her right. The door clicked and she pulled it open.

She walked down the cool fluorescent hallway to an employee break area. There, just past two o'clock right on schedule, she saw an identical blue lunch tote waiting for her.

Her timing was excellent today. It had to be.

She placed her tote next to the one sitting in the chair, stooped to retie her white shoe, then picked up the other tote and left with it. Everyday Alecia was in school, this was the drill. Her original blue tote was empty. This tote was heavy. It contained a three-hundred milliliter transfer unit of fresh blood for her.

Timing had to be exact. If she arrived a few minutes early, no tote would be there. If she arrived as much as ten minutes late, the tote would be gone, too. Because the transfer unit contained no anti-coagulants, the fresh human blood had to be consumed within no more than a fifteen minutes timeframe.

Jeanine headed south and out a different building exit from the one she entered. It would not do for the security video to show her exiting a doorway she had entered just a few minutes before. This would attract the wrong kind of scrutiny. She was still within her five minute window. Jeanine quickened her pace, but not to the point of attracting attention.

Her Mustang engine gave a growl as she revved the engine up. Quirky. Not attracting attention to herself but driving a car that made almost every male she encountered turn their heads to stare. She hurried to a nearby dead-end street, backed into a parking space, made absolutely certain she was unobserved, then opened her dinner tray.

Almost ten minutes had passed. She was still safely within her window of opportunity. She pulled out a special tube with a one-way valve from her locked glove compartment, exposed the sharpened end, and jabbed the filled transfer unit with her straw. The cusp of the straw would seal against the plastic of the blood unit. The special valve would only release blood when she sucked on it. Nolan had given it to her five years ago.

Nothing but high tech for my girl, he said.

Before that, she had to actually open the bags with a knife or tiny scissors and sip it. The blood was still warm.

Tasty.

No mess. No fuss. No awkward blood stains to explain. Her stash of straws were hidden behind a panel in the kitchen wall of her trailer and beneath the floor in the cupboard of Nolan's remote cabin. They had gone disposable, so she only needed seal the entire bag and allow Nolan to dispose of them somewhere. He made a point of not telling her when she asked. This was, she believed, deliberate to keep her in the dark and as helpless as possible. She drained the blood within five minutes.

Over thirty minutes to wait to get Alecia.

When she finished, she usually just stared at the little buildings around her. Old people lived in many of these homes. Some had been converted for use as old-folk-homes. She remembered a few times she had gained employment in these little old-folk hideaways. Another ready blood source to be had.

She thought often how she got into this condition. When Bobby plunged her into this blood cult hell, he died.

She didn't.

And from what she could tell, she didn't age at the same rate as normal people. She pondered. She was human, yet not human. Forced to live by blood alone.

I'll be with you forever, he had promised her. Like everything else, her life had become a total lie.

Alecia beamed at Jeanine, chatting excited about a hundred things at once that happened to her in the day. A boy made a face at her and caused her to laugh in class and get in trouble. A girl got sick and had to go to the school nurse. She had a drawing she had done in crayon and a paper her teacher marked with a smiley face and an "A." She chatted about anything and everything in her world as Jeanine drove Nolan's daughter to her trailer. Until Nolan returned the following week, Alecia would stay with her. After all, she mused, Nolan did actually have to see clients, service video and surveillance systems, and generally run the actual business.

She thought about Nolan as she knew him and the public Nolan the community thought they knew. She spoke his name in her mind: Nolan Ciucevich. She smiled at Alecia, still chatting. Alecia Ciucevich. She considered herself. Jeanine Nobody.

She stopped at a red light adjacent to SafeWay. Jeanine considered stopping, but decided against it. Alecia had enough at her home to go a few more days. The grocery store had been a haven for her in caring for Alecia from the beginning, from diapers, to formula, to healthy snacks; then as she began eating regular food, Jeanine wanted her to eat what was good for human little girls and not too many sweets.

She had to watch Momma Lillian. Her peach cobbler was to die for and Alecia loved it like nothing else. She had come home with a stomach ache more than once.

Jeanine drove past the SafeWay shopping center. Maybe, she considered, her and Alecia could go to a movie this weekend. The movie houses would, no doubt, be packed. Alecia liked popcorn, a soft drink, and gummy bears.

Years ago, it hurt Alecia's feelings when Jeanine had to refuse to eat a gummy bear snack Alecia was offering her. That afternoon Alecia even cried on the way home. Jeanine tried to somehow explain that she, herself, could not eat food. *Human* food. She tried to explain, but simply could not find a way to tell her in a way Alecia could grasp. That evening, Jeanine held and rocked Alecia on her tiny sofa for hours. The little girl's hands, so tiny even then, reached around her neck and hugged her as hard as she could.

Jeanine smiled at Alecia, so proud to have her, so proud of the little girl she is and, no doubt, the beautiful confident young lady she will become.

Her thoughts suddenly became dark.

Where did she expect Alecia to be when Nolan left at the end of the year?

Her heart suddenly began pounding in her chest. This wasn't right! This wasn't fair! This was cruel and unusual punishment! She would likely lose Alecia in a few short months anyway. Jeanine gradually calmed herself, and tried to present peace and tranquility to the little girl she clearly loved more than life itself. From the beginning, Alecia had quickly become her mainstay and anchor in her world.

Well, three months was a long time.

Anything could happen in three months.

Nolan could get run over by a bus, or something equally deadly. Her problem was, though, once Nolan was gone (one way or another) another blood cult leader would appear and be worse than the one before. She repeated to herself what her Papa always said, *If anything can go wrong, it will.*

Jeanine decided she did want to take Alecia to a movie this weekend. She would make it the best girl's day out that she can. Alecia was also a few years older since the gummy bear incident. Maybe she can better understand.

Jeanine awoke to thick peals of thunder and heavy rainfall. She was instantly awake. Alecia was afraid of thunder. She pushed her way free of the bedcovers and bounced to her feet. She pulled her house robe over her tiny slip and padded barefoot to Alecia's bedroom. She slid the bedroom door open slightly.

Alecia had curled in a fetal position, but she still appeared asleep. Soft whimpers came from the bed. Jeanine finished sliding the door open and said, "Honey?"

Jeanine knelt beside the bed and reached for Alecia. The little girl was clearly afraid. Her face was contorted and she had been crying. "I'm trying to be brave," she said. Her little fist was clenched next to her mouth.

"C'mere," Jeanine said. She reached for Alecia. In an instant, Alecia was in her arms. The frightened little girl wrapped her arms around her Jennie's neck and both legs were tight around her waist.

Jeanine held her body close and carefully maneuvered through the tiny hallway. She pushed her own sliding bedroom door open with her foot and placed Alecia in her own bed. The little girl stopped crying.

Jeanine tossed her house robe over a tiny chair and slid into the opposite side of the bed. Alecia reached for her. Jeanine put her arm behind Alecia and pulled her into a hug.

"Honey," she said, "I don't want you to ever be afraid.

You can come to me whenever you're scared. I'll never let anything bad happen to you."

Alecia's hand reached across her abdomen. Jeanine pulled the bedcovers higher, to her waist, and bundled the rest of the covers over Alecia's back. "You're always so cool," Alecia murmured.

"Yes, honey," she whispered. "Now go to sleep."

She was silent for a moment.

"Jennie?" Alecia said quietly.

"Yes, honey," Jeanine replied in a daze; she was starting to feel sleepy.

"Why does Daddy hurt you?"

Jeanine's eyes instantly snapped open. Her mouth felt completely dry. So long she had tried to keep the violence apart from Nolan's daughter.

"What do you mean, honey?"

"You come home with bloody stripes on your butt, legs, or back every time you go away on a business trip." Her voice was small. "The time before this one – when he told me to stay downstairs, I sneaked back up. I saw him hitting you with a rod thing."

Oh God, Jeanine thought. What could she say? The welts would still be visible for another day or two.

What must the baby be thinking of her Daddy all this time?

"Have you been bad?" Alecia offered.

"No," she replied, "no, honey, I haven't."

Her face started to well up with tears. "When I hear the thunder, it sounds like that rod thing hitting you."

Jeanine felt what Alecia said like a heavy blow to her abdomen. Alecia had been afraid of thunder and lightning storms for years. She felt telling Alecia of the adult drama and interactions, especially in bed, would be too much to say, but the little girl had obviously been aware that Nolan hit her regularly for years. Beat her bloody to tell the truth.

What else did the baby see him do? she wondered.

"Honey," she said stiffly. "This is something we can never tell anyone else. It has to be a secret, between you and me. You haven't told any of your teachers, have you, sweetheart?"

In a small voice, Alecia said, "No, Jennie."

Jeanine sighed in obvious relief. She rolled to face Alecia and scrunched lower in the bed until her face was right in front of Nolan's daughter. The rain was beating so hard on her trailer that it sounded like an army marching just outside.

"Baby," she said. She reached both hands to cup Alecia's face. "Your Daddy hits me because, uh, because it makes him feel strong and powerful – and in control over me. Some men become like this and your Daddy is one of them."

The little girl was silent for a moment.

"Why?" she asked.

Alecia was asking why her father was such a cold hearted bastard. Truth be told, Jeanine had no idea what made him the kind of man he was except his need to control.

"Baby, he just does is all I know." Another crack of thunder made Alecia wince.

"I don't want him to hit you ever again," the little girl said resolutely. Strangely, the tone in the little girl's voice was so much more knowing and aware than for a girl of seven. Jeanine lay next to Alecia a bit stunned.

Waves and waves of rain were pounding on the aluminum siding now. The rain was coming in sheets and the wind whistled through the sliding window across from her bed. Alecia seemed to turn to cuddle now. It would be morning in a little bit.

"I love you," Alecia whispered.

Jeanine felt tears spill down her cheeks.

"I love you, too, sweetheart," she replied.

In Jeanine's heart, there was nothing in the world but Alecia until morning came.

By light of morning, the day was still gray and overcast. It would probably rain on and off throughout the day. Gloomy morning to go with a gloomy night. Alecia awoke normally at six. Jeanine usually had to prod her a few times to get her to actually get up. Alecia giggled when Jeanine tickled her lightly.

Jeanine slipped into a school day routine.

Alecia's usual breakfast was cereal and milk with a piece of cinnamon toast made with butter on the stove. Jeanine heated the sauce pan, put butter on the toast, and grilled it on both sides before adding the cinnamon spice. She smiled to herself. Momma Lillian had gotten her baby girl hooked on cinnamon.

Jeanine watched Alecia eat. She seemed again the same innocent seven-year-old girl she was yesterday. She kept waiting to see if Alecia would mention anything they had said in the night. Behind them, Jeanine turned on her black-and-white television. The TV sat on the counter between the kitchen and living room. When she and Alecia watched TV on the couch, she turned the little TV around.

She adjusted the rabbit ears antenna to make the wavy picture a little better. It was grainy because of the storms, she guessed. The banter of the familiar couple on the morning variety show filled the silence.

Nothing but high tech for my girl, Jeanine remembered.

"Yeah, right," she said sarcastically.

Alecia finished eating. Jeanine put her bowl in the sink and ran water in it. She prodded Alecia to go get dressed and ready for school. Jeanine dressed in her own bedroom, careful that Alecia not see the fading red welts on her backside. When she pulled her tight jeans up, the welts did not burn like they did yesterday.

Alecia met her in the kitchen.

"Honey," she said, "get your raincoat."

Alecia rushed to her bedroom and came back with a bright yellow slicky raincoat with a hood. Jeanine bundled Alecia in the coat. As she knelt in front of Alecia buttoning the coat, the little girl turned to reach for her book pack and took out the crayon drawing she had made for her yesterday.

Jeanine smiled. It was a little house drawing with two people outside. One obviously her, with yellow bouncy hair and a smaller girl beside her with dark brown hair. The house had not been fully colored in, but there was a flower blooming in the window. There was grass and a tree behind the home.

"Let's put it up here," she said. Alecia's face brightened as Jeanine found a spare magnet and stuck the picture on her refrigerator. She gazed at the picture.

It was now obvious that there was no man in the picture. Jeanine choked a little bit.

She prodded Alecia to go for the door. Jeanine picked up a piece of newspaper to use as an umbrella. Funny, she thought, how she did not have a raincoat herself. She took Alecia to school and came home.

Alone, the silence in her little trailer was deafening. Jeanine turned on her TV just to have some noise in the home. She glanced at it briefly. Some exercise show, it looked like. She kept the TV pointed toward the kitchen. She kicked off her sandals and raked her fingers through her tangled wet hair. There was a little mirror in the ceramic candle holder on her wall. Her hair was getting past her shoulders and it was time to get it cut.

She picked up odds and ends in the living room to tidy up the place.

Then she remembered the new phrase Nolan had said at the sacrifice. She went to her bedroom and found her old Latin college textbook stuffed under her bed and browsed the index.

"*sacrificium primogentium*" she remembered.

She hummed a Fleetwood Mac song that had been in her head since yesterday as she looked.

Jeanine found the word she was looking for and stopped breathing. "Oh God," she muttered. "Oh, no!" She frantically doubled checked the roots of the words for any alternate meanings. Black swirls seemed to float around her head.

The phrase meant *firstborn sacrifice.*

Oh God, oh God, oh God!

Nolan meant to ... to ... *kill* his own daughter!

"Sonofabitch!" she swore. Everything she had seen the man do from the time she met him flooded her consciousness. He was just cold and cruel enough to do it, too!

But, why? Why would he kill his baby?

Alecia was good and right and sweet and loving. Alecia was everything that Nolan was not. But, she was his firstborn child. She knew vaguely of Nolan's ex-wife in California. Sarah, she thought her name was.

Still, for Nolan to plan to kill his own daughter meant he had a reason for doing it. The murdering sonofabitch never did anything without a reason. Her mind reeled as she stuffed her Latin textbook back under her bed.

She pondered as she plodded mindlessly to her living room.

Nolan obviously meant to kill his own daughter. His firstborn. In ancient times, children were often sacrificed to false deities to gain favor of the gods.

Something else Nolan did bothered her because of what Alecia had asked her.

Why? Why did Nolan beat her bloody after every sacrifice? The prattle of the talking TV ruined her concentration. Jeanine bound up and snapped the TV off. She stood with her hand on her chin in the middle of her living room. She had to think.

Jeanine closed her eyes. She had seen gushes of blood from so many sacrifices through the years that she would always see it. The images were indelibly etched in her mind's eye. She would see blood forever. The life of the flesh is in the blood, she recalled. Raised Catholic in a Catholic high school, some of her past Bible study classes came to mind.

The life of the flesh is in the blood.

Jeanine looked at her slender hands, her slender youthful body, and her face in the ceramic mirror. She still looked much as she did, even to the day she ran away with Bobby. She stifled the pain in her memory.

I'll be with you forever, she remembered.

Although she felt the passage of over twenty years gone by, she had changed little, if any at all. She aged, she thought, but the effect of aging on her body was not the same as a normal human. Jeanine rubbed her eyes with her fingertips. Black swirls again. She made space between her sofa at the tiny table in front of it and collapsed the length of her sofa. The fake leather, really cheap plastic, she thought, squeaked as she settled down.

Blood everything, she reasoned.

What was she? She recalled a late-night movie she had seen years ago. A vampire movie. A circus, she believed. The movie looked to be old, even by her standards, and the undead creatures sprouted fangs and drank the blood of the living. She felt of her own normal teeth with her fingers.

Fangs – pleeeaaassse.

Another term bothered her. Undead.

Undead, as in once dead, and came back.

This didn't sound right either, because she, obviously, was very much alive. If she had died and came back, she would surely know it. She squeezed her fingertips with her thumb and saw the skin pale and turn pink.

Blood flow, obviously. Yep, she thought, very much alive.

Mother Rosalind taught that Jesus said the rich man died and went to hell. As a Jew, he saw his father Abraham in Abraham's bosom and cried for Lazarus to bring him water. Abraham said, There is a gulf fixed between us. You cannot come to us and we cannot come to you.

Jeanine pursed her lips. Dead was dead and that was it as far as she was concerned. She really couldn't explain these creatures that people called vampires. She shivered. Whatever they were, they were not people come back from the dead.

She didn't even *like* black.

However, whatever she was, she knew that she knew that she knew she could only drink blood to live. She lived by blood, fresh blood, and did not age in the normal human way. By all accounts, she reflected, in the natural, she was like them in the only way that mattered. She had to drink blood to live.

She remembered the movie. Within a hour the show had started getting gory and she had turned it off.

The movie did make one other point.

Vampire blood made more vampires.

According to legend, drinking vampire blood made a normal human turn into one of these creatures. Whether you drank it, or bathed in it. She remembered her beautiful mother Roxana telling her stories of evil Elisabeth Bathory, who bathed in the blood of servant girls she sacrificed to stay youthful forever.

In her mother's village, actually.

Vampire blood made more vampires.

Jeanine sat upright at once.

Nolan was beating her bloody after every sacrifice to get *her* blood! Suddenly, the seemingly endless ritual sacrifices of the blood cult made sense.

These were people, twisted people, trying to become like she was. Nolan was going to sacrifice Alecia to whatever god he believed was the vampire god to make himself, with her blood offering, like one of these creatures!

Jeanine hunched forward and placed her head in her hands with both elbows on her knees. It made cold and cruel sense. Nolan would surely kill Alecia if he thought it would do for him what he was wanting. This was beyond ludicrous. This was beyond impossible. Nolan was aging. His coal black hair now had streaks of grey at his temples and in the back of his head. His hairline from the front was slightly receding.

Well, she asserted, whatever Nolan was trying to get from her blood, it was not working for him. Nor any of the other blood cult zombies she had encountered through the years!

Jeanine's mind reeled. She had no other choice now. She had to take Alecia away from him, take her far away, find a place where he would never find them. She pulled on her sandals and grabbed her keys off the counter.

A desperate plan formed in her mind.

Escape with Alecia was her only thought.

Chapter Three

Kimberly reviewed her impossible-to-read scrawling on her yellow notepad at the family breakfast table. Thomas had already gone and Momma was on the telephone in Dad's office planning a wedding for one of her friend's nieces.

That left her and Dad at the table.

Donald Kline ruffled the paper, then finally put it down to look at her. "Not working today?" he inquired.

"Personal day," she replied. Her mind was on her notes.

She wanted to see the dimensions and angles of what was bothering Thomas – it was there, she just had to see it. Kimberly was vaguely aware that her Dad smiled at her, then got up to place his coffee cup and breakfast dishes in the sink.

Thomas had barely eaten anything again.

She was careful when she came down for family breakfast. After last night, she really didn't want to see Thomas. He didn't glare at her over breakfast, but he didn't talk to her either. He really didn't seem angry at her. He seemed resigned.

Actually, he seemed hopeless.

Kimberly wrote "hopeless" at the bottom of the page. The specific things she'd heard him say last night were written along the right half of the page.

I'll be fine, meaning, I am not fine now.

I don't even know where to begin looking for her, that is, the elusive Mary Harris. Meaning they had a sudden parting of the ways and it had not been her brother's idea.

Momma said, He still thinks of her. I see it in his eyes when he looks straight ahead. And even when he smoothed the photo she had stolen and he slipped it into his jeans pocket, he said, It's her. She saw pain and loss in her brother's expression.

She had to make a few assumptions to even have a place to begin, but as any journalist knows, assumptions may change as new facts present themselves.

Brother plus girl meant happiness.

Brother without girl meant misery.

Yet Thomas had practically knocked her down when she suggested she put out a few stringers to find where his Mary had gone. He said, You can't even begin to understand, and, Leave it alone.

Patricia came into the kitchen. She carried a ballpoint pen in her mouth and a little notepad of, apparently, a to-do list for the wedding. Momma loved weddings and any social event she could get involved in. Kim was aware that her father left for his study. "Mom, could you take me to town today?" Kim asked.

"We'll go in a little bit, dear," she said.

Kimberly knew from experience, that answer meant at least an hour. It was about nine o'clock and the day was bright and pretty. Kimberly collected her notepad and went to the back deck to enjoy the sunlight.

I don't know where to begin to even start looking for her, Thomas had said.

By light of day, the hammock he laid in was less imposing. It was just the familiar hammock under the tree now.

Kimberly uncapped her fountain pen, turned to a new page, and drew two lines that divided the page into fourths. She labeled the boxes Who, What, When, and Where. A thinking trick she'd learned from her photographer friend during her internship last summer at the *Observer*.

In the Who box, she listed: Thomas Mary.

In the What box, she listed: brother girlfriend student coed.

In the When box, she listed: May June July and August. The first of May was when they had gotten their first call that he had met this girl. About the first week of August was when he cryptically called to say he had been in an accident and wanted to come home. Kim went back and wrote the word *accident* in the What box. The term stuck in her mind. She underlined it and wrote a question mark beside it. What accident?

Kimberly stuck the end of her fountain pen in her mouth, then stopped chewing on it. In the Where box, she listed: Trenton New Jersey college – then pondered, and added the word *city*.

What had Thomas said? He had last seen Mary the morning she had brought him to the hospital the morning of his accident. Again, she pondered, What accident? What did Mary have to do with it?

She knew in her gut that there were serious questions here waiting to be answered. Begging to be answered.

Thomas had to be hiding *something* because his life had changed so abruptly. In the photo of him and his girlfriend, they looked to be happy and unafraid. Now her brother was hopeless and extremely despondent.

Well, Kimberly thought, finding out things was what she did. She folded her 4W chart in her notepad and went back inside. Mom was chatting on the telephone in the living room. About another thirty minutes, was 'Kim's guess. She went through the home to her father's study, a bright studio open on the southern side of the home. Two rows of drafting tables were arranged by the double insulated windows. Hanging flower pots gave the open skyline some green and color.

Her dad was sitting on a swivel seat in front of a blueprint spread out on a level desk. She loved to watch him describe an idea for a construct, then make the design real on paper, then produce the final architectural drawings that could be then used to actually build what he had once envisioned.

Finding the truth was like this. Start with a basic idea and build structure and detail until you see everything. She came beside her father. He was putting his readers on his face to examine a small handbook and taking his readers off to view the blueprint.

"Whatchadoing?" she asked.

He hugged her waist and pointed to the schematic with his free hand. "Just checking the materials in the foundation of the Gibbons Office Project." The structure as he envisioned it did not turn out like the builders actually built it. There had been delays, shortcuts, and work-arounds the general contractor had done that seemed to endlessly frustrate her father.

He turned to her. "Why didn't you work today? It's a pretty enough day."

"Research," she said.

Donald Kline seemed to give his daughter a knowing look. Like when he told the story of playing baseball in a cow pasture and slid into what he thought was second base, then he went home. Watch what you slide into.

Yuck, Kim thought.

"Did Thomas say anything to you about why he suddenly came home?" Her voice had become formal, like she was interviewing a celebrity in front of hundreds of cameras showing this the world over. She held her fountain pen like a miniature microphone.

"No, baby," Donald said, "he didn't."

That word again: *baby.*

Kim fumed silently. Her father's work telephone rang and he turned to answer it. "Excuse me, dear." She listened to half of a conversation, only a few minutes, then her father hung up.

His brow was furrowed in puzzlement.

"That was the bank," he said. "There are charges on my credit card to the VA clinic and a pharmacy in town. They were just calling to confirm that the charges are legitimate."

"What did you tell them?" Kimberly asked.

"I'm not going to dispute the charges until I know what they are. Thomas is on that account, but hanged if I know what he was doing at the VA clinic or why."

Kim considered prompting her dad to call the clinic itself, but stricter confidentiality guidelines severely restricted what medical personnel were allowed to say about a patient without explicit granted permission.

Kimberly pursed her lips.

Having information restricted made her rear end hurt. Assuming this was, indeed, her brother, it was a very juicy bit of intel. Not only was something wrong with him in his head, like staring into space wrong; he must have thought something was wrong with himself physically too.

Oh, how she wished for a special set of headphones. When you put these on a person, you can see and hear everything they think whether they want it or not. She could easily see herself interviewing her captive brother. Patricia came into Donald's studio. "Ready, dear?" she asked.

The captive brother image suddenly dissolved. Kim instantly switched gears and gave her father a small kiss on his cheek.

"Bye, Daddy," she said.

"Be safe, Kimberly," Donald said.

In her mind, Kimberly saw herself interview that celebrity before the entire world. Thomas was hiding something and she intended to find out exactly what.

* * *

Two blocks past the downtown fountain was the coffee shop. Two blocks past the coffee shop was the newsroom. Kim liked balance and symmetry. She could get a cup of mint coffee, then go up to the third floor of the former Sentinel daily paper and research the newswire like a real journalist.

Her mom dropped her off at the usual place. The brick enclosed thoroughfare was a favorite place for people to meet and have lunch outside on a pretty day. She pushed past the swivel iron gate and headed for the old Sentinel building.

Now somewhat scrappy, the red brick building was looking in disrepair. The tattered blue canopy over the door had faded and was ripped in a few places. The upper story windows, once brilliant red, were now a dull rust color, and they were peeling.

It's what was inside that counted.

Kimberly entered the first floor where a new small business had renovated the bottom floor. A man she did not know in a long white shirt and striped tie waved at her. She smiled but did not wave and kept going. The stairwell at the back was sealed with a padlock, but she – as former trustee of the Sentinel, was one of the few residents of the town that had the key.

She unlocked the padlock and clipped it to a belt loop in her jeans. When she left she would re-lock the door. The little stairwell was steep and she had to make two turns around the building, again coming to the front of the building before she entered the top newsroom that was the communication center of the little newspaper. Stacks of newspaper racks, like in the library, were in the middle of the room. On the far side of the wall, to the west side of the building, was a huge map of the entire state. On the aisle nearest her on the east side a row of tables held the newswire terminals.

Her first exposure to the newswire terminals, antique by modern standards, was when she was brought here on a seventh- grade field trip. She thought she was in love with her seventh-grade teacher anyway, a young man who had just started teaching the year she was in seventh.

Mr. Colbert was a radical for his day. His hair was longer than the accepted norm of the day. He wore a rainbow-colored tie and pale blue shirts. And he was oh, so passionate, about the freedom of the press, the need for information in our lives, and tried to instill his former career in journalism into his students.

Kimberly shook herself from her reverie.

She saw the old teletype machines, too. Although now silent, she remembered them printing messages on rolls of paper. She pressed several round keys as she walked by.

The newswire terminal was a dumb terminal hooked to a mainframe in Charlotte. A newsperson could research a story or article by entering keywords or date parameters, similar to finding a book you wanted at the public library. It was a big, big news catalog. All you had to do was find the right way to ask it what you wanted to know.

The old dot matrix printer was still attached and it still had form feed paper. Kim turned the little printer on and it buzzed to life. The little green phosphor glyph blinked at her. She began typing her login and password.

She was rewarded by the main screen.

Mr. Colbert called it a splash screen.

She limited the searches to New Jersey, then the city of Trenton. Kimberly began her first inquiry. She simply typed her brother's name. Hit the return key. The blinking cursor blinked and sat there. Nothing.

Likewise, she typed Mary Harris and found nothing.

Kim entered the keyword *headlines* and saw screens of titles pass by, up to twenty per page. Each time she pressed the return key, a new set of twenty titles scrolled past. In a big city like Trenton, a lot of stuff happened all of the time. Her search was too broad.

She took out her 4W chart she had put in her back pocket and uncapped her fountain pen. She looked for help how to narrow the date range of the search. Kim looked at her months in the When box and chose July, the month before Thomas called to come home.

The titles of newsworthy items scrolled by.

Even if the list was much shorter, it was still too broad. If a person had a new recipe for chicken soup, or if a person wrote a complaint to the newspaper about the mayor, or if garbage collection was delayed for a week for a strike, the array of clutter was obscuring the facts Kim wanted to see.

Thomas said, You can't even begin to understand – *what* ?

Kimberly when back to the help screen to seek inspiration. She found the way to filter out national, weather, business or financial titles. The list was much more promising, now only about four screens of titles.

She scrolled the list several times, just letting her eyes absorb the words.

A word caught her attention: *slasher*.

Kim selected the titles with the term *slasher* and was rewarded with screens of information. Kimberly wrote *slasher* in her Who box and kept reading.

Apparently, the city of Trenton had a mass murderer on the loose. Many of the articles Kim spotted were either demands that police do something about this crazed killer, or paranoia of where he might strike next. Kim wanted facts – who did he kill, where did he strike, and so on. The mindless blathering about where the killer may strike again was meaningless.

On a hunch, Kim checked Associated Press and Reuters for this lead. Nothing came back. If the story had not been picked up by the national newswire services, then it was either below threshold as not newsworthy or it had been highly suppressed by authorities who did not want the bad news to escape the Trenton local newspapers.

Kim felt a chill, even though warm afternoon sunlight poured into the once active newsroom. A literal murderer had been on the loose in the city where Thomas' college was. Although she did not know that it fit, or why, she kept the name *slasher* in her Who box. Kim stared at the names.

In the What box, she poised her fountain pen over the blank space several moments before she penned the word: *killer* . She also circled the word *city* in her Where box and connected a line to the word *killer* in her Who box. This was huge!

She considered the inferences of what she had just written, and tried to connect the dots, but in her mind – she did not know enough. She turned to her terminal and continued to read articles as she found them on the mass murderer called the *slasher*.

Something Mr. Colbert always said came to mind. The truth always comes out.

Majken moved carefully, silently, through the wasteland that was once the basement of a lively commercial building near the French Quarter, but the red brick building now had been boarded over and abandoned for years. Old desks and cluttered paper littered the dusty concrete. This was *her* building. Stefan's spotters had seen drug and prostitution activity spill over into this quiet business neighborhood.

Faint glow of lanterns cast spooky long shadows along the abandoned desks. She heard the sound of men talking in murmurs and some type of laboratory glassware being used. A drug lab, she assumed. She had left Josè and the limo at the far end of the alley two buildings down. She bent low and straddled two desks, bending and stretching from her waist. She flexed and straightened her arms and clenched her fists. She moved barefoot and silent, having left her shoes dangling on the third-floor fire escape where she had entered the building.

These men would surely try to kill her.

Didn't matter, though.

Footsteps from the corridor behind her made her pause, then leap straight up into the ceiling suspension framework. Majken hid as two men unsuspectingly walked under her as she melted into the shadows. When the men entered the room, she stretched down and touched her toes on the desk near the wall.

She moved to the wall opposite the open doorway. Shadows within. Someone in the room had a small radio playing, a nameless announcer talking about football.

Majken steeled herself and prepared to strike. Sensitive to human bodies, even when she could not see them, she felt inside at least four in the center of the room around the lab apparatus. Two or more along far side in the shadows. Maybe another guard or two. They were obviously armed and ready to kill.

Didn't matter, though.

She wanted more than blood tonight.

Majken ran and jumped, skirting the nearest wall. The white lantern light made her a wraith shadow as she literally ran along the side of the vertical wall, then

jumped across the fifteen or so feet to tackle the men in
the center of the room.

She kicked two of the men as she landed, then straddled a particularly large man over his shoulders behind
his head. She used her momentum to pivot her body as
she fell and they tumbled into a heap. She reached for
the fourth man just beyond her. The man she rode cursed
and swore, but dropped as she tightened her legs around
his throat. His neck snapped. The man in front of her, the
lone man standing in the center of the room, was reaching for a gun in a holster.

His hand just barely pulled the gun free before she
caught his arm and twisted. His wrist and forearm shattered and the weapon he thought he was going to use
dropped to the cold concrete floor. She landed lightly on
her toes as she pushed the gunman – his right arm dangling useless – into the lab apparatus and lantern in the
center of the table.

Majken immediately dove for the floor.

At least one of the men across the room, near the
east corner, was firing his weapon. She felt the vibration
stream of hollow point ammunition over her head. The
bullets tore into one of the men she just kicked down.

The makeshift laboratory was plunged into chaos. In
the shadows below the ghostly white light from the single
working lantern in the corner of the room, Majken stayed
low and sprang forward. She knew she had to move to the
end of the table on her right, then strike up and to her
immediate left.

The man she was facing was only firing at waist level
or above. Nearly ten feet away, she ducked, rolled, and
landed on her back in kicking position just in front of
him. Majken kicked straight up with her heel into his
groin. Blood oozed through his pants. As he doubled over,

she kicked a solid blow to his stomach while sweeping her other leg behind his knees to take him down.

When he fell, his upper body knocked the other lantern to the floor. The basement room was turned into darkness.

Majken squeezed her eyes shut and listened; the lantern afterimages faded from her vision. The room had become pitch dark to human eyes. Her dark adapted eyes could still distinguish black upon black shapes moving around her.

Two men left. One man was fleeing and had run straight into one of the tables kicked sideways in her initial attack. He groaned when he hit and appeared to be dragging his leg as he stumbled into the wall. The other man, by her estimate, was now huddled in the corner and was holding his hands over his head. The swishing of blood through his body sounded loud in her ears.

Ignoring the man in the corner for a moment, Majken sprang after the man trying to run. Before he got completely out the door, she caught his throat from behind and pulled him backwards. Her grip tightened, but not to the point of crushing his neck. She simply stopped and allowed his body to flop forward, then she reversed his momentum and tossed him on the table behind her.

As the man she threw on the table went motionless, she took three strides back to the assailant huddling in the corner. She simply lifted the man from the corner and slapped him. His head jerked sharply and he slid to the floor, unconscious, but alive. She then returned to the man lying on the table.

Dinner rush, she thought.

These types of people usually carried a knife or two in every boot. Majken hopped onto the table with the fallen man and used her right foot to pin his chest down as she searched for a knife. When she found the knife she wanted, she ripped the man's sleeve off, baring his arm, and made a slantwise cut along his upper arm.

As blood flowed from the cut, she drank.

Her body started to absorb the flowing nourishment.

Whatever she did, didn't matter.

However hard she tried to keep Thomas from being hurt, it didn't matter. Stefan had refused to allow her to bring Thomas here. Although he had good reason to protect the infrastructure they had carefully built through the years and she understood his decision with her mind, her heart ached.

Nothing she could do now would matter.

The man before her lay still in the darkness. The cut on his arm was starting to clot. She could hear this man's heart beat slower as he faded from consciousness. Didn't matter. Thomas was not part of her life now.

Nothing mattered.

Less than an hour after she had entered the office building, Majken exited the same third-story window facing the west.

The setting sun spread a golden-red glow behind a layer of clouds in the far western sky. The faint breeze off Lake Ponchartrain carried ozone, metallic tang of industry, the slight distillery scent of diesel fuel, and all of the combined scents from the people in the city. This city itself seemed to have its own characteristic scent found nowhere else.

Majken found Josè and the limo in the alley where she had left him. Alert to her arrival, he opened the door to the luxury compartment behind the driver. She smiled at him, but opened the passenger-side door up front where he sat, tossed her shoes into the back seat, and curled into the front with him.

Merely twenty minutes after she had fed, her body would compel her to lay down soon. She felt restless, as if she was a bottle with contents under pressure about to explode.

Josè joined her in the limo. "Home, James," she said.

James was the old black servant and driver she had when she was here in the sixties. He had long since retired. He was still living in his nineties now. She had not visited him yet. She affectionately called any driver Stefan sent her "James."

Josè knew not to ask. He was a very humble and discrete man with his little wife and two children. As Josè pulled into the normal city traffic, she said, "Cleanup." He nodded and apparently understood. Majken noted they were heading toward Metarie. "Josè?" she said. "May I ask you a personal question?"

"Yes, señorita," he replied. The gold of his front teeth flashed when he smiled.

"If you knew that your Conchetta had less than a month to live, what would you do?" She turned to the side so she could see him as he drove. She knew from how he spoke often of his little wife that he loved and protected her fiercely. He seemed to consider her question carefully.

Then he answered, "I would be with her."

"Suppose you were responsible for her condition. That she would die because of something you did."

"I would still be with her," he said.

Majken watched the late afternoon traffic thin as they were leaving the business district and entering the residential area.

"Your young man, señorita?" Josè asked.

Majken smiled to herself. Stefan must have briefed him. Then Josè would likely know all or most of what had happened. She said, "Yes."

"If you want to be with him, then you should be with him."

Oh, such a simple answer. In her mind, simple answers only worked in a far less complicated life. Josè was the kind of man who believed everything just works out. Yet, his answer *did* appeal to her greatly.

"What if he dies because of me?" All of the time they were together passed through her mind at once. Everything Thomas was to her, and could be to her, bore as a crushing weight on her chest. She had done this terrible thing to him. Her heart started beating faster.

Josè seemed to shrug. "If you stay here and he dies, or you go to him, and he dies, what is the difference, señorita?"

Majken calmed herself.

If he does die, she thought to herself, then the outcome is the same. Josè was nearing her home. Home at the end of the road, just like Thomas' parent's home in South Carolina.

"Señorita, may I ask you to consider a thing?" Majken nodded yes. "Would your young man have a better chance of survival with you here or with you there?"

The weight mercilessly boring on her soul suddenly lifted.

Josè stopped the limo in front of the small two bedroom white frame house. Its only distinctive feature setting it apart from any other home nearby was the very large palm tree that reached over the home.

She planted that little tree years ago.

"Thank you, Josè." She opened her passenger-side door, turned around, and leaned down to look back at him. "Start preparing for a trip. I have a feeling we'll be going to South Carolina in a few days."

She closed the limo door and watched him back the

length of the block before he could turn around. Dusk had settled over the peaceful neighborhood. If she was going to reenter Thomas' life, she would need a cover.

Majken walked barefoot to her front door. She pushed open the little wire gate with her foot and closed it as she passed. Smooth flat river stones formed a path through the grass. A set of wind chimes tinkled in the breeze.

Yes, she was going to him, she decided.

First, there were contingencies to prepare for. Majken entered her home. Her living room and adjoining kitchen were simply furnished. Two green plants hung in each corner next to the closed drapery. Her sofa was a burnished copper and gold twilled pattern she liked. She had several throw pillows, forest green, deep maroon red, and sunset orange to brighten the décor. A single oval rug covered her polished wooden floor.

Two incandescent lamps in her living room turned on as she approached and cast soft yellowish light through the lampshades. Her one concession to living in New Orleans at all were the rows upon rows of beaded necklaces draped over the wooden model of a sailing ship behind her sofa in her living room.

She listened throughout her home. She was alone and unobserved. Majken placed her shawl on a hanger between her kitchen and living room and reached for her telephone.

It was only past six in the afternoon.

She dialed the long-distance number by heart. Christopher would probably be home now. The phone rang twice before a young man answered. "Hello, Christopher, it's your distant cousin calling." Majken smiled. She could hear the noise of a baby over the line, surely his baby girl Maria born two years ago.

"Majken!" he shouted. "Good to hear from you. How've

you been?" She also heard over the line Christopher's wife exclaim happily. Francesca was probably holding Maria close to the phone. Majken pictured in her mind the young couple as she last saw them in their uptown Chicago apartment. Christopher's black curly hair, so much like Luigi's, and Francesca's freckled face, long tanned legs, short shorts, red flip-flops, and Florida Gator's sweatshirt.

"I am very well," Majken said. "I'm calling because I need another loaner." She toyed with a braided sash across her counter. She knew Christopher understood. She needed an alias, a contrived identity that would pass inspection. "Same as my prior loaner," she added. She reached under her cabinet and found a small pan to boil water and make herself a cup of hot tea. Stefan made her install a water filter device on her sink tap. She really was not used to it yet.

"Same specs as the last one?" Christopher asked. Her former alias, Mary Harris.

"Almost," Majken said, then switched her intonation to a Cockney accent, "but this one needs to be from England."

She heard Christopher exclaim under his breath. He would be tracking in his mind the path from birth certificate, to social security ID number, to visa or naturalization papers.

Challenging, yes. But four generations of Cappelli Investigations had never let her down. From great-grand Pa Luigi, to grand Pa Giuseppi, to Pa Michael, and now to son Christopher – her life with this family had been so intertwined from the day she rescued Luigi in Chicago in 1924.

"Yes," Christopher said, "we can do it. Expect a courier package in a few days."

* * *

Kimberly worked the newswire terminal until her stomach growled and she checked her watch and realized she was late meeting her Mom to take her home. She quickly collected the sheaves of form-fed, dot matrix printing of articles she found on the *slasher* and other seemingly insignificant events that had transpired in Trenton a few months ago.

She was careful to log out and watch the green screen terminal properly shut down before she turned the machine off.

The lamps from streetlights below shone in the bay windows next to her. Kim hurried down the stairwell, locked the Sentinel door, and went out of the storefront building. It was well after five and the other business had closed for the day. Kim passed the familiar businesses along South Main street back to the water fountain. She found her Mom parked to the side and sitting on a bench next to the fountain. She bundled the sheaves of paper out of sight. "Mom," she said, "I'm so sorry I'm late." She was a little winded from having run the last few blocks.

Patricia greeted her daughter, smiling.

"I know when you research, you lose track of time altogether." Kim smiled at her mother and was grateful for her Mom's gentle understanding. Mom's white Trans Sport was parked across the street. She glanced toward the fountain clock as she passed. She had kept her mother waiting for over an hour.

Kim hugged her mother as they walked.

"Love you, Mom," she said.

Patricia hugged her back. "Thank you, baby. I love you, too." For once Kim didn't mind being called baby. When her mother said it, all of the warm and right feelings of literally being her baby once upon a time came to

Kim's mind. According to Momma-logic, she felt her Mom was thinking more in terms of grandchildren right now. She knew her mother hoped that she would soon marry and soon thereafter make the great announcement that she and her new husband were now expecting.

Kim secretly laughed at the idea of marrying. Absolutely no one came to mind in this sleepy little town that she was even remotely interested in. And most of the guys she had known in high school were really not interested in her either. When Mr. Right comes along, she thought, I want him to share my dreams as well as my life. She paused dreamily to gaze up at the sparkling early night sky before her mother unlocked her door.

Kimberly got in her mother's car for the ride home. Oh, how she wished for a car of her own! She stuffed the sheaves of printed articles beside her seat and fastened her seatbelt. Kim considered as her mom drove. Speaking of marriage, Kim thought, there was Thomas and his evasive girlfriend. The elusive Ms. Harris was also a puzzle in Kim's mind. She wondered why the word *evasive* popped into her thinking.

Kim quietly shivered. She had spent much of the day researching a mass murderer who had been in the same city as her brother's college. Strangely enough, as she checked and double-checked the timeline, the *slasher* had come and gone during the summer months, but no references to an actual attack were mentioned beyond the first of August.

Kim actually felt a chill, an icy cold finger of realization, wiggle up her spine. There had been no *slasher* incidents in Trenton beyond the time of her brother's mysterious accident. This redoubled her confusion over her big brother's assertion that he had an accident on the highway and somehow fell out of his own car. I mean, re-

ally, here. How does one fall out of his own car, especially if he's alone?

The puzzle of what her brother had said returned to her thinking: the last time he saw his girlfriend was the morning she took him to the hospital after his accident! Somehow the scars, cuts, and bruises her brother tried to casually dismiss and explain away were not so easily explained away. Although she could not see how exactly he would have such marks on his forearms, if he had actually fallen on a roadway, she would've expected his skin to be like a rash or scrape and not literal cuts.

She noticed they were almost home. Kim really hoped that Thomas was there. She really needed to talk to him now, and have him tell her that her fears were unfounded and no one had literally tried to kill him.

Tonight after family supper, Kim went up to his bedroom in hopes of talking to her big brother. Thomas said he was not hungry and wanted to skip eating altogether. When Mom questioned him on it, he said he'd gotten a burger in town and wasn't hungry. He did come down and raid the kitchen ice pitcher twice for water before supper was served.

There were no sounds from his bedroom, not even music, and no light appeared under his door. The catatonic brother image popped in her mind. What was he doing in there?

She tapped lightly on his door.

No sound. Not even, Get lost brat!

Kim tapped again, a little harder. "Thomas," she called.

She turned the knob and opened the door a crack. She could see across the bottom of his bed. She called again and tapped on the door as she opened it. When the door completely opened, Kim said, "Huh." His bedroom was empty. Like a magnet, her eyes were drawn to the flapping curtains, white and gauzy in the moonlight and from the yard light reflected outside.

"Thomas!" Kim called. She reached his window and stuck her head out, looking right and left. He did not answer her, but she saw a shadow from the top of the roof and heard a scratching sound, like him sliding on the tile. She found him sitting above the gable of his bedroom window, cool and comfortable in only a T-shirt and shorts. Kimberly stretched to look out the window, then stepped up and half climbed out. "Hey," she called.

Thomas seemed to have a wry smile on his face. He knew heights were not one of her favorite things. "Hi, brat," he said lowly. Kimberly gathered her courage and stood on up, but she kept her feet on the window sill.

"Mom's making cherry pie for dessert. Thought you might want some." Thomas smiled and seemed relaxed.

"You came all the way up here to tell me Mom's making cherry pie. I appreciate it, but I'm not hungry tonight."

Kim scrambled around the gable and felt better as she straddled the gable itself. It was secure and solid, unlike her brother's weird behavior. "Well," Kim acceded, "Mom's not actually making cherry pie. I just wanted to talk to you and apologize. I'm sorry I went through your stuff. When I think of a lead, I just follow it. Peter called you a looney toon and I just wanted to prove him wrong."

"History repeats itself," Thomas quipped.

Kimberly stared at him. "What'da'ya mean?"

"Phillip, my roommate at school. He had a few choice things to say to me before I came home." Thomas clasped his hands and propped his arms on his knees.

"Like what?" Kim asked.

She noticed faint white line scars on his knees as well. His once tanned legs were starting to look pale. "All about Mary," Thomas injected. "How she was stringing me along, how she would hurt me, how she was seeing other men, uh, yadda, yadda, yadda."

"Did'ja prove him wrong?" she asked.

Thomas chuckled, but no humor was in the tight sound. "Phillip was so wrong about Mary, and so right about her, all at the same time."

Kim started. "How can he be right and wrong at the same time?" she asked.

"Point of view," Thomas replied.

Kimberly hesitated for a moment. The slight breeze tonight was stirring the limbs of the hardwood trees in the yard. "I went to town today," Kim said.

"I know," Thomas said, "Dad told me."

Kim's voice became tight and strained.

"I found out things that happened in Trenton during the summer. Bad things."

Thomas was just sitting, watching her.

Her words tumbled in a rush, spoken in a single breath. "Please, please, please tell me no one was trying to kill you."

He made a pained sound in his throat. His grim smile did not reach his eyes. His eyes were hard in a way she'd never seen in him before. "Kill me," he finally said. "What on earth gave you that idea?"

"I found articles on this *slasher* suspect. His killing spree started in mid-summer and ended, so far as I know, about the time of your accident. I couldn't find one instance of an actual attack attributed to him after you called us and wanted to come home."

Thomas clapped his hands in a mocking salute. His voice became totally void. "Well, well. Give the journalist a Pulitzer prize." He stopped clapping. "I'll at least say, Kimberly Denise, you're good. You're better than good. You're brilliant in your own way." Thomas rose to his feet and towered above her. "The only thing you don't know how to do is stay out of business that doesn't concern you."

Kim felt afraid. Anger from him she could handle. They'd had their arguments and fights before. But this, this was vindictive. She wondered if he would throw her off the roof or something equally bizarre.

Kimberly let out a slow, calming breath.

She was Barbara Walters material, she just knew it. Composure under fire. Kim stiffened her stance and re-played what her brother had just said. She would be on safe ground again if she could get to the facts. Her thoughts seemed to gel at one place. "Your accident wasn't an acci-dent. This killer called the *slasher* was your accident."

Kim's heart started beating very fast. She could feel and see her brother stiffen as she said it. This was it! This mass murderer had tried to kill her brother! This was beyond bizarre.

Thomas ... her brother ... in the hands of a literal killer.

For once Kimberly was speechless. She couldn't think of a single thing to say. She had no rebuttal, no reply, no answer. She had only the gentle swaying of the leaves around them and the promise of autumn. "I don't under-stand," Kim finally said. "What do you have to do with a killer like this?"

Thomas laughed humorlessly. "I have friends in low places."

Kimberly just stared at him.

Thomas filled the awkward silence. "The *slasher* took me to use as bait. He wanted to kill Maj – Mary, and she came after me." Thomas knelt before Kim and pointed his finger in her face.

"You'd better thank God that she came after me. If she hadn't I'd have been another statistic and you would've never heard from me again." Kimberly felt very, very small.

"How'd you get hurt?" she asked.

"John kept pushing me on the sharp rocks next to this cliff. Over and over again." Thomas looked at both hands as he spoke.

Kim could instantly see it. If her brother had been pushed onto sharp rocks, he would certainly have the kind of injuries he had come home with. She felt another chill. The *slasher* murderer had not been named in the newspaper. Not named at all. Kimberly gawked. "You know this man's name!" she exclaimed. Thomas spread his hands.

"Suuuurrrre," he said, "I'm on first name basis with the scum of the earth right now."

Kim held her head with both hands.

This was absolute overload! She had wanted her brother to calm her fears, but this, oh, this was so bad that *bad* couldn't even begin to describe it properly. Mom and Dad could never take this. The only thing she could think to do would be to grab the next guy who said, Hi, to her and elope. Or maybe run naked down main street. Oh, sweet Jesus, she kept thinking.

Her brother stood again. The moonlight cast his face and the front of his body in shadow.

"Told you, Kimberly, to leave it alone."

Chapter Four

Jeanine drove to the SafeWay shopping center off Prospect and parked in her usual spot. Some of the rain had lightened and it was not pouring as it had been that morning. Jeanine still felt numb. In front of her people milled about doing what they do everyday. A middle-aged woman was pushing a cart toward the store; an older man was pushing a cart away from the store.

She felt her heart racing.

Jeanine struggled to compose herself. Panicking would not help the situation. Nolan would be out of town a few more days. Alecia was safe at school right now. No one was going to kill her baby girl today. Jeanine bowed her head on her steering wheel.

She gripped and released the steering wheel as she prayed, "Oh, God, help me. Help me get Alecia away from Nolan."

Jeanine looked up and gazed around the shopping center. She fished her wallet from between the seats, found her ATM card, and made her way purposely to get cash.

The maximum she could withdraw at any given time was one hundred dollars. Money meant freedom from Nolan. She stepped up to the ATM, inserted her card, and punched the codes to make the withdrawal. The machine gave her the cash in twenties and returned her card. This was routine. Nolan insisted she make only cash purchases. She was given a weekly allotment of cash just to meet basic expenses and to care for Alecia. She stared at her reflection in the ATM glass. Jeanine stepped back quickly from the ATM. She was suddenly concerned whether he could tie in to the ATM surveillance.

This would drive her crazy. She couldn't start second guessing herself now. This was just another day. She stuffed the cash in her pocket and walked in a normal fashion to the grocery store. A few minutes walking through the store would be a normal thing to do. She needed normal right now.

She pushed a cart and walked the aisles.

When she saw something she knew Alecia would like, she put it in her cart. Snacks, food that could be carried in the car and not need refrigeration, a few sweets, and two coloring books with a new pack of crayons. For herself, she glanced over the plasticware. She found several packages of cheap plastic bowls. She also got several boxes of fresh razor blades.

Jeanine purchased her items. She put Alecia's things on the right side of her trunk and stuffed her bowls with razor blades in a paper bag and hid this beneath her spare tire.

The rain started again.

She was soaked before she got under the wheel. Over half of her cash was gone, but she could stop at a different ATM and make more withdrawals.

Jeanine wiped the water from her eyes and straightened her hair. With a heavy heart she pulled into the normal morning traffic. Her mind was clouded. The situation was causing her to go numb. Little by little she found herself in the Wal-Mart parking lot and was walking to the rear of the store where the automotive department serviced vehicles. She saw no one she recognized behind the counter.

A young black man who worked on the cars waved at her. She smiled and nodded but kept walking. After passing through the auto service department, Jeanine wished she had remembered his name. None of the other employees seemed to know her.

She felt like an outcast. The brightly lit store depressed her. Everyone else around her had normal lives. They had children of their own. They had husbands and wives to love and cherish them. They had names.

How many of these people ever had to deal with blood cult zombies?

She wandered to the children's section.

Jeanine picked up and lay down small toys as she passed them in the aisle. Alecia played with dolls sometimes; she had a stuffed Winnie The Pooh toy when she was littler but it was at Nolan's cabin. She passed by the books without picking any up. Alecia wasn't much of a reader.

The child was about to be uprooted from everything she knew. Jeanine decided not to purchase any toys and went back to the automotive department. Several men were making purchases when she passed by the counter. The young black man was gone. He must be on break, she thought. She found herself staring at a box of bungee cord tie downs. She counted her cash and bought six long ties.

Jeanine left the Wal-Mart store and found another ATM at a nearby bank. She withdrew another hundred in cash and felt better. This cash, she locked in her glove compartment. It was just past ten o'clock. Already Jeanine felt weary from the day. At least for now it had stopped raining.

She considered going home, but knew she would not rest peacefully. She drove north into a part of Helena she had not traveled for years. She rolled her window down and let the breeze dry her hair. The county road that ran parallel to the north-bound Interstate was busier than she remembered. More businesses littered both sides of the road. Within thirty minutes, she found a bar she had worked at over sixteen years ago. Same dull siding the color of sage. She knew it would be closed at this time of day. The small lounge appeared as she remembered it.

When she parked and got out of her car, memories of the place flooded her memory. She had taken a bartending course in her earliest vampyric days. This gave her an excuse to be in a public place, but not be expected to either eat or drink. She made some friends here, including her Hispanic coworker Manny.

She smiled at the thought of Manny.

He could serve liquor, but he couldn't drink much before he passed out. Useful kind of thing to know.

She was in this establishment four years.

Two blood cult leaders ago, almost twelve years, they put a stop to her job. Jeanine resisted going up and trying the door. No one there would know her. Jeanine got back in her car and headed back the way she came. Unfamiliar shopping malls and businesses sprouted everywhere. Manny's place was nearby.

She found a small subdivision of trailers just west of the Interstate. Jeanine slowed to better get a feel of this area again. The entire subdivision had been cleaned up quite a bit from the time she was here before. More trailers lined the street on both sides. His trailer had been a beige brown, but over the years that could have changed. He was in his fifties when they worked together. Now he would be, what, in his late sixties.

She remembered his kind round face and laughing eyes.

Jeanine found a trailer that seemed in the same spot relative to the landmarks she recognized. The trailer itself had a framed roof and a porch on it now. The driveway was empty. No vehicle. She parked, got out of her car, and walked to the porch.

The curtain blinds were drawn and she could not see inside at all. She rapped on the aluminum frame of the door. Several minutes passed. She rapped again. She waited another minute or two, then turned to leave when she heard the door open.

The man that came to the door was a slight old man with frizzled white hair. He used a walking stick to balance himself. His weathered face was taut and the line of his jaw was severe.

Jeanine turned to the man. "Sir, I'm looking for Manny Ruiz. I think he used to live here." He seemed to glare at her through the door. Jeanine wondered if he heard her. His voice had the sound of cracked dry parchment.

"I'm Manny Ruiz," he said. He looked her up and down. "Who are you?"

"Manny!" she said, "I've missed you so much." Jeanine reached in the doorway and hugged the startled elderly man. "We used to work at Vito's lounge together. I was your bartender buddy on Friday and Saturday. I'm Jeanine, uh," she paused to remember her name at the time. "Jeanine Brown," she said.

The man's eyes finally registered that he recognized her. "Wha –" he made noises.

He seemed to be trembling and shaking.

Jeanine reached for his arm to help him steady himself. He started backing away from her. She glanced inside his living room. The same oversized stuffed chair was in the same place. "Let me help you," she offered.

She helped the elderly man back to his lounge chair. His hands were shaking when he reached back to sit down.

"You're not the Jeanine I knew. The Jeanine I knew had dark hair. She'd be in her late forties now." The man eyed her warily. She realized he was afraid of her.

Jeanine slowly stood and moved slightly away from her old friend. She started backing toward the door. "I'm sorry, sir. I must have the wrong place. I'm sorry to have disturbed you." She reached with her hand behind her.

His walking stick had fallen on the carpet. She nearly

tripped on it backing up. She set his cane next to the door and reached behind her to get outside.

This had been a big mistake.

Jeanine ran off the porch to her car. Her Mustang engine revved when she started her car. There was no hiding the distinct growl of that engine. Although her car had since been reworked and painted, it was the same car she drove when she worked at the bar. "Oh, God," she prayed as she backed into the street, "don't let him remember me and have a heart attack."

Jeanine could no longer see Manny or his trailer. She slowed to a respectable pace and quietly left the subdivision. She stopped at a service station down the street and used the rest room. The look of wild fear in his eyes would haunt her for a few nights. When Jeanine again reached the more recently familiar part of town, she felt a little better.

That was delightful, she thought. Go scare an old friend to pieces just because you don't show age the same as humans. Not only did she feel alone, and an outcast, now she felt like a freak. To top everything else off, it started raining again.

Jeanine drove home just because she did not want to be out right now. The little trailer was as she left it. The place seemed to have it's own weight bearing down on her.

I'll be with you forever, stabbed in her thinking.

Everything in her life since Bobby was here. She remembered Alecia's high chair she had fed her with as a baby in her kitchen, the times she played with Alecia on this living room floor, having a talk with Alecia about her body as she started maturing as a little girl to prepare her for womanhood.

Yet her life was a lie. A fabrication of the blood cult

leadership. Secrets abound.

She did have a few secrets of her own.

Jeanine opened her silverware drawer and found the small screwdriver she kept there. She unscrewed the wall panel beside her stove. Hidden in the wall, journals she had kept through the years, were wrapped in plastic and stored for safe keeping. Jeanine took the top journal and sat with it on her couch. She fished around her couch cushions for her pen and found it.

She dated the next blank page and wrote her revelation of the day. There were dates, times, places, events, and what she had seen and experienced in life from the beginning. She didn't know what she would ever do with these, but at least she had them. Soon it would be time to get her hospital care package, then Alecia. Manny's reaction to her bothered her. She wrote all that down, too. What was she? In her mind, she resolved that no matter what, she was going to get Alecia away from Nolan

Going to a new place frightened her a little.

She would have to acquire new blood sources herself.

Somehow they would make it.

The corridors of Smith Elementary were bright and colorful and cheerful. Even in the gloomy rainy day like today, the walls were brightly decorated with happy children playing in the sun.

Jeanine came a few minutes early to get Alecia. She entered the school office. A young woman behind the counter looked up and greeted her. The clamor of little voices from the hallway could be heard. Students were ready to go home for the day.

She asked for a release form. This would give her permission to keep Alecia out of school next week because of a family outing. Jeanine filled in the form and signed it.

At least Nolan had made sure Jeanine herself could sign or speak on behalf of Alecia's care in his absence. The entire school had seen her with Alecia for years. There was no question. The school office aide wrote a hall pass and gave it to what looked like a high school student, and sent her to get Alecia from class a few minutes early.

Within five minutes, Alecia came to the office with her book pack and yellow slicky raincoat on, smiling brightly at her Jennie.

Jeanine led Alecia to her car. The rain was pelting the metal canopy overhead like machine-gun fire. The sky was still overcast with thick dark clouds. Dreary day, she thought.

She had parked in the bus stop. Two yellow busses were waiting to pull up to the stop behind her. She opened the passenger door for Alecia, helped her get in the seat without flooding her car interior, then waved in thanks to the first bus driver. She didn't have a raincoat herself.

Jeanine got soaked getting into her car behind the wheel. She pulled out of the school driveway. Alecia chatted non-stop on what she did today. Jeanine started to head home, but turned at the last minute to enter a shopping center near the school. She saw a small pavilion and parked next to it.

"Honey," she said to Alecia, "come with me."

Jeanine braved the pounding rain and went around her car to open Alecia's door and led the little girl to the pavilion. Alecia was still bundled warmly in her yellow slicky raincoat. Jeanine got on her knees before Alecia and loosened the hood and unfastened a few of the clasps so she could see Alecia's face better. She smoothed the water from her baby girl's face and smiled at her. Alecia smiled at her, and reached for a hug. Oh that hug! Jeanine held Alecia close. Tears pulled at her eyes.

"Baby," she started. "I have to talk to you about something important. You need to listen and try to understand what I'm saying to you." Alecia was attentive. "I have learned that your Daddy wants to hurt you. He's going to hurt you like he hurts me." Her voice caught for a second. "I can't let him get to you, because he will kill you." Alecia was strangely silent.

Then she asked, "Why?" in a small voice. Jeanine thought of a million vindictives.

"Your Daddy does things – I think because he wants power. He does bad things to people just because he can. It doesn't bother him when he hurts someone." In her mind, Jeanine added, *It doesn't bother him when he kills someone.*

"Do you understand me, baby girl?"

Alecia looked like she did when she was hiding from thunder and lightning. Her lips quivered a little and her mouth was drawn. She didn't cry, but she looked like she was on the verge of crying. "Why does my Daddy want to hurt me? I've been good." The little girl's voice was fragile.

Jeanine reached for her. "Baby, it has nothing to do with you." Jeanine smiled at her and caressed her pouty face. "You're the sweetest, most loving child I've ever known. You're an angel to me, honey. He wants to hurt you because he's bad."

Alecia's voice seemed to take a tone of greater knowledge that a little girl could know. "He's evil," she said flatly. Jeanine could only nod in agreement. She had choked up on what Alecia had said.

"Yes, baby, he's evil." Jeanine held her baby's arms to gently direct Alecia to face her and looked intently at her baby girl. "I can't let him get you. We have to go far away where he can never find us. We have to leave here, honey. Do you understand? We have to get away from him."

"I understand," she said. She was being extraordinarily calm for a seven-year-old girl who just learned her father wants to kill her.

Jeanine sighed. Now was the hard part.

She looked down at the wooden beams she was kneeling on. The wet grass was visible in the gaps between the wood. That's what her life had done. She had fallen through the cracks.

"Honey, I have to take us far away from here. We can never come back. You will never see your Daddy again if I have anything to say about it. Will you come with me and stay with me?"

Alecia nodded. She would!

Jeanine felt a great surge of relief. Alecia seemed to understand about her father. Now Jeanine had to make her understand about herself. *What am I?* she thought.

Not human. Not entirely.

"Honey," she began slowly. "There's something else I have to tell you about me." Oh, God, she thought, this was harder than she'd thought it would ever be. She squeezed her eyes shut and looked away from Alecia's trusting face. Then she looked back at Alecia. Jeanine put on a brave smile.

"Baby girl, do you remember me, how I looked when we first met?" She fluffed her honey blonde hair and primped a little for Alecia. Alecia giggled.

"Yes, Jennie."

"Well, honey," she paused, "I don't age the same as normal people." She recalled the shock of recognition on Manny's face. "Well," she corrected, "I age, but I don't show it."

Alecia asked, "Why?" *Million dollar question.*

"I –" she began. "I'm different. I really don't understand all of it. I grew up in a family with my Papa and

Mamă far away from here. My Mamă died when I was only ten and my Papa raised me. I went to school like you and grew up. I knew this boy in high school." *I'll be with you forever.*

Jeanine scooted off her knees to sit on the small bench inside the pavilion. Alecia sat next to her. Jeanine put her arm around Alecia to make sure the wind and rain didn't blow on her too much. She lowered her voice. "He was sooooo good looking." Alecia giggled when Jeanine poked her.

Jeanine laughed with her baby girl. It had been too long since she'd actually laughed, she thought. Jeanine liked it. It lifted the gloomy feeling that had been clinging to her all day long.

"What happened?" Alecia asked. Her eyes and her gaze was total innocence and total trust. Jeanine always wanted Alecia to trust her, to be able to come to her, no matter what she did or how she felt, no matter how bad it was – whatever it was.

I'll be with you forever, she remembered.

Jeanine sighed. She just couldn't look into Alecia's bright trusting eyes. "He died. He got sick and died."

Alecia was clearly disappointed. This was girl talk of the best kind. Jeanine realized just how little she'd spoken of her own life and dreams before – her life changed.

"Baby girl," she said. "I have to live different from your teachers at school, or your friends, or their parents. You know when you go to the school cafeteria and they fix your plate with what you want to eat?"

Jeanine vaguely remembered school food. Maybe this wasn't the best analogy to use.

Alecia nodded.

"I can't eat food or drink milk or, I can't even have a slice of cinnamon toast. I have to drink water, and I know

I can drink some things, like hot tea, but most everything else, I cannot take it in like normal people do."

Gummy bears, fresh on her mind.

Alecia looked at her with the same trusting expression as before. Jeanine felt somewhat relieved. "Why?" Alecia asked.

"Something bad happened to me years ago."

Alecia was starting to squirm a little in her seat. Jeanine tried to force herself to say it. She'd been skirting around what she had to say, what Alecia would likely see her do since they would be travelling and living together.

No way around this, she thought.

"Honey," she said, looking straight into Alecia's eyes, "I can only take blood to live."

She waited for the inevitable fear to creep into her baby girl's face, for Alecia to draw away in horror at what she was and how she had to live. Nothing happened.

Alecia just looked at her with the same trusting expression she always had. "Baby girl," Jeanine emphasized, "you do understand that I can only drink blood to live?"

Alecia just looked at her. *She's afraid of me*, she thought.

Oh, God. If Alecia bolted from her now she would have no protection from Nolan. *This is hard*, she thought. *I have to make her understand what I am without her being afraid of me.*

"Honey," she said, her mouth gone dry.

"You know that I would never hurt you?"

"Yes, Jennie," Alecia said lowly.

Were those tears on Alecia's face or was water dripping from her wet hair?

Oh, God. *What was she?*

Jeanine bowed her head. The shame of what she was now and how far she had fallen was just too much. Alecia's love for her had become the core of her life, her very existence. If she lost that, what would be the use in going on? Cold tears, like when Nolan beat her, started to drip down her cheeks. She felt so totally alone. Alecia reached her tiny hands for her. Her own little face had drawn up in tears. Tears for her, Jeanine thought.

"Don't cry," the little girl said.

Jeanine thought again of the little picture Alecia had drawn for her. The both of them together. Safe. Happy. Free from Nolan and the likes of the blood cult.

Blood spurting from the sacrifices, she vividly remembered. Years upon years upon years of blood. People dying.

What was she?

Jeanine looked up. Her gaze fell directly into Alecia's eyes. Her baby girl's eyes seemed so open and loving right now. Jeanine knelt in front of Alecia again. Alecia reached for her. Oh, that hug! Jeanine pulled Alecia close and whispered over and over again, "I'll never let anything bad happen to you, baby girl. I'll protect you with my life, if need be."

That look of absolute trust was in Alecia's face again. Somehow they'd make it. She held Alecia close for what seemed like forever, even if it was only a few minutes, in the pouring rain. Somehow, they'd make it.

Cold rain. Cold tears. Cooler body temperature. Jeanine took Alecia home and they settled into their normal routine at night. She watched her baby girl for signs of fear or a reaction to what they had discussed at the pavilion, but Alecia seemed okay.

Alecia's dinner was a heated TV dinner. The little girl

didn't say anything when Jeanine brought the dinner to her and set it up on the collapsible tray in front of their sofa. Jeanine considered it far more obvious that she, herself, did not have a dinner tray. She guessed that Alecia probably believed she ate during the day while she was at school.

She remembered the blue lunch tote and the emptied blood bag she dined from today. Jeanine made a mental note to get rid of the blood bag somewhere. Maybe bury it in the yard – too many nosy neighbors. She guessed it was considered hazardous medical waste. She couldn't just throw it in the regular trash.

Jeanine turned her black-and-white television around so she and Alecia could watch the evening movie together. Alecia got cold, so Jeanine covered her with a quilt.

With nightfall, it had finally stopped raining. At bedtime, Jeanine made sure Alecia got her bath, brushed her teeth, and got ready for bed on time. Tomorrow would be a big day. After Alecia finished, she let her baby girl sit up and watch the evening news while Jeanine got a shower and prepared for bed as well.

When she got out of the shower, Jeanine checked her backside as she stepped beside the toilet onto the cold linoleum floor. The former bloody red welts had completely faded to barely pink. By tomorrow, she thought, the scars would be completely gone. If only her feelings and everything else that had happen to her would fade and heal as quickly. She found Alecia bundled in the quilt in the center of the sofa. She'd propped her feet on the table and she was wiggling her legs like she often did.

Jeanine smiled and plopped down beside her baby girl. She seemed unusually quiet. Jeanine reached over the quilt to hug Alecia and gave her a kiss on the side of her cheek.

Alecia smiled vaguely. She seemed far away. Maybe what they'd discussed at the pavilion was bothering her. "Honey, what are you thinking about?" Alecia looked at her, seeming to look through her.

"It wasn't your fault," she said.

Again, the tone of her voice had become so much more knowing and aware than for a child of seven. "What do you mean, baby girl?" Jeanine almost held her breath in anticipation of what Alecia would say.

"When that bad thing happened to you years ago – it wasn't your fault."

Fresh tears welled up in Jeanine's eyes. Truth be told, Bobby had dragged her into this miserable life. In her heart, she had always looked back and thought if she'd only done this, or didn't do that, he might be alive today and none of this would've ever happened. *I'll be with you forever*, in her memory. She stifled the pain and looked at her baby girl. She was so proud of the remarkable young lady Alecia would surely become.

"What a treasure you are, baby girl. Nolan'll never know what he missed when he didn't see you."

Jeanine nudged Alecia up and prompted her to go to bed. Before Alecia entered her own bedroom, Jeanine asked her, "Want to sleep with me, baby girl?"

Alecia turned with a sudden smile and practically leaped into her Jennie's arms. Everything good and everything right in her life lay next to her that night. Jeanine watched Alecia sleep a little while before she, herself, closed her eyes and slept.

When morning came, the sky was the color of ash. The sky was full of turbulent clouds – the wind was blowing, but, thank God, it was *not* raining.

Jeanine got up first and prepared Alecia's breakfast as usual. Alecia came out after her in about five minutes.

Today was Saturday. Alecia was not going to school today. She turned on her television to listen to weather and any travel forecast.

Generally, she intended to go south, but away from California. She didn't have a map but she could get one on the road. She had withdrawn an extra hundred yesterday and she planned to stop by several ATMs before she left beautiful Helena and Nolan forever.

When Alecia finished breakfast, Jeanine reminded her that she did not have to go to school next week and they were leaving this morning. Alecia perked up when Jeanine told her to go to her bedroom and lay out all of her clothes and anything she just had to take with her. She watched her baby girl happily hop to her bedroom to find her clothes.

While Jeanine washed Alecia's breakfast bowl in that sink for the last time, she was considering herself what to take and what to leave behind. Her journals were safe behind the wall panel next to her stove. What few personal possessions she had kept from her old life were long buried there as well.

If everything went according to plan, she would be rid of Nolan forever today. The thought of being free filled her with both great happiness and certain anticipation. She would have to start acquiring her own blood sources, starting today. She planned to leave by nine o'clock, travel for six or so hours, then stop early enough in the afternoon to find a place where men were, travelers, people's large dogs, bars, elderly – she was certain she would find what she needed every day.

Alecia called Jeanine from her bedroom.

When Jeanine stuck her head in Alecia's bedroom, she found that Alecia had laid out all of her clothes in neat stacks. Panties, socks, shorts, tops, dresses, and a few playthings she had here.

The few toys Alecia had made Jeanine a little sad. She smiled at Alecia and praised her for being so organized, but she silently promised herself she would find money to get Alecia that bicycle she always wanted or that doll she saw on television last Christmas that she could not afford to get her last year.

Life would get better from here on.

Jeanine picked a few of Alecia's dresses for school, her new school, then clothes Alecia would be comfortable riding in the car, then a few changes of underwear. She didn't have a suitcase. Plastic bags would have to do. She went into the bathroom and got her and Alecia's toothbrushes, then remembered her shaving kit also to shave her legs and underarms. She primped in the mirror.

Had to look sexy for the gentlemen, she thought.

Alecia picked only two toys to take with her. Jeanine beamed with pride. She loaded everything she and Alecia had packed in her car. She gave Alecia one of the new coloring books and pack of crayons. Her baby girl squealed happily and started drawing in her coloring book.

She noticed that Alecia did not have a warm coat. There was probably a coat at Momma Lillian's trailer. Before they left, Jeanine thought to say goodbye to the one person in this town that had known her all of her twenty-four years here.

Jeanine slipped in her dark contacts, then went to her bedroom for a final look around and to gather a few clothes. She took a plastic bag with her and stuffed a few changes of underwear, some sexy underwear she never had a chance to wear, and a handful of jeans.

In her closet she collected several of her comfortable blouses, and two blouses with skirts that were pretty and dressy. She picked a few dresses and saw, in the back of her closet, her old prom dress wrapped in plastic. Jeanine took her prom dress out just to look at it a final time. She unwrapped it.

It was a satin silvery material that her Papa paid an arm and a leg for just so his only daughter could even go to her senior prom. She held it up. It still fit. Yesterday, in her mind, and over a quarter of a century ago.

That was where Bobby had first promised her, *I'll be with you forever.* She turned and saw him in her memory, dying on her bed, reaching for her. His body was covered with sweat. He had alternating chills and high fever, nausea and abdominal cramps. Purple blotches were around his ankles and along his arms. Blood in his urine. Jeanine savagely shoved the unwanted image from her memory. She couldn't help that he'd gotten himself killed by drinking blood and getting her to do it too. Yes, she'd loved him dearly once, but it was time to move on. A better life awaited her and Alecia. She wrapped her old prom dress back in the plastic and shoved it deep into her closet and even farther out of her memory. Time to move on, she thought.

She gathered her plastic bag of clothes, a pillow and quilt for Alecia to sleep in the car, and her car keys from the counter.

Jeanine thought to lock her trailer, then reconsidered. Why bother? She wasn't coming back anyway and Momma Lillian could find another poor soul to take under her wing. She dumped the plastic bag of her clothes in her trunk, told Alecia she would speak to Momma Lillian a few minutes and get her warm coat, then they would be off.

What could she say to Ms. Daugherty?

Thank you did not even begin to cover how she felt. She pushed back the first stinging of tears and she held herself in check. She didn't want the last thing for this precious lady to see was her crying. Jeanine hit the aluminum screen with her open palm a few times. "Momma Lillian, it's me, Jeanine," she called. She heard the elderly woman moving inside from, she guessed, her back bedroom. Jeanine traced the elderly woman's hobbling steps through her home with her sensitive hearing.

When the door opened, she called to her elderly friend, "Momma Lillian, I need to get Alecia's coats." She found herself speaking louder than necessary. It was an ingrained habit from working in old folks homes.

Ms. Daugherty probably had good hearing.

"Why, child, yes. Come in."

Jeanine hugged her landlady as she passed by, then went to Alecia's bedroom and gathered two of her baby girl's warmer coats. The smaller of Alecia's two coats was camouflaged and could be used if her father took her hunting. He never did. Her big coat was white and had a fur-lined hood. She didn't know if it was real fur or not. Nolan probably paid a bundle for it.

With coats under her arm and a heavy heart, Jeanine stood before Momma Lillian in her living room. She grasped the elderly woman's bony hand with both of her hands. "Momma Lillian, Alecia and I are leaving."

The elderly woman smiled at her with that cherubic face.

"Where are you going, dear?"

Jeanine hesitated. "I don't really know. Maybe south or southeast. That's not important. I wanted to thank you for taking care of me and taking care of Alecia. We love you and we'll think of you often."

The elderly woman seemed taken aback.

Jeanine hugged her again.

"Leaving?" she said. "But dear, the world is a dangerous place. Where are you going?"

In her mind, Jeanine replied, *Far away.*

"I don't know yet. My trailer is unlocked. Anybody who wants whatever is left is welcome to it."

Her landlady seemed to stammer, "But dear, what about your young man? Alecia's father." Every foul thing she could think to call the sonofabitch popped into her mind at once. She barely managed to calm herself and put on a fake smile.

"He won't miss us," she said with cold certainty.

With that, Jeanine hugged Momma Lillian and went out the door. Alecia was watching. At the gravel, Jeanine turned and waved at her former landlady. Momma Lillian just stood, transfixed, in her doorway.

Jeanine opened her car door, tossed Alecia's coats in the back seat, and whispered, "Wave, honey."

The little girl waved at Momma Lillian.

It was more than time to leave.

A better life awaited her and Alecia.

Jeanine got into the moulded driver's seat and smiled at her baby girl. Alecia gave her two thumbs up and Jeanine laughed. She revved her Mustang engine, for once not concerned that her former neighbors would complain. She pulled out of the trailer park. Before she left the city, she stopped by her SafeWay again and asked Alecia if she wanted anything to eat or snack on. She had about two hundred locked in her glove compartment and about forty in her wallet.

Jeanine fished her card from her wallet and walked to the ATM. When she entered her code to make a withdrawal, the little screen displayed a code and did not eject her card. She punched the cancel button several times, but the machine kept her card. The polite little machine displayed a message that she should contact her financial institution.

A trap, she thought.

Jeanine quickly walked away from the ATM and got into her car. Alecia resumed drawing in her coloring book. Jeanine turned into the street, eager to leave Helena far behind.

Jeanine throttled her Mustang on the expressway and downshifted as she rapidly approached the highway exit. They had been travelling for half a day, now in Wyoming, and were approaching a town called Sheridan.

For the first time in many years, she started to feel the pull of her blood needs. Her immediate concern was feeding Alecia. Then she, herself, would need to find a blood source somewhere. This had to work. She had no other choice.

Alecia was irritable and tired after riding for almost six straight hours. Jeanine also felt the sting of irritability, but not because she was tired. In the early days of Nolan's tenure, he deliberately withheld blood from her just to see what effect it would have on her body. The first effect was a type of edge on her perceptions. Her sensitive hearing increased and she became acutely aware. The second effect was irritability. She knew to make adjustments in how she reacted to things that happened around her when her blood needs started pushing her.

Nolan said the edge effect was her body gearing up for the hunt. Predator response.

Jeanine stopped at an economy motel with a gas station, first refueled and topped her Mustang, then found a room for herself and Alecia. Alecia needed to eat first. She found a Dairy Queen on the main street. Once Alecia had eaten, they went back to their room. She left Alecia watching a color television and toured the motel. Jeanine walked the perimeter of the second floor. Too few travelers had checked in. Jeanine checked on her baby girl. She warned her to stay inside and not let anyone in but her. The sky was starting to get dusky dark, and the overhanging clouds made it appear darker than it would have been.

Behind the hotel, a hill rose steeply. Beyond the incline on the far side, she heard trucks hauling on a road nearby. She stopped by her car and got two razor blades and slipped one in each pocket. She hiked to the top of the hill.

A strong scent of diesel fuel assailed her senses. There was a meandering trail to the top of the hill and a truck was coming. A man was driving. She quickly unbuttoned half of the buttons of her blouse. Not all of the buttons.

Give him enough to see to get him interested.

"Hi," she said as he pulled up.

His window was down. He was a big man with long reddish-brown curly hair. His face was largely unshaven. She smelled his body odor from outside his truck, but she smiled at him anyway.

He stopped. "Whew, wee, little girl. What are you doin' up here all by your lonesome?" She sashayed to his truck and propped one arm on his driver's side door. The way she leaned made her blouse come open a little. He could see she wore no bra.

"I'm lookin' for a man. You happen to know where I can find one."

He cleared his throat. "Little girl, you're lookin' at one. What's your name, darlin'?"

Jeanine replied, "Rose." Her middle name.

When she smiled at him, she wet her lips a little and bit her bottom lip. Something about big pouty lips on a girl guys just liked. When she smiled at him, she could hear his heart beating faster and he was drooling.

That, in her book, meant he was interested. "What's

your name?" she asked with her best Southern accent.

"Brody." His chest heaved.

"Nice to meet you, Brody. You see, my daddy says I have a bad habit. I like my men tied up so I can do things to them while they can't move." She pushed her hand into her blouse just enough. "That wouldn't be a *problem* for you, now would it?"

"Huh," he stammered.

Definitely drooling, she thought.

"I ain't into no kinky shit," he said. He opened his door and came toward her. She turned and started walking away.

"Too bad," she called back at him.

She heard him slam his door and say several choice swear words. "Hey," he called, "don't just run off. We can talk about this."

Jeanine slowed, then stopped and looked over her shoulder. "Go home, Brody. Get a hot shower. Meet me in the motel parking lot in one hour" – she pointed in the direction of her motel – "and I'll give you a night you'll never forget." Brody gave a whoop, and drove off the hill like a madman.

Jeanine felt certain she would see him in an hour. Several more cars and a truck were parked in the motel parking lot. She got her ties, three bowls, and additional razor blades and took them to her and Alecia's room.

Alecia was laying lopsided on the second bed. The television show she'd been watching went off and she had gone to sleep. Jeanine set her supplies behind the first bed and sat on the bed with Alecia.

She stirred a little when Jeanine ran her fingers gently through her curls.

"Honey," she said lowly, "wake up."

Alecia rolled on her back and looked up at Jeanine.

"Honey, we're going to have a visitor in here for a little while. I have to take blood from him." She glanced at the digital clock. "He'll be here in about forty minutes. If I make you a pallet in the bathroom, can you sleep there, baby girl?"

Alecia seemed out of it.

Jeanine lifted Alecia to her own bed and took the quilts and bed cover from the second bed, with pillows, and made a square pad between the toilet and the bathroom door.

She helped Alecia out of her clothes and into her little gown, then kissed her as she lay in the center of the bathroom floor. Jeanine locked the bathroom door from the inside. She knew how to open these locks from her old folk home days. She arranged the ties carefully on the bed and laid her bowls and razor blades out of sight, then removed her dark contacts.

With barely five minutes to spare, Jeanine took the room key and went out in the parking lot to await her "date." Brody wheeled into the parking lot a few minutes after the hour. He gave a whoop when he saw her and parked sideways in two parking spaces.

His aftershave, or whatever he'd splashed on himself, arrived long before he did. Brody got out and planted a sloppy wet kiss on her right cheek. Jeanine caught her breath and smiled at him.

She'd asked for this. She turned and led him up to the second floor, listened inside to make sure Alecia had not come out of the bathroom, then brought Brody inside.

She gave him her sweetest smile and told him to get undressed to his skivvies. He seemed more interested in pawing her, but she slid out of his grasp until he got the clue that there would be no interaction until he did what she wanted.

While he was undressing, she slipped out of her sneakers, jeans, and she unbuttoned her blouse completely but kept it on.

She made a hitching loop like she had seen Nolan use and tied his right arm, then his left arm. The only thing he had on was his underwear. She used the next three ties to secure his thighs, above his knees, and his ankles. With the last tie, she looped through the binds at his ankles and secured him to the bedframe at the foot of the bed. She pulled off her blouse and started crawling up his legs.

Yes, Brody was interested.

She rolled a pillow case into a makeshift gag – she shoved a knot into his mouth and looped it around the back of his head.

She deliberately tickled him to make him jerk. She made it playful, but she had to make sure he was really secured. Jeanine brought out two bowls and set them on the bed under the bend in his elbows. Jeanine held a razor blade where he could see it. His eyes grew very, very wide.

"I promise I'll try not to hurt you."

She made superficial cuts into his fleshy forearms. He squealed, but the gag muffled whatever he would have said. His blood dripped along his arms to his elbows.

While he was bleeding, she reached into the open fly of his underwear to go exploring. When he turned his face and saw himself bleeding, his eyes rolled to the top of his head and he kinda passed out. His blood dripped from the bend in his elbows into the bowls she used to collect the precious blood. When the bowls were half full, she looked for a rag or cloth to staunch the flow of blood.

She had poorly prepared.

The only thing she had handy was her blouse. She

ripped the gauzy material in half and bound each forearm to stop his bleeding. She untied the gag from his mouth and made him look at her. He seemed out of it, but he was at least partially conscious.

Jeanine poured the blood from the second bowl into the first, making a full bowl, and lifted that bowl to drink. Behind her, she heard Alecia unlock the bathroom door and come into the bedroom. Jeanine finished lifting the bowl and drank. She *needed* the blood. The young vampyric girl's body began immediately absorbing the blood.

She closed her eyes for just a moment.

When she opened her eyes and looked around, Alecia was standing beside the bed frightened. She was just looking at her with wide eyes. Alecia backed up when Jeanine reached for her.

"I had a bad dream," she said shyly. "Daddy's here."

Jeanine scrambled off Brody and went to the window. Nolan's white van was parked on the far side of the parking lot, lights on. The headlights each were a slightly different color, left to right, and was instantly recognizable.

"Oh, God!" she exclaimed.

She glanced around the motel room. She had no weapon. Alecia only had on her little gown, and she, herself, was half naked. Jeanine pulled on her jeans, at least. She glanced at Brody as she pulled on her white hospital sneakers. His forearms seemed to have stopped bleeding. Her torn blouse strips were stained with blood completely. When she unfastened his arms, he just flopped over on his right side.

"Thank you," she said.

She planted a kiss on Brody's lips.

She had other issues to address at the moment. Jeanine had to go out there. She checked the room telephone and made sure it had dial tone. Alecia was still between the beds. Jeanine knelt before Alecia.

"Baby girl," she said. "You remember how to dial 9-1-1 and get help?" Alecia nodded. "I'm going to lock you in here and try to get him to follow me. If anyone else but me comes to the door, dial 9-1-1 and cry for help. Tell them a strange man is trying to kidnap you. Tell them you're in room 217."

With that, Jeanine took her car keys but left the door key inside with Alecia. No one was on the second-floor walkway. The door clicked behind her. She pulled the handle to make sure it locked. She listened around herself. People were walking and entering a room just below her to her right. She watched around Nolan's van and swept the parking lot, now somewhat fuller than when she and Brody went inside.

Jeanine made her way to the stairwell and started down to the first floor. Halfway down, she passed a man and a woman coming upstairs. The man ogled her and the woman with him punched him. Yes, she thought, you just passed a half-naked girl on the stairwell. She exited the stairwell and looked in all directions she could see across the parking lot. Several large utility trucks of some type had parked lengthwise. Her view was restricted so she listened for footsteps or movement.

Nolan could be hiding anywhere.

She felt of her car keys and contact case in her jeans pocket and started toward her car on the opposite corner of the parking lot near the office. When she got to her car she did not open it, but knelt between her car and the car next to her.

Sharp metal spikes had been positioned just in front of her back and front tires. If she had driven forward, her tires would have been punctured. Jeanine bent low and pulled the spikes away from her back and front tires on the passenger side. She threw the spikes over her shoulder onto the sidewalk.

The driver's side of her car was exposed to the roadway and the nearby office. Jeanine stayed down to better look for feet beneath the other vehicles around her. She made her way around the front of her car.

At that moment, another car with a host of people pulled into the motel parking lot. She shielded her sensitive eyes from the direct headlight beam. Her face flushed red. These people pulled around to the front of the motel.

She worked to get the spikes from under her front driver's side tire and was moving to the back when Nolan jumped her and tried to shove her onto her own car. A nozzle spewed a yellow gas in her face. She fought him to push the nozzle away.

The gas doesn't work on me, she thought.

Jeanine managed to kick him, and tried to knee him. The canister he carried fell. He tried to tackle her as she ran from him. They fell together and the pavement scraped her right arm. She rolled on her back and kicked him in the face.

He scrambled on top of her again.

Jeanine twisted and fought. If she could get her car keys out of her front pocket, she could rake them into his eyes. He climbed on top of her and tried punching her. She grabbed both of his wrists and held him, but he was sitting on her and she was pinned under him. She bucked with her hips and tried to hook her right foot into his chest or neck to push him backwards.

He got an arm free. He punched her in the face. She saw black swirls. She saw him drawing back to hit her again.

Then, suddenly, he was lifted from her body.

Two other men, she assumed construction workers from those big trucks, had lifted Nolan bodily off her and the third man was punching him none too gently. When Nolan collapsed to his knees, the man standing nearest her asked if she wanted them to call the police. Jeanine said no.

"He wants to hurt my baby girl," she said.

She just wanted to get away with Alecia. By the time she explained her version to the police – and could not prove Alecia was hers, Nolan would have them arrest her for kidnapping.

Nolan started to get up.

The man went back to hitting him.

Jeanine got on her knees beside her car and pulled the last spike from her back tire. While Nolan was distracted, she ran back up to her room to get Alecia.

At her room, Jeanine slapped the door with her palm three times. "Honey, it's me," she called. "Open the door."

Alecia opened the door. Jeanine saw with great relief that Alecia had dressed herself. Jeanine picked Alecia up and made her way back down the stairwell to her car.

Nolan was on the pavement by now.

Two other men had joined the melee. Three of the men were taking turns kicking him. Jeanine shielded Alecia's gaze as much as possible from the men hitting her Daddy. She felt utterly vile things come to her mind as she saw him getting the stuffing beat out of him. She worked her key out of her pocket.

"Jennie?" Alecia said lowly.

"Yes, baby?" Jeanine replied.

"These men saw your boobies." Her face was totally serious.

"I know, honey."

"You said we weren't supposed to let men see our boobies."

Jeanine got her passenger door unlocked. She cradled Alecia's head and set her in the passenger seat. Jeanine reached over Alecia to snap Alecia's seat belt securely around her.

"I did, baby girl, but sometimes you've got to do what you've just got to do." She made her way to the driver's side, slid into the moulded seat, fastened her seat belt, and started her car.

The powerful engine growled.

Half of the men beating Nolan stopped to stare at her.

Jeanine peeled out of the motel parking lot and headed back to the Interstate. On the straightway of the ramp, she punched the accelerator and quickly passed two cars in the slower right lane. In less than a minute, she was easily going over a hundred and forty miles per hour. After several exits whizzed past, she slowed down to seventy and kept looking in her rearview mirror.

She knew from experience with the man.

He never, ever, gave up.

Black swirls swam around Nolan's vision and dried blood caked over his forehead. When he moved his shoulder, it hurt with a fire-hot poker jab of sharp pain, but he gritted his teeth and moved it anyway.

The men beating him had dumped him in tall grass behind the service station building.

Jeanine was a fool to try to run with Alecia. Caring for the little girl would only hinder her efforts to get away. He swayed unsteadily on his feet when he passed the service station corner.

He made his way to his van and punched the unlock

code in the keyless entry. A glowing electronic display with a map of the immediate area greeted him with soft glyphs. Jeanine had never seen him use this. Her car had tracing electronics all through it.

Sooner or later, she would pass an indicator mounted in light poles or hidden in telephone relays along the roads. Sooner or later, she would slip up and contact social services for help to care for Alecia. The number of eyes watching were endless.

Jeanine would be found quickly.

Chapter Five

Thomas felt nauseated at the display of meats slathered in bar-b-q sauce ready for grilling. This was a family tradition for Dad to cookout on Labor Day weekend. The sun was hot and bright already over the east facing back porch.

His father was decked out to cook with his chef's hat, long red apron, and mint tea cooler Mom made just for him. He brushed the red sauce on the pieces of meat grilling.

Thomas caught himself on the banister but managed to straighten himself before his father noticed. He wiped his burning eyes with his hand and started moving toward the kitchen door.

Rather jovially, his father asked, "What'da'ya say we put on the brockworst next?"

"Can't say," Thomas muttered as he passed his father. In the dimmer hallway to the kitchen, Thomas felt a little better, but his eyes literally burned now.

Thomas steadied himself along the wall.

When he closed and reopened his eyes, his entire field of vision was white glowing spots. His mother passed him carrying an aluminum pan of more meat with vegetables and corn to be grilled as well. It was more than the nausea he was now accustomed to. It's like his blood itself was now on fire in the sunlight. Thomas went to the refrigerator and poured himself a glass of cold ice water. Water, the colder the better, seemed to assuage the symptoms.

He thought he heard his father calling him.

Thomas sat at the kitchen table.

From upstairs, he heard Kim's light footsteps on the stairs. She had stayed out of his way since their roof discussion.

Patricia came into the kitchen.

"Don't you hear your father calling?" she asked.

Thomas gave her a sideways glance.

"Yes, ma'am," he said.

Kim came into the kitchen. She was dressed in shorts and a cotton blouse. Off until next Wednesday. "Good morning, dear," Patricia said to her daughter as Kim kissed her on the cheek.

"Morning," she said to Thomas.

She seemed especially ready to make peace after their rooftop discussion. In a small way, Kimberly knowing what she knew relieved Thomas of the entire burden of the secret he carried. Even if Kim wanted the scoop of the century – he knew she was also tenderhearted enough to show compassion and discretion when required.

Thomas drained his glass of water and got up. "Morning, brat," he said as he walked outside into the furnace.

He glanced back at his baby sister.

Quite proud of her, actually.

Dad wanted Thomas to take over the grilling for a while. He plopped his chef's hat on Thomas' head. It was too large and slipped onto his eyebrows.

Thomas took the tongs and the spear fork used to turn the meat and set about placing the foil-wrapped vegetables on the upper grill rack. His Dad went inside to get a refill on his mint cooler. His vision was becoming blurry. First he thought it was the heat distortion from the grill, but the effect was the same wherever he looked.

His fingers felt numb. He placed his right hand inside the kitchen mitten, and felt better, but his hand would not close tightly. Thomas glanced at Kim sauntering on the porch and eyeing the steaks, onions, and corn Dad already grilled. It was only mid-morning and she was probably hungry. Dad followed her outside with a fresh mint tea cooler in his hand.

Thomas turned several pieces of meat.

"Want to take over, Dad?" Thomas asked hopefully.

Donald sat on the lounge chair at the far side of the porch. He swung lightly. "No," he said, "you can take it for a while."

Kim had come out with a tube of sun lotion. Her legs had tanned some from her graduation trip to Florida, but she was rubbing the lotion on her legs and arms likely in the hopes of getting a deeper tan.

Thomas remembered Majken on their camping trip. She used some type of thick cream on her skin, and later at the motel just before they were hunting John in the city, she told him it was a concentrated sunscreen she used to protect herself from the sun.

Mom came out on the porch and joined Dad on the lounge. It was just big enough for two and she swung with him. She had on the kind of hat he'd seen people wear who play cards – a hat with no top, but the visor.

He remembered Majken had worn sun glasses most of the time outside. Thomas absently turned the meat again. He took off a few pieces that looked done and laid them on the top rack, and picked a fresh piece of meat to grill.

In his head, pressure seemed to start above his ears. It was as if the sun was boring a tunnel into his brain, into his vital organs, searing flesh. He was not sweating like he would suppose if he had some type of heat stroke – his face felt cool when he touched his forehead with the back of his hand.

It was as if his blood itself had caught fire.

He was burning from the inside.

From the pit of his stomach and lower he started to feel waves of the most incredible yucky feeling he'd ever had. It was like he'd eaten this gigantic burrito with everything on it in the blistering hot sun, and he was turning literally green.

Then it was like he was falling – the uplifting vertigo

sensation causing his insides to twist. Thomas swayed in the sunlight. He felt like the sun itself, pure burning light, was pouring directly into his exposed brain, causing his entire cranial cavity to sear and bleed and whither in the light.

Out of the corner of his eye, Kim had finished slathering the lotion on her legs and arms and she was laying back to soak up the sun's light.

This must have been how Majken had felt as they trekked across the open field to reach the cooler forest on their long ago camping trip. If he didn't understand how she felt then, he certainly did now. His stomach seemed to lurch and he lost feeling in his right hand. He watched as the tongs he held dropped to the wooden deck, then his vision blurred. His vision dimmed.

As if from a great distance away, he heard his mother call his name. Then, the next thing he knew he was lying on his back on the deck, his parents above him and Kim hovering nearby. His mother was in his face.

His father was attempting to shake him awake. His mother called his name over and over. He heard them like they were calling him in a great long tunnel that stretched into the darkness. Their voices became dimmer and farther away.

Thomas completely lost consciousness.

He saw only blackness around him.

Darkness. Eternal night beckoned him.

The faint sound of wolves howling across the landscape and Majken's light laughter played in his mind.

When Thomas again came to his senses he was lying on their living room couch. An oscillating fan was blowing cool air across his supine figure and several bags of ice mixed with water had been placed under his arm pits and along the outside of his legs, chest, and neck. He didn't feel the burning anymore and the ebbing of nausea, a totally gross and sick feeling that seemed to grip his entire body centered in his abdomen, had just subsided into stillness.

As Thomas moved his right arm, the ice water bags sloshed. He held his right hand before his face and flexed his powerful fingers. Only a slight tingling remained. The pervasive numbness was gone. Thomas looked around. He could hear his mother's voice from the kitchen, talking as if she was speaking on the telephone. Their family doctor, he assumed.

He tracked his mother's half of the one sided conversation. Keep him still. Keep him cool. Make sure he drinks plenty of fluids. *No problem there, doc*, Thomas thought. Stay out of the heat. In his mind, Thomas translated "heat" as "light" and he replied, *Amen*. He heard his father's shuffled steps on the carpet behind him from the opposite direction before his father stepped into the living room.

"Hey," Donald said, "there's my young man." The couch dipped as Thomas' father sat alongside the wide cushion next to Thomas.

"How are you feeling?" Donald asked.

The pate of his father's prematurely bald head was shiny in the diffuse light from the curtains on the opposite side of the room.

Thomas reflected.

He'd need thick dark curtains in his bedroom now. So much for the thin gauzy curtains and his mother's taste in decorating.

Thomas smiled at his father.

"I feel okay," he said. "Just a little light-headed." The ice water bags placed around his body sloshed as he tried to sit up.

His father's smile was tight, as if strained.

"You gave us quite a scare, young man."

Donald patted him on the arm as he arose. "I'll let your mother know you're awake."

As Donald left the living room, Thomas noticed Kim hovering in the arch just outside the living room.

Thomas waved weakly at Kim.

"Hi, brat," he said. Relief seemed to flood her tightly drawn posture. Behind Kimberly, Thomas easily heard his mother's footsteps as she quickly approached from the kitchen. Patricia darted around Kimberly and came toward Thomas with her hands forward to cup his face. She sat next to him and squeezed his cheeks. He suddenly felt like a chubby squirrel.

"Son," she said, obviously exasperated, "you gave me and your father a terrible scare." Her voice wavered a little. "I think you should go to the hospital emergency room for a check up, just to make sure you're all right."

Thomas scrunched on his elbows to lift himself higher and took his mother's hands in his own.

A distinct scent of sandalwood soap flared in his nostrils. His mother's favorite soap. "I'm fine," he said, forcing a smile. "Just a little light-headed," he explained. Patricia felt of his forehead. Like she was checking him for temperature.

Thomas shifted more on his right side and began to pull the bags of ice and water concoction away from his skin. The ice itself felt okay, but he was tired of the sloshing.

He grimaced inwardly. *Light-headed.*

Patricia looked back at Donald.

Thomas noticed her eyes pleading with him. His father stood with both hands in his pockets, just relaxed and calm, as if his son collapsed on the deck every day of the week.

He slipped his arm around her shoulder.

"Patty," Donald said, "he'll be all right."

Thomas saw his mother's lips purse, like she was suddenly angry. Her eyes were tight and crinkled. She seemed to force a smile for his benefit. "Thomas," she said, softly just to him. "Don't you want to go to Dr. Michaels and have him look you over?" She brushed her hand through his thick ash brown hair. "You might have gotten a concussion or a brain aneurysm when you fell. I want to make sure you're really all right."

Dr. Michaels, Thomas remembered, had graduated from high school with his mother. His sandy hair was now turning light silver-gray. Kind enough man, but Thomas quickly said, "No, thanks."

Thomas' father's smile seemed to broaden, "See, I told you, he'll be all right."

Patricia seemed to relent, just for now.

When she smoothed his hair above his left ear, she seemed to be stroking her fingertips over his scalp, as if she could feel a hairline fracture. Thomas presumed. He must have fallen and hit the deck with the left side of his head. Thomas smiled broadly at his Mom.

"I'm fine," he said. "I'll just rest for a while. Either here or up in my room."

Donald turned off the fan that had been blowing cool air over him. Patricia stood next to her husband. From the look in his mother's eyes, he knew his Dad was about to get it.

Thomas actually finished sitting up.

His parents left for the kitchen and beyond.

Kimberly had come into the living room fully now. Concern for him was certainly in her light brown eyes, but also a hint of conspiracy. She had kept his secret, what she knew of it, from Mom and Dad because she knew they couldn't take it.

She sat on the living room table a space away from him. Thomas dropped the last ice water bag on the carpeted floor. His body was very, very tired. Thomas suddenly felt such an overwhelming urge to sleep, he actually yawned in Kim's face. He covered his yawn with the back of his hand and muttered an apology.

"It's all right," she said.

Kimberly paused. "What happened?" The tone of her question was more than he just fell out on the deck during a family cookout. She was really asking him, *What just happened to you?*

Thomas considered his sister – all the times they had fought in the back seat of the family wagon while going on vacation, all of the times she'd gotten into his Christmas presents before he did, all of the times as a preteen she'd tried to embarrass him in front of his high school dates, and all of the times her infernal snooping into everybody else's business drove him crazy.

What just happened to you?

More question than he could answer right now.

Before Thomas could mask his facial expression or give her an offhanded comment, he saw her eyes carried such love for him. Yes, she was a pain in the rump most of his life, but, dammit, she *was* his only sister. He reached his hand behind Kimberly's neck. When he pulled her head close to his, as if to hear him whisper the greatest secret the world ever knew, she leaned forward with him. "I don't know," he said, confessing his worst nightmare.

He was alone and, he knew, his body was changing.

He could no longer deny it.

He was becoming like Majken. Vampyr.

* * *

In the stillness of his bedroom, Thomas rested fitfully. He raided the spare bedroom between his and Kim's bedroom for quilts; he found newspapers and stapled them to the wall around his window, sealing out the bright sunlight.

The family cookout went bust.

Dad probably finished grilling whatever Mom took outside, but no gathering of the family around the picnic table today.

Forgive me for becoming vampyric, Thomas thought morosely. It was just the kind of thing that put a dent in any family celebration. Thomas wanted to laugh, but found his sense of humor had withered with the bright morning sunlight.

Once, his mother came to his bedroom door. He finally convinced his mother that he was okay and she should wait for him to come out later. Twice during the afternoon he heard Kimberly go into her bedroom for a while, then come out and bounce downstairs.

He started making lists in his head. Sunscreen. Dark glasses. Night job. More sunscreen. Blood bank withdrawals.

He reflected on things he had seen Majken do and not do.

In the month and so many days since he'd left Trenton to come home, his symptoms had not gotten any better. He knew they were becoming progressively worse.

Whatever had hit him in the sunlight was to be avoided. As bad as he felt outside, it seemed to subside when he came inside out of the direct sunlight.

Majken had said something about being sick in the daylight. Oh, how he understood now! Thinking of her made Thomas sad. He reached in his bedside night table and got his picture of her in a happier time.

He looked at her, known to him then as Mary Harris. He knew and remembered, even when that photo was taken, he was already falling in love with her. Little by little, she let more of her true nature slip through. Was it really that big of a surprise when she drank his blood in the mansion that night?

Well, yes. But everything she told him about herself made sense in the light that she was a vampyric blood drinking person of an indeterminate age. Another sticky spot. She never told him how old she really was. Maybe she was hundreds of years old, but the mere thought of her actually being over a hundred boggled his mind. How did she survive for so long?

One thing was certain. She was a literal blood drinking person. He'd seen and felt enough of being with her and watching her to know that she wasn't a crazy person like he first mistakenly believed.

And she was incredibly strong.

It wasn't just the fact that she'd held him so easily as she was feeding on him that night in the mansion; it was her fight with John later. He visualized again how she dropped on John from above and fought to save his life. Thomas felt of his own abdomen, just below the line of his ribcage, about halfway above his navel to his breastbone. He remembered the deep gash across her midsection when John cut her with the blade. Anyone human would have clearly died just of shock. Yet, she managed to half drag, half carry him back to safety, then survive them crawling out of the fire and tumbling on the soft earth outside.

His eyes saddened as he looked at her face in the photo. The last he'd seen of her was when she took Albritton's car down the block. Then she stopped and leaned over, probably in great pain.

In this photo, he mused, he was totally innocent.

After exposure to her blood during the fight and what he now knew of vampyric people living in the world, he could no longer think of himself as innocent.

He thought of her, judging what had happened to him in light of what he knew now. She didn't mean to expose him to her blood. He was certain, if she could have prevented it, she would have. Where was she now? he wondered.

Million dollar question.

Thomas considered getting Kimberly on Majken's trail. No doubt his brilliant but naïve sister would unearth some trail that was believed long buried and lost. If anyone could really find Majken, his sister could.

Herein was another problem. Majken's survival, and likely his also, depended on no one knowing that vampyric people existed. They were superstitions of countless nations. Thomas decided to exhaust his other alternatives before he told Kimberly the whole truth. He put his and Majken's photo back in his night table and laughed bleakly.

What other alternatives did he have?

Thomas got up because he was just tired of lying on his bed. He considered for a few moments, then went into his bathroom and started a cold shower. He made the water tepid warm, then undressed and got under the stinging spray. He let the water stream pour around his face. He adjusted the temperature slightly, then let the water pulse beat him on the shoulders and back. One thing Dad believed in was water pressure.

His parents, particularly his mother, was another aspect of his problem. Kimberly might be able to take the news of what he would tell her about Majken, her true nature, and all of the gory details about blood drinking people.

He considered. His parents, no way.

As soon as the word "vampire" came out of his mouth, he envisioned a one-way trip to the rubber room – complete with straitjacket.

No wonder Majken herself shied away from the word.

In the dim light of his bathroom, he thought of her pretty smiling face and the depth of her dark violet eyes. He would do anything just to see her again and know she was all right. He had to believe she survived her wounds, as bad as they were. He had to believe she was alive somewhere. He had to believe he would see her again.

As he soaped himself and rinsed off, he was very much thinking of her. Well, Thomas thought, why not?

When he finished, the tepid warm water had grown cold. Cold as in the trail to where she'd gone – deserting him in Trenton.

He guiltily squelched the thought of her deliberately deserting him. Everything she'd done, including her fight with John, was to protect him. He didn't know what hazards she was navigating now. He didn't know what she had to do to merely survive – and deep in his heart, he trusted Majken still.

Thomas laughed in spite of himself.

He still trusted her.

Kimberly kept her Dad company much of the afternoon. Mom came around a few times but really didn't say much. Thomas was okay and would be okay. Her dad said so.

She watched him finish grilling what Mom had prepared. She wrapped what he cooked to store in the refrigerator.

Her Dad didn't say much either. Ever so often, she'd glance up at the second-story window to his bedroom on the far left side. Maybe she should've told Mom and Dad that a mass murderer had tried to kill her brother, but it was too late to tell them now.

In her mind, she mused over what she had learned from him. Now that she had a chance to think over Thomas' behavior and the type of injuries he'd come home with, it was the most natural conclusion of all that led her to exactly what he tried to hide. Everything made sense, except what part his girlfriend played in all of this. What Thomas said was very clear – his girlfriend had saved his life. His girlfriend had come after him and this John *slasher* suspect.

This neighed at her mind. Far more was going on than was apparent on the surface.

Finding out things was what she did.

The next move had to be his.

She munched on bar-b-q chicken and grilled corn on the deck. The thick red sauce stained her fingers as she ate. Every coin had two sides. What she was seeing was from one side only. The missing aspect was the part Mary played in all of this.

When her Dad took the last of the food inside, she stayed on the deck to enjoy the late afternoon sunset.

The elm and poplar tree leaves were turning the color of russet and gold. With leaves swaying gently in the breeze, this was her favorite time of the day. Kimberly sighed. Maybe someday she'd be able to share the sunrises and sunsets with her Mr. Right.

She heard Mom in the kitchen.

Kimberly went inside and found Thomas sitting at the kitchen table and Mom fixing him a plate of food. She poured him a large glass of orange juice, too.

Mom didn't exactly hover over him as he started eating, but she was hovering over him as he ate. Dad went to his studio. Kim sat in her spot and thumbed through a *Woman's Day* magazine as Thomas ate. He didn't touch his orange juice. Apparently satisfied, Mom went to Dad's studio. By the time he'd eaten even a few more bites of the grilled hamburger she knew he stopped eating altogether. When they were alone, Thomas picked up his plate of food and dumped all of it into the garbage compactor. He dumped the orange juice down the drain and ran water in the sink.

He propped both arms at the sink and just stood, then threw up everything he'd just eaten. Gross. Furtively wiping his mouth with a towel, Thomas turned on the sink garbage disposal and rinsed the refuse down the drain, then turned without a word to her, plucked his car keys from the key holder, and went outside.

Kimberly heard his car start. He was leaving.

She started to call her mother, but it would take far too long for her Mom to get with it and follow him. Kim grabbed her Mom's car keys, slipped on her sneakers at the door, and ran after her brother.

What just happened to you? she recalled.

Kim hopped in the car, pulled on her seat belt, and backed her Mom's Trans Sport out of the place she parked next to the porch, which took longer.

The gas gauge was almost on empty.

Great goin', Mom.

Kim looked both ways on the little road and went after her brother. The sun had set below the treeline. Shadows reached across the road. At the highway, she saw her brother's car taillights to the left. She followed.

He was heading generally west.

She managed to close the gap between them with only two cars between them. He turned abruptly right, and followed a second highway directly west. She started to turn after him, when the car in front of her stopped at the red light and sat there.

Kim bit back the swear word again. So unlady like. Thomas' car was not visible when she finally turned on the secondary highway. She resisted the urge to just race ahead. Many old buildings and factories lined this road. If he'd turned off she didn't want to shoot past him. She caught a glimpse of his car parked in this abandoned factory place as she passed. She passed it entirely, had to turn around and double back.

The wire fence around the place was old and bent along its length. Piles of old timber and some type of metal bindings littered the weed strewn expanse. A huge rusting lift lay silent in the middle of the near vacant field. Kimberly parked next to him, turned off her Mom's car, and got out. He was no longer in his car. He was nowhere to be seen. Her shorts had no pocket. She stuffed her Mom's keys above the visor and left the driver's door unlocked. She suddenly realized she didn't have her license with her either.

Great goin', Kimberly.

Well, now wasn't the time to fret.

A large metal building with a cavernous maw was reddish yellow in the setting sun. She couldn't see Thomas anywhere. There was no other place for him to go.

She started across the littered field.

It was becoming imperceptibly darker as she made her way through the piles of timber and weedy broken concrete. She tried to envision what they'd built here, but couldn't see it. Halfway across the lot, beyond the rusting lift, Kimberly started worrying about guard dogs. She glanced back at her Mom's car and how far safety was.

Ahead of her, she was certain Thomas had gone into the building. The inside was darker than the rapidly fading sunlight. Now that she was closer she could see shapes inside of huge stacks of bins lining both sides of the center passage.

She entered the cavernous maw.

Long shadows from the ancient rusting equipment on both sides of the weed infested concrete floor reached for her. The building itself was a type of pre-fab metal. She could not see through to the other side, but light was coming in holes in the roof. Kimberly heard something to her left shift in one of the bins about midway into the dark.

She debated whether to call her brother or not. Right now, she just walked quietly into the face of the unknown. Never occurred to her that someone else may have been in this building. Not her brother.

Great goin', again, Kimberly.

No guard dogs had attacked her yet.

She kept moving. Something shifted again on the pile of timbers and rusting metal to her left.

Kim turned and called, "Thomas!"

After a few exasperated seconds, she heard him call back, "Go home, brat!" As she got closer to the rusting pile, she thought she heard dripping water.

"Where are you?" she asked.

She clearly heard her brother utter a swear word. His dark shape appeared at the top of the metal piles. There seemed to be a faint glow, like candlelight, behind him.

He reached a hand for her.

She took his hand and he carefully guided her up. The metal seemed to be a stack of girders. They had been stacked for so long they were probably rusted together. As she topped the rise, she did see several candles arranged in a circle. Beyond the light was a precipice, an almost perfect oval cavity that seemed to shimmer like water on the surface.

Thomas spread an old oily towel he had for Kim to sit. It was either sit on the oily towel or get scraped by the rusted pitted metal framework.

Kimberly realized she was poorly prepared and poorly dressed for saving her brother.

When Thomas stood fully, his upper body was in the shadows. He propped his left arm on the nearest vertical girder and seemed to be staring at the water surface. Occasionally some water from above would drip into the pool, causing the surface ripples to fan out.

She couldn't tell if his head was bowed, but it seemed to be.

"Thank you," he said, "for keeping my secret from Mom and Dad." He seemed to look at her. "Thanks, brat, for being you."

Kimberly choked a little. This was the kind of speech someone gave who is about to say goodbye.

If he needed to talk, she would listen.

Thomas pulled a heavy looking chain from the wall. It was old and rusty, for sure. His entire hand would fit in the hole of the links it was so big. He pulled it until a pile of chain lay at his feet. He still said nothing.

The silence drew on. "Why –" she started.

He looped an end of the chain around his legs just above his ankles and looped it in a type of square knot. He pulled the other end of the chain around his torso and wrapping it higher around his body until he looped the opposite end over his left shoulder.

This is not good, Kim thought.

"What are you doing?" she asked.

The dripping water sounded ominous to her now. She could see him looking into the pool before him. Its black surface rippled slightly as more water dripped from the ceiling far above.

Thomas spoke lowly.

"They say it has no bottom."

Kim stood, now frightened.

"What are you doing?" she said. "You don't need to do this."

He seemed to shuffle toward the precipice. The chain links clinked as he moved.

"Stop!" Kim shouted. He stopped.

"What are you doing this for?"

His voice was very faint and soft when he spoke. Kim had to strain to even hear him.

"It's not stopping," he finally said.

"What are you talking about? Don't do this," she pleaded. "You have everything to live for – you don't want to die. This is not right." Tears started to stream down her face. "Nothing is so bad that you should take your own life."

He snapped angrily at her. "What do you know? This is so bad, even if I told you, you wouldn't believe me."

Kim stepped toward him. She was too small to stop him if he really threw himself into that pool. She had to make contact with him somehow. He had to look at her.

"I'm with you," she said with certainty. "Whatever this is, we can handle it together." He raised his left arm and held to the vertical beam in front of him.

"You really don't want to die, do you?"

Thomas coughed. "I don't want to die."

Kimberly raised both of her hands to him.

"Please, Thomas. Back up and take the chain off." He looked at her. "Please."

He moved back from the pool. Her voice was completely hoarse. "We can talk about this – I'm a good listener, I promise."

Kim remembered his behavior all week.

Hopeless. She felt suddenly chilled.

Thomas stepped back and unloosed the chain from his shoulder, then twisted his upper body until the chain fell at his feet. He kicked free of it.

With a hard scream, he grabbed an armful of chain and heaved it forward, dumping the serpentine chain into the cistern. The rusty chain disappeared into the dark water. The sound of it reverberated as it scraped the metal sides going down and down and down.

When he stood, he was breathing hard.

"I want to live," he said. "I don't want to die."

Kim's heart seemed to break. She rushed forward and held to him. She was shaking as she held him. The gravity of what almost happened to her brother hit her at once. She felt a deep queasy feeling in the pit of her stomach.

She'd almost watched her brother die.

She kept saying over and over, "You're not alone. We can handle this together."

Thomas hugged her. "I'm okay, brat. I'm not done yet." He walked with her to her oily towel and helped her sit, then sat beside her.

"Well," Thomas started. He propped both arms on his knees, like he did on the rooftop. Kim was still shaking. She stared forlornly at her brother. Recognition seemed to dawn in his brown eyes. Thomas sat closer and placed his arm around her. She was still shaking. He looped his other arm and linked fingers. She wasn't going anywhere until he let her up.

"I –" she began. Her voice faltered.

"So," Thomas began for her, "this is really the first time you've ever faced death first hand."

She stammered and looked up at her big brother. "Uh, yes," she said softly.

Thomas laughed lightly. This time there was humor in his voice. "Think nothing of it. It's something you get used to."

She glared at him. He was actually smiling. His eyes were gentle again. He was not laughing at her, but with her. "Oh, brother," she said weakly. Little by little, she stopped shaking, at least on the outside. She tried to draw a purifying breath, but she felt completely giddy inside.

Now she wanted to smack him. Big brother smile and all.

"Please don't ever do that again," Kim pleaded.

Thomas' gaze fell on the pool and the splash made by the chain as it disappeared. "I won't," he promised. He sighed and bowed his head. "It just seemed so – so impossible."

Kim wrapped her hands around both of his. "I'm with you," she promised. "We can handle this together."

Thomas hugged her. "I know you are, brat. But this is bigger than you, me, and the entire state of Texas." His eyes rolled up as he said that. Now, he looked tired.

She felt the silence thicken around him.

Finally, she asked, "What happened to you up there? What really happened?"

His voice was flat when he spoke.

"A lot more than you know," he replied.

So, Kim thought, her brother faced a serial killer and what happened to him is a lot more than I know. "Tell me," she prompted.

"It's more than me, Kimberly Denise. My former girlfriend's life is very much at stake here, if she's still alive."

"Why do you say – if she's still alive?"

Thomas began, "Maj – Mary. Ah, first of all, her name is not Mary Harris. I really can't tell you her real name, since it doesn't exist anyway. I'll call her Mary just to have something to call her. She was the one John was after. He took me just to get to her."

Kim nodded, like she understood any of this anyway.

"John took me to use as bait. He wanted her to follow us and she did." Kim just stared at her brother. He continued. "The short version of all of this is Mary got me away from John, but she was injured very badly. John kept pushing me on the rocks, over and over again. He shoved me down in the roots of this tree and I saw him draw his knife."

Thomas was looking up, Kimberly noticed, his eyes forward – as if he were seeing it all again. "Mary dropped from above him, and she fell in the clearing. I'm not sure what John did, but next thing I know he's trying to kill her with a blade of some type. I saw him swing the blade several times, and miss, but he finally cut her" – Thomas stopped talking, unlaced his fingers, and drew an imaginary line across Kim's upper midsection below her rib-cage – "here."

Kimberly glanced at her own midsection. She nodded for Thomas to continue. He laced his fingers again and held her. She was not shaking as badly as before.

Thomas continued. "She fell against me when he cut her. I don't really know what happened exactly. I saw John in the moonlight lift the blade high over his head, like he was going to strike. Majken kicked him I think. The next thing I know, she's crawling back to me from the edge of the cliff and John is gone."

Kimberly blinked as the scene shifted in her mind. She got the part where John was lifting a blade to strike. Then the picture got blurry. She remembered that her brother was lying on the ground injured when all of this took place. She noted the name he called her also.

"So this John *slasher* suspect is dead."

"Not exactly," Thomas added. "Mary helped me get up and half carried me to the mansion. I didn't know she was so badly injured until we got to her study and she lit a lamp. She'd been bleeding all the way up the hill as I was holding her. Her blood got on my wounds without either of us knowing it."

Kim thought – mansion? Like *Gone With the Wind* mansion? The more Thomas talked the worse this was getting. He was sounding more and more like a looney tune than ever before.

By the flicker of candlelight his face became very grim.

"We'd only been talking for a few minutes when John came charging in the room. She'd already heard him coming. Somehow she was on her feet before he reached us. John hit her hard in the stomach. I saw her double over and fall. He started choking her. I grabbed the only thing nearby – an iron poker from the fireplace – and I threw the lantern at his head. The place started burning around us. I kept hitting him 'til he got off her."

Kim adjusted her seat. By now her body was completely numb.

"The last I saw, John was burning in the doorway. He must've run out the back way. Majken was lying still. I thought she was dead, but when I pulled her up she coughed up this wad of blood. I kept pulling her toward the door and we made it out before the whole place burned down."

Kimberly settled down after listening to his incredible tale. If she didn't think he was a prime candidate for the funny farm before, she thought so now. Yet, she did promise to listen to whatever he said.

He was looking at her, possibly judging whether she believed him or not. Kim kept her gaze neutral and tried to avoid looking directly into his eyes.

"Then what happened?" she prompted.

"I fell with her as we came out the front door. She'd stolen this professor's car to have a way to reach me. We got in his car and left. I drove her to the hospital. When we got there she pushed me out the driver's side door and slid under the wheel. She had a cache nearby and she told me she'd see me in a few days. I saw her drive around the corner. After two days I knew she'd left Trenton and wouldn't be coming to see me. That's how it left off between us."

Thomas paused thoughtfully.

"I still miss her."

Kim scrambled in her mind to assemble the pieces of this jigsaw puzzle into place. Between the mansion, burning lanterns, his girlfriend so badly injured but still able to get up and help him climb uphill, serial killers who fall off cliffs but – apparently – don't die, and a girlfriend with a name that no longer exists, this was getting weirder by the second.

Thomas propped his hands back on his knees. "That wasn't even the bad part."

Kimberly cut her eyes at him.

"Ah, ha," Kim breathed. In her mind, Kim started at the end of his tale and backed up.

"How do you know she left you?"

Thomas paused thoughtfully. Her question, apparently, took him by complete surprise. He answered, "I felt that she was no longer in the city. I don't know how I knew, I just knew it." His expression had become thoughtful and he was looking, staring really, straight ahead.

The catatonic brother image popped into Kim's mind again. Yet he seemed hopeful again. "If she left you in the city, then she's at least well enough to travel," Kim suggested.

"That's right!" Thomas exclaimed.

"Hey, big brother. Can we go home now?"

Thomas helped her stand. "Yeah, let's go."

* * *

Dusk had settled over the city of New Orleans. In the center of the newly renovated business district, Majken got out of the limo – she had Josè park on the street – and looked up at the three-story office building in front of her. She knew the opaque windows at the top floor clearly showed the entire region when viewed from above.

Stefan was waiting for her.

Majken glanced upward before entering the front office of the building. Out of sight from the street, she pressed a panel in the wall and a circular staircase appeared. She walked down. Once inside the panel closed behind her. She knew she had to enter the basement, traverse a long corridor jammed with security devices, before she could enter the single lift that brought her to the top floor apartment. This was the only place in their whole schema that her biometric data had been used to validate her identity. No one human would ever make it this far. The sensors would distinguish human from vampyric and activate the appropriate protocol.

On the second floor the lift stopped.

Majken got out and went to the elevator bank on the opposite side of the building. She entered her unique nine digit code in the metal keypad and allowed her hand scan to process. The elevator opened and took her to the secured third floor. Majken kicked her shoes off and stepped onto the thick pile carpet. The hallway before her was decorated with wooden sculpture and bright ancestral weapons used by tribal people to draw blood in the covenant rituals.

At the end of the hallway, a circular panel moved open at her approach. Once inside the entire tube rotated ninety degrees and she found herself in the inner sanctuary.

She found Stefan leaning in front of his desk with his shirt sleeves rolled up. Locks of his dark hair curled over his forehead.

Majken's eyes swept the room. From the new CRTs mounted in the wall to the far left, to a huge acrylic globe that glowed aqua blue with pinpoints of deep red, yellow ochre, and forest green – business interests and contacts all over the globe, to the bedroom with the sleeping girl to her far right.

He smiled at her approach.

"Welcome home," he said.

She kissed him lightly on the cheek in greeting.

"You know why I am here," she said. Her dark violet eyes measured his obsidian black eyes. His features appeared severe under the tungsten lamp overhead. Stefan reached for a glass and poured himself a snifter of bourbon. The amber liquid glistened as he swirled it.

"Yes," he said. "I know."

Without having to look, Majken felt the girl in the bedroom stir and get up. The pretty brunette slipped on a silken robe and stood quietly at the foot of the bed watching. Stefan's intended Michelle. Now at twenty-one, over the last three years he had brought her three-fourths the way to the full vampyric condition. Her dazzling aqua blue eyes were visible even in dim light. Stefan would share and tell Michelle everything, even about her. Majken liked Michelle and felt she would be a perfect partner for her long-time friend.

Stefan drained the snifter and set the glass down. "Don't bring him here unless you know he is going to survive. Don't even tell him about us until you bring him here."

Majken sensed him tense as he spoke.

"I agree," she promised.

The tightness in his shoulders and back eased with her agreement. Did he think she would argue with him? Majken kissed him lightly on the cheek and left.

* * *

Michelle watched Stefan and Majken with mixed feelings. Older than Stefan by almost eighty years, Majken's diligence and maritime skill had brought her love safely to this far American shore over a century ago.

She owed her so much just because Stefan was here. Yet the ache in Majken's soul also caused her love great worry and distress. This latest mishap, with her young man in Trenton, had only made Majken's sense of loneliness worse. Michelle joined Stefan at the large bay window overlooking the street. She rested her head on his shoulder. Far below, Majken got into her limo and the black vehicle pulled into the street.

"She loves him," Michelle said.

Stefan's gaze met hers. Then he bowed his head. "I know," he said solemnly.

The huge grey wolf waited in the shadows.

Light snowfall sprinkled around its head and over its thick coat. Thomas stood in the cold, sere, white landscape. It was fully night with the barest hint of moonlight behind thick clouds. Thomas was amazed he could still see. Even between the trees where the darkness was the most pronounced, vivid detail gray upon gray and black upon black registered in his mind's eye.

He stepped barefoot in the snow. He felt the rocks and bramble beneath the blanket of snow. Thomas looked at himself. He was wearing only his underwear. It was probably very cold on his bare skin. His breath made frost clouds appear in the air. But he was not freezing. He wasn't warm either.

The wolf turned and loped through the treeline along a narrow trail.

Thomas followed.

As he walked uphill, there were many larger stones and fallen branches littered across his path. He stepped lightly and surely between and across the branches. His body instinctively moved with preternatural grace and rhythm.

They came to a campsite. A small pile of rocks lined a campfire, long since silent and cold ashes. Thomas felt into the ashes. No warmth was there. The embers he touched died and went out in his palm. Sadness swept into his feelings like a broken dam letting floods of water gush through a peaceful sleeping valley.

Now the snowfall was a little harder. His own shoulders were covered with thick flakes of snow. Resting against a broken tree trunk across from the cold campfire was a backpack. It was green and looked much like the one he'd used as a teenager camping years ago.

Thomas opened the pack and found warm clothes in his size. He pulled on the quilted white undershirt first. He found jeans, woolen socks, a long sleeve red and black checkered wool shirt like a lumberjack might wear, and a cap like he'd never seen before with flaps that covered your ears and fastened under your chin. He dressed and pulled on the oiled hiking boots he found beside the backpack.

In the bottom of the backpack, he found a folding knife. The blade was a quick opening type with a thumb catch. Holding it deftly in his palm, Thomas flicked the knife open with a snap. The blade glinted razor sharp in the scant moonlight. Thomas looked up through the trees overhead.

The high thick clouds were moving faster and allowing more natural moonlight to bathe the mountainous landscape.

The wolf waited patiently while he dressed. When the wolf again took to the invisible trail, Thomas followed. He flicked the knife closed and placed the clip in the waist of his jeans. Normally one would place a knife like this in your pocket, but Thomas wanted to feel the metal against his skin.

That way he would know exactly where the blade was when he needed it. The feel of this knife against his skin comforted him. The landscape had, indeed, become very mountainous. The type of trees and landscape reminded Thomas of pictures he had seen of the Rockies. Although he'd never yet been that far west, the terrain was familiar to him as he followed the wolf.

When they traversed a ravine, Thomas approached a huge rock slab balanced on four vertical rocks half buried in the ground.

The moon in the sky was only a crescent, but the rock slab itself was clearly visible. It was mostly flat but with grooves and channels carved into the surface. As soon as Thomas touched the stone, the wolf that had led him there started howling.

Obviously, the dominant male of his pack; within a moment the other wolves nearby started howling in unison. Thomas shook, chilled, in spite of himself. The more he looked at the desolate stone slab the colder he felt.

He wanted to get away from there.

Thomas reversed his path and went out of the ravine the same way he entered. He rubbed his arms to generate heat. When he topped the next ridge, he saw a soft yellow-white glow from a cabin nestled in the forest.

Snow crunched under Thomas' hiking boots as he climbed the rough-hewn stairs. The inside of the cabin looked to be warm and inviting. Thomas felt only a moment of silent trepidation before he reached for the door and opened it. He had the right to survive. A large rock fireplace with a stone hearth commanded one end of the main family room. The fire was softly crackling pine and birch. It was a smoldering fire where half charred pieces of wood dropped ashes and embers in silence. Thomas heard soft breathing of a girl asleep on the sofa bed facing the fireplace.

When the girl rolled over, it was Kimberly.

Thomas watched his sister sleep with quiet amazement. She had slept in the same Tigger pajamas for years, since before he left for college. She was curled on her right side. Her left arm was above the covers and before her face on the pillow.

He knelt with his knife drawn. He flicked the blade open.

Suddenly, from overhead he heard a sharp thwack, thwack, thwack. Each time the sound came, a girl cried in pain. He imagined sharp cutting lashes and bloody bruised welts.

Thomas ignored the crying girl upstairs.

He had come for blood.

He found a place on his sister's forearm and made a cut. He quickly replaced the knife in his waistband and put his mouth over the wound. Fresh blood oozed into his mouth and he drank. His sister was starting to awaken.

He held her arm still as she struggled.

Kimberly screamed, now fully awake.

Thomas found himself in his sister's bedroom kneeling next to her bed. She was struggling and he was holding her arm.

Wild fear was in her eyes.

She drew her fist and punched him between the eyes. She hit him harder in the mouth and drew blood. She hit him a third time in the jaw with her right fist.

Thomas' jaw hurt with that one.

He let her go.

She kicked backwards from him and sat up to reach her bedside lamp at the head of her bed. She cradled her left arm in her right arm tight against her waist.

In the glaring white light, Thomas saw blood on her pajamas and blood on his hands. He cried in alarm and shock when he looked directly into his sister's fearful light brown eyes. He turned and fled. Downstairs, he punched the front door open. This was no dream. Thomas ran out of his parent's house into the night, no longer merely a college student at home on leave from his studies.

He was no longer just Thomas Kline.

The wolf had come home.

PART II

THE WOLF AT EVEN

Chapter Six

Jeanine squinted into the bright morning sunlight as it rose above the city skyline as she traveled due east on Interstate 90. She rubbed her tired eyes. Her eyes felt gritty and the glare of the sun bothered her even with her dark contacts. She had driven most of the night, except for two fitful hours sleep under an overpass off the main drag. There she pulled on a fresh blouse before they started travelling again. To make sure Nolan was not following her, she took a circuous route on and off the main Interstate. She kept travelling east. In her mind, east was away from Nolan and the likes of the blood cult in California.

Alecia was now curled asleep, wrapped in a blanket in the front seat. In the middle of the night, while Jeanine was running on pure adrenaline she let her baby girl climb into the back seat and lie down to sleep. With morning light Jeanine became extra cautious. An hour ago, just at sunrise, she moved Alecia back to the front seat and buckled her in. Take no chances, she thought.

The weight of the previous eleven hours were starting to drain her concentration. She adjusted her sunvisor again to the morning sun and glanced at Alecia.

Alecia was stirring. She had a pouty sleepy look on her face and her eyes were still almost closed. "I'm hungry," she said.

They were approaching a large city. In fact, they had been approaching this city for a bit. The larger the better. In Jeanine's mind, big was what she wanted to disappear into.

Jeanine merged right. She passed under several overpasses onto a street named Pulaski. She considered the layout of the city. The streets here were wider and had names instead of numbers. The city blocks were somewhat rectangular, but the thoroughfare streets cut at odd angles.

She matched the flow of morning traffic. Her first task was to find a place for Alecia to eat breakfast. Jeanine took note of the blue and white police cars as she drove. "Help me find a place, honey," she said. Alecia perked up in her seat, watching.

Many car shops, liquor stores, pharmacies, and large buildings lined the street they were travelling. She passed a sign that called this place the Windy City. At an intersection off Belmont, she noted a tavern on the corner. The door was open and a black lady with tightly braided hair was talking to a crippled man in a wheelchair.

Unusual for a place to be open so early.

She slowed at the traffic light.

Alecia called out, "Turn here." Jeanine made a smooth right hand turn and saw a McDonald's restaurant ahead.

"Is McDonald's okay, honey?"

Alecia perked up in her seat and looked expectantly. Jeanine took that to mean, Yes, and she pulled into the restaurant parking. She pulled the next to last twenty from her wallet and got out. She grimaced. She would have to refuel with the other twenty. That left only pocket change and the last hundred in her locked glove compartment.

Jeanine circled around the back of her car, and helped Alecia out as they went into the restaurant. The restaurant was busy. Alecia slid into a plastic seat and Jeanine ordered and purchased her breakfast for her. She sat next to Alecia as she ate hot cakes and sausage. Several men in the booth next to them and a lady in business attire across from her were busy eating breakfast and drinking coffee. It was conspicuous that she, herself, was sitting there and not eating or drinking anything. This was why she most often fixed Alecia's breakfast at home.

In a pique of regret, she remembered her little trailer and every detail of her kitchen. This was behind them now. Jeanine smiled at Alecia and stroked her baby girl's hair.

Bright morning sunlight flooded the windows of the restaurant. Across the street Jeanine noticed what first appeared to be a hospital, but saw it was an assisted living home for elderly, St. Joseph. She had done menial jobs, like laundry, and they'd passed a laundromat one block back. And she'd worked as a bartender. Maybe she could get a job at the tavern, or another bar, nearby.

Her first task was to refuel, then find shelter for her and Alecia for the day. They found a little motel next to a shopping center nearby. Alecia wanted to play in the pool, but did not have a bathing suit. Jeanine paid for two days, which took two-thirds of the last hundred dollars she had. By the time she bought Alecia food for two days, they would be without cash. She made a deal with Alecia to take her to the pool in shorts and a top that evening. For now, Alecia could watch TV in their room. Jeanine kissed her on the head and turned the volume down.

Hours upon hours of driving and the stress of running hit Jeanine at once. She felt suddenly weary and wanted to sleep. She went to her car and gathered comfortable clothes for Alecia, something for Alecia to swim in, and a few dressy clothes for herself. As Jeanine picked through the plastic bags in her trunk, the family in the car next to her had actual suitcases and they were leaving the motel. The boy and girl stared and pointed at her as their parents ushered them into their car.

Bag lady, she overheard.

Jeanine felt ashamed, but smiled tightly to herself and tried to show indifference. She tried to pass it by, but it bothered her. *Let it go*, she said to herself. These people did not know her or her situation.

Inside her and Alecia's room, she pulled the heavy curtain closed, dimmed the light over the circular table, and turned up the air conditioning. She lay coins and dollar bills on the dresser and told Alecia she could go only to the vending machines nearby if she wanted something to eat or drink. No farther.

Jeanine lay their clothes out and went to the bed away from the TV and undressed. She removed her dark contacts, put them away, and went to the bathroom and splashed cold water on her face. The fluorescent light in the bathroom was glaring bright to her tired eyes. She turned it off. She turned on the shower and ran the water until it got hot. Her body felt cold to her, no matter how hot the water was.

Cold tears. Cooler body temperature.

What was she? Not human, not exactly.

After her shower, she felt better, but still very tired. She turned down the covers of her bed and sat there. Her slip and Alecia's gown to sleep in had been left at the other motel.

Jeanine slid under the covers and rolled to her right side facing the floral wall-papered wall away from the TV. Mother Rosalind, her saintly Bible teacher, came to her mind as she drifted off to sleep. She remembered Jesus said we had to forgive or our Heavenly Father could not forgive us. Jeanine felt so alone. How much farther from God could you fall? Cold tears trickled onto her pillow.

Yet, Jesus said forgive.

Mother Rosalind's gentle and kind face, so many years of love and acceptance as she was growing up, filled the void in her heart after her mother's untimely death. Apart from her Papa, it was the one time in her life, until Bobby, that she felt she had been really loved. Now she was alone.

Yet in her heart, she kept feeling, Forgive.

Before she drifted off to sleep, Jeanine whispered to herself, Yes, Lord.

Somehow she and Alecia would make it.

When Jeanine again opened her eyes, she was aware that hours had passed. The light and TV were off and Alecia, too, had curled under the covers of her own bed in her clothes. It was almost two o'clock in the afternoon.

Although she felt a little groggy, Jeanine became instantly awake and ready to search for a blood source. She yawned and stretched, got up, pulled on underwear, and went into the bathroom to straighten her hair and put on makeup.

She combed the tangles out of her naturally curly hair and placed two clips to keep her hair out of her face. She brushed on light powder base, applied mascara and eye shadow, and put a subtle gloss on her lips. Jeanine carefully slipped her dark contacts on. She gargled with hot salty water. Salt seemed to help remove any residue of blood in her mouth. Then she brushed her teeth. Jeanine smiled at herself. She wanted to feel confident and ready for her job interviews. First, she would try the tavern on the corner they had passed, then the assisted living home, then the laundromat. She wished she had some jewelry.

In the bedroom, she heard Alecia stirring. She found Alecia sitting up. Jeanine put on her dressy crème colored ruffled blouse and the matching black skirt, and pulled on her sandals. Jeanine felt the first tugging of her blood needs. The perception edge on her hearing made her aware of the people's conversation and sound of their television in the next room.

Alecia said she was hungry.

Jeanine knelt in front of Alecia and smoothed her dark brown hair out of her face. "Baby girl," she said, "I have to go get a job and find a blood source." Alecia stared at her. Jeanine picked up on the rumbling of Alecia's stomach. The coins and dollar bills she'd left on the counter were still there. Alecia had stayed in the room all morning.

"I want to go, too," she protested.

Jeanine considered. "I can't take you with me this time, baby girl. I'll only be gone a few hours. I know you're hungry. I can order room service for you, but I need you to stay in the room while I'm gone." Alecia's face twisted in a frown.

"You said I could go swimming," she protested.

"You can, honey," Jeanine promised, "but it will have to wait until I get back." She found a room service menu and let Alecia pick something. The cost would be double what the cost would have been if they had gone to the restaurant, but Jeanine needed to go now to start hunting for a blood source.

A male voice on the telephone said the food would be delivered in ten minutes. While she was waiting, Jeanine scanned the phone book to see what types of businesses were in downtown Chicago. Jeanine thought of Momma Lillian and all the times she had kept Alecia on the spur of the moment.

She pictured the dear park manager as she last saw her standing in her doorway. When she found a job, she would need to get Alecia enrolled in the school system here and find daycare help to keep Alecia during the after school hours as necessary if she needed more time to acquire blood that day.

There was a gentle knock on their door.

Jeanine opened the door and saw a rather handsome young man with dark hair carrying a food tray. He seemed to look her over, too. Gave whole new meaning to the phrase, Room Service. Jeanine quickly considered

Alecia and simply paid the hotel employee with a tip. She set Alecia's food tray on the table and helped her baby girl into the seat. She had to place an extra cushion to boost Alecia high enough to eat comfortably. Jeanine also turned on the television to have some noise in the room. A Western movie was playing.

"I'll be back soon," Jeanine said.

Alecia looked up with a mouth full of mashed potatoes.

"Stay here until I get back."

Jeanine left the motel and drove to a street adjacent the tavern and elderly home. It wouldn't do to have a car that attracted the wrong kind of attention in this new city. She saw small squat garages along the alleys and beside larger homes. To hide her car, such a garage would be ideal.

Belford Tavern was open for business. Jeanine walked in and quickly eyed the place over. The liquor was arranged on glass racks in front of a mirror. The bar was a polished mahogany and the place was clean and well kept. A man who looked to be in his thirties was tending the bar and a few patrons were at the farthermost booths next to the wall. The black woman Jeanine had seen that morning was wearing a white apron and standing at the far side of the bar talking to a man wearing a suit. She looked at Jeanine as she approached. "You have to be twenty-one to be in this joint," the woman said to Jeanine.

Jeanine met the lady's level gaze. "I am."

And then some, Jeanine thought. "My name's Jeanine Bishop. I'm a bartender. I'm looking for work."

"Licensed school?" the woman asked.

"Yes," Jeanine replied. "Certified."

The black woman shook Jeanine's extended hand. "My name's Mari. I'm co-owner of this joint." She took off the white apron and tossed it to the man behind the bar.

"You may be in luck. My man Tony here is having foot surgery next Monday. We don't have his replacement yet."

Mari walked around Jeanine. "Let's see your ID." Jeanine pulled her recent California driver's license from her skirt pocket. The photo was severe and her hair had been pulled back tight. She was nineteen, so to speak, two years ago. Wrong birth date, as usual. According to her license, she'd turned twenty-one only two weeks ago. Mari gave her license back. She glanced at Tony, who seemed to nod. To Jeanine, she said, "Make me a margarita."

Jeanine took her place behind the bar, slipped on a black apron, and took a few minutes to familiarize herself with their setup. She found the cocktail glasses, limes, tequila, and Cointreau – then set to work.

Her hands moved deftly and easily.

Shaker. Ice. Tequila. Cointreau. Lime juice. Rim glass with lime. Coarse salt on plate. Swirl. Strain. Slice of lime with a twist as garnish. Jeanine set the finished drink before her prospective employer with a flourish.

Just like Manny taught her.

Her presentation and mixing speed were still superb.

Jeanine smiled to herself. It had been over twelve years since she'd mixed a drink, yet she knew what to do like it was yesterday. Mari gave the drink to Tony, who sampled it, and gave Jeanine a thumbs up. Mari's smile broadened and she placed her hand on Jeanine's arm across the bar.

"I'm impressed," she said, "and I'm never impressed."

She glanced at Tony, who nodded yes.

"If Tony says you're good, then you're in. Let's step into my office to get all this legal paperwork handled. Once we check your background, you can work from five until closing at two."

Jeanine stiffened slightly but kept calm.

"What kind of background check?" she asked.

"Just the usual. We need birth certificate. Social security card. Three references. And a letter from your bartending school." Jeanine slipped off the apron and came around the bar. She'd never been asked to provide a birth certificate or a social security card. She had no valid references and her bartending school was over twenty years ago. Her license was legitimate, although, Jeanine wanted no one to try to contact anyone in California to verify her credentials.

"I don't have any of those documents. I had to leave home in a rush." Mari did a turn around and faced Jeanine with her right hand on her hip.

"Sorry, girl friend. Without the legal, I can't use you."

Jeanine glanced at Tony then back at Mari. "Can I work temporary until I can get those things? Just until Tony's back on his feet?" She looked expectantly at Mari.

Mari's face hardened. "We're a reputable establishment. If the authorities find out I worked you, they'd take our serving license."

Jeanine felt crestfallen, but tried to put on a brave front.

She extended her hand to Mari.

"I understand. I appreciate your time."

As she was turning to leave, Mari called her back.

"Promise me you're not an illegal alien."

Jeanine demurred. "I'm an American citizen. I promise." Mari glanced at Tony; Tony seemed to shrug.

Something was up, Jeanine thought.

"If you work for tips, you could pull two hundred a night. It's just until Tony's back on his feet."

Jeanine was elated. "Thank you."

"You have to apply for your documents in the meantime. When you get your paperwork we can hire you permanent."

"We only just arrived today. Can I have the documents mailed here?"

"We?" Mari asked.

"My daughter and I," Jeanine replied.

Mari seemed to look her over.

"We need a place to stay. She's at the motel now."

Tony spoke up. "I live on Karlov, a few blocks from here. I have to go stay with my sister and her husband until I can walk again. My place'll be sitting empty anyway."

She regarded the man behind the bar.

"This is very kind of you, but we wouldn't want to impose."

No free lunch, Jeanine remembered.

Tony shrugged. "Up to you. The place is clean and I have an extra key. You can pay me a hundred a week out of your tips. Leave the money with Mari. That, and restock the fridge when you leave or when I come back. My ex wouldn't understand a new roommate."

Jeanine reconsidered. "Thank you. Write down your address and we'll be happy to come by tomorrow to see it – say, about two in the afternoon." Tony nodded, wrote his address on a small white piece of paper, then went to serve a new customer at the bar. Mari seemed to be studying Jeanine carefully.

"Haven't quite figured you out," she said, "but I will. Always do." Jeanine thanked Mari and Tony for helping her, shook Mari's hand, and promised to return tomorrow to see Tony's place.

Next stop, old folk's home.

Jeanine stood outside St. Joseph Village examining

the huge facility. This was larger than any place she had worked before. At least now she had an idea of the types of documents they would likely ask for. The lobby reminded her of her former Catholic high school. St. Joseph had been founded by a religious order. The inside was well kept and had a peaceful feel to it.

She spoke to a number of ladies before she reached the woman in charge of hiring temp laundry workers. She was very pleasant, but very businesslike. Jeanine filled out an application and patiently answered questions. She was eager to see the actual rooms where the residents were boarded.

It was starting to get dark outside when she walked out of St. Joseph Village. The street lights were starting to come on.

On the street Jeanine took stock of what was around her. Across the street behind the tavern, the same crippled man she had seen that morning exited the tavern from a rear metal door. He was pushing himself down an alley going east. Jeanine crossed the busy street and followed.

She examined him as he pushed himself down the alley and around the corner of an apartment complex. His hair was long and unkempt. He was unshaven and wore gloves with the fingers cut out of them. A knapsack was slung over the back of his wheelchair. When he turned the corner, Jeanine quickened her pace and stopped to watch at the corner of the building. A few paces down the block, he pressed some button and was admitted to a gate. Jeanine sprinted and caught the gate before it closed. The man had wheeled himself through a garden area and was entering the double glass doors.

She reached the doors after the man had disappeared inside. She could hear the chime of an elevator changing floors and the whisk of air conditioning. Jeanine slid the door open and stole inside. The elevator had stopped on the third floor. Jeanine took the fire stairs up.

The third floor was deserted. She heard the tinkling of keys at her far left down the corridor. The man opening an apartment door with a key attached to a chain. Jeanine moved quickly behind the man and wrapped her arm around his neck.

He reached and grabbed around her head, but she held him until he stopped moving. His heartbeat slowed as he became unconscious. Jeanine finished opening his apartment door and wheeled him inside. He appeared to be a man in his late twenties. His arms were massive, but his legs were half the size they should have been and emaciated.

Jeanine wheeled him to his living room, took a wrapped razor blade from her skirt pocket, and went to this man's kitchen for a bowl. She slipped up the sleeve of his coat and made a cut on his right arm midway down his forearm. He obviously lived alone.

She did not cut him deep, but blood quickly seeped down his lowered arm. She smelled something rotten. Now that she was close enough to the man, she smelled an odor on him. It was even stronger – overpowering the normal scent of his blood. Jeanine only collected a half bowl before she drank. As soon as she drank the blood, her body began absorbing it. He was starting to come to. She found a whiskey bottle and tumbler in a well-stocked mini-bar and left the man at his kitchen table with bottle in hand.

She poured a little on his cut to sterilize it and some whiskey on his shirt. She left him sitting in his wheelchair pulled up to his kitchen table with tumbler in hand. She hoped he would assume he came in, started drinking, and just lost an hour or two of his life. He would fill in the gaps himself.

Jeanine made her way out and locked the man's door as she left. She felt a numbness in her body that was unusual after feeding. By the time she made her way to her car, parked four blocks away, her fingers were tingling. By the time she pulled into the motel parking lot, her vision was blurry.

Her head had started hurting and her ears started to buzz. It was now fully night. Jeanine heard the splash of children playing in the motel pool.

Jeanine found her room. Alecia was standing in the door. Jeanine stumbled past her and reached to steady herself. "I want to go swimming," Alecia started. Everything was going dim. She lay down.

In all of her vampyric years, she had never been sick until now. Jeanine passed out and everything went black.

Jeanine saw starlight. The night sky full of sparkling, radiating stars. Bobby pressed himself against her and kissed her again. She felt a flutter and lightheaded when he held her and kissed her that way.

He was sooooo good looking!

She looked into his blue eyes and twirled the stubborn lick of thick brown hair curled on his forehead. She was a poor Catholic girl. *What does he see in me?*

He lived on the rich side of town. His parents had given him a new Mustang for his sixteenth birthday. He even went to East Meck! Robert Trenton Blaylock was loaded! He could have any girl in town. *Any* girl. Yet in the two years, six months, eighteen days, four hours and twelve minutes since they'd met – not that anyone was counting – he continued to pursue her. Tomorrow was the prom. She'd decided. Tomorrow would be their night.

He looked into her hazel green eyes with wonder. When he smiled at her, everything inside her turned mushy.

What started warm grew hot, then grew to a blazing inferno. She couldn't imagine loving anyone this much, but here he was in her arms. All hers. The entire world lay before them at sixteen.

When he pulled away from her, his kiss lingered like a brand on her soul.

Oh, God! she thought.

She liked the way his eyes smiled at her.

"I have something for you," he said. He drew a shiny black rectangular box from his letterman jacket. He was smiling at her. That grin drove like daggers into her heart. He opened the box for her. A small gold heart necklace gleamed in the light of street lamps. She touched the small necklace. It was the most beautiful thing she'd ever seen, and it was so much more precious because it came from him. His heart to her's.

"I couldn't wait to give it to you," he said.

He unfastened the tiny gold chain clasp and placed the necklace around her neck. It glistened just above her silver crucifix. She couldn't wait to go inside to see it in a mirror. Jeanine reached both arms around him and hugged him close. "Thank you," she whispered in his ear as she drew him close. She could stand out there all night with him.

He drew her into a kiss again, then stepped back from her holding both of her hands in his. Regrettably, it was late.

Papa was waiting. They would be together tomorrow.

He walked her to her steps, kissed her a final time, then got into his car and drove away. Tomorrow, she breathed.

She took half a day off from school just to get ready. Hair coiffured, nails polished, skin glowing. His necklace shone as a gold braid on her pearly white skin binding her heart to his. Her prom dress was a satiny silver flowing gown. The most beautiful gown she'd ever seen.

When she stepped out of her bedroom, her Papa stood transfixed in the hallway. "So like Mamă," he breathed. He carried a Polaroid camera he'd bought at the drug store. His medium blonde hair had been slicked back. The stubble on his face was rough and his hands were calloused from years and years of working with concrete.

He motioned her to the hallway and snapped a few pictures of her. In that moment, Bobby pulled up outside. He raced the engine of his new car a few times before he shut it off and came to the door. She smoothed her skirt and waited for her Papa to answer the door. He knocked.

Jeanine felt butterflies in her stomach.

Would he like the dress? Would he like her hair?

The smiling handsome young man in the door was dressed in a black tuxedo with a deep red sash around his waist. Jeanine caught her breath as she saw how he was looking at her. He had a corsage for her wrist. He placed it on her right wrist and held her close as her Papa took photographs of them together. She kissed her Papa on the cheek. "Thank you, Papa," she said.

He kissed her on the cheek in return and released her hand. To Bobby, he cautioned, "Drive safely with my Rose."

Bobby replied, "Yes, sir."

As he took Jeanine's arm they were finally off on this enchanted evening together. She slid into the passenger seat of his car. He made sure her dress was fully inside, then closed the door. When he got into the driver's side, he just stared at her. "You're so beautiful," he said. Jeanine demurred. Much of her beauty came naturally from her beautiful mother Roxana. Pale skin with medium brown hair and green eyes, she could have been a gypsy. When

Jeanine saw the photos of her Papa kept, she thought of her mother in her native Romanian village. She had been brought to the United States as a little girl six years old.

She smiled adoringly at her date.

"And you are so handsome, sir," she replied.

The evening passed elegantly. They danced, dined, stood for photographs from a professional photographer, then danced some more. After ten o'clock, many couples had started leaving. At eleven o'clock, Bobby took Jeanine by the hand and led her out to the patio under a million stars.

The concrete table and benches made Jeanine think of her father's years of labor at the concrete plant.

Bobby held her and kissed her in the night.

Oh, how she wanted to be with him!

He led her to the edge of the roof. A fence separated them from a fall. The lights of the city sparkled in their eyes.

A blustery wind tousled Jeanine's hair.

Bobby took her in his arms and stood behind her. When Jeanine was in his arms, she felt safe. It was not the same as when her father held her. This was far more. "I have something important to ask you," he said lowly. He kissed her on her earlobe then kissed her neck. His fingers traced the thin golden strand necklace. He turned Jeanine to face him. They embraced. "Jen," he said, "I met some guys that have some cool things goin' down in San Mateo. I'm leaving after graduation and I want you to come with me." Jeanine frowned. Across the country?

"What do you mean? I thought we were going to stay here."

Bobby let her go and stood apart from her. "This is something I have to do. I thought you would want come with me. You have to come with me." He was starting to scare her. This was not the Bobby she knew. His blue eyes were intense.

"Jen, all my father ever thinks about is business and money. I've been born with a silver spoon in my mouth and one up my rear. I've been given anything and everything I could ever want. But I have to live life for myself, for us, and find what life is all about. All the money my family has is nothing but another chain on me. Help me break free."

He held his wrists before her like he was shackled. Jeanine wanted to take his face in her fingertips and kiss away the worry on his brow. She took both of his hands in hers. "Bobby," she said, "it isn't you having money that's the problem. It's money having you. Money doesn't make you who you are. It simply reveals the person you already are."

He bowed his head and looked away from her. "I love you," he said. "I know you love me whether I have the Midas Touch or not. You'd love me if I was flat broke. Jen, you have to come. Whether you come or not, I'm going."

Jeanine followed his intense gaze into the cityscape below. She could not see what he was seeing in the darkness.

"I'll be with you forever," he promised.

Jeanine awoke with Alecia curled beside her on her bed. Her baby girl's face was pressed to her sleeve and her sleeve had been soaked. The white lines of tears on Alecia's face were still visible. It was very early in the morning. The motel room was dark and quiet. Jeanine could hear the rumble of traffic on the nearby street and the shuffling of perpetual wanderers in the city night.

Her sensitive hearing had become acute.

She heard the light clicking of a dog walking on the

sidewalk, a stray probably. She heard a rusty screeching, like a sign was swinging in the breeze. She heard Alecia's heart beating. She counted the thump-thump sounds and grinned. Jeanine reached over and smoothed Alecia's hair. People all around her were living, breathing, dreaming, hoping, and sleeping. She felt an intensity in her awareness that she had never known before. She was still dressed. Her crème blouse was wrinkled.

Jeanine sat up and took stock of her surroundings. Alecia had laid next to her fully clothed as well. The last thing Jeanine could remember was coming in the door.

She must have passed out.

Jeanine slid to the end of the bed, kicked off her sandals, and slid out of her skirt and blouse. She removed her bra but kept her panties on. She removed her contacts. Alecia stirred slightly. Jeanine sat Alecia up and pulled off her shirt, shorts, and let her curl in the center of the bed. She saw the clothes she had laid out for Alecia to go swimming in. She felt guilty but nothing could be done to fix the situation now. Their time was spent in the morning and she did not have enough to pay for another night.

She felt badly because Alecia had to just sit alone for so many hours unsupervised. When she worked the tavern job, she would be gone from Alecia most of the night. If she got the part-time laundry job at the old folk's home, she would likely work in the mornings. Child care took money. A home took money. Running away from blood cults took money. Everything boiled down to money at some point. She remembered Tony's kind offer. She checked her skirt pocket for the piece of paper Tony had given her. She still had his address. She would show Alecia the tavern where she would be working, too.

Jeanine decided she had to find someone trustworthy to help her take care of Alecia. With at least three hours until dawn, she decided to lay down and rest on the bed while they still had one. As Jeanine took her place beside Alecia, she gave her baby girl a kiss on the forehead. When Alecia reached for her, Jeanine made room for her baby in the bend of her left arm.

Everything right and everything good in her life lay next to her. Being in St. Joseph reminded her much of her high school. The same air of peace dwelt there and the staff and tenants seemed happy. After years of Nolan happy was what she needed. Alecia stirred beside her. "Jennie?" she said in a whisper. Jeanine kissed her baby girl.

"I'm here, honey," she replied.

Alecia snuggled and closed her eyes.

In spite of every other wretched thing that had happened to her, at least the decision to run with Alecia was the right thing to do. All she had to worry about now was making the next right decision, one choice at a time.

Jeanine found herself lying awake. Sleep would not come. When she focused, she could easily distinguish Alecia's heartbeat against the myriad of other sounds. Alecia had said it was not her fault when that bad thing happened to her. Alecia had called her own father evil with an insight that defied description. Alecia had known in a bad dream when Nolan had tracked them to the motel in Sheridan.

In a sudden start of revelation, Jeanine almost stopped breathing. Many times her Mother Rosalind had spoken of the truth of the spirit world we cannot see or touch with our five physical senses. Yet it was just as real as the traffic in the city outside. She remembered the women in scripture called prophetess. Deborah, Mirriam, the daughters of Phillip – it struck her suddenly that Alecia had to be a prophetess also. She considered this manifestation of the anointing with awe.

Jeanine kissed her baby's forehead. She was so much more precious because of the gift of God that lived within her. This gave her great hope.

Somehow they would make it.

The woman behind the desk gave Jeanine a stack of paperwork to fill in. The school office of Monroe Elementary was a hustle and bustle at the beginning of the school year. She had to give them Alecia's real last name so she could get her records from her prior school. They wanted Alecia's birth certificate, her social security number, and proof Jeanine was Alecia's legal guardian.

Jeanine claimed to be Nolan's common-law wife because Alecia's former school had seen her with Nolan for years. She had no choice but to call for Alecia's records. In a brief conversation by telephone with the aide in the Smith Elementary office, Jeanine learned that Nolan had not filed a missing person report on Alecia. He told the school that he and Alecia were moving back to California to explain Alecia's absence. She knew he would not involve the police. Blood cult problems were always handled internally and permanently.

When the Smith Elementary aide faxed copies of Alecia's paperwork, Monroe Elementary requirements were satisfied pending receipt of her actual documents by mail. Jeanine toured the school grounds and walked Alecia to her classroom. The recently added annex to the facility almost doubled the size of the school. She toured the new annex gymnasium, auditorium, and classrooms with a group of other parents taking their children to meet their teachers. Alecia's teacher was a slender Asian woman who took Alecia in and introduced her to a group of students sitting at a circular desk. Two girls Alecia's age started talking with her. It was good to see her interact with her new classmates so readily.

Alecia was a charmer, Jeanine noticed.

When Jeanine took her to the tavern, Mari had liked Alecia immediately. Tony's fifteen year old niece Rachel had taken up residence with her and Alecia at Tony's apartment. Rachel cooked for Alecia and watched after her while Jeanine worked odd hours at the assisted living place and worked nights at the tavern.

Jeanine left her contact information with the school office – the telephone number at the tavern and the number at the assisted living home. She took the long way out. She exited the school building through the auditorium exit on the street. Adjacent to the new annex building, Jeanine looked up and saw Alecia standing in the window on the top floor with two other students, a black boy and an Asian girl.

Jeanine smiled and waved, then walked to the playground, got into her car and drove back to Tony's apartment. She topped off her car at a gas station, then took her time cruising the haphazard streets to consider her options.

Everything was working out so well. She was almost afraid something would happen. What her Papa always said, *If something can go wrong it will*, nagged her thinking.

Well, it was high time something went right in her life.

Mari seemed to like her and gave all indications that she wanted to hire her permanent even after Tony returned to work. The tavern was busiest Thursday through Saturday. She would notice during the course of a night Mari just watching her. Jeanine would smile at her and continue working. Tavern business actually picked up because word got out about the pretty new bartender. The regular patrons liked Jeanine and this was to her advantage.

Several blocks from the assisted living home, Jeanine backed into the garage she'd negotiated with a nearby home owner to use so her car was not visible on the street.

She kept her change of shoes and the powder blue dress uniform she wore at St. Joseph in the back seat. Not wishing to be left destitute again, she kept at least two changes of clothes for her and Alecia plus sleepwear in the trunk. She checked her supply of cash in her glove compartment. In spite of paying Rachel to buy food and keep Alecia, she was still making money just in tips alone. How much better it would be when she could earn a real paycheck!

Jeanine bought and kept a small notepad. She made notes of street names, directions, people she saw on the street, buildings, and places she might be able to find blood sources.

She now worked at the old folk's home Monday, Wednesday, and Friday mornings. The west wing of the facility was reserved for patients in such a mental state that they were unable to interact much with anyone. Jeanine was able to feed discretely so far on two of the least responsive tenants. She wished she knew how to withdraw blood by venipuncture. Her range of suitable blood sources would increase if she could get a job in a hospital setting – like whoever withdrew her weekday transfer unit of blood at St. Peter's.

She flipped through her notepad to refresh her memory, jotted down new street names she saw next to Alecia's school, then locked it in her glove compartment with her extra cash.

With the rest of the morning and the early afternoon off work, she could start planning for her and Alecia's future. She stood in front of Tony's apartment. Jeanine studied the two-story brick building from the sidewalk. Some homes in the area were older. The crayon drawing Alecia had made for her was in her mind, but she didn't think she could afford a home with a real yard – at least not yet. Their future depended on her finding another identity for herself and Alecia. She had no idea how this was done. She might tell Mari the truth, but decided to wait until she knew the black lady much better.

The tavern was full Thursday night.

Jeanine hustled to fill drink orders and keep tabs on the regular patrons who liked for her to talk to them. Nothing chatty. She had to focus on what she was doing. A group of young men in business suits were new. They were drinking at the far left booth and Mari's twenty-five-year-old daughter, Keisha, was busy carrying drink orders from bar to booth. Mari had left unexpectedly at five and did not return until just after six when the first rush of the after-work crowd started piling in.

When she came back, her face was tight and pinched, like she was worried or distressed. She would stay close to her office, Jeanine noticed. Jeanine waited for Mari to make eye contact with her or even to engage with the customers. Mari seemed to be in a world all her own. Just before eleven, a heavyset bald man shoved the front door open and wheeled in the young crippled man Jeanine fed upon last week. She kept her face neutral as the heavy man wheeled him to a spot at the far end of the bar. He locked the young man's wheelchair in place and turned to Mari.

They disappeared into Mari's office.

Jeanine approached the young man in the wheelchair cautiously. His long hair was unkempt. This time he wore no coat. His sleeves were rolled up and she could see a white gauze bandage on his arm where she had cut him. The same little backpack was slung over his wheelchair.

"Hi," she said brightly, "what can I get for you?"

He looked up at her, staring.

"Scotch and water," he said dryly.

She remembered his well-stocked mini-bar.

From Mari's office, she overheard a rather loud discussion between Mari and the heavyset man. For appearances, she had to check his ID.

"Are you at least twenty-one?" she asked.

He nodded and pulled a wallet linked to a chain on his belt to the bar top and pulled out his driver's license. She read his birth date and name. He was twenty-three.

She smiled at him. "Nice to meet you, Patrick. On the rocks, neat, or straight up." He put his license and wallet away.

"Straight up," he said.

Jeanine mixed his scotch and water, chilled with ice, and strained into a highball. He seemed to be staring at her when she set his drink in front of him. He sipped and nursed his drink.

"Have we met before?" he asked.

Jeanine picked up her tab and the empty glassware of a customer next to Patrick that just left. She replied, "I don't think so. We've only been in town less than a week." Jeanine let the implied "we" hang in the air. Perhaps he would think she was married or had a boyfriend and drop any other association.

Patrick went back to staring at his drink.

Jeanine thankfully moved down the bar to wait on two other customer orders. At that moment, the heavyset bald man and Mari left the office. The man seemed to glare at her as he strode past the bar and out the door. Mari stood next to Patrick with one hand on her hip and another on his right arm. Jeanine made her way to the far end of the bar. She checked with Patrick, "All good?" He nodded.

Jeanine caught Mari's gaze. "What was that all about?"

"Porter doesn't like that I'm working you."

Jeanine assumed this man was the co-owner of the tavern. She suddenly wished Mari's co-ownership was at least fifty-fifty.

"I promise that I am not illegal," Jeanine reminded Mari.

"I believe you," Mari said. Several men jostled by as they were going to a table. Mari gave Jeanine a tight smile. "It'll be all right. I'll talk to him and he'll come around." She swept her hand at the people filling the bar.

"You're good and the patrons like you. Porter will listen to his customers. If they say you stay, then he'll have to keep you just to keep business in the place." A customer from the other end of the bar called her. Jeanine squeezed Mari's hand then left to take care of the customer's order. She glanced back at Patrick, who listened to the entire conversation. As she and Mari were talking, she picked up the rotten scent on him that she smelled in his apartment. He was just sitting, like the old folk's home tenants who were not in their right mind.

No matter what else happened, she knew Patrick would die and very soon.

Before Jeanine entered Tony's apartment, she breathed a prayer of thanks that she was able to find a lone derelict wandering the streets in search of food. She had money from her tips and she bought him two hot roast beef sandwiches from a grocery store deli that was open twenty-four hours. She made a deal with him. I get you food. You give me some of your blood. There were more transients in this city than she ever saw in Helena. She was getting better at cruising the overpasses and parks. The tavern closed at two a.m. – this time it had taken her only an hour and a half to find a suitable blood source. And today, Friday, she would be back at St. Joseph at nine in the morning.

Jeanine quietly entered the darkened apartment on the second floor. She was in the living room. The night breeze blew in the two open windows at the front of the building. Although the air was generally dry here, she was starting to distinguish the myriad scents from Lake Michigan to the east. She heard soft breathing from Tony's bedroom to her immediate left. Jeanine checked on her girls. Alecia and Rachel had taken Tony's king- sized bed and the bedroom. She kicked off her sandals in the hallway, then padded softly to Alecia's side. She gave Alecia a kiss on her forehead and tucked the cover around her.

Sleeping peacefully.

Jeanine went back to the kitchenette and pulled two twenties from her skirt pocket and left the money on the kitchenette table for Rachel's babysitting fee. She left her skirt, slip, blouse, and bra over a chair, then went to stand next to the window to enjoy the night air a little before bedding down on the couch. The gentle night breeze stirred the white curtains. The white street light from the corner of the block illuminated Jeanine with a soft ethereal glow as she stood watching the street below. Everything was quiet. Just how she liked it.

When Jeanine slept, she awoke to the jarring sound of an alarm clock. She stirred under the quilt on the couch and hit the snooze button. She felt as if she had only slept ten minutes. Eight fifteen all ready? Her alarm jangled again at eight twenty-four. Jeanine forced herself to get up. Rachel and Alecia's breakfast bowls were in the sink.

Oatmeal and milk were the choice today. Part of the babysitting deal was for Rachel to make sure Alecia got on her bus each school day before taking the transit to her own school.

Within twenty minutes, Jeanine got a hot shower, brushed her hair, put in contacts, put on makeup, dressed in her powder blue work uniform with white sneakers, and dropped her change of clothes for her tavern job in her car before walking to work at St. Joseph. Her little uniform did not have a place to keep razor blades, so Jeanine had to stuff them in the padding of her bra.

At work, the laundry tasks were divided between two Hispanic workers, a black lady, and Jeanine. As they branched out, Jeanine took the west wing. She tried the third tenant, an elderly man who was just sitting in a lounge chair. His hands shook when he lifted them. His skin was a sallow color. She tried to engage him in some conversation, but he did not respond.

Jeanine gathered his bedclothes and towels and left them by the door. She found alcohol and swabbed his arm above his right elbow. She made a slight cut on his flabby skin and, at the first trickle of blood, she knelt beside him and lapped the blood that oozed from the wound.

Her body began to immediately absorb the blood.

Because she had fed early that morning, she did not need much. Within a few minutes, she was through. She took unwrapped square gauze pads from her skirt pocket and secured the squares with clinging gauze wrap. She used a damp washcloth from the bathroom to clean up any drops of blood that were on the floor under his chair. The man remained unresponsive.

Moments later, a nurse came into the room. Jeanine had a bundle of sheets and towels in her arms as the nurse entered.

"Are you Jeanine Bishop?" the nurse asked.

Jeanine replied yes.

"There's a call for you at the nurse's station from your daughter's school."

Jeanine dumped the laundry in her cart and followed the nurse to her station. Jeanine picked up the telephone and said hello. The girl on the telephone sounded young, like an aide. "I'm not sure I should be calling you," she said, "but Alecia's father is with the school administrator right now. He wants to check her out and take her with him." Jeanine's blood turned cold.

"Describe him," Jeanine said quickly.

"Black hair, pretty muscular, hawk-like gaze, kinda mean dark eyes."

"Stall him," Jeanine said, "Don't let him take Alecia with him. I'll be right there." With that, she dropped the receiver and ran to the stairwell at the end of the east wing, and punched the metal door open. Oh God, she thought, Nolan was here!

Two flights down, she reached the bottom, and pushed open the door. An alarm sounded. Jeanine did not care. She raced across the grass, the open field, with an iron wrought fence next to the sidewalk. She jumped the fence and reached her borrowed garage a few minutes later. She kept her car key on a chain around her neck. She fished the key out of her blouse, unlocked her car, and slid into the moulded driver's seat.

The engine growled when she raced it.

She pressed forward and moved down the one-way streets as quickly as possible to find Monroe Elementary.

As she circled the Schubert Avenue side, she saw Nolan's white van in the parking lot. Jeanine circled the school and parked on the opposite playground side of the school. She ran back to the front of the school and came to the main office. No one tried to stop her. Older students were milling around in groups led by teachers.

They appeared to be having some type of assembly.

Jeanine looked in the glass window of the main office. The girl who called her, a student intern, pointed right and mouthed the words, That way. There was a stairwell leading up. She waved at the girl who warned her. She took to the opposite stairwell adjacent to the office to her left.

Alecia's classroom was on the top floor.

Nolan would be escorted to Alecia's classroom by the school administrator. Jeanine pictured in her mind the rows of classrooms on the front of the main building. Alecia's classroom was at the end where the ledge made an "L" shape and merged with the chimney.

Jeanine came from the stairwell and stepped onto the highly polished top floor hallway. A teacher was guiding her class into her classroom. Jeanine saw Nolan with the school administrator. They were midway down the hall, waiting for a class to pass by.

She bound into the nearest classroom across the hall in front of her. A black man, the teacher, was at the front of the classroom writing on the board. A class of third graders, Jeanine assumed, was in progress.

"Sorry for the interruption," Jeanine said as she raced to the opposite side of the room. She pushed and broke the window latch and the huge window panel opened outward. She stepped back and jumped the chest high wall through the open window, and stepped onto the wide ledge outside.

A sea of third graders closed behind her.

Jeanine made her way quickly to Alecia's classroom. The lowest window nearest the bend of the building was ajar. Jeanine pushed it open completely.

She dropped to her knees and rolled through the window and onto the tile floor. She scanned the full classroom for dark-brown- haired girls. Alecia was sitting near the front of the class. Their teacher had gone to the door and did not notice that an intruder had entered the classroom. When Alecia turned and saw Jeanine, her face registered complete surprise.

Jeanine motioned for Alecia. "C'mere baby!"

Alecia bound up and ran to Jeanine.

Nolan pushed his way past the teacher and school administrator and saw Jeanine. He charged her.

Jeanine quickly placed Alecia behind her. With a side glance and a shove, she told Alecia, "Climb out the window, baby, quickly." Nolan shoved a little boy out of his way.

The child smacked the floor and started crying.

Jeanine met him in the aisle and pushed as hard as she could. His blood sounded loud in her ears. Her own pulse had quickened. When Nolan swung for her she dodged the blow and wrapped both arms around his chest and pushed him backwards.

Her hospital white sneakers squeaked on the tile floor.

She pushed Nolan over the teacher's desk at the front of the room. With a quick side glance, the teacher and school administrator were just standing there – mouths gaping open. Alecia had pulled a desk chair to the window and had halfway climbed outside. When Nolan fell on the floor behind the heavy metal desk, Jeanine shoved the desk onto him. She heard him grunt in pain. She quickly ran after Alecia and, pushing the chair out of her way, bound out onto the ledge with Alecia.

Jeanine picked Alecia up. "Bear hug, honey," she instructed.

Alecia wrapped both arms around her Jennie's neck and tightened her legs around her body. Jeanine used one hand to steady Alecia and the other hand to help her navigate the ledge back to the third grade classroom at the other end of the hallway.

Behind her, glass was breaking. Nolan was following them onto the ledge. Jeanine reached the farthermost point on the ledge and used the elbow of her free arm to break another window lock. She knelt with Alecia, balancing on one knee, and lowered her baby through the open window panel into the classroom. Hands reached for Alecia.

Nolan tackled Jeanine. They fell together to the end of the ledge. The rough surface of the ledge scraped Jeanine's forearms and palms as they fell. Both of her arms were pinned under her chest. Nolan was trying to reach around her, but he could not get an adequate grip. Jeanine's powder blue uniform ripped from the left sleeve and Nolan lost his hold. Jeanine turned over and smashed Nolan on the side of his jaw with her left elbow as she turned over. She managed to hook her knee into his stomach and heave him off of her. He lay on the ledge unmoving.

She lay still for a second. Her head was pounding.

Alecia's face was pressed to the closed window. The black teacher and a host of third grade students were around her.

Jeanine got up and stepped through the open panel window. Her arm shook as she steadied herself to lower herself to the floor.

As soon as she touched the classroom floor, Alecia embraced her. Jeanine could hear Nolan stirring. When she turned to face him, she met the murderous gaze in his coal black eyes.

"Hurry, baby," she urged, "that way."

She coaxed children out of her way and made a path for Alecia. Her right palm was bleeding. Jeanine grabbed a white cloth used to clean the board off the wall clip and wrapped her hand as she led Alecia into the hallway. She took Alecia's hand with her uninjured left hand and led the way down the stairs back to the school office. The hallway downstairs was empty.

She heard Nolan running behind them.

Jeanine led Alecia out the main entrance. Her car was to the left. Nolan's van was in the faculty parking lot to her right. They ran. She heard the van engine. Nolan had reached his van and was coming for them.

Jeanine picked up Alecia and raced to her own car. No students were in the playground area. The pebbly surface made Jeanine slip and nearly stumble. She set Alecia next to the passenger door and ripped her key free of the chain around her neck. She unlocked Alecia's door and pulled it open.

Nolan was circling the one-way streets around the school and would likely try to cut off her exit.

"Hurry, honey," she panted, "climb in and fasten your seat belt." Jeanine rushed to the driver's side, unlocked and pulled open her door, slid into the moulded seat and clipped her own seat belt quickly. Alecia was in her seat and buckled in. Jeanine jammed her key into the ignition, and sped out of the little lot. She turned left on the one-way street.

Nolan came around the block after them.

Jeanine raced ahead in the residential apartment section. Some pedestrians and a man on a bicycle were ahead of her. She was looking for Pulaski. She made an abrupt left hand turn onto the thoroughfare and merged far right to make a right hand turn.

Alecia was crying. Jeanine saw Nolan turn after them

in her rearview mirror before she made the next turn. She was heading in the direction of the old folk's home and Belford's tavern. She regretted not being able to even say goodbye to Mari.

They were on Milwaukee. Some type of road work was going on ahead. The traffic was merging to the left and slowing.

Jeanine pulled into the left lane, then cut over into the face of the oncoming traffic lane. Two blocks away, she faced an onslaught of cars coming toward her.

She punched the accelerator and passed the row of stopped vehicles in her lane, and barely managed to get back to the right before the oncoming traffic met her.

Nolan was trapped for a moment behind her in the construction traffic and the traffic light.

Jeanine passed the gas station she remembered fueling at when she came into the city. Pulaski should be two blocks down.

The traffic was heavy here. Jeanine slowed. She stayed in the right lane and hoped to get onto the expressway and have a free run of places she could go before Nolan found them again.

How had he managed to track them to Alecia's school? She'd figure it out later.

Alecia had stopped crying. Her nose was runny. She used her sleeve to wipe her nose and her free hand to dry her eyes.

Jeanine glanced at her baby girl as she merged and flowed with the traffic.

"Baby, are you all right?" she asked.

Alecia answered in a little girl voice, "Yes, Jennie."

"You're a brave baby girl," Jeanine coaxed.

Alecia seemed to perk up.

She had to stop at the light just before the overpass and

the turn lane to the interstate. Jeanine did not know the interstate very well. They traveled due east, then south, she thought. When the light changed, Jeanine surged forward and entered the ramp with two slower cars in front of her. She glanced in her rearview mirror and did not see Nolan's van. She double checked with a quick glance over her shoulder.

Jeanine accelerated and merged into the mid-morning expressway traffic.

For now, she stayed in the center lane. She glanced at Alecia several times as traffic flow permitted to see if she was all right. "I hope we lost him, baby girl," Jeanine said. She saw out of the corner of her eye, a white van racing parallel to the expressway on an adjacent street. Jeanine looked around her for an opening.

The high barricade wall separating the roads gradually got lower. Nolan had gotten to an access ramp and was trying to pull ahead of her. Jeanine made sure Alecia had buckled herself in securely. "Baby, hang on," Jeanine called. With that, she punched the accelerator and dove between the two cars in the passing lane beside her, then further to the median and the concrete barricade wall between the expressways. She passed the two cars, then narrowly missed another car in the center lane to pull past a tanker truck in front of her.

Nolan was behind her now, by her guess, a truck and two cars back on her right.

As she changed lanes she saw him in her rearview mirror. The windows of his van had been tinted so no one could see who is driving. They had given chase on occasion when people attempted to flee. His van was as fast as her Mustang if Nolan chose to drive that fast. She expected him to try the same maneuvers that State Troopers used to cause a car they are pursuing to spin out.

He moved several cars closer.

Jeanine could see his outline in the driver's seat of his van.

She looked in desperation at rows upon rows of cars in front of her. The heavier traffic in front of her prevented her from outracing him. She had to cause him to wreck somehow, without him disabling her vehicle in the process.

Jeanine merged left, toward the median barricade.

Nolan was two vehicles behind them now.

He stayed in the center lane next to them.

Alecia glanced back at her father's van. She was holding onto her shoulder strap of her seatbelt. Her tiny fists were white and strained. Jeanine kept watching the flow of traffic around her, calculating, counting seconds.

The first impact sounded extremely loud to her sensitive hearing. Nolan hit the passenger back panel of Jeanine's Mustang. Jeanine was ready. She counter-steered.

He came closer, driving faster, and matching her pace.

He was aiming for her back quarter panel again.

Jeanine accelerated and he drove into thin air. She jabbed her brake to force him to turn aside. He swerved back into his lane. The traffic thickened ahead of her.

Jeanine passed under several overpasses. Each time, her eyes adjusted instantly to the shadows, but the sun blinded her for a few seconds each time they emerged into sunlight.

Nolan had pulled even with them.

He swerved left and hit Jeanine with the full force of his van. She steered into him, metal grinding against metal.

Alecia screamed. Jeanine accelerated.

Nolan hit them again and Jeanine swerved off the road into the median. The median narrowed at a bridge ahead.

She barely made it back into the far left lane. Nolan was no longer beside them. Jeanine looked all around her. He was behind them now. Several slower trucks were in the left outer lane ahead. Traffic was backed up in the far-right lane with cars leaving. Jeanine stayed in the middle lane and Nolan was forced into the channel also. When the way was clear in front of her, she surged ahead, but kept Nolan in her sight and counted in her head.

Ten. Nine. Eight. Seven. Nolan broke out of the channel and came racing toward her. Six. Five. He was taking his stance to hit her on the driver's back quarter panel. Four. Three. Two. Jeanine shifted far right, so he would miss her, then doubled her steering wheel far left. One. The vehicles impacted, and Jeanine steered Nolan as her back panel locked with the protective grill on his van and forced him off the road into the concrete barricade.

Jeanine steered free and accelerated away from him as he crashed and spun around. A large freight truck behind him swerved into the center lane and narrowly missed him. A line of vehicles behind the truck wobbled and dove into the middle lanes of traffic. Somehow no other vehicles crashed.

Jeanine drove frantically until she no longer saw him in her rearview mirror.

Nolan swore quietly to himself as two blue and white police cars pulled behind him into the median. He disengaged the map grid he had been using to track Jeanine's car. At this point, he would have to rely on the lawyers discretely retained by the blood cult to get him out of any legal difficulties.

He rolled down his window and smiled at the officer. Several scenarios came to mind to explain this incident. Security work-related. The officer seemed to take note of the sophisticated electronics in the cab of the vehicle. So much more was in the back. Even if the stupid police searched his entire van, they would not likely find the hidden places under the side panels he could store a person they wished to transport to a sacrifice site.

Nolan presented his public face, calm and tranquil. The officers asked him to get out of the van. He complied. The remote kill switch in the motor of Jeanine's car had not worked.

When all of this bother with Jeanine was done, he promised himself to kill the man who had installed the kill switch relay – very, very, very slowly.

Chapter Seven

Thomas stumbled at the edge of the woods and pushed his way into the bramble that blocked his passage. Blue-white moonlight made everything appear the same washed out gray.

He was shaking. He looked at his sister's blood stains on his hands. Black stains in the moonlight. He could no longer trust himself to be with people anywhere. His family. Friends. Strangers on the street. Anyone.

He made his way with more caution now.

He did not know exactly where he was.

Thomas came to a large tree trunk that had fallen silently in the woods. It came to mind, if a tree falls in the woods and no one is around to hear it, does it make a sound? He often thought mind puzzles like this were fun to think about and debate.

Thomas felt a distinct stitch in his side as he passed the fallen tree trunk. He sat down. It was a wonder he didn't break his neck just running through the darkened landscape and woods like that! Thomas remembered some of his dream. The moon above was the same crescent, but strangely the blue-white light it gave was enough to see by. He could distinguish shapes in the gray upon gray landscape. Details on the ground were clearer to his eyes than they should have been.

He tested the air around him and sniffed. An acrid scent was to his left. The mint sweet tang of foliage was to his right. The air was damp and full of the scent of furry animals, birds, larger animals, and the decaying damp mustiness of dying moss far away. Everything he felt, touched, smelled, or saw was likely affected by what was causing him to become like Majken.

Thomas looked at himself. He was dressed like he imagined a lumberjack would dress. At least he had the good sense not to cut his sister's arm in his underwear.

He felt cold metal at the band of his trousers on his right side. His fingers found the cold metal of the knife – the knife that he'd used to cut his own sister's arm. He shivered. He pulled the knife out and looked at it in the moonlight.

The backpack he remembered from his dream was his father's old backpack. Thomas thought he'd last seen it years ago on a dusty shelf in the old family garage. That was way back when they still had the family wagon. Since then, the old garage had been taken down and a new carport built.

The backpack had to have been in the basement.

But Thomas had not gone down there for years. Or had he?

Yet here he was dressed in the same clothing he had seen in his dream. Thomas closed the knife and put it away. The attack on his sister had clearly been premeditated. Any court would convict him. He had gone into his sister's bedroom with the knife. He had gone into her bedroom for her blood.

Thomas wished he had water to wash the blood stains away. Now that he thought about it, he was thirsty, too. Where was he supposed to go and what was he supposed to do in the middle of nowhere? At least, he was not around people – the thought of hurting anyone else scared him.

Thomas pulled the tail of his shirt out and used the cloth to clean his hands as best he could. He considered for a moment going home, then squelched the idea. The look of fear in Kimberly's eyes and the shock of seeing her blood on her pajamas and his hands was enough. He knew his parents loved him, but this was out of their league.

He felt very guilty. Kimberly had kept his secret. She had become his confidant. Now, she was his victim. No telling what she'll tell Mom and Dad now, he thought morosely.

Thomas stood and looked around himself.

If he was going to make his way on his own, he'd best be movin' on. Amid the myriad of sounds, squeaks and squeals, rustling of paper dry leaves, and the soothing sounds of a small gurgling stream some distance to the west, Thomas heard cars and trucks on a road somewhere north.

He checked his back pocket for his wallet. It was not there. Like he purposely left his identification behind.

Thomas started walking toward where he thought the traffic noise was coming from. As he walked, he imagined his parents calling the sheriff's department to arrest him. He didn't want to go to jail. He kept playing the courtroom scene over and over in his mind. He imagined his sister accusing him. His mother was quietly weeping and his father had a sternness that he had never seen before. All in the guise of helping him, they would put him away and destroy him. There was nothing much to be done about his home situation now. As he walked the stitch pain in his side was less, but he was getting weak and he was still very thirsty. He had been walking for a while. He was getting tired. He wanted to sleep.

Thomas looked up. The moon was high in the sky. The air had a chill with the approach of autumn, even in South Carolina. It was not easy to tell how long it would be until morning but he had his survival to think about now.

He knew he would need shelter in the daytime.

Just great! He sighed.

Thomas pushed himself farther into the woodlands. The land had become denser and rougher to traverse. He took a sideways path up the side of a hill, past the bramble and foliage that reached for him. He remembered going into Majken's dorm the morning after she had been walking all night to remove John from the campus after he killed a guard and attacked one of the girls. Seemed walking all night was par for the course.

Oh, how he missed her!

He distinctly heard the gurgling sound of water. A little stream had to be nearby. He crossed a small ridge and found the source of the sound meandering through the woods.

Thomas knelt on one knee and used his hand to cup water and drink. He didn't want to be one to lay on his face. A Bible story from a backyard Bible school came to his mind. It was a story in the Old Testament, where Gideon had too many soldiers to deliver Israel from the oppressing army. So the LORD told Gideon to send everyone who was afraid home. Still too many. Then the LORD told Gideon to send the army to water to drink. Most of the soldiers lay on their faces to drink. Only three hundred knelt and drank water by cupping it in their hand and bringing the water to their mouth while they were upright and alert. From that point on, Thomas wanted to be the one that drank upright and alert for danger. He'd been ten years old that summer. His parents sent him to summer camp that year.

Bible stories, fun activities, and evening worship were one of the best times in his life. He remembered going forward near the end of the summer to accept Jesus as Lord and Savior. That is, become a Christian. Since the church split when he was twelve, he'd not thought much about the Bible or Jesus or God at all. Kimberly was the only one in the family that still went to church regularly.

Go, Kimberly, he thought.

Thomas finished drinking the water in his hand, sluiced his hand and wiped it on his pants, and stood up. The sky was becoming a faint pink on the horizon to the east. Sounds of the road traffic were more distinct. He was getting closer, but the road was still miles away.

Morning was about an hour away.

When Thomas moved, he felt a sharp jab of pain under his ribcage, in his midsection, and along his lower left side. It was like someone had viciously punched him in the gut.

Thomas steadied himself by placing his hands on his knees and leaning against a nearby tree. Whoa, he thought. The sharp immediate pain subsided, but it sent subtle reminders to him as he hiked to reach the road. He walked by pushing his way through the thick bramble. He felt so tired. He used the back of his sleeve to wipe his brow. The ground he was stepping on changed from foliage to grass and he found himself with his face pressed against the cool white hull of a boat.

What the ... Thomas exclaimed.

He backpedaled and found himself looking at a large boat placed on stocks in someone's back yard.

Thomas looked up and around. In front of him was a large yacht covered with a tarp. The place where he had exited the woods was an abrupt ending to the forest. He stood on well maintained grass. He felt with his hand along the sides of the sleek craft. His Dad had once in his life talked about living on a boat, free to sail the world.

Thomas circled the bow of the boat and began walking to the stern. Wonder what happened to his father's dream? The morning sky was getting lighter. He found a ladder extending halfway down the hull – high enough for him to leap his chest height and step up to the tarp rope to loosen it and climb inside.

Thomas worked the knot free and reached to unfasten the tarp. As the sky lightened, he could see the two-story brick home across the lawn. The covering of the yacht slipped free. Thomas crawled into the open space and pushed the tarp closed. The light along the rim of the tarp gave light enough for him to see. He found the inner passage to the yacht interior, and discovered the galley. He found bottled water. It was not cold, but it was cool. He drank two immediately, then found a place to lie down.

His head was swimming and he was very tired. He yawned in spite of trying to stay awake. Now was not the time to worry about anything – there was nothing he could do. He closed his eyes and somehow slept.

Kimberly stared at the early morning sun from her bedroom window. She had slept fitfully and her left arm was wrapped with gauze and an elastic bandage. Her forearm hurt where Thomas had cut her. She rested her head in her other hand, then raked her fingers through her hair.

After Thomas ran out of the house, her father had come into the living room to see what the commotion was about. Kimberly knew her brother was a looney tune, but something in his eyes were lost as he was – he was – what?

Something bad had happened to him in Trenton. He came home a different person altogether. She pieced together enough from his rambling about his Mary, also called Majken, that she was the focal point. She was the epicenter in this mystery. To protect her brother's secret, she went to her bathroom and smashed her water glass on the tile floor. She picked up the curved edge and smeared her blood on the shattered glass.

Momma fussed over her for an hour in the kitchen. Dad said very little. His brow was furrowed in worry. She did not know if she would need stitches or not. Would this leave a scar?

Her head throbbed from lack of sleep and worry for her big brother. He owed her big time after this!

Momma told her years ago of the time just after she was born that Thomas wanted to run away. He may have been eight or so. He had just gotten his Labrador Bud, a little puppy then. Dad had snapshots of him in a scrap book holding Bud in both arms and eating a cheese and bologna sandwich.

He made himself a sandwich or two, got a paper sack for his supplies, and set out for the edge of the yard. Kim smiled. She could picture her big brother as he looked in the album snapshots standing at the edge of the yard with Bud and just sitting on the stump of a tree that was near the woods. Momma tells the story best. When it started getting dark, Thomas changed his mind and ran for the back porch. Bud was loping behind him, barking.

Momma was there waiting with the door open. She didn't say anything, she said. He didn't say anything, as Momma told it. She knelt before her son and smiled at him. He reached for her and Momma hugged him. He said he was sorry he ran away. He cried and spoke through the tears. He didn't think Momma loved him anymore because she was taking so much time caring for Kimberly. Momma smoothed the tears off his cheeks.

"I'll always love you," she said, "and I'll always love your sister. You are both the best part of my life. You'll always belong here." Kimberly felt stinging tears. Thomas had simply run away. His car was still here. Mom and Dad didn't know what to do. There was no reason to involve the police. Thomas was a grown young man. Now in the morning light, she was glad she acted to protect his secret.

Oh, how she wanted to see her brother appear at the edge of the woods. She could picture him in her mind. Even she would run out and embrace him! But this time, he did not stop at the edge of darkness.

Kim tore her gaze from the edge of the woods. For whatever had happened to him, as bad as it was, he was still her brother.

* * *

Thomas awoke groggy and his head hurt. His mouth was pasty and dry. He had laid on the small bunk next to the galley. It was a little better than sleeping on a rock. Thomas squinted in the dim light. He could tell that the day was well spent, and that it was near twilight again. Time to move on, he thought. He sat up and steadied himself, then lumbered to the galley for more water. It was wet. That was all he could say for it. He wished he could have a huge pitcher of cold, cold ice water. Like the kind his Mom kept in the refrigerator at all times.

He drank all of the water that was there. The empty bottles littered the floor of the yacht. Thomas really didn't care. He walked stooped over and made his way to the side to climb out and depart. From beneath the tarp, he glanced at the thick clouds and the beautiful sunset. It really was late in the day. Strangely, he had not been hungry at all. Maybe once he started moving he'd feel hungry. As he climbed from beneath the tarp, a dog started barking. Thomas wished it would stop, but it raced toward him, wagging its tail, and the man of the house was walking toward him from the two-story brick house.

Well, he was caught red-handed for sure.

Best to face the consequences and try to make amends, if he could. The man approaching had thick sandy gray hair. He wore aviator sunglasses so Thomas could not see his eyes. Even in casual clothes, he was well dressed and presented himself with an air of authority. This was a man of means and wealth.

Thomas jumped to the ground and wiped his wet hands on his jeans to prepare to shake the man's hand.

The man extended his hand. "My name is Dwight. Dwight Gibbons." Thomas was momentarily stunned. Gibbons. As in his father's employer on the Gibbons Office Project. This was definitely not good. "And you are?" the man prompted.

"Joel," Thomas replied. His middle name.

"Joel Thomas." He shook the man's hand.

"Good to meet you, Mr. Thomas," he said.

The dog wagged her tail and circled through Thomas' legs. Thomas petted her. She was a gorgeous silver Labrador. "And that's Sassy," Dwight said with a smile. The dog continued to lick Thomas' hands as he played with her ears. "If Sassy thinks you're good people, then you're good people," Dwight commented.

Thomas liked this man and felt that he owed him some explanation of why he was on his property. "Sir, I was on my way to Florida when I met these guys. They took my wallet and I don't have any money. I didn't mean to impose. I'm not really sure where I am."

Thomas let his monologue hang. Dwight did not appear to be listening to him. There was a matronly woman standing at the back of the house motioning to the man. Probably his wife. The dog Sassy laid down at Thomas' feet and curled on her back. He could reach down and pet her belly if he wanted to.

The woman at the back of the house was pointing to a telephone, Thomas noticed. She called to the man, "You have an important telephone call," Thomas clearly overheard.

"What?" the man called to the woman.

"You have an important telephone call," Thomas remarked.

Dwight glanced back at him, then said, "Well, c'mon then. You might as well meet the missus." He waved for Thomas to follow and Thomas did. As they drew closer to the back of the house, Thomas noticed the two-story brick home had a garage at the lower level of the home.

A lot of debris was cluttered in the right half of the two-car parking space. It looked like the scrap remains of old ducts and part of an old furnace that had been replaced. Dwight called uphill, "I'm coming."

The woman who was calling Dwight was a slight woman, but her hair was the color of pewter and bundled tight in a bun on top of her head. She seemed emaciated, like she had some type of disease that caused her to waste away. Thomas wasn't sure. She may have been only extremely thin.

Dwight started up his back steps.

Thomas stayed at the bottom of the steps.

The man called back at Thomas when he was halfway up. "This is my wife, Eleanor. Eleanor, this gentleman is Mr. Thomas." Thomas followed Dwight up his back steps. The landing at the top of the steps was a concrete with metal railing. Eleanor kissed Dwight on the cheek as she gave him the telephone. She smiled at Thomas as Dwight went inside to take the call. Sassy bound past Thomas' legs to reach Eleanor. She was wagging her tail, but she did not jump on Eleanor. When Eleanor put forth her palm, Sassy lay flat but continued to look up with expectancy. In a second, she reached into a bag and threw Sassy some type of treat. The Labrador pounced on the treat and gulped it, and wagged her tail even harder.

Thomas smiled. She was a very pretty dog. Eleanor extended her hand.

"My name is Eleanor. Sir, you are?"

Thomas shook her hand. "Thomas, ma'am," he replied without thinking. He quickly corrected: "Uh, Joel Thomas."

Dwight's voice could be heard from inside the house – what was probably their kitchen. He was getting a bit pointed and abrupt with whomever was on the receiving end of the call. Thomas hoped it wasn't his Dad.

Eleanor smiled at Thomas. "Well, sir, what brings you to our humble home?" Thomas noticed that Eleanor had kind blue eyes and her smile seemed genuine. He considered she would have to be a very graceful lady to put up with her husband's demeanor. His voice had gotten louder, then silent as he was listening.

"I was on my way to Florida. Some guys that picked me up took my things and my wallet. I apologize for intruding. I really just need to be on my way." Thomas considered his makeshift story. His father had an older brother in Panama City Florida that he'd not talked to in years.

This was as good a destination as any.

Dwight seemed to finish his telephone conversation. He came out of the house. He had taken off the aviator sunglasses. His gaze was sharp and shrewd. He smiled at his wife but seemed to take Thomas in at a glance.

"Mr. Thomas has been trespassing on our yacht and our property. Tell me why I shouldn't call the sheriff to pick you up."

Thomas held up both hands. "Hey, I apologize for intruding. I was lost and I didn't know where I was. If I had any money I would gladly pay you for your trouble. As it is, all I want to do is be on my way."

Eleanor looked at her husband. "Dear, he may be hungry and in need. The Good Book says we are to take care of strangers." Dwight was scowling, but seemed nonplussed at his wife's comment. Thomas decided he liked Eleanor much better than her sour husband.

"Sir, I don't have money to pay you for your trouble, but I can work. If you have anything around here that needs to be done, any chores, I would be happy to do it. All I want is to find out where I am and be on my way in peace."

The man seemed to be considering.

Eleanor asked Thomas, "Can I get you anything to eat?"

"Ma'am," he replied, "I could really use a drink of cold water, if you have some." Eleanor smiled at her husband, then went inside. Thomas overheard the tinkling of ice in a glass and water being poured into it. She reappeared with a glass of ice water for him. Thomas reached for the glass gratefully.

"Well, Mr. Thomas," Dwight said, "I've got all of this scrap in my basement. If you could load it on the trailer so it can be hauled away, we'll call it even, and you can be on your way."

The afternoon sun was setting below the treeline. A faint breeze had picked up and clouds the color of pale red and yellow ochre in the desert spread across the sky. Dwight took the lead and led Thomas to the cluttered basement. When he pushed up the other garage door Thomas saw just how much junk was piled on the concrete floor.

He may be hours piling it on the flatbed trailer in the yard.

Thomas raked his fingers through his hair. "Well, uh, this doesn't look like much. I should be able to do this in a little while." His gracious host was all smiles again. Thomas walked into the basement area and prodded a piece of duct with his sneaker. "Sir," he inquired, "if you have work gloves I can use, that would help."

Dwight produced a pair of work gloves for him and Thomas stood overlooking the pile of debris. He set to work as the sky grew imperceptibly darker.

It did not take as long as Thomas first thought. He separated the debris as he was pulling it out. He flattened the ducts he could reach and placed what he could extract on the trailer first, then bundled the bands of metal supports by wrapping it around a piece of wood he found. The last part was pushing and rolling the heavy furnace to the edge of the trailer, then lifting and rolling it on top of the heap. He used nylon rope to secure the debris to the trailer.

All in all, it took him about an hour. The sun had set while he was working. Eleanor brought him two more glasses of ice cold water. He gently refused any food, but his left side was burning and he felt the initial stages of nausea. At Eleanor's insistence, her husband fished out his wallet and gave Thomas a twenty and a ten dollar bill for his trouble. Dwight gave him a lift in their Lincoln Towncar to the road. Sassy leaped out of the car with Thomas and wagged her tail. She chewed on a stick she found in the yard and picked it up.

She wanted Thomas to play fetch with her.

Thomas thanked Mr. Gibbons. The man got into his car and called his dog, but Sassy remained with Thomas.

The dog is obviously a great judge of character, Thomas thought. He kept a fake smile on his face as his new good friend Dwight drove back to his house alone.

The pain that was starting on his left side was more than subtle throbbing. It was like his insides were in vertigo, a sensation of falling although both feet were firmly on the ground. Sassy barked at him.

Thomas petted her, then threw the stick far into the yard. "Stay, girl," he said. The dog obediently took off after the stick. Thomas opened the gate, then closed it, and started walking down the little county road. The road went east to west. Thomas considered. If he walked east, soon he would reach a highway. He heard a sound behind him. Sassy had come after him and was loping toward him with the stick in her mouth.

He became acutely aware of the cold metal of the knife against his waist. "Go home," Thomas yelled at the dog.

Sassy only lay flat, like she was expecting another treat, and wagged her tail. A truck was coming by. Thomas stepped completely off the road into the ditch and looked to make sure the dog moved off the road with him. The driver of the truck didn't even slow down. The roadway was again desolate.

Vertigo and a sensation of burning on his left side. Before he had attacked Kimberly he went to sleep like this. His blood chilled as he stood there. He had cut his sister's arm in a dream state and he'd found himself literally drinking her blood when he woke up. Thomas led Sassy forcefully back to her yard by pulling her collar. When he had her at the gate, he looked for a chain or rope he could use to fasten her to the gate so Dwight would come and get his dog. As he walked back with Sassy in tow, his blood swishing sounded louder and louder in his hearing.

Rapid heart beats. Thomas became aware of his own slower heart beat. He was not hearing his heart beat. He heard the blood circulating inside the dog.

Thomas left Sassy at her gate and walked quickly away. The dog stayed.

Something was wrong inside his body.

Thomas tried to walk down the silent road, but he grew very weak. It was like the malaise that had overtaken him that morning was returning full force.

Behind him, he heard the light clicking of dog claws on the asphalt. Thomas uttered a swear word under his breath. He knew without looking that Sassy had followed him again. The dog came toward him with a stick in her mouth. Her tail was wagging. The cold metal of his knife seared his skin.

Thomas knelt and Sassy bound into his arms. She started licking his face. "Easy, girl," he said as he wrapped his arm around her body. He drew his knife and flicked the blade open. He became aware of the blood flowing inside the dog's body.

"Oh, God," he said as he led the dog to the ditch and thought to kill her. Sassy only wagged her tail and licked his fingers. He knew he needed blood. Thomas bowed his head. A broken piece of concrete block was half buried in the leaves of the ditch.

Thomas placed the blade of his knife in his teeth and wrenched the concrete block loose.

He closed his eyes to keep from seeing what he was about to do. He swung the block at the dog's head and hit her. He hit her twice more before she lay still in the ditch. He used his knife to cut her fur at her throat, seeking still warm blood. Her head swung from side to side, her tongue extended loosely.

Thomas didn't know what to do except pick the dog's body up and hold it upright with the new gash in her neck at his mouth and try to drink as much of the blood as he could.

The dog's blood was strangely salty. He detected a subtle difference between human blood and animal blood. Blood would seep out of the dog's neck and Thomas would lap it. He was aware that some blood trickled on his shirt. The knife he had used was buried in blood and leaves at his feet.

He choked in sorrow. He could not cry, although he wanted to. It seemed like an eternity he held the dog upright with her torn throat against his face. The county roadway was dark and desolate, but Thomas could see the gray upon gray landscape clearly. This was what he was now. Vampyric.

* * *

The Sumter downtown streets were strangely still as the black limousine drove into the main thoroughfare. Next to the water fountain with a lighted clock overhead, a young woman stepped out of the back of the car. She wore an overcoat and carried a satchel strapped over her shoulder.

The driver's opaque window opened slightly and she spoke in hushed tones. Then the driver rolled up the window and drove away. Her instructions were clear. Return in four hours. Majken looked up and considered the lighted clock. It was just past seven o'clock local time and she was finally here. It had taken two days to travel to lovely South Carolina, including an overnight stay in one of Stefan's safe houses outside Atlanta.

Dark impressions seeped into her consciousness. Impressions soaked in the ground of cruelty, old blood, and great violence. This was exactly why she avoided the rural south in favor of cities to the north. It would take her a little time to acclimate and re-tune into the voice of Thomas' blood. Her first priority was to acquire her own blood sources in this town.

Several cars drove by, paying her no heed.

Majken removed her dark glasses and let her eyes adjust to the ambient street light. She placed her dark glasses in her satchel and set out down the street. A few pedestrians were on the opposite side of the street. There were a few cars passing by.

The little town had very little activity at night. All shops and businesses were closed. There were no night spots and places to meet after dark, as she expected.

Yet every city and town had its secrets.

She left the main thoroughfare to search the nearby underpasses and unused buildings. It was here she hoped and expected to find one or more transients to tell her the secrets of this place. She found such a man under a bridge. His clothing was tattered and he wore gloves with no fingers in them. When she came into view, he reached a hand up to her.

She glanced up to make sure they were not visible from the road nor the sidewalk far uphill. She listened for other movement in the near vicinity – all was silent but her and this stranger. They were alone. Majken studied the man, then decided.

She reached into her satchel and pulled out a roll of used bills, several hundred dollars in ones, fives, tens, all used currency. The man's eyes widened. He had long unkempt sandy hair. His face was full of stubble and several days of growth. His fingernails had layers of ingrown dirt, like he seldom washed. The scent of his breath told her he was not likely drunk. His eyes were alert. Majken held the money up so he could gaze at it, then placed it in her coat pocket.

"I can give you money if you give me information about this place. Are you a long-time resident here?" He pulled at the loose knit scarf around his neck. He appeared nervous.

"Yes, mistress," he replied.

Majken listened to his heartbeat. Still slow and steady. The fact that his heart rate had not picked up greatly since they started talking meant he was probably in good physical condition.

Just a man down on his luck.

"What is your name?" she asked.

"Mark," he replied.

Majken lifted the satchel off her shoulder and took a place beside him on the mattress he was sitting on. "Well, Mark. Tell me what you know about this place. How did you come to be lying under a bridge with nowhere to go?" The man started his tale of woe. Majken listened to him talk for well over an hour. He was a contractor. Mistakes were made on a building project that were not his fault. Yet, as the general contractor he had been blamed and barred from the construction business.

He knew the mayor, city council, many church leaders, the people with money in this place, influential families, the police chief and several of the officers, a baseball coach, and Thomas' father the architect.

Majken took special note of Thomas' father and what this man knew of him. She would be meeting Thomas' family very soon anyway. Mark had it in for Thomas' father as the ultimate cause of his problems. He spoke of the judgment that would come to Thomas' father because of his misdeeds.

She questioned him into the second and third hour. By this time, she had removed her overcoat and opened her blouse. She let him kiss her. When the man removed his shirt, he was indeed powerfully built and a strong man.

She rendered him unconscious when he rolled to face away from her for a moment. Using her puncture set, she removed blood from him and fed quietly under the bridge. When she had finished feeding, she covered him with his shirt, coat, and scarf and placed the roll of money beside him. As her body began to absorb the blood she had consumed, she looked into the night. A distant light over an industrial site shone blocks away. The trees were gently swaying in the breeze and the air carried the scent and sweet tang of approaching autumn.

Thomas was nearby, somewhere. She could not yet pick up his direction, but that would come to her soon enough. She faced the southeast direction from where Thomas' parent's home was. Still, nothing. Her four hours were almost up. She put on her overcoat and gathered her things. It was time to return to her pickup spot. She would rest in the limo for tonight.

Tomorrow, she thought, I will see Thomas again and meet his parents and his younger sister Kimberly.

Kimberly sat at the kitchen table long after her mother and father went elsewhere. An empty notepad sat in front of her. She had stared at the page for an hour and nothing was coming forth. Dad was probably in his office for the rest of the morning. Mom had gone to town for something. From the open window beyond the sink, she heard someone nearby sawing with a power saw. She had not yet returned to work because of her arm. Mom had rewrapped it this morning and it would probably leave a scar. She closed her right fist and imagined smashing her brother's nose. Now, she wished she'd hit him harder.

Mom and Dad kept on like nothing was wrong. Thomas was away hiking or visiting friends or at the mall or ... couldn't they see that something was seriously wrong with him? With that thought, she had a pique of guilt. She had kept Thomas' secret about the killer in Trenton because – as he put it – Mom and Dad would freak out and be no use to anyone.

Kimberly agreed.

She considered telling them that a killer had tried to kill him in Trenton and that his former girlfriend had something to do with it – at least so far as saving his life. Thomas was adamant about that point. His Mary had saved his life by coming after this killer. Everything she had learned had become a mishmash inside her head. Nothing made sense any more. She took out her other notes from her research session at the Sentinel and smoothed them flat. Mom and Dad didn't see this either.

Something had to be done!

Kim decided that she would tell Mom and Dad that evening at supper if Thomas had not come home or called by then.

It was mid-morning.

A vehicle was pulling into the yard.

Kim hopped up, hoping her mother had returned. She slipped her notes in her pocket.

A long black limousine had pulled off the road next to the house. The windows were tinted so the interior could not be seen. She stood at the back door waiting. The limo drove into the yard and backed next to Thomas' parked car in the shade.

Kimberly walked out onto the porch.

A young woman stepped out of the back of the limo and came toward the house. She had long chestnut hair, dark glasses, a scarf and an overcoat. As she came closer, Kimberly recognized that face – this was Thomas' Mary, his missing girlfriend!

Majken came up the stairs of the back porch where Kimberly was standing. She smiled at Thomas' sister and reached her hand out. "Hello," she said with a Cockney accent, "I am a friend of Thomas from college. Is he here?"

Kimberly yelled, "Dad!" She turned and looked into the house. She turned back to Thomas' girlfriend. She shook her hand. "Uh, I'm Thomas' sister. He's not here right now." She glanced back again at the kitchen. Her father was puttering down the hallway in no special hurry. As soon as he stepped on the porch, he raised his eyebrows in surprise. Kimberly quickly escorted him to Thomas' elusive girlfriend. Kim introduced her father. "Dad, this is Mary Harris – Thomas' friend from school. Mary, this is my father, Donald Kline."

Donald Kline shook her hand, but seemed to stand there stupefied by her appearance. Kim nudged her father. "Oh," he said, "would you like to come inside?"

Majken nodded and went inside the house.

Donald and Kimberly followed. She removed her scarf, dark glasses, and overcoat once inside. She seemed to take stock of her Mom's well kept kitchen. Kim noticed she looked around and casually strolled by the living room to make sure no one was there before she stood next to the kitchen table.

"Thomas isn't here," her Dad began. "You're certainly not what we expected. He said so much about you, Patty and I consider you family."

"Your wife, Patricia?" Majken asked.

"Yes," Donald said. He reached behind him to draw Kimberly forward. "And this is Thomas' baby sister, Kimberly."

Kimberly waved at her. "Dad, we already met," she said with a sidelong glance at her father.

"You said Thomas was not here. When will he return?"

Her Dad backpedaled and reached a hand to the fringe of hair around his bald scalp. Something Kimberly had never seen her father do before. "Weeee don't know exactly when Thomas will be back. But you are very welcome to stay in the meantime."

Kimberly prodded her father, "Tell her Dad."

"Tell me what?" Majken asked.

"We don't know where Thomas is or when he'll be back," Kim injected before her father could stop her.

Thomas' girlfriend took the news in great stride. She just regarded them while standing in their kitchen. At that point Kimberly noticed her eyes were a striking deep violet color. Rare.

"When did you last see him?" she asked.

Straight to the point. Kim liked that.

"Late," Kim said, "two nights ago. He just ran out without any explanation or anything."

"Where?" Majken asked.

Kimberly shuffled. Her parents did not know that Thomas cut her. They thought he just barged out of the house. By coincidence, I just happened to cut myself on a broken water glass in my bathroom. Pleeeaaassseee.

Thomas' father commented, "When I got up he had just ran out of the house. As you can see," indicating the key holder on the wall, "he ran out without taking his keys, wallet, or anything. Patricia and I are getting concerned about him. He has never done anything like this before."

Kimberly noticed Thomas' Mary watching her father closely. In fact, other than herself, his girlfriend appeared to be as observant of other people as Kimberly was.

In a moment, she seemed to look Kimberly over carefully.

"How did you get hurt?" Majken asked Kim. She stood open mouthed for a moment. With her long-sleeved sweatshirt on, the bandage on her forearm could not be seen.

"I cut myself on a broken glass."

With that, Thomas' mother appeared at the back door. "Donald, what's a – oh, hello." Majken turned to greet her.

"Hello," she said, "my name is Mirriam, but Thomas knew me as Mary Harris. Rather awkward to explain. Mr. Kline was just telling me that Thomas has gone out and you are uncertain as to when he might return."

Patricia seemed to stammer a moment at Thomas' girlfriend's straightforwardness. She gave Dad the Look, as if it was his fault this stranger knew our secret family business.

Majken glanced around Patricia to the limousine out-side.

"If you would excuse me for a moment, I need to speak to my driver," she said, placing her dark glasses on and stepping outside.

Kimberly, Patricia, and Donald gravitated toward their back porch en-masse. As the young lady approached the black vehicle, the driver's side window rolled down slightly. She leaned over and spoke to the driver. She opened the door behind the driver and took a valise and a second overcoat, then closed the door.

The driver's window widened some more. She grasped the hands of the man driving with her hands and placed her head down. She kissed his hands then released them. Kim thought she heard her say, "Home, James," as the driver rolled up his window and pulled out of the yard. The limousine quickly circled the road and drove out of sight. Gone, Kim thought, just like that.

Majken returned to Thomas' house.

As she approached the door, Kim felt her mother and father draw back. She reached for the door and strode inside like she owned the place. She draped the second overcoat on a chair in the kitchen and set her valise out of sight under the kitchen table.

She removed her dark glasses and hooked them in her blouse. Kimberly followed her Mom and Dad back into the kitchen where their new houseguest waited. She was looking at the décor. "You have a beautiful home," she commented. "I remember Thomas saying you had it built to your specifications." Indicating her father. "Your bed-rooms are upstairs," she said to Kimberly. It was near-ing the lunch hour. Patricia went to the refrigerator and picked over several covered dishes.

She said to Majken, "Can I get you something to eat?

You must be famished. We have a spare bedroom upstairs. I would be happy to help you get settled."

Majken waved off lunch. "I'm not hungry and I do not wish to be a bother." Kimberly kept trying to place her accent. She directed a question directly to her father. "Do you have any idea why Thomas would have just left and where he might have gone?"

Donald glanced from Majken to Patricia, then Kimberly.

He held his hands open. Craftsman's hands, Kimberly always thought. "Thomas called us a month ago saying he wanted to come home for a while. Of course, we agreed. He hasn't really been our same boy. He was in a slump of some kind and we waited on him to come to himself and snap out of it."

Kimberly went around her mother to draw closer to Thomas' girlfriend. Now that she was actually here, she wanted a private discussion with her.

Patricia commented, "I know he thinks of you often. He really didn't talk about you much after he came home. That left us wondering what happened between you and why you separated like you did." Majken looked around the kitchen again and drew closer to the sink and the open window. Kimberly noticed she breathed deeply, as if testing for a scent.

"I will be happy to explain all of that after we find him." Kimberly noticed the hopeful glance between her Mom and Dad. Talk about a way to make the family start eating from your hand. Mom and Dad seemed to be hanging onto her every word.

To her father, she asked, "Do you have a map of this area? If you do, mark on it in yellow highlighter the places he knows." To her mother, she requested, "Mrs. Kline, if you would be so kind as to make me a list of people, friends he knows nearby. Mark these on the map in red."

Kimberly recalled what her brother had said about his Mary: She came after me.

Instantly, her father went to his office and her mother went to find pen and paper to start writing the list. Kim was momentarily alone with Majken in the kitchen.

The bandage on her forearm itched.

"How did you know I was hurt?" Kim asked as she cradled her left arm.

She seemed to overlook the question.

"Can you show me Thomas' bedroom, please?" she asked. Kimberly perked up. Private conversation opportunity.

She motioned for Majken to follow and led the way to the stairs. As Kim padded up the stairs barefoot, she noticed Thomas' girlfriend wore soft slippers that made little or no sound on the polished wood. She made an immediate right at the top of the stairs and led Majken to the last bedroom door to the left. The door was still ajar. Kim pushed the door open and went inside.

Thomas' bedroom was still cluttered.

Lived in, as Mom would say.

She watched Majken walk around the bedroom slowly, as if savoring the moment. Kim could see no details that would explain where her brother had gone, but she was very interested in seeing what facts her brother's love would uncover.

She glanced in Thomas' closet. She browsed through the garments until she came to Thomas' rugby jersey, the orange and white one he wore the most. She pulled the garment from the hanger and pressed it to her face.

She seemed to take in the scent of it by breathing deeply, Kim noticed.

She laid the rugby shirt on Thomas' bed and knelt on the hardwood floor. Her hands lingered where drops of dark stain were on the floor next to his bed. From there she stepped into Thomas' bathroom briefly without turning on the light, then came out and stood in the center of his bedroom.

She addressed Kimberly.

"How did you know me by sight? I had not mentioned my name before you introduced me to your father."

Kimberly was undaunted.

"Thomas has a photo of you and him together. I found it and went to him with it. He said it was you."

Majken browsed Thomas' bare desk for a moment, then came to his night table. When she opened the little drawer, the snapshot was there. She lifted it and smiled. "This was taken on our third date. To a game. The first game they had won, at this point." Kim noticed that her eyes seemed to soften in the memory the photo represented also.

So her brother *was* important to her.

"You just happened to find it?" she inquired lightly. Kim felt her face blush a little bit. Majken's eyes and smile held a hint of shared conspiracy and secrets she would keep.

Oh, Kimberly thought, *I like this girl!*

Kim noticed that she slipped the photo in her skirt pocket instead of placing it back in the night table.

She walked to Thomas' bedroom window.

Her hands lingered on strips of duct tape and parts of newspaper that had once covered the window. She knelt and ran her finger over the white flakes of paint, like a window long ago painted had been pried open. She placed her dark glasses on and pushed the window open. Kim remembered her brother sitting on the roof and their conversation thereon. The sky was partially cloudy, but it was a beautiful cool day.

"He likes being on the roof at night," she commented to herself. She left the window open and the gauzy curtains fluttered in the light breeze. She slipped her dark glasses off and hooked them to her blouse at her neck.

She stood for several moments in silence.

"What do you think?" Kim prompted.

"I think that Thomas is not here," she said dryly.

Kimberly turned at the sound of her mother at Thomas' bedroom door. She held a piece of paper in her hand.

Patricia waited at the door.

Majken took the paper from her hand and looked at the list of names. Not very many. Six. Four men names. Two female. Majken inquired about the names. They were friends he had known since high school or earlier. But many of his former school mates and friends had either married and started new lives or had moved away. Kim watched her eyes as she read the list.

She handed the paper back to Patricia.

"If you can call these friends, ask them if they have seen him. Simply say he left the house a few days ago to visit a friend and you are trying to track him down. Ask them to call you if they see him." Patricia left. Kim noticed she was standing in the center of Thomas' bedroom, very intently concentrating on something. Her brow furrowed with thought and she pressed her right hand to her temple. In a moment, she stopped. Kimberly watched her closely. Something was definitely up.

Majken dropped her head and sighed. Kimberly wanted to ask, Do you know where he's gone? She knew to be silent now. Let Mary or Mirriam or Majken think. What's in a name anyway? Kim considered.

"We will find him," she said with quiet certainty. Kimberly let out a breath that she was unaware that she had been holding.

Again she asked Kim, "How did you get hurt?"

Now they were alone. Kim glanced in the hallway to make sure her mother had not returned. "I cut myself on broken glass," Kimberly parroted. She rubbed her left forearm. "How did you know I was hurt?"

Majken replied, "First, can I see your bedroom?"

Kimberly led her from Thomas' room to her bedroom. Her bedroom, too, had been lived in. Majken gently closed the door to the hallway. "May I see?" she asked Kimberly.

With a moment's hesitation, she pulled her oversized sweatshirt over her head. Her petite bra was pale pink today. The flesh-colored gauze wrap on her left forearm had a dark reddish splash, like her cut had opened and bled through the gauze. Majken gently reached for Kimberly's arm and unwrapped the stretchy gauze bandage. It hurt a little. Blood had soaked into the white gauze pads. Maybe it was when Kim was thinking of smashing her brother's nose.

After looking at the ugly wound for a second, she replaced the white gauze pads and rewrapped her forearm in the flesh-colored gauze bandage. Kim felt a surge of these powerful feelings flooding her heart.

Her own brother had hurt her!

She was keeping his secret and protecting Mom and Dad from this ugly thing, whatever bad had happened to him.

"Thank you," Majken said solemnly. "That is not a cut made by broken glass."

Tears trickled down her cheeks. She hated to cry. It made her feel like a baby. Yet before this stranger, this woman her brother clearly loved, she, too, had to confide in somebody.

"He cut me," she said quietly.

"I know. He was not himself when he did it. When

he spoke of you in Trenton, I could tell that you and he are very close. Thank you for protecting him. We have to find him before anyone else does." Majken got Kimberly a wet washrag to wipe her face. Runny nose and all. She held the towel for Thomas' sister to make herself presentable.

Kimberly pulled on her sweatshirt.

"I found news articles on this *slasher* suspect in Trenton at the time you and he were there together. He came home claiming to have had an accident. When I checked the newswire, I couldn't find any trace of an actual confirmed attack by this suspect after the time of his accident. I got scared. I came to him wanting him to calm my fears, but he said this John suspect captured him to get to you. He said you came after him and that's why he's alive today. When he went to this old construction place he once worked at, I thought he was going to drown himself, but he didn't. I asked him what really happened up there. He talked about burning mansions, serial killers who fall off cliffs, but don't die, and you. You're in the middle of all of this.

"Who are you? What's really going on?"

Majken smiled a winsome smile, kind of fragile but tender at the same time. Her eyes were gentle when she reached around Kimberly and hugged her.

When Kim reached around Majken, she felt very solid muscle. Lithe and very strong. "Oh, Kimberly," Majken said, "Thomas was so right about you. He told me you're a snoop into everybody's business, and you're good at it."

Kimberly smiled at that. She looked into those dark violet eyes with her light brown eyes, seeking truth, seeking hope.

"I cannot promise that I can tell you everything – certainly not until we find him. But I will say that I will do anything I can to protect him and give him back his life, if it can be done."

In that moment, Kimberly looked into this stranger's eyes and believed her. Even if her brother's problem was bigger than the whole state of Texas, she saw that this woman loved her brother and vowed she would do anything to protect him and give him back his life. That was good enough for Kimberly.

After several moments, they parted and went back downstairs. Kimberly sat at her place while Majken spread the map her father had brought on the kitchen table.

Patricia busied herself making lunch for their impromptu houseguest, but the plate she prepared went untouched. She questioned Donald and Patricia at length about the places they had highlighted. Kim noticed her Dad had placed a gold star on the spot of their home. Also, since Thomas had left on foot, he had drawn concentric circles around ground zero representing every five mile radius. The question of why Thomas would run off in the middle of the night was left hanging. Now everything was focused on finding him.

For a little while, Kimberly showed Majken the second bedroom upstairs, the one between her's and Thomas'. Their houseguest carried her valise and overcoats, and unpacked an over-the-shoulder leather bag that looked like it came from the Middle Ages. Before her vanity mirror, she spread a white cream on her face. A sunscreen, she explained to Kim. She had several jars of the cream in her valise and she placed two of them in her shoulder bag. When Kim asked why, she said the second jar was for Thomas. She also asked Kim if Thomas had any dark glasses, sunglasses, or the like. Kimberly replied no. She had never seen her brother wear sunglasses before in her life. Not even at the ocean or lake. She packed a second

pair of dark glasses in her shoulder bag that looked like
Thomas could wear them.

Kim remembered her brother's sudden collapse in the
sun during their Labor Day cookout. *What just happened
to you?* she vividly remembered. As they went downstairs, Majken asked Kimberly if she had a driver's license. Kim said yes. She said, "Get it." Kim went back to
her bedroom to get the little strap purse with her license,
chewing gum, mascara and light powder blush, a small
fingernail clipper, and two postage stamps that were no
longer enough to mail a letter.

It was just past three in the afternoon. She tossed
Thomas' car keys to Kimberly and said, "Drive." The
search was on.

Majken stopped Kimberly on a bridge overlooking
stagnant water and mossy pine trees. She walked to the
edge and considered the treacherous terrain below. She
knew, as in the bayous of Louisiana, the hazards of walking through a swamp. Although the area of swamps increased as you made your way to the ocean, they were
still numerous enough to be hazardous to a lone hiker out
at night.

She and Kimberly had criss-crossed the general area
within ten miles of his home and no spectacular impressions had come to her mind. Thomas was probably travelling at night and sleeping during the day. Whenever
she tried to feel him, all she could get was an impression
of wet and cold on his back. Her directional sense of him
was still too vague. She kept feeling he was to the west.
Majken returned to Thomas' car and motioned Kimberly
to join her. She unfurled the map on the hood of the car.
Kimberly came to her side. She had offered a few pointers
and ideas when they first started searching.

Majken followed these suggestions to give herself time to acclimate and sense Thomas her own way. She was still trying too hard.

Let it come, she reasoned.

Thomas had moved beyond the concentric circles drawn by his father. Yet he was still near enough, Majken sensed. He had not gotten a ride out of the immediate area. He was still in the woods. She traced her finger along a little county road that ran southwest from Sumter. There were blocks of undeveloped land in that area and, keeping with Thomas' thinking once he found he had cut his own sister, he would try to stay away from everyone.

There was no logical reason to choose this road.

She just knew. Majken pointed the road out to Kimberly and asked her to mark this with her fountain pen. She felt she could get close enough to him as they toured this road to distinguish the voice of his blood over the blood-soaked ground of this place. The sunset spread a beautiful gold and mauve cloud tapestry across the west.

She suddenly looked up with a start. In her mind she saw a flash of Thomas. Sharp pain shot up his leg. He had somehow slipped and jabbed his right calf on a sharp branch. He was bleeding below his knee. "Hurry," she said to Kimberly.

They reached the county road twenty minutes later.

Majken stopped Kimberly at places along the road so she could get out and walk. Thomas' Honda tipped at an angle as Kim was forced to park along the ditch sometimes. Her directional sense of him was now distinct. The little road was almost deserted. The occasional truck would pass by. The light in the sky was gently receding. Majken looked up and watched the gently swaying leaves stir next to the telephone lines above.

Closer. Yes. Closer now.

Just beyond an overpass, Majken stopped Kimberly at a forest road that had a barricade in front of it. Trash had been strewn inside. Thomas had recently passed this way. She just knew it. Majken retrieved her leather shoulder bag from the back of Thomas' car and instructed Kimberly to wait here. Wait here, no matter how long it took.

As the sky darkened, she followed him.

Thomas limped into the clearing as he topped the gentle hillside. He pushed bramble out of his path and walked downhill until he stepped on a weed strewn road. It was little more than a cow trail. No vehicles had been on this road for a long time. The little road meandered ahead. Thomas decided to follow it. He was very thirsty. The stream he found a while back did little to quench his thirst. When he bowed his head, the subtle dark stains on his reversed shirt reminded him of the dog he killed to get blood, leaving her body on the road in such a way as her owner will hopefully assume she had been hit by a car.

He grimaced as he walked. Hurting, let alone killing, a dog was something he never ever wanted to do. He grieved, but he guessed he just had to do what he had to do. He had plans of finding a job on a farm with lots and lots of animals – where he could get blood without hurting anyone else. Thomas thought of Majken as he walked. He kept wondering what she would do if she was in this situation. He sighed deeply. The chances of him seeing her again, he reasoned, were slim and none.

The blue-white light of a waning moon was rising in the sky. It was nighttime. The cool night air had a crispness to it. Clouds in the daytime became gray ghosts billowing across the low horizon. Dry grass and weeds crunched under his boots.

Around the bend, he came to an open space. Tall clumps of grass hid grave markers and cinder blocks to denote a cemetery. In the waning moon, a small wooden chapel lay desolate and abandoned. Mossy trees lined the field, posted as silent sentinels.

He could barely read the carved rock face.

Grant Chapel.

Thomas abruptly stopped in his tracks. Momma talked about her family chapel, years and years ago when her great grandfather Joel ministered in this area. The name Joel had been passed down from generation to generation – Momma had named him Joel. He found this place by accident. In the moonlight, he could see a silvery sparkle and amber, blue, and crimson shine of the little oval stained windows. They were intact. Not one was broken. Momma had a scrapbook of sorts. It had news clippings and faded sepia photographs from that era. He could imagine people riding up to this chapel on horse and buggy.

He forgot about his tiredness and thirst. Momma said her father brought her here as a little girl and told her stories about the wondrous things that happened when the power of God would fall in this place. He wanted to see it. Thomas made his way between the river rock tomb stones and crusty ground to the little chapel. When he got to the entrance, he guessed the back, weeds partially covered the door. Thomas pulled them away.

A gigantic lock and chain had been placed across the door. It looked like the door had been sealed. Thomas backed away, saddened. The rustic look of the little chapel reminded him of the time he and Majken found the old cabin in the woods on their long ago camping trip. If she were here, he thought, she'd be able to open that lock and they could see what was inside. He just sat on one of the rocks that made the foundation of the chapel.

Oh God, how he missed her! He sat on the desolate little rock in the middle of the desolate forgotten cemetery. What good did all of this do? he wondered. The thought of living your entire life, dreams and hopes included, to only end with your name carved on a faded rock in a cemetery made him angry.

Angry at his parents for insisting he finish that degree. Angry at his high school sweetheart for breaking his heart. Angry at himself for choosing to leave the state and go to a college as far north as possible just to get away from Julie.

Angry at stupid fate that had thrust this condition upon him. Why? He asked himself why a million times. He placed his head in his hands, but the tension inside him snapped.

Thomas sprang up and stomped to the nearest clearing. "Why God?" he shouted. "Why'd you let this happen to me?"

He saw a clump of dirt, picked it up and threw it. Momma always said, If you're gonna have a hissy fit – have a good one.

He threw another clump of dirt, then another, then another. Each time his throw became sloppier. Dirt rained from the heavens. He shouted until his throat was hoarse. Exhausted, he collapsed. He lay panting on his hands and knees.

A figure stood in front of him.

She was outlined in a silvery halo of moonlight.

"Majken!" Thomas shouted.

He stumbled to his feet, then tripped sideways. He righted himself and she reached for him. When he held her, she was solid and real. It was really her! She wasn't just his imagination – she was really here! He tried to talk, mumbling.

She took his face in her hands and drew him to her.

She kissed him with fervency, an urgency born of deep hunger and loss. Thomas panted. Words tumbled out of his mouth. "I thought – I thought I lost you. I didn't know how badly you were hurt, I didn't know if you survived, or if you died, or where you were. I was so worried for you. I –" he had to pause to catch his breath "– thought I would never see you again."

She smiled at him. "I think if you're actually going to hit God with those rocks, you're going to have to throw them a lot harder," she quipped. He grinned, now embarrassed at his rant.

He staggered before her. She helped him back up and sit on the crusty weed strewn ground and she picked a spot beside him to sit. She lay her heavy leather shoulder bag down between them. He heard a sloshing sound when she dropped it. Did she – did she bring – water? She produced two large containers of bottled water. Bless her, Thomas thought.

He quickly uncapped the first and directed the spigot into his mouth and leaned back. It was not cold, but it was cooler than the night air and what he very much needed. When he finished the first one, she held the second one down as he reached for it. "Slow down," she told him, "wait."

"I missed you so much," he said. "How did you find me?"

Majken glanced upward at the waning moon. "I can hear the voice of your blood. I can feel you, even from a great distance."

She touched the torn right leg of his jeans.

"How's your leg?"

Thomas was startled. He felt of his right calf where the sharp branch had punctured his skin. Somewhere it had stopped hurting, he noticed. When he pulled the torn fabric aside, pink scar tissue had already formed over the puncture wound.

"What the —" he stammered.

He just stared at his leg. It was all too unreal. She let him drink the second container.

"It's healing," Majken told him. "Your senses will now be sharper, your metabolism faster, and you will heal, unless you are significantly damaged, very, very quickly."

Majken resumed, "I knew you were in The Change, and I discovered that you had come home. I am here to see what I can do for you, and to see if you survive."

"If I survive?" Thomas asked.

Majken crouched to a kneeling position, then stood.

"I can explain all that when we're back at your parent's house. Kimberly is waiting. There are deer in the area. You and I must feed before we take you home."

Thomas stood and followed her.

Chapter Eight

Home. Jeanine blinked again as the once familiar sky-line came into view. She had come home to Charlotte. She changed lanes smoothly on Interstate 277 as she glanced at sleeping Alecia in the passenger's seat. They had been driving all day, stopping only at Lexington for Alecia to get something to eat.

She did not believe she would ever come back here again. Faint memories danced and twirled in her mind as she sought an exit so she could find a place for Alecia tonight. Jeanine mapped her body's internal signals. Her need for blood tonight was not immediate. She had fed that early morning and again in the old folk's home just before Alecia's school called her about Nolan. She could wait until morning to search for blood.

She said a quick prayer of thanks.

Jeanine found an exit and entered the heart of the city she once called home. The streets were both familiar and strange. She did not immediately recognize where she was.

She oriented relative to the concrete plant.

Her Papa had worked at the concrete plant for years, even before she left with Bobby. She vividly remembered its spires reaching heavenward as silent monoliths in the night sky. When she saw the plant from North Carolina 16, her heart quickened.

Papa! Papa would still be here alive in his seventies now. He was in good health when she left with Bobby. *Chances are he's still alive.* The mere thought of seeing her Papa again filled her with excitement. Tomorrow would be soon enough to find him.

As she turned on the brightly illuminated city street, she felt bone weary. Her body was telling her to stop now.

She followed Tryon Street into the heart of the city.

She took note of several taverns and bars as she drove. She passed Dunhill Hotel and remembered her Mamă speaking of once working there. Jeanine had always wanted to see it, and perhaps, some day, actually stay there. Dreams and memories, long denied and buried, began to resurface. She guessed she had to leave the Fourth Ward to find a hotel that she could afford. She had only two hundred and twenty dollars.

Alecia stirred in her seat, now awake and bedazzled by the glittering streets. Jeanine smiled at her baby girl. "This is where I grew up," she told Alecia proudly. Alecia seemed to take it all in, suddenly animated and pointing at different things of interest to her. Seeing her home again made her feel not so isolated and alone. It was only fear that had kept her away for so long. The farther she and Alecia got away from Nolan and the likes of the blood cult the better she felt.

She headed south to McDowell street and eventually found a promising hotel next to Marshall Park. It was large enough to have a swimming pool for Alecia and other amenities. Jeanine pulled into the parking lot and drove to the front entrance. Alecia perked up when she saw the swimming pool as they passed by.

The trees in the park stirred in the breeze; as soon as she stepped outside, she distinctly felt the air from the south held moisture. Her heart told her she was home. Their hotel stay cost a hundred and she had to show her driver's license. She refused to spend the rest of her life in fear and hiding.

Jeanine found their room on the seventh floor and went to the window straightaway.

Alecia was already changing into her swimming clothes. Maybe later she would buy a swim suit for herself and join her. Warm memories of her Papa and Mamă teaching her to swim at the Y when she was five years old came to her mind. It had been years since she had even thought about her family – before.

She remembered Mamă so vividly. Her lovely mother Roxana was so beautiful. Eyes as green as emeralds. Jeanine considered her own eyes, hazel green, part from her mother and part from her father. Her hair color much from her father. Her pale alabaster skin from her mother.

Jeanine kicked off her sandals and found the oldest pair of jeans she had. Holes were in the knees and the legs.

She followed her baby girl to the pool.

So proud of her baby girl, she really wanted to teach Alecia to swim as her Mamă and Papa had taught her. She laughed when Alecia reacted to the cold water. Alecia played in the swimming pool until it closed.

Jeanine awoke at three a.m. in the dark hotel room. Quiet air conditioning whispered in the night, the closed curtains let a sliver of streetlight into the room, and Alecia breathed softly in the bed next to her. She listened around her. The carpeted hallway was silent. No unusual sounds were coming from the rooms nearby. She gently sat up and scooted to the end of the bed and stood up. Her body's internal signals were telling her to feed. The edge on her perceptions were acute. A wave of light vertigo passed. Jeanine slipped on her robe, went to the window and drew the curtain aside. Maybe she was simply excited at being home. She bowed her head in the stillness. A lone street cleaner circled Marshall Park far below.

Uprooted from Chicago, she now had time to ponder how Nolan managed to track her. Likely Alecia's school records. If she wanted a new life for Alecia, she and Alecia needed new identities. Aside from a few counter-culture things she had read in her hippie days she had no idea how to get another name, social security number, birth certificate, and other documentation that identified you. Wherever she took Alecia next, she vowed not to give them her last name. She also considered her California license. That, too, was a link she wanted to lose forever.

Jeanine considered time remaining until morning. Alecia should sleep until six. If she had three hours, she considered touring the lounge downstairs to see if any patrons were out early. Nolan had shown her surveillance tapes early on and many of these were taken in public buildings and hotels such as this one. She knew most, if not all, areas of this hotel were under twenty-four-hour surveillance. If she was going to go, she really needed to go now. Jeanine went to the bathroom and quietly dressed. She needed little makeup. She pulled on her sandals and decided she needed higher class wardrobe to catch the kind of men who frequented the city bars and nightspots. She hated selling herself, but this was her only other way to get blood.

Jeanine wrote a note for Alecia and left it on the bedside table in case she woke up and quietly slipped out. She found the lounge still open and several men still drinking. She walked up to a man sitting alone at the bar.

"Hi," she said. "Want some company?"

The man with silver-gray hair and heavy copper chains on his wrists regarded her. He took a sip of his drink – cognac Jeanine knew by the scent – and motioned for her to sit. He wore a Hawaiian type shirt that showed some of his hairy chest. "Name's Bob," he said. "What's yours?" He swirled the red liquor in his tulip glass. His lips were full and sensual.

"Rose," Jeanine replied. "Rose Bennett."

Everything inside her screamed predator when he

slipped his arm around her waist. She smiled at him and scooted a little closer. *So, he wanted some,* she thought. She listened to his heart beating, just a little faster when she moved. Jeanine returned his caress by rubbing her hand along his left thigh twice, then rested her hand in her own lap. *Make him wait,* she thought. Over the next hour, he offered to buy her drinks, take her dancing, let her visit his penthouse, go to the gallery at the museum, and tour the countryside with him. He did everything but invite her to visit his mother. She touched his arm and hand, stroked the hair on his arms, and generally moved to rub his thighs again.

He was starting to pull her closer.

When he leaned over her to kiss her, Jeanine pressed herself against him. Her voice was hot and breathy – "Can we go to your car?" she asked. His eyes widened. He wanted her.

She let him escort her to the parking deck behind the hotel. An air conditioner unit hummed nearby. When she passed his driver's side door, she noticed leather straps and buckles in the floorboard behind the driver's seat. She also saw the glint of silver metal – she was almost certain to be handcuffs.

She smiled at him as he led her to the passenger side and opened her car door. Before she slid into the seat, she pulled the drawstring knot of her blouse open and rubbed her breasts through the fabric. He already knew she did not wear a bra.

He went around to the driver's side and slid into the seat. His shirt was already open and his belt was undone. She started caressing him, but she was very aware where his hands were. His body shifted as his left arm reached behind him. Jeanine heard the light clink of metal against metal. If Mr. Romantic had plans, so did she.

With a sudden motion, he tried to pull her left arm with his right hand while trying to fasten the handcuff to her wrist.

Jeanine jerked her left arm free and hit him hard in the nose with the ball of her right palm. Blood splattered down his chin.

While he was stunned she wrenched the handcuffs from him and quickly fastened his right and left wrists between his steering wheel. Jeanine quickly grabbed his keys from the steering column and tossed them in the back seat. Bob, naturally, started swearing. She reached her right hand over his privates, pressed, and squeezed very hard. Her mouth was very close to his ear.

She whispered, "If you want to keep these, shut up."

He whimpered. Jeanine got out of his car and sauntered to the back seat to see what other goodies he had stashed. She cooed as she picked through his bondage accessories. "Mmmm," she hummed, "quite the collector." She noted with satisfaction he had Alaska plates as she circled his car.

The gag was put to good use. Several leather belts immobilized his arms. She dragged him out of the driver's side door long enough to strip off his shoes, socks, pants, and underwear and fasten his ankles and knees with two other leather belts. By the time she pulled him back inside his car and across his own seat, he straddled the front and back with his butt and hairy legs in her face. Jeanine unwrapped the razor blade she had hidden in her skirt and made several cuts on the inner sides of his thighs. She wanted to finish feeding quickly and get back to Alecia. Already the sky was getting brighter. It was only just past five in the morning.

Mr. Kinky squealed when she cut him.

Heaven forbid, he may like this and try to invite her

back. She wanted to be long gone from this hotel before someone found him. When she finished feeding, and then some, she circled around to the driver's side door and removed the gag from the man's mouth. His face had turned beet red.

Jeanine grabbed a handful of his hair.

He was paying close attention.

She gave him a little peck on the cheek. "Had fun, Bob. But let's not do this again. Okay?" She rolled his driver's window down enough for him to be heard when another driver came by in the parking deck and left him trussed up in his own vehicle.

It was not yet five thirty when she slipped back into her room. Alecia had just woke up. Jeanine stepped inside and Alecia came to her at the door. Her little face was twisted up, afraid, but Jeanine knelt and took her in her arms.

"Baby, I'm here," she said lowly.

"I woke up and you weren't here," she said. Jeanine smoothed her dark brown hair and smiled at her.

"Honey, I had to go find a blood source. I wanted to do it while you were sleeping." She shrugged, and said, "Didn't you see the note I left for you?" When Jeanine led Alecia between the beds, she found her note sitting on the floor untouched. Jeanine reminded herself to never step out on Alecia again unless she told her that she was going out. They had been fortunate so far.

She kissed Alecia on the head and prodded her to get her morning bath since she did not get one last night. Jeanine felt she needed a hot, hot shower after her session with Bob, but she also wanted to leave the hotel as soon as possible. While Alecia was bathing, she laid out fresh clothes for her, then she undressed and got more comfortable clothes for herself today.

Today, she thought. Today.

She was excited about seeing her Papa – thoughts of anything else were secondary. Jeanine heard water being let out of the tub and Alecia came out of the bathroom wrapped in a towel like they had seen girls in a movie they watched a few days ago.

Jeanine kissed Alecia and went to get a quick shower. Within fifteen minutes she was finished, and they were packed and leaving the hotel ten minutes later. Alecia was not too hungry this morning because of all the chocolate she had eaten last night. She thought of Momma Lillian again and the times she had cared for Alecia on the spur of the moment. Jeanine gave thought to find someone reliable to care for Alecia when she, herself, was working or otherwise occupied.

Jeanine refueled in the Second Ward and found a fast-food place for Alecia to eat her breakfast. The sky was cloudy and it would be breezy throughout the day. The air had a crispness and soft quality to it that spoke of home sweet home.

The streets were still not familiar. She knew the few streets that were in her mind but the city had changed. The rows of new buildings and apartments on the street she thought she remembered looked unfamiliar.

Everything had changed in her former neighborhood.

She oriented relative to the concrete plant. She remembered she could see the silos from her bedroom window. She drove around until she saw the concrete plant in the same way she remembered it. Yet the lot in front of her was vacant. No buildings had been here – by the look of weeds and broken concrete – for many, many years. Alecia got out of the car with her. They walked up and down the vacant lot until Jeanine saw a street sign: Smith Street. She backed up, stunned.

The home she knew and remembered was gone. Her Papa was gone. Jeanine sat back against her Mustang and just stood there looking at the vacant lot. She was stunned. In her mind she pictured the loving home she remembered and the older houses nearby. Yet, all she once knew was gone.

Alecia seemed to sense her distress. She came up to her and wrapped her arms around her legs. Jeanine wrapped her hands around Alecia's head and pulled her close.

In the years since her Change, she had long pushed memories of home and family out of her thinking because of the ache in her soul over what she once had. But, in her heart of hearts and her thinking, she had assumed her home would always be there – waiting and ready for her to return. In her memory, she could see her Papa as she last saw him. His sandy blonde hair, both arms muscular from years of working with concrete, and the blue work shirt he wore. He had been angry at her when she left with Bobby. They'd had words. Yet, now, the echo of those once angry words faded in the breeze that stirred the weeds among broken concrete on an empty lot.

Alecia looked up at her. "What's wrong?"

Returned to a semblance of now, Jeanine took Alecia's face in her hands. "My home is gone," Jeanine said. "The place I grew up at, the place I remember, is not here anymore. This is where I left with Bobby, the boy I told you about, twenty-five years ago. This was where I last saw my Papa –" she motioned to the empty lot "– standing there angry at me for choosing to leave with Bobby. At the time I thought it was what I was supposed to do."

She rubbed her eyes. Black swirls again.

Alecia looked up at her and seemed to regard what she said. Her eyes were as soft as gentle sea foam spray, with depths upon depths of understanding. Jeanine gazed into

Alecia's eyes as her baby girl watched her.

For now her love was enough.

Jeanine's heart stirred, although she was too numb right now to even cry. She knew she had once been much loved by her Mamă and Papa here. Now Alecia was her family. She held tightly to Alecia. She sighed in the desolation. "Whatever can go wrong, will," Jeanine breathed.

Then she saw the concrete plant. "C'mon," she told Alecia.

Jeanine and Alecia loaded up and Jeanine drove purposely to the concrete plant. She kept her pace gentle as to not rev her engine too much. She crossed backroads and railroad tracks until she reached the entrance to the plant. A guard stopped her at the entrance. The older man came to her driver's window. Before her, the silos were to her right and several brick buildings were in front of her with a loading dock. What she assumed was employee parking ran along a chain-link fence in the middle of the yard.

"I want to talk to someone in Personnel," she said. The guard pointed to the building and entrance she should go to and directed her to park in the visitor's parking to her left. Jeanine got out and took Alecia's hand. She walked with her to find administration. Several workers entering a nearby brick building watched her as she passed. She followed the dock under the metal canopy until she came to the blue door. She opened it and she and Alecia went up the stairs to the second floor. They went all the way down to find the office on the end to her right.

Jeanine stood in a little reception area with two plastic chairs and a little table with a telephone and telephone book. She faced a reception window with a small hole in the glass to speak through. A woman who looked to be in her sixties was talking on the telephone in the reception office. She had several folders on the desk in front of her and Jeanine could tell she was looking at a computer screen also.

Jeanine had Alecia sit while she stood in front of the window waiting to get the lady's attention. Alecia fidgeted a little.

When the woman finished speaking and hung up the telephone, she was writing on the folders and said, "Can I help you?" without even glancing up.

"I'm looking for my father," she said. "He used to work here. His name is Steven Bryer."

The woman looked up at her. She had half spectacles, like Jeanine had seen on a pharmacist once. "It is against our policy to give out employee information to anyone except immediate family."

Jeanine stammered, "I'm his daughter!"

The woman studied her, Jeanine guessed.

"I don't recognize the name," she said, "and I've worked here for nearly fifteen years. When was he supposed to have worked here?"

Jeanine thought back. Her Papa had met Mamă in New York, then shortly thereafter they married, and he moved here for work. "The nineteen-fifties and sixties," Jeanine replied.

The woman took off her half spectacles and regarded her through the window. "What was his name?" she asked. "How are you related to him?"

Jeanine bent over to speak into the hole cut in the glass. "Steven Bryer. Like the ice cream. My name is Jeanine Rose Bryer. I'm his daughter."

The woman pursed her lips and crossed her arms. "Hummph," she said in an exasperated tone, "I dare say, you can't be older than twenty. And you want me to believe you're the daughter of a man who worked here in the sixties?"

Jeanine instantly realized her mistake. She should have claimed to be his grand daughter or great-grand daughter.

Well, the mistake was made now.

Jeanine placed both hands on the glass. She felt she could break it if she wanted to. "All I need is his address. Our home on Smith Street is gone. I have no idea where he lives now. Would you please help me?"

The woman reached for her phone and dialed an internal number. She spoke lowly into the receiver, but Jeanine heard her clearly. "Security, come to Personnel." Within moments, Jeanine heard footsteps coming down the corridor she and Alecia came up. Jeanine backed away from the window and stepped into the corner with Alecia. She wrapped her arms around her baby girl, ready for whatever or whoever came through that door.

Two uniformed men stepped into the little reception area. They filled up the tiny room. Jeanine held one arm around Alecia and held up her other hand in submission. "We're leaving," she said. "I don't want any trouble."

She and Alecia quietly left. The men escorted her out of the building, and one man followed her down the dock and watched her as she got into her car and left the plant.

Her heart ached as she pulled onto Smith Street. But she had learned through bitter experience that she was a survivor. Although her emotions were rolling right now, what she felt was not necessarily what she must do.

She made a few turns just to reenter Fourth Ward and drove slowly on West Ninth Street. After a few moments, she passed a playground. Alecia looked expectantly at her. Jeanine found a parking space halfway down the block and thought, Why not? The playground was set on the corner of the block next to what appeared to be a market. The backdrop building was gaily colored with children playing and a little picket fence to her said, Home – come and play. She laughed as Alecia headed directly for the huge swing.

Jeanine sat against the wooden table and bench in the middle of the playground. She watched a man lead a little dog on a leash around the metal bench on the walkway. He paid no particular attention to Jeanine and Alecia and soon he left by the sidewalk. Jeanine had to make some quick decisions. She had less than a hundred dollars after refueling and buying breakfast for Alecia. She wanted to see her Papa and the reaction of the woman at the plant made her angry.

Then she glanced at her youthful hands and body and guessed, if the roles had been reversed, she wouldn't have given private employee information to any teenager that walked into the place either. The wind was blowing the leaves of the ash tree next to her. Every sense opened up around her. It felt right for her and Alecia to be here. Now it was up to her to make her former home a new home for herself and Alecia.

Her first decision was to fervently avoid the public school system. The bureaucracy was impossible to avoid and links to Helena and Nolan were part of the public school bureaucracy. Her second decision was to, somehow, find another identity for herself and Alecia. Only in this way could they live in peace and stay away from Nolan and the blood cult forever.

Jeanine took a seat and motioned for Alecia to come. Her baby girl was getting a little tired now anyway. She sprang off the swing and came traipsing to the bench.

Another woman with two young boys entered the playground. Jeanine assumed she was their mother. The boys immediately went for the climbing set and she cajoled them to be careful. Alecia sat on the bench across from Jeanine.

"Baby girl," Jeanine said, "does this city feel right to you, or do you think we should move on?" Alecia's face was a little flushed because she had been swinging so high.

"I like it here," she said without hesitation.

Jeanine rephrased her question.

"Baby girl, I don't mean the playground. I mean this city, the area" – she waved her arm to encompass the whole of Charlotte – "What do you feel about this city and whether we'll be safe here?" Alecia started playing with a leaf that had fallen on the table from the tree. She was acting just like any other seven-year-old girl. Her attention was on a bug crawling on the pebbles beneath the bench.

Jeanine tried not to be exasperated.

Alecia was still her baby girl.

The woman who had been corralling the two boys came over and sat at the far end of the table. Her brunette hair, with streaks of gray, was wind blown. She wrapped a scarf over her head and tied it under her chin.

"Hi," Alecia said brightly.

The woman smiled at her and Jeanine.

"Hello," she replied. She called to the smaller of the two boys. Jeanine assumed this was the younger one.

When she turned back, Jeanine extended her hand. "My name is Jeanine. This is Alecia. We're new in town. I was wondering if you might know of a good daycare."

The woman smiled at Jeanine.

"My name is Rebecca. Rebecca York. I keep children –" she stopped to call her oldest son this time "when I am not wrangling my own two boys."

"How long have you been keeping children?" Jeanine asked.

"For the last eighteen years, or so. My husband and I both work at St. Peter's Episcopal Church. It's just off Tryon Street."

"Oh, really," Jeanine said, "are you taking applications right now? I would really like to find a safe place for Alecia."

Alecia wanted to play on the climbing set with the two boys. Jeanine said yes. She started climbing in the tunnel after the smallest of Rebecca's two boys.

"How old is she?" Rebecca asked.

"She's seven, but very smart."

The largest of Rebecca's two sons noticed Alecia was there. Alecia reversed course and the boys crawled after her in the tube. When she reached the end, she jumped out and went for the swings again. The boys followed her to the swings, one on each side, and they started swinging as well.

Jeanine asked Rebecca, "Don't you have parishes like the Catholic church?"

Rebecca replied yes. The women talked for thirty minutes or so. Jeanine decided she liked Rebecca and wanted to see the church. She motioned for Alecia. After several more swings, she skidded to a halt and came running. Rebecca's children flocked around her. With Rebecca in the lead, they all walked the five blocks to the church facility.

A pretty brick church, Jeanine thought.

She promised to return Monday.

As she and Alecia left the church, Jeanine noticed several nearby taverns and lounges she might hunt at later that evening. Finding her Papa was on Jeanine's mind as they made their way back to her car. She found a place for Alecia's lunch, then headed for Norland Road and Evergreen Cemetery.

Her old middle school, where she was attending when her Mamă died, was just across the street.

Memories flooded her mind. She was starting to remember places and directions again. When she saw the dried grass, white brick columns, and wrought-iron fence, she stopped at the entrance and just could not drive in right away.

"Where are we?" Alecia asked.

Jeanine turned off her Mustang engine and rested her hand on top of her steering wheel. "Baby girl," she said lowly, "this is where my Mamă is buried. I was only ten years old when she died."

Alecia was silent for a moment. Then she asked, "How did she die?"

Jeanine bowed her head.

"Ovarian cancer."

Jeanine gathered her courage and started her car engine. She idled, placed the car in gear, and moved slowly forward.

Her eyes were on the north west corner of the cemetery. If her Papa was here, or not, she just had to know.

She started talking: "My Papa loved my Mamă very much. When she died, it nearly destroyed him. But he had me to take care of and he couldn't just quit. When Mamă died, it came sudden. From the time she was diagnosed to the end was only four and a half months." Tears trickled down her cheeks.

Jeanine made the turn at the end of the road and started circling the cemetery. She picked out the Bryer headstone from the distance. Oh, God, she thought to herself.

"My Papa has no family and most of my Mamă's family is still in Romania. I'm from the Mihnea lineage." Jeanine lifted her head proudly. She tried to steady herself. If her Papa was here, then her Papa was here. She parked and saw the tombstone with the family name etched on it. Cold stone. Cold tears.

"C'mon baby. We have to know."

Jeanine got out and stood at her door until Alecia came

beside her. She instinctively reached for Alecia and Alecia slipped her hand into her's. The dry grass crunched under step. They circled the tombstone. The spot beside her mother was ... empty.

Her Papa was not here. If her Papa was not here then he had to be alive somewhere. The youngest boy of an old family, her Papa had no family other than she and her Mamă. Surely, he would still be in Charlotte somewhere. She just needed to track him down.

Alecia stood at the headstone and drew her finger along Jeanine's mother's etched name. Roxana Mihnea Bryer. Jeanine felt the distinct ache of missing her Mamă again, but also sweet memories of the happiest time when her Papa and Mamă were together.

Jeanine knelt on the dry grass and reached for Alecia. Alecia came to her. She wrapped her arms around Alecia and said, "Remember, baby girl, that death is not the end of life. When we trust Jesus as Savior and believe in His blood, God can forgive our sins, then we have eternal life in Him."

Alecia seemed a little puzzled. "Aren't you angry at God for taking your mother?" she asked. Jeanine hugged Alecia and kissed her.

"No, I'm not. We live in a sinful and broken world. We have to trust God to take care of us. But I don't think He causes us to die. God is love and truth and all life."

"What about when that bad thing happened to you?" Alecia looked like she did when she was hiding from thunder. Her little pout turned Jeanine's heart inside out. It was like when Alecia cried for her in the pavilion.

"I made the mistake of following Bobby and staying with him. It was my own stupid choice that put this on me. I certainly can't blame God for my own ignorance and fear."

"What were you afraid of?" Alecia asked.

"Not being loved," she replied. "Not being loved like my Papa loved my Mamă." Jeanine wiped slow pooling tears from Alecia's eyes. She held her baby girl in her arms.

"I want you to know how much I love you and how proud I am of you. I don't regret one moment we've ever spent together. I don't ever, ever regret having you in my life, and I solemnly promise I will be very proud of the remarkable young lady you will soon become."

Alecia's eyes were bright, clear, and trusting. Her baby girl reached for her. That hug was worth all of the tears and the ache in her soul over her past. She felt in her heart that God didn't make the bad thing happen to her, but she was so thankful, that since she was coming down this broken path anyway, that He put Alecia on the same path with her.

Her Papa was not here. That was settled.

Jeanine stood up and gazed at her Mamă's grave a little longer. She took Alecia's hand and they walked back to Jeanine's car. It was early afternoon, by Jeanine's internal sense. She had to find shelter for Alecia then start hunting blood sources.

The charcoal gray clouds billowed rapidly in the upper atmosphere. Jeanine could feel the moisture and drop in pressure and knew the weather would be changing abruptly.

Jeanine pulled onto Norland facing her former middle school. She used to sneak out of class and hang out at Eastway Square. She turned into the school parking lot and took the back way to Biscayne. She turned on Argus into the strip mall. The Food Lion was still there. Anna's Linens was still there. She made a loop in the mall just for old times sake. She pointed to an old drink machine next to the grocery store.

"That's where I used to hang out after school when I was a little older than you," she told Alecia. Jeanine resumed her course down Eastway to Central, back to South End to find a cheaper motel than The Blake. She found a Super 8 off Clanton.

The manager was a wizened man with long chalk white hair. He wore a faded yellow and orange Hawaiian print shirt with tabasco stains dribbled down his chest. He said for them to ignore the knocking. Jeanine did not comment.

She purchased two nights. Alecia asked her why they couldn't stay at the place with the swimming pool again. She replied, as she opened their little room, "We're on the cheap until I get a job." The sky was getting dusky dark, made even darker by the pending storm. Jeanine made sure Alecia had blankets and towels. The edge on her perceptions meant she had to go hunting now. She took a quick shower and dressed in hunting clothes, then took Alecia out for her dinner.

Jeanine took a tour of Dilworth just to refresh her memory and found a pizza place off East Boulevard, then she bought bagels for Alecia at a bakery just in case she got hungry that night. Finally, back at the sleazy motel, as Alecia called it, she had to leave her baby girl. At this rate, she may be hunting all night. The television picture was grainy at best. There appeared to be only one other traveler at this motel and it was nearly nine o'clock in the evening. Chances were, this is all they would have. Jeanine knelt in front of Alecia.

"I have to go find a blood source," she said. "I'm going to hit the taverns we saw Uptown first. Maybe I'll get lucky and land a job and get blood at the same time."

Alecia looked sad. "Do you really have to go now? Can't you wait until morning?"

Jeanine silently mapped her body's internal signals. She had to feed soon. "I'm sorry, baby girl. I have to start hunting now before it really gets bad for me."

"I know," Alecia said. "But I'll miss you anyway." Jeanine reached for Alecia and immersed herself in that hug. She'd done for Alecia all she could do for right now.

She reluctantly let Alecia go.

Jeanine bowed her head as the man approached her naked. Her skin was covered with a fine sheen, but not sweat. Her skin was still very cool and cold tears dripped down her cheeks. He was barrel-chested and very powerful. His short black hair was spike cut and his face was Polynesian. His entire body was covered with tribal ceremonial tattoos. She'd been worn out by this man and his bountiful enthusiasm. He grabbed a handful of her hair with his right fist and jerked her head down to the bed, bending her at the waist. He felt her up with his other hand. It wasn't really as bad as what Nolan did to her, but it was still humiliating.

The first man she approached, she made the initial advances. As he got close to her, she detected the same rotten scent she remembered from Patrick. She dumped this guy in a hurry. She actually made it to the second guy's apartment. When she got to his place, a thousand people were in his living room and she could find no hope of getting blood without being seen. She excused herself, saying she had a headache, and dropped this guy.

The Polynesian guy was actually a lounge and restaurant owner. She was talking to the maitre d' on a bartending opportunity when he walked up and escorted her to his private office. She played a dumb innocent girl from out west. She laughed at his jokes. He was pretty slick, not grabby, obviously loaded, and he smelled okay to her. Maybe a wealthy businessman in Charlotte would be a good friend to have. She hoped to meet people and establish herself here.

She went with him to his luxury Uptown apartment. It was lush and well appointed. He wanted her for sex, just straight sex. So she obliged.

After the second or third time, any other man she had ever been with fell asleep. She then tried to get him unconscious by enticing him to drink liquor but this did not work well either. Then he wanted to tie her up.

She avoided anything that involved being tied up herself because of Nolan. Her need for blood was now increased due to the physical pounding she'd been taking. She held the sash of his bathrobe and wrapped it around her hands. She intended to use it as a garrote to render him unconscious.

Finally, he stopped and lay back still.

His eyes were closed. His breathing had become shallower. She listened and tuned in to his heart rhythm. His heartbeat was slower. She had long since been stripped in front of this man. She found her skirt tossed over a vase in the hallway and found a hidden wrapped razor blade in the hem. When his mouth opened, he actually started snoring.

Jeanine straddled his chest and poked the sharp end of the razor blade against his arm above his elbow. He flinched slightly, but otherwise did not move. She jabbed him harder and drew blood this time.

He still did not move.

Now reasonably certain he was not going to awaken, she made four deliberate cuts along the fleshy part of his forearm and let his arm dangle off the bed. She did not have a bowl to collect her evening meal, but she did have the wine glass she drank from earlier. She dumped the last of the wine out and used the glass to collect the blood she now so desperately needed. When it was one-third full, she drank quickly and replaced the glass under his arm.

Blood had splattered on the crisp white bedsheet. No way to explain that away, she thought. He bled until she half filled the wine glass again. As his blood started to clot, she held the wine glass between her legs on the floor and used his bathrobe sash she was going to use to throttle him to bind his arm and stop the bleeding entirely.

Finally, she lifted the glass and drank.

Her body was already absorbing the blood.

Jeanine got on her knees and gently lifted his arm to his bed. He rolled on his left side in front of her. She got up and used his bathrobe to cover him against a chill, then started picking through his living room in the dark to find her own strewn clothes. She finally found all of her clothes. She dressed and wanted to leave quickly so she could get back to Alecia before daybreak.

When she looked out his window to the street below, it was raining. The rain was driven by the wind in sheets. This man did not say anything, one way or another, about actually hiring her. She decided she would keep him as a lover, but she would not work for him. He lay still behind her.

She felt cold. Jeanine rubbed her arms.

Jeanine got soaked as she left the man's apartment. When she got to her car, sleet gray rain drummed on her windshield.

She was so tired.

Too tired to drive right now. She just wanted to close her eyes for a moment.

She slept dreamless sleep.

When she opened her eyes, the sun was a handspan above the city in the sky behind a thick canopy of gray clouds.

Jeanine was instantly awake.

By her internal body clock, it was about nine-thirty in the morning.

Alecia!

Jeanine jerked awake with a start and oriented to the people milling on the city street before her. The Uptown pedestrians were busily going about their business. When she started her car, more than a few turned to stare at her. She let her Mustang throttle down and she gently eased into city traffic. Her light sensitive eyes ached in the bright daylight.

She headed for South End and Alecia.

As she idled beside a bus, she realized her blouse had been soaked by the night rain and was almost transparent on her skin. She flushed when she realized people in the bus above her were staring. She made a left hand turn and found a less populated path. When she pulled into her motel, a black lady was pushing a cleaning cart into the open room two doors up from her and Alecia's room.

Jeanine parked, got her room key from her locked glove compartment, and unlocked her room. She hung the DO NOT DISTURB sign as she locked the door. The room was dark when she shut the door. Jeanine kicked off her sandals.

"Alecia?" she whispered.

She found Alecia curled in her clothes on top of the cover of the first bed. The other bed had not been disturbed. She had curled in a fetal position and was so still. White lines of tears were on her face. Jeanine knelt quietly on the carpet and ran her fingers gently through Alecia's dark brown curls.

She vividly remembered Alecia and the thunder storm in her trailer several weeks ago. A lifetime ago. She'd promised her baby girl that she would always be there to protect her – and last night, it had thundered, she was sure of it.

Alecia stirred slightly.

Nothing says failure quite like a little girl's tears.

She rolled over and opened her eyes.

"I'm so sorry, baby girl," Jeanine started. She felt a distinct ache at the wounded way Alecia was looking at her.

"You were gone all night!" Alecia wailed.

Jeanine's eyes saddened. "I know."

Alecia rolled back over and faced away from Jeanine.

"You don't care that I cried all night, and you weren't here. You don't care about me! All you care about is your stupid blood needs!" Her fists were balled up. Alecia pushed Jeanine's hand away from her shoulder.

"I love you, Alecia, and I do care."

She gently turned Alecia to face her.

"I tried to explain to you what I was and how I have to live before we left your father. I wanted to get back before morning, but the man I eventually got blood from would not go to sleep. He had me up all night."

Alecia's eyes welled up with tears.

"You only care about yourself," she said angrily.

Jeanine sat on the floor next to the bed. There was very little light in the room, only a sliver of light from the part in the curtain, yet Jeanine could see Alecia clearly in the dark.

"I won't argue with you, baby girl. You are my life. Your father and all the others before him kept me enslaved to their way, and I was forced to do things I regret to this day. But I never ever regretted you. I would rather die than go back to the way life was for me before you came into my life."

With that, Jeanine got up and went to the bathroom.

She used the bathroom, got several drinks of water because she felt dehydrated, then undressed and slipped into a large t-shirt that came down to her thighs. She pulled the covers aside and slid into the crisp white sheets. Outside, she heard the cleaning lady push her cart past their room to the next room in line.

The bed across from her squeaked.

Alecia stirred and sat up.

She guessed that Alecia could only see a black outline on the bed before her. Jeanine waited to see what Alecia would do.

Alecia moved to the edge of her bed, sitting still and saying nothing. Her legs dangled off the edge of the mattress and did not reach the floor. Her bare feet knocked the frame a few times. Then she stood and tiptoed over to Jeanine.

Jeanine could see that Alecia held her right hand over her mouth. She was starting to cry. Jeanine swept back the covers and made a place for Alecia.

"C'mere, baby girl," she said quietly.

Alecia bound toward her.

Jeanine guided her to the empty space beside her so they would not bump heads or any other body parts. Alecia was crying, but Jeanine smoothed the tears from her face and softly said, "I know you missed me, honey. I'm not angry at you for your feelings."

Alecia cuddled next to her.

Jeanine held her baby girl.

"I'm disappointed, too, that I didn't get back sooner. You see, baby girl, I miss you, too." Jeanine lay back and Alecia curled at her side. Everything good and everything right in her life lay next to her. Jeanine did not sleep for a while. She focused and listened to Alecia's heart beating. She found she could also hear the swishing of blood through Alecia's body, the slight gurgling of water through the air conditioning compressor, and several cats meowing outside somewhere. She finally slept peacefully.

Sunday evening she found a blood source sooner and a promising lead to a job. She was able to get back to Alecia before midnight. Monday she returned to St. Peter's Episcopal Church and enrolled Alecia under an assumed name in their daycare. Rebecca and her husband were glad to care for Alecia in the evenings just for a while until she could find a place to live. The waitress job lead did not work out. Jeanine continued to look for a bartending job because it paid more money.

Jeanine drove down Independence and Idlewild to her former parish SJN. She drove past it on Tuesday but she did not stop. The landscape had changed a little and it looked like a new building wing had been added to the sanctuary. Wednesday morning, she went to St. Peter's and checked Alecia out early to go with her to SJN. The sun was bright and clear that day. Jeanine felt miserable as she pulled into the parking lot and made her way to the sanctuary. Alecia took her hand again. She drew strength and courage. Wherever her Papa was, someone here should know.

Jeanine opened the door and stepped onto red carpet. The interior was cool and very comfortable. She went to her immediate left to find the church administrative offices. A girl was seated behind the counter. Jeanine asked for the secretary for the congregation. She was directed three doors down.

A woman sat behind a desk with a banker's lamp and a fluorescent lamp mounted to the side. A volume was open and sheaves of papers with handwritten notes were scattered over the top of the desk. The gold and black nameplate on her desk was written S. Beechum.

She looked up when Jeanine and Alecia approached.

Jeanine directed Alecia to the chair beside the desk. The woman stood and extended her hand. "My name is Stephanie. How can I help you?"

Truth, Jeanine thought, in God's house.

"My name is Jeanine Bryer. This is my daughter Alecia. I'm looking for my father, Steven Bryer. He and my Mamă once came here. I want to know if you have a current address for him."

Stephanie lifted the volume off her desk and placed a bright yellow piece of paper in the book and slid it back into the massive bookshelf behind her. Rows upon rows of massive hardbound books were behind her. She walked to the end of the bookshelf. Under her desk was carpeted, but along the bookshelf itself was a strip of hardwood floor. Her heels clicked as she walked. She found a particular volume above her head and pulled it out. Jeanine gathered that it was some type of alphabetic index of parishioners. Jeanine lifted Alecia and took the seat beside the desk. She let Alecia sit in her lap.

Stephanie lay the volume on her desk and perused what appeared to be a table of contents in the front of the book.

"Bryer, Steven" she said.

She found the marker she was looking for and turned to the page spread two-thirds into the volume. Jeanine could read from the side her Papa's name with his family members. She was listed as his daughter. The page spread had their former address on Smith Street. A line was drawn through it. Two other addresses were listed. Lines were drawn through them.

The fourth address did not have a line drawn through it.

"He lives on Yadkin Avenue. It's just past East Thirty-Fifth street in NoDa." Stephanie took a slip of paper from the memo tray next to her telephone and wrote his address for her.

Jeanine took the piece of paper. If Ms. Beechum noticed that Jeanine's name was written in the volume, she did not comment. As Jeanine stood to leave, Stephanie added, "He has not attended mass regularly since the late nineteen seventies. Our elderly support team took him Christmas dinner last year. We've had no other contact with him all this year. He drinks heavily and we know that he's had at least one mild stroke."

Jeanine steeled herself, stood, and shook Stephanie's hand.

"Thank you," she said quietly.

Alecia took her hand as they walked out. Any touch was comforting right now. She felt very, very guilty for leaving him. Yet the decision she made to leave with Bobby had been made over a quarter of a century ago. All the things she wanted to say to him jumbled in her mind. Her heart ached at the news of her father's condition, but she had been expecting something like that.

That's why I brought Alecia, she thought. Alecia seemed to catch her somber mood. "He'll be okay," she said hopefully.

Jeanine pulled her car keys from the chain around her neck and opened Alecia's door. She was going to see her Papa and face whatever she had coming.

Would he rant or scream at her?

Would he be angry or break down and cry?

Would he be happy to see her at all?

The ache of anticipation in her heart and mind seemed to intensify as she came nearer to the North Davidson region, called NoDa by locals.

She found Yadkin Avenue. She looked again at the piece of paper where Stephanie had written her father's address. She found a cream-colored house with light gray trim. The house number on the porch column had been knocked off. The top number was broken, the next number was missing, and the two bottom numbers were skewed side to side.

The house looked deserted.

Jeanine pulled off the street into the adjoining patch of gray sere ground. A large twisted oak tree spread across the left side of the home. The grass around the porch had clumped in tufts of weeds. She got out and went around to Alecia's side and opened her baby girl's door. Jeanine hesitated just a moment. Alecia waited, looking back and up at Jeanine. She knew her heart was beating very fast. She tried to calm herself and relax. It was hard to relax. She sighed deeply. "C'mon, baby girl."

Jeanine stepped onto the porch and rapped on the door. She strained to listen for movement inside the house, like she did while waiting on Momma Lillian to come to the door. She rapped on the door again, harder.

The door latch clicked. The door opened.

The man standing in the narrow crack of the open door was slight. Gone was the robust man in his fifties as Jeanine remembered him. This man was stooped and rail thin. His hair had turned gray, like the color of pewter. His eyes were red-rimmed and bloodshot. The bones and veins of his hands were protruding. He padded silently on bare feet. His toenails and fingernails were yellowed and too long.

"Papa," Jeanine breathed. Oh God!

This was worse than she imagined, but at least he was alive.

Alecia had slid behind her and was holding to her

right hand. She seemed to pull back as Jeanine stepped into the doorway and eased the weathered peeling door open.

He didn't say anything when she came inside. He just turned away from her and started a shuffle walk back into his living room. Instantly, the stink of long dried excrement and rotting food assailed her. The only furniture he had was a tattered couch with one arm broken off. It was the cheap foam kind and tufts of padding were protruding from the sides and middle of the cushions. The little table beside the couch was littered with empty bottles. There were bottles around the couch all over the floor too. He made a grunting sound as he flopped down. He had not yet spoken to her.

Jeanine had seen bad and she had seen worse. Her Papa was avoiding eye contact with her. She stood full in the archway to his living room. Alecia was lingering in the hallway. Jeanine held her right hand behind her to warn Alecia back.

"Baby girl," she said looking behind her, "you don't need to come in here. Wait there." Alecia obeyed. They had left the front door wide open. Jeanine could see clearly in the dim living room, but she looked for a light to turn on so her Papa could see her. The lamp next to the couch had a broken light bulb littering the floor and was covered with cobwebs across the lamp shade. She found a floor lamp to turn on. Soft yellow-orange light filled the room. Jeanine took her father's hands and knelt in front of him.

"Papa," she said, "it's me – Jeanine."

He made some noises from his throat. She waited for recognition to lighten his eyes, but he did not seem to know her.

"Papa," she said more forcefully, "I'm your daughter, Jeanine. Roxana's daughter. Your Rose. I've come home."

His hands were shaking.

She tried to get in front of him to make him look directly at her. He made some incomprehensible sounds, more grunts than anything else. She wondered how he could have come to this. The guilt she felt for leaving him multiplied in the yellow-orange lamp glow in his sparse living room.

Jeanine looked around her. There was nothing much in the room that identified family. She was looking for pictures, pictures of Mamă or herself. Pictures of them together as a family. Nothing there. Alecia had come to the arch of the hallway. She was halfway hiding behind the wall and peering at the shell of a man who had once been Jeanine's father.

His face and hands were dirty.

Jeanine stood and went to the kitchen. She looked for a dishrag or a towel she could use to clean him up. The dishrag she picked up fell apart and shredded in her hands. She heard Alecia approaching from behind her. Without turning, she spoke, "Baby girl, go to the car and get me some cloths from the bag in the trunk. On the left hand side in front of the tire jack." She pulled her key and the chain from her neck and tossed it to Alecia. She caught the key and went out directly.

The kitchen table was a cheap Formica brand with numerous cigarette burns on the once pastel surface. No one in her family had smoked and she saw no ash trays. The metal frame kitchen chairs with plastic seats were rusty on the bottom.

While she was in the kitchen, Jeanine hazarded a peek in the refrigerator. There were boxes of partially eaten meals. From the pile of disposable refuse in the garbage, Jeanine gathered that he was getting meals for the elderly delivered. This may be the only thing that was keeping her Papa alive.

Alecia returned with a handful of rags.

Jeanine thanked her and took the handful of rags and split them into two piles. When she tried the hot water at his sink, pipes under the cabinet made a knocking noise and some type of sludge splattered into the sink. She turned off the hot water and turned on cold. At least it worked. She rinsed the sink clean and got new rags to moisten to wipe her Papa's face and hands.

Alecia had resumed her post in the arch.

Jeanine found her Papa on the couch but he was leaning to the right. She adjusted the little table of bottles out of her way and knelt in front of him again. She wiped his hands first, then started on his face. He tried to speak. He made motions with his hands. "What?" she asked.

"Who are you?" he asked.

His voice had become coarse, like broken concrete. His speech had a slur and rasping quality. She remembered that Stephanie said he'd had a stroke. Jeanine positioned herself in front of him. "I'm Rose, your daughter."

He was silent a moment. Then he said, "I have no daughter. She died a long time ago."

Jeanine got on her knees.

"Papa, look at me. I'm Jeanine, Roxana's daughter. I'm your daughter. Remember, I left with Bobby. I didn't die. I've come home."

He shook his head violently from side to side. "No," he vowed sternly, "my daughter is dead. I have no daughter."

Jeanine felt a numbness spread from her knees upward, a cruel twist in her midsection as she knelt before her Papa. He did not know her. He was in denial and clearly delusional. Jeanine stood up. She knew from her time in old folk's homes not to argue. It took her a few moments to gather her wits.

She simply replied, "My name is Jeanine and I will be taking care of you from now on." He seemed to settle down at that. He rolled on his side on the part of the couch that had an arm and curled his legs. Jeanine made the floor lamp dimmer and searched for a blanket or something to cover him as he napped. Alecia was balanced in the archway. She cast Jeanine a hopeful glance as she approached.

Jeanine stopped and hugged Alecia.

Alecia reached around Jeanine.

"Oh, baby girl," Jeanine said lowly. "I'm so sorry you had to see all this. Thank you for being with me today. I don't think I would have handled it as well if I didn't have your presence here now." Her baby girl was looking up at her with sad eyes. She kissed Alecia on her forehead, then went to search the rest of the house. The bathroom was ancient, but functional. The hot and cold water worked in his tub. She killed a huge roach in the floor. He had no toilet tissue. She used a piece of rag from her car to dispose of the smashed bug. She found an extra blanket on his bed and searched his closet. He had few clothes.

When she moved one of his coats in the closet, she heard a tinkling sound. He had a key ring with a Fiat emblem, two keys she remembered were to the Fiat he once drove, what looked like a house key, and another key she did not know what it was.

She stuffed the keys in her skirt pocket.

She took a blanket to cover him and kissed his head as she turned off the lamp in his living room.

Jeanine gathered Alecia and quietly left her Papa. Before she shut the front door, she tried the house key on his key ring, and it unlocked the door.

It was early afternoon. Jeanine had to get Alecia back to the church before quitting time. Rebecca and her husband had been faithful to care for Alecia in this interim time.

Jeanine counted her blessings.

Her Papa was alive.

Alecia had a clean safe place to stay with adults who cared.

She had good prospects of getting a job and starting to work. The lounge manager had wanted her to return at eight. She would likely be bartending that very night.

Her search for blood sources would get easier as she adapted to the ebb and flow of this city, now her home again.

Jeanine got her key from Alecia and opened her baby girl's door. Alecia slid into the moulded seat and reached for her seat belt. In a flash, Jeanine saw Alecia as a beautiful young lady with long dark brown hair and soul searching, penetrating eyes.

Then she was her baby girl again.

Jeanine smiled to herself all the way back to St. Peter's.

By early morning, Jeanine had worked and earned some money. Her new manager paid her an advance on Friday's paycheck and even tossed in a bonus because of how quickly she adapted to the scores of new customers who came in that night.

Her hunt for blood was delayed because she was working until two in the morning, but she found a large stray dog in one of the city parks. She reduced the stray dog population of Charlotte by one. By nine, she visited Alecia at St. Peter's.

The large black lady who was leading the crafts did

not seem to mind Jeanine's daily intrusion in her class. Rebecca probably explained her situation. When Alecia saw her, she jumped up and ran to her arms. She borrowed Alecia from her class and walked out front with her. A man was cutting the triangular patch of grass next to the sidewalk. Jeanine took a right and circled around to a place where she and Alecia could talk but not be overheard. "I'm going back to SJN to see Stephanie to see what help I can get for my Papa." She reached into her skirt pocket and drew out the folded bills she had. "I'm finally working." She peeled off two twenties and gave them to Alecia. "This should pay for your snacks and drinks at the concession. I'm not sure if I can get back this afternoon. Depends on what I find out and what can be done." Jeanine rattled off for a few more minutes, then distinctly noticed that Alecia was not looking at her. She was looking at the grass.

She caught herself. She had been literally ignoring Alecia because her mind was so crammed with what she wanted to do for her Papa. Her baby girl had needs too and Alecia had not been with her since yesterday.

Jeanine stopped talking and knelt in front of Alecia. Something was wrong. "I'm sorry, baby girl. Hug?"

Jeanine held her arms wide for Alecia.

She was being very quiet. Almost shy.

Her voice was almost inaudible, except for vampyric hearing. Alecia spoke while looking down. "Are you going to give me away now that you have your Papa?"

"Oh, honey! No!" she exclaimed. "What on earth made you think that I would ever give you away?"

Alecia sniffled; her voice was thick with emotion. "Bradley said I was an orphan. He said you were gone all the time. I heard Ms. Rebecca and Mike saying how much they would like to have a little girl. I'm tired of sleeping under the desk in the den. I want to be with you." Jeanine sorted names. Mike – Rebecca's husband. Bradley – Rebecca's youngest. She saw that maybe she had been relying on Ms. Rebecca's generosity too much.

Now that she had cash flow again, that could change. But she was not yet well enough established that she could spring Alecia from her captivity. Still ...

Jeanine took Alecia's arms. "Well, baby girl. We can go back to your favorite motel. I just hate leaving you alone for so long. Right now, I don't have anyone else I can trust to keep you."

Her baby girl's eyes were so hopeful.

"Okay," Jeanine said. "I'll get us a room and I'll get you at the end of school today. You can stay with me all weekend."

Alecia finally reached for Jeanine and hugged her. Jeanine held her for a few minutes then led her inside. As she was leaving, she spoke to Rebecca and told her she would be back before three to get Alecia at the end of the day.

As Jeanine left the church and crossed the street to her Mustang, she realized she had made an important decision. If it came down to caring for her Papa or caring for Alecia, Alecia had to be first. Although she loved her Papa and grieved for his condition, she was not responsible for him. She pushed back the waves of guilt that would cloud her thinking.

Her Papa was the adult. Alecia was still a child and needed her. She drove to SJN in peace and entered Stephanie's office just after ten o'clock. Stephanie smiled and arose when Jeanine entered. Jeanine shook her hand. "Thank you for your help yesterday. I found my Papa, but his condition is very bad. I wanted to know what kind of help we can arrange for him, or even better, an elderly care facility we can move him into."

They talked about home care options and what few facilities there were operated by Catholic nursing or elderly care management that could give him a better quality of life. All options were either very expensive or had a waiting period of years. Stephanie invited Jeanine to lunch at a local restaurant she frequented. Jeanine accepted, but only ordered hot tea. During lunch, Jeanine mentioned her Papa's Fiat. They found it. Stephanie and Jeanine went to the garage where it had been stored. Her Papa's Fiat had been parked in an old garage covered by a tarp for the last fifteen years.

Stephanie arranged for a mechanic friend to come and see if it could be put back into operable condition. The car started with a new battery and fresh plugs.

Jeanine took her leave of Stephanie before two and stopped in NoDa to see her Papa. He was generally unresponsive. She heated his dinner for him and set it on the little table in his living room. She left him eating his mid-day meal. Before three, she returned to St. Peter's to rescue Alecia from her captivity and they went back to the Super 8 motel on Clanton. Alecia seemed very content. Jeanine kicked off her sandals at the door and sat cross-legged on her bed. She patted the place next to her for Alecia to sit with her. Alecia kicked off her sneakers and crawled on the bed next to Jeanine. "Baby girl, we have to make a plan."

Alecia sat with her legs curled behind her.

Although their room was quiet, Jeanine could hear the television in the room next to them. The edge on her perceptions meant she had to feed better this night than last night. She also had to report to work before eight.

"I talked to Stephanie about my Papa and some about you. She's willing to help me get him into an old folk's home. There's a place in Monroe, but it's expensive. I will have to raise over twenty thousand dollars – on a bartender's salary, it would take me years to raise that kind of money, even with good tips."

"What can we do?" Alecia asked.

Jeanine liked seeing the sparkle in Alecia's eyes. They were conspiring together against the whole world.

"I can sell my Mustang," Jeanine said.

"What?" Alecia said. She looked alarmed.

"The blue book value of a vintage Mustang kept in pristine condition is one hundred thousand. I think I can get at least seventy-five thousand. This would give us the money at one shot we need for my Papa and to set aside an account for you when you get older."

"What would we do for a car?" Alecia asked. Jeanine lifted the Fiat keys from her skirt pocket. She laid the keys on the bedside table. "Stephanie found my Papa's car in storage. It still runs. I could use his car until I can do better. The other advantage for us," Jeanine added, "would be the down payment on an apartment of our own. As it is, we have to wait for me to earn two months rent as a down payment."

Alecia seemed to understand the gravity of the decision before them. Jeanine wanted Alecia to be involved in these decisions because they could affect her quality of life and choices for years to come. Alecia nodded yes. Jeanine lifted the ragged telephone book from the bedside table and started looking for dealers in exotic cars who would likely buy her car.

Nolan accelerated over the highway plateau to reach the signal source ahead of him. Travelling Interstate 20 toward Atlanta, the signal tracers in Jeanine's car had finally passed a register. The LED indicators on the display in front of him made tiny blips as he came closer.

He rubbed his hands over the stun gun in the seat next to him. Military issue, this could put down a rhino – he was confident it would work on Jeanine.

Finally extricated from cumbersome legal entanglements in Chicago, he left the lawyers to work out details. He angrily sought out Jeanine's car ahead, but the only thing in front of him were rows of trucks.

Nolan surged forward. Suddenly the LED display reversed. She was behind him?

Moving slowly beside him, a car transport pulled alongside. In the middle of the carrier he spotted Jeanine's Mustang. Nolan swore vehemently. She was no longer with the car!

He gradually idled back and allowed the carrier to pass him, then he set in to follow it until the driver reached his destination or stopped to refuel.

The driver finally stopped at a truck stop service station and pulled into a parking space at the back of the station. Nolan drove slowly along a gravel road that led to a cemetery.

Nolan took note of the driver hitching his pants as he made his way to the men's room. He parked near the men's room and took his chemical mace with him. The man he wanted appeared to have taken the second stall. Another man was washing his hands and left the restroom a moment later.

Nolan used the urinal while he was waiting. The driver came out of the stall. Nolan rinsed his hands as the man came to the sink. Smooth velvet. "Hey, man. I saw a car in your load of cars that looks like the one I gave my old lady. Where did you pick up the orange Mustang?" Nolan smiled wolfishly.

The driver seemed to regard Nolan for a second before

making a rude gesture. The man punched the hand dryer knob and started drying his hands.

Nolan's smile never wavered.

He sprayed the man in the face with the mace. The man screamed and covered his face with both hands. Nolan kneed him in the balls just to get his attention and shoved him hard against a urinal. He pressed his forearm against the man's throat. When the driver started gasping, Nolan let the man breathe. Nolan smiled at the man. He liked the wild fear in the man's eyes. This was respect money couldn't buy.

He enunciated slowly and clearly.

"Listen to me. I am going to ask you politely one more time where you picked up the orange Mustang and who bought it. What you tell me had better line up with your paperwork."

The man squirmed. "Charlotte," he said, "I picked it up in Charlotte North Carolina from Streetside Classics." Nolan followed the stupid driver to his truck and confirmed the sale of the Mustang and the buyer.

He watched the driver leave the truck stop. Alone, in anguish, he pounded the side of his van in sheer frustration. Jeanine had eluded him again, although she did not know it! "Whether it be midnight or the noonday sun, all is darkness," he lamented. He squeezed his fists in mindless rage.

"Charlotte," he repeated to himself.

Chapter Nine

Thomas received a hearty welcome from his mother and father at the back deck of their home just before midnight. Kimberly was behind him. Majken brought up the rear. He glanced back. She was smiling with him.

She saved his life again.

He hugged his father. Something he rarely did. His mother kept fussing over the dirt and the tear in his jeans. He assured her his leg was all right. Better than all right thanks to his faster metabolism. It was all too much to process right now.

Majken made sure they fed on blood before returning to his home. Now Thomas was sleepy. This whole episode of becoming vampyric was wearing him thin.

Play along, Majken had said before they rejoined Kimberly in Thomas' car. When she spoke to Kimberly, she spoke with a British accent. He didn't know she was from Britain. She winked at him as she got into the back seat, letting him ride up front with Kimberly. Thomas yawned. He needed rest.

He stopped in the kitchen. The overhead light bothered him. It seemed startlingly bright and glaring. Thomas went to the refrigerator and, bless Mom, found the ice water pitcher full.

Thomas filled and drank two glasses of ice water. Something inside of him was changing. He had just drank blood with Majken only thirty minutes before. The water inside of him felt like it was going through a sieve. He thought to talk to Majken about it later. But right now, he needed rest.

Patricia went to Majken and hugged her.

She replied in her British voice, "You are quite welcome. Glad I could help. Everyone is tired right now. I suggest we all turn in and get a good night's sleep."

Thomas caught Kimberly's eye as he started toward

the stairs to go to their bedrooms. The knife he had cut her with was still in the waist band of his pants, although out of sight. She seemed only happy that his Mary had found him.

He was quite proud of his baby sister.

Majken joined Kimberly heading upstairs.

Thomas brought up the rear. He had not believed she would actually be with him in his parent's house, but here she was. She paused at the top of the stairs, likely waiting on him. When he was two steps below her, she leaned forward to kiss him.

Thomas responded. He kissed her.

So much of his life had been placed on an abrupt hold when she disappeared from his life. Now he was in motion again. He felt he had a lot to learn, so he withheld judging her. When they had the chance to really talk, then he expected to better understand her for the person she really was – vampyric and all.

Kimberly's face was a little flushed as she paused next to her bedroom door. Majken told Thomas and Kimberly good night and withdrew. She seemed to sense that Thomas had something important to say to his baby sister.

Thomas looked down at his own hands.

The hands that cut her and held her arm to drink her blood.

He choked. He couldn't think of anything to say. Her light brown eyes were misty. "I'm so sorry ..." he stammered. She bade him lean closer to her. She gave him a little peck on the cheek.

"I'm glad you're home."

With that, she opened her bedroom door and slipped inside. Thomas listened for her door to be latched from the inside, but she did not lock her bedroom door. The habits of a lifetime were hard to break. They had never locked bedroom or bathroom doors.

Thomas tapped once on Majken's room. She said he could come in. Her room was darker than his, but the thin moonlight in the window illuminated the narrow bed she lay in. Her clothes were piled on the floor and she was apparently undressed under the covers. Her long chestnut hair spilled around her face. She stretched and closed her eyes. He remembered from the mansion when she lay against him and went limp. After feeding she goes under, he remembered. He gently kissed her forehead.

"Thank you for coming after me."

She was breathing softly. He could tell that her breathing was much slower. All that he had to say could wait until tomorrow. He quietly slipped out of her room and went to his own bedroom.

Inside his own bedroom, he tossed his rugby jersey on his desk and pulled down the covers of his bed. Waning moonlight spilled onto the wooden floor. He saw the blood stains beside his bed. He didn't know how Kimberly kept from telling Mom and Dad that he'd cut her, but it was a miracle to be sure.

He was bone tired. Too tired for even a shower.

Thomas undressed and changed into a pair of pajama bottoms from the pile of clothes beside his desk. He found himself listening closely to the household. Majken was surely in her comatose sleep by now. He heard the mattress in Kimberly's room squeaking. She was in bed. His parent's bedroom was almost directly below him. Under Kimberly's bedroom was much of Dad's office. He could hear a muffled sound, not distinct enough to tell what was being said, but his father's voice.

He opened his window so the cool night air would stir the curtains. Then he lay on his bed on top of the sheet.

Where his life would go from here, he didn't have a

clue. At least he was not struggling alone anymore. It was more than a sinking feeling in his gut. She'd said nothing medical could be done for him. Exposure to her blood was causing him to become like her. She called it the Change, he remembered.

Change indeed.

As he lay in bed he felt around his abdomen. When he pressed on his left side, it hurt a little. That side of his body seemed larger or puffier. Before he closed his eyes to sleep, he thought of Majken as he knew her on campus, the coed named Mary Harris. Some of the happier times floated through his memory. Before he learned the truth. Before he learned that vampyric people existed.

He slept.

Thomas awoke sometime in the early morning with sharp pains in his upper left abdomen. He felt a distinct nausea, like his insides were twisted. He had an urgent need to go to the bathroom. He stumbled on the smooth wooden floor and staggered to his bathroom. He jerked down his pajama bottoms and sat on the toilet. His gut was on fire. He was doubled over and gasping to breathe. Finally something passed.

When he wiped his bottom with toilet paper, the tissue came up bloody and full of yellow puss. The tissue was slimy, too.

He stared into the toilet. What came out of him looked like bloody coffee grounds. He could see pink tissue streaming in the water. Thomas threw the tissue away and flushed the toilet. He was dizzy. Thomas started his shower and let the water get tepid warm before getting in and lathering up. The strong water pressure made him feel better. When he finally felt clean, he got out, dried himself, and found a fresh pair of pajama bottoms to put on. He remembered what she said in the cemetery.

If you survive.

Thomas finally slept and awoke sometime in the mid-morning. His mouth was pasty dry and he was very thirsty. The sun was glaring, but not yet unbearable.

He listened to the household around him.

Majken was up because the shower in her bathroom was running. No sounds from Kimberly's bedroom. She was mostly an early riser anyway. His Mom was in the kitchen. Dad was likely sitting at the breakfast table reading the morning paper.

What day was this? he wondered.

Thomas sat up slowly. He gingerly swung his feet to the wooden floor. The sunlight was reflecting golden light off the polished wood of his floor. He winced and stood completely up. He wasn't really dizzy, but he felt not quite in his own body either.

He took a few steps toward the pile of clothes next to his desk, then decided, with company, he'd better put on something clean. Thomas found a clean pair of jeans that his mother had folded. He kept socks and shoes off for now. From what he'd seen of Majken, she went barefoot most of the time anyway. He rummaged through his closet and found an older, long sleeve buttoned shirt to wear.

He stepped into the hallway and heard Majken singing. Thomas was drawn like a magnet to Majken's bedroom.

He tapped on her door once and entered.

She was singing amid the water spray in her shower. Pretty voice, but the words were foreign. He went to her. The shower door was frosted glass, but he could see enough of her with the ambient light in her bathroom. He walked softly toward her.

Before he reached the threshold of her bathroom, she stopped singing and reached for her towel draped over the shower door. She held the towel decorously over her front as she slid the shower door open from the wall. She smiled at him, her long wet hair plastered to her shoulders and back.

"Good morning," she said.

"Morning," Thomas replied.

Majken was smiling at him, obviously aware of how much of her body he could see and how much he could not see. She'd never had occasion to tease him before.

He came to within a few inches of her.

Her eyes beckoned him. The shower was still running. She seemed to lift her chin and smile at him, like she wanted him to kiss her. He smiled warmly at her.

"What were you singing?" he asked.

She seemed a little self-aware, but told him, "My mother used to sing to me when I was little. I sing what I remember, especially when I'm happy."

"What language was that?"

"Norwegian," she said. Her dark violet eyes saddened, then she added – "My mother was from Norway."

Thomas listened to her deep breathing.

"A woman of mystery," Thomas said as he leaned forward to kiss her. He had not shaved in several days and the stubble of his beard probably scratched her. She reached for him.

Behind them, Thomas heard his mother at her bedroom door, "Thomas!"

Majken quickly recovered her composure and towel. She was still behind the frosted shower door. She seemed bemused at the stricken expression on his face as he turned to face his mother.

It was like the time she caught him – well, nevermind.

"Yes, ma'am," he said.

Her hands were on her hips. "Young man, what on earth are you doing in there?"

Thomas shrugged. "Just offering to scrub her back," he replied.

Patricia stood in Majken's bedroom door.

"Young man," she directed, "you march yourself down those stairs right now and wait for her to come down like a proper gentleman." He glanced around at Majken and shrugged.

His mother swatted him with a folded newspaper as he passed her. She closed the door and followed Thomas down the stairs. His father sat at the breakfast table with his morning paper. It was thicker than the standard daily paper. Thomas reached for the funnies from his father's stack. Sunday, he realized. Kimberly would be at church. It was just past eleven. She would be home in an hour and a half.

Thomas raided the ice water jug.

Majken came downstairs fifteen minutes later. She had braided and wrapped her long damp hair on top of her head. She wore a white ruffly blouse he had never seen her wear before. She wore a long skirt that looked like wool, and she was barefoot.

He stood and pulled out a chair for her.

She sat elegantly.

Thomas' father had put down his morning paper. Patricia stood beside her husband with a glass of orange juice in her hand. She set it down in front of Thomas.

She smiled at his parents. "Good morning," she said airily.

They exchanged pleasantries and morning chit chat for a few minutes. Majken said she was fasting and did not wish anything to eat. Thomas said he was fasting also. She asked Patricia if she had any tea. Thomas joined her at the counter. She picked through the canisters. She opened one by one and held them under Thomas' nose. Under her breath, she asked him if any of these smelled okay to him. He chose the orange pekoe. She heated enough water for him and her, then prepared a cup of hot tea for them both.

He carefully took the first sip and watched her. Majken sipped her hot tea slowly.

She whispered to him, "If you can keep this down, it will help you." He'd never been a hot tea drinker before. Its taste was bitter, but the hot liquid soothed his stomach.

When they had finished their tea, Majken took Thomas' hand and announced, "Thomas once promised he would take me to see the sights where he grew up. If it is not too much bother, he and I need some time to just be together. We shan't be gone too long."

Majken made a subtle nod and Thomas followed her upstairs. From the shoulder bag she got a jar of sunscreen for him and a jar for herself. She opened her jar and began to slather the cream on her exposed skin. "Rub it in thoroughly," she cautioned.

Thomas opened his jar. The cream was thick and had a slight astringent smell. When he rubbed it in, the cream turned transparent and was absorbed by his skin.

She next found him a pair of dark glasses.

He put them on indoors. He felt like a gangster. Majken hooked her dark glasses on her blouse. She pulled her overcoat from the hanger in her closet and bid him don his coat as well.

When they were garbed alike, he let her lead the way. "Whereto, milady," Thomas said.

Majken smiled as he opened her door.

"Start with your elementary school."

* * *

High clouds spread a thick mauve and lavender tapestry across the western sky before Thomas returned home. He showed Majken every place he could think of, from the field where he first played soccer in fifth grade, to the downtown fountain where an eighth-grade boy punched him in the mouth and broke a tooth, to the place where "she who would not be named" once lived.

She laughed with him over the different misadventures of his life. When they were in school together, he'd often dreamed of showing her his home on just such a day as today. It was a little odd viewing the world through dark glasses, but his eyes did not hurt and his brain did not wither in his skull.

During the middle of the day, he took her to the old construction site, Kimberly's least favorite spot. He was a little ashamed of his feelings of hopelessness, but Majken listened to him talk about what he was thinking and feeling. She had again become the coed he could talk to about anything and everything.

But there were moments when he looked into her dark violet eyes – something inside her just took his breath away.

She asked him what he and Kimberly had discussed and how much she knew. While they were waiting out what she called the high time of the day, Thomas tried to explain how his naïve but brilliant sister's mind worked to Majken. Kimberly had uncovered his connection to the *slasher*, and she knew Majken was in the middle of all this. She also told Thomas of her and Kimberly's discussion before they found him. His sister's research skills would easily allow her to poke holes in any cover story Majken could come up with. She had not counted on Thomas' sister.

Yet all was not lost. Majken reasoned with Thomas.

Kimberly had acted to protect him and his secret, the

brutal facts of his kidnapping by the *slasher* and Majken's rescue (albeit, he was also exposed to her blood). She knew Thomas had cut her, but likely she could not fathom why.

Thomas voiced his profound belief that Kimberly could be trusted with the truth if it came down to it. Majken said she would keep this in mind. As they got on the road home, Majken broached the subject of Thomas leaving with her. "Why do we have to go right away?" he asked.

"I cannot stay here. You cannot stay here either. You are too well-known in this place and there is not sufficient population for me to find people on both of us to feed. As it is, you are in The Change. You cannot stay at home or keep your family. You will only hurt them far worse with the truth. You must leave with me, for your sake and their sakes."

Thomas immediately felt angry. The whole thing was totally unfair. She breezed in here and now she was demanding that he just leave his home entirely.

She apparently read his disdainful expression and commented, "I came here at risk to help you. I cannot help you if you fight my choices and what I know to do to keep us both alive. Your Change is very serious. As it is, you could die."

Thomas became numb. He stared hard at her. His turn was coming up. Brick house at the end of the road, just like he described for her when they were in school. They were home. Thomas' mother was on the back porch arranging flowers in a planter box. What Majken just said shocked him to his core. Thomas sulked as he parked in his spot under the oak tree. She immediately slipped into bright sunny mode and waved to his mother. She changed gears so fast, he had to remember to smile at his mother, like he had a good time today.

He got out of his car and followed her onto the back porch. His mother was showing her the flower boxes she had arranged. He pasted a smile on his face as he wrapped his arms around her. Her dark violet eyes held a moment of sadness, then the impression faded like mist in the morning sunlight.

Majken begged off the evening meal, claiming to have dined in town with Thomas. They sat at the kitchen table drinking cups of hot tea and socializing after dinner. She claimed to be exhausted and wanted to turn in early. She kissed Thomas on the cheek as she passed by him. He went upstairs after her within fifteen minutes. She pushed open her bedroom window and met him on the roof as the cool evening breeze stirred the leaves of the elm and poplar trees planted around the house.

A waning moon hung idly in the sky.

Thomas placed both hands on his knees.

"I'm sorry," he began. "I'll do whatever you want us to do without further flack. As it is, I owe you my life about two dozen times already anyway." Majken scooted closer to him on his right side. She placed her arm around his back and rested her head on his shoulder.

"I know this is difficult for you. I can see that you love your parents and sister. But there is nothing they can do, nor I can do, to stop what's happening inside your body." She placed her other hand over his arm and reached around his wrist, probably to take his pulse. She added, "The next three weeks will be the hardest part of your Change. If you survive that, then you'll live."

"What do you mean Change?" he asked.

Majken spoke lowly, moving closer to him.

"We call it The Change because your entire body adapts to drinking blood and blood becomes the only sustenance you can take to survive from then on. In most cases it is triggered by exposure to a vampyric person's blood, like in your case. In rare instances, a person can become vampyric by drinking blood and they Change. The survival rate is low. If a person is too young when they're exposed to vampyric blood, they die. If they are overage, they die. I don't know of any person older than twenty-two who has survived a reactive Change such as yours."

Thomas stammered, "I'm twenty-four!"

"I know. That is why I say if you survive."

He sat still, unmoving, and bowed his head. Majken adjusted her position so he could look into her eyes. "Do not give up," she said firmly. She waited until he looked into her eyes. "You are a strong young man and I think your desire to live will be the deciding factor on whether you live or die. I do not wish to lie to you. What you are facing is not easy. But others have survived and you can too if your choice is life."

Thomas sat stunned for a few moments.

"You called my Change reactive. What does that mean – how many kinds are there?"

Majken adjusted her position so she was facing the same direction he was. "I know of three ways: adaptive, mutagenic, and reactive. Your Change is reactive because it's like throwing hot oil into cold water. From the age of twenty to twenty-two, your body is in the fastest growth and is at the peak of sexual and physical maturation. A reactive Change means that your entire body seizes upon the vampyric condition and your body is forced to adapt so quickly. I knew your Change would be reactive because of your age when you were exposed to my blood."

"How did you Change?" Thomas asked.

"My Change was adaptive. I was young, barely in puberty, when I was attacked and exposed to vampyric blood. My body took two years to adjust to the vampyric condition, from the time I was fourteen to sixteen."

"How old are you?" he asked.

Majken smiled wryly.

"I was born in the winter of 1698. I will be two hundred ninety five on my birthday the fifteenth of December."

Thomas gasped and exclaimed, "You're two hundred and ninety four!"

"Yes," Majken replied.

She laughed and prodded him when he just sat with his mouth hung open. "Are you okay?" she asked.

"Yeah," he said. He whistled low and stared at her up and down. "You look good. You don't look a day over two hundred."

Majken grinned and took his arm.

"Why, thank you," she replied.

Thomas watched the light evening breeze stir her long chestnut hair. "The last Change is mutagenic," she continued. "This is when a person drinks blood and, for reasons we do not fully know, they survive and become vampyric. A friend of mine became vampyric this way. He was drawn to drink blood from his youth. When he succumbed to it, he became vampyric in the true sense."

"What happens if someone is too young?" he asked.

"No vampyric person I know would ever deliberately expose a child to their blood. Children are not mature enough physically to Change. It causes a collapse of their immune system, very high temperature, and swelling of their brain. It is very brutal."

"What happens if someone is too old?"

Majken replied, "If a person, say older than twenty-five, was exposed to vampyric blood, or worse tried to drink it, their body is already in a state of decline. For a brief time their body can handle the acceleration of The Change, but they quickly start hemorrhaging and generally die of heart failure."

Thomas paused thoughtfully.

"You said exposed to vampyric blood or drink it. What other kinds of blood drinkers are there?"

Majken sighed, then replied, "Other than true vampyric people, people of all types drink blood even from ancient times. Some drink in ritual, some drink ceremonially, some drink to attain immortality or extended lifespan, some drink because they like the cruelty and death associated with it, and some drink because they want to become a vampire in the classical sense – my advice to you, avoid them all."

Thomas raked his finger through his thick ash brown hair. "Whew," he said. "Who ever thought there'd be this much to it!" He told her about his reaction to the sun on the fateful family Labor Day cookout and what came out of him just last night.

Majken explained. "You were exposed to my blood. Unfortunately, you have acquired my sensitivity to sunlight also. Your body is hyper-reactive right now. Later on, it will not be this bad for you, but you will always have to be careful to avoid radiant energy, like sunlight, to avoid being sick."

She paused thoughtfully. "What is coming out of you marks the second phase of your Change. The entire inner lining of your former digestive system is sloughing off and passing. I am sorry to say it will only get worse."

Thomas pressed his fingers to his eyes.

"Don't you have any good news to tell me?"

Majken brushed the roofing tile grit from her palms and stood. She reached down for his hand. When he touched her hand, she grasped his and pulled him forcibly to his feet. At this point, he had not yet seen her fight or use her tremendous strength. "If you survive, you have a future on the arm wrestling circuit." Thomas rotated his right arm and rubbed his shoulder.

"Got it," he said lamely. Majken glanced to her left.

"Kimberly has gone to bed. Now is our opportunity to feed."

Thomas grabbed Majken's arm.

"Wait a minute," he said, "that's my sister!"

Majken regarded him calmly.

"Trust my judgment, Thomas. Your sister is the youngest, most viable donor we have here tonight. I will be careful with her. I do not want to hurt her, but we both have to feed tonight and it is better to do it while you're still in control. You were out of control when you came into her bedroom in a dream state and cut her." Thomas released Majken's arm.

"You are vampyric now. You must drink blood just to survive. You must learn to blend in with humans, be part of their lives without getting too close. Yet the ache of your life and existence apart from humanity will sometimes cause you to tell too much, to want to be seen and be recognized for who and what you really are. This is very unfortunate. That is what happened between you and me in school. I let you gradually see and learn too much about me, and now, here we are. I regret, Thomas, that you were exposed to my blood. If I could have prevented it, or if I could change it now, I would. I hope one day you will forgive me."

Majken led Thomas through her bedroom window to her bedroom and showed him her puncture set. She retrieved another puncture set from the bottom of her valise and gave it to him. This was not the happiest moment of his life, but he was at least thankful she knew how to get blood from donors without killing every person she got blood from.

She told Thomas to sit on her bed and wait until she came for him. She padded silently on bare feet to Kimberly's bedroom and entered.

Kimberly slept. Her dream was idyllic and romantic. It was a reverse on the classic story of Sleeping Beauty. In her dream, she was approaching her sleeping Prince to awaken him with a kiss. She was in medieval times.

Her Prince had long golden hair and wore a homespun tunic of bright red, blue, with woven gold filigreed stitching, and he wore a deep purple sash around his waist. He lay on a dais where moonlight spilled over his supine form. She drank in his beauty, the curve of his stately chin and the majesty of his brow. She longed for him to open his eyes and gaze into her light brown eyes with such love and tenderness. She ached in her bosom for him to touch her and for them to frolic in the most intimate manner. She dearly wanted him to kiss her and to press his full, luscious lips to hers. My Prince, my Prince, she thought.

Kimberly climbed onto the dais and knelt beside her future love. The dais stone hurt her bare knees. Her love lay on a straw pallet. She placed her hands on his chest and knelt forward to kiss him. She closed her eyes and pressed her lips to his.

She became aware of someone in her bedroom. Her bedroom was brighter than usual because Mary had drawn her curtains aside to let the moonlight outside spill across her bed. Her brother's girlfriend's long hair was shiny in the soft moon glow.

She sat beside Kimberly and rested her arms on the quilt Kim had wrapped up in.

Kimberly, now awake, stretched and yawned.

"Hi," she said to Thomas' Mary.

She wondered why she wasn't afraid.

Her guest's normally dark violet eyes appeared almost black in the scant moonlight. When she smoothed Kimberly's hair around her face, her touch was gentle.

"I wanted to talk to you away from your parents overhearing us. This seemed like the best way." She smiled at Kimberly. "When I came in, you were dreaming so peacefully. I hated to awaken you."

Kimberly stretched again. "It's okay. I don't know what I was dreaming anyway." She rolled on her right side. The gauze bandage around her left forearm had been replaced by a single rectangular bandage.

"While Thomas and I were out today, we had a long talk. I let him tell me most of the day about himself and how he's feeling. We also talked about what he's told you about his condition and me. Thank you for protecting him. In protecting him, you've protected my life and his also." Kimberly adjusted her position so she was partially sitting up.

"Who are you?" she asked.

"Thomas realized later as he was talking to you at the construction site, he slipped up and gave you my real name. My given name is Majken. I have to use other names, such as Mary Harris, to give me an identity in society. The student called Mary Harris, as such, nor Mirriam do not really exist."

Kimberly frowned a little.

"Why are you telling me this? What are you? Some kind of secret agent?"

Majken smiled. "No," she said, "nothing quite so exotic. I live a sojourner's existence to survive and live among people wherever I can find a safe place. Thomas discovered that I was not the coed I pretended to be. As he told you, John kidnapped him to get to me."

"Who is this John suspect and what does he have to do

with you?" Kimberly asked.

Kimberly watched Majken's eyes turn downward, like she was seeing. She seemed to be looking far, far away.

"John is a stranger in this modern world, like me. He has chosen to kill wantonly to get what he needs and he is very dangerous. I cannot tell you any more about him or myself without putting your life in grave danger. As it is, you know too much already and I have to swear you to secrecy."

"I don't understand," Kim replied.

"I know," Majken said. "I have to ask you to trust me, as Thomas trusts me. I am doing what I can do to see that he survives. He will never again be the same brother to you he was before he left for Trenton. His entire life has now Changed and it cannot be reversed."

Kimberly persisted.

"What really happened to him up there? Why are you in the middle of all of this?"

Majken rested her hand lightly in Kim's hip and gently grazed the elbow of her injured arm. Her eyes seemed to soften. "I've told you all that I can for right now."

Kim bit back the ten thousand questions on her mind. Majken's eyes had become very sad, deeply forlorn, and lonely. She wasn't really sure how she knew, but the eyes looking at her had touched antiquity and great pain.

She clearly loved her brother.

She had vowed to protect him and give him his life back, if it can be done.

She'd found her brother.

"What do you want me to do?" Kimberly asked.

Majken smiled.

"Just keep our secret," she replied.

Kim nodded her head. Yes.

It went against everything Mr. Colbert had taught –

that the truth must come out for the better good of the public, that the public always has a right to know, that everything is fair game to be told. Kimberly muffled her rising journalistic aspirations.

She smiled back at Majken. "I agree."

"From this point on," Majken added, "I call you friend. Thomas has such confidence in you that I believe in you also. He implicitly trusts you and so do I. I know you will not tell anyone what we have discussed tonight."

Majken adjusted her position on the bed so she was directly beside Kimberly's waist facing her. She prompted her new friend to lie still and try to sleep. She listened and focused on Kimberly's heartbeat and breathing.

There were layers of perception.

Majken focused. Calm. Stillness. Sleep.

Kimberly closed her eyes.

When Kimberly visibly relaxed, Majken rendered her unconscious. She checked her pulse and breathing, then rolled up her pajama sleeve on her right arm.

She turned on Kimberly's bedside lamp and got Thomas.

When he saw his sister lying unconscious, he became alarmed. Majken checked her pulse at her throat, then lifted her eyelids to check her pupil dilation. She used a pressure point on Kimberly's upper arm to cause the veins of her lower arm to swell, then selected a suitable vein at the bend of her elbow.

Majken sterilized the puncture site.

She made the puncture into the vein.

"You feed first," she directed. Majken adjusted the bevel of the needle in her vein. Thomas fed from the tube attached to the butterfly needle.

He stopped after a few minutes.

Majken fed next.

She immediately felt the blood being absorbed by her body. Her senses seemed to close off around her. She was only vaguely aware of Kimberly's heartbeat when she withdrew the needle, then applied a pressure bandage around her elbow. She recapped the needle and put it away.

Thomas looked stricken.

How was one supposed to feel once you've drunk your own sister's blood?

Again.

"Is she all right?" Thomas asked.

Majken checked her pulse at her right wrist. Her breathing seemed deep and normal and her pulse at her wrist was strong.

"She will be fine," she assured him.

Majken turned off Kimberly's bedside lamp and adjusted the covers around her so she would sleep comfortably. She shooed Thomas toward the hallway.

He ambled reluctantly to the door.

"I will get up in a few hours and remove the bandage from her arm. She'll probably have a bruise there in the morning, but that is all." Majken stepped into the dark hallway with him and closed Kimberly's bedroom door. Majken opened the door to her bedroom.

"What do you do with the used needles?" he asked. She grinned at him. Now he was thinking like a vampyric person.

"My sunglasses case is metal. I keep them sealed until I visit a hospital and can make a deposit into a sharps container."

Thomas looked mournful.

Majken could think of nothing to say.

She gave him a small kiss on his cheek and told him to get a good night's sleep. By this time tomorrow, they would be gone from his home. Majken undressed and lay on her borrowed bed. She listened to Thomas move about a little, then lie down. Her body began to feel numb and she was going under.

Morning was about five hours away.

Nothing further could be done for Thomas. He would simply choose to live or not.

Morning sunlight streamed into Majken's bedroom window. By her internal sense, she reckoned the time was about seven thirty. No sounds were coming from either Kimberly's or Thomas' bedroom. She had gotten little sleep herself. Majken awoke at three to remove the bandage from Kimberly's arm and to make sure she had good circulation. She checked Thomas' sister again just past four to make sure she was sleeping normally.

She heard Thomas up more than once in the middle of the night going hurriedly to the toilet. The most pressing need was to get him away from his family to a place where she can hunt before the crippling abdominal cramps in the next phase of his Change.

Majken slowly sat up and took stock of her surroundings. She had left the window open from her night musing and the early morning breeze was refreshing. She arose, gathered her clothes off the floor, and got a hot shower. She had much to arrange for today if she and Thomas were going to leave by nightfall.

She put on her sunscreen and dressed to travel. She checked on Thomas and Kimberly. Both, sleeping fitfully. She went downstairs.

Thomas' mother Patricia was washing breakfast dishes. Her husband's usual spot was empty. She explained that he went to town early to meet a client on a new project. She washed the last few dishes, drained the sinks, and draped the dish towel over the drying dishes.

Majken made herself a cup of hot tea and sat at the kitchen table with Mrs. Kline.

"Mrs. Kline, I want to thank you for your gracious hospitality."

"Call me Patricia."

"Very well, Patricia," Majken replied.

While Majken sipped her hot tea, Patricia put on a fresh pot of coffee and poured herself a cup. She put in two packets of granulated sugar and idly stirred the cup.

To Majken, she seemed distracted.

"May I ask if anything is on your mind?" she asked.

Patricia stopped stirring and folded her hands in front of her on the table. "It's nothing, really. Just hot flashes I get from time to time. Donald is a wonderful husband; I just – I just wish he would be a little more forthcoming, if you know what I mean."

"I understand," Majken replied.

Patricia took Majken by the hand, and said, "Oh, my dear. You have quite a few years to go before you have to worry about hot flashes, night sweats, or cold husbands."

Majken heard Kimberly's bedroom door open. The teenage girl padded down the stairs barefoot. When she turned the corner and came into the kitchen, Patricia greeted her daughter.

Kimberly's light brown hair was tousled. She wore a short sleeve white blouse and dark blue pinstriped shorts. The bandage she had on her arm last night was missing. An angry red cut slashed diagonally across her forearm.

"Good morning," she said to Majken.

Majken replied and took note of the bruise in the bend of her right elbow. Her mother offered to cook her some breakfast, but Kim said she only wanted cold milk and buttered toast with grape jam. The telephone rang in the hallway to Donald's office. Patricia answered it. In a moment, she covered the receiver and told Kimberly it was her carpentry boss asking when she could come back to work.

Kimberly shrugged. "I still don't feel quite right." To Majken, she said, "I feel tired, like I have no energy." Then to her mother waiting, "Tell him I'll be there Thursday."

She spread more jam on her toast, then yawned widely. "Ahh," she said, "if I'll ever wake up, I'll be fine." Patricia relayed Kim's message, wished Kimberly's boss a good day, and hung up the telephone.

Patricia rejoined Majken and Kimberly at the kitchen table. When she looked at the exposed cut on Kimberly's forearm, she said to her daughter, "Let me bandage that." She used a little first-aid kit. While Patricia was bandaging Kimberly's cut, Majken checked the pulse in her opposite arm by admiring her ringed bracelet a boy at school once gave her. Kim decided to go back upstairs and lounge around in her bedroom.

Majken traced her departure up the stairs and in a few moments, her bedroom door closed and music was turned to a moderate level. After the music started, very soon thereafter she heard Thomas ambling down the stairs. His footsteps were heavy.

He looked somewhat haggard.

Majken got up immediately and went to him. She kissed him good morning and let him sit in her seat. She got him a clean glass and the ice water pitcher from the refrigerator then began making him a cup of hot tea.

He drank four glasses of water quickly.

Thomas thanked her when she set his hot tea in front of him. She poured herself a new cup of hot tea and sat beside him on his left. She saw him wince a few times as he probed the upper left quadrant of his abdomen. His mother appeared to not notice especially.

"What are you two going to do today?"

Patricia had asked Thomas a question.

Majken countered, "I think Thomas needs to rest today." To him, she added, "When you have finished your tea, would you like to go back upstairs and lie down for a bit?"

He nodded lamely. He was out of it.

Majken thought to make an excuse to take him back upstairs. She could not tell how much pain he was in or how much he actually slept. By the look of him, little or no sleep.

He has to rest today to be fit for travel tonight, she thought.

Thomas finished his tea and trudged back up the stairs. Majken excused herself to brace him as he plodded up one step at a time. His skin felt warm to her, but she could only know if his Change was accelerating if she took his temperature over several days to see what his basal temperature was.

He thanked her when she guided him into his bedroom.

Alone, Majken helped him undress and climb under a sheet. She propped an extra pillow along his left side where he was hurting and tried to make him comfortable. A reactive Change was hard on a person even under favorable circumstances. Majken kissed his forehead and told him to get as much rest today as possible. She closed his bedroom door. She considered for a moment stepping in on Kimberly as waves of Bon Jovi songs pelted the atmosphere. She decided to wait.

Kimberly needed rest too. Majken returned to the kitchen.

She found Patricia talking on the hallway telephone. Majken drank several glasses of ice water because she expected to be outside. Mrs. Kline finished her call and came to the table where Majken was standing.

Majken asked, "Patricia, would it be possible for you to take me to Sumter so I can post a letter?" She glanced at the little round clock over her refrigerator. It was past ten in the morning.

Patricia brightened up. "Certainly."

Majken put on her dark glasses and wrapped a scarf around her neck. She put on her overcoat and followed Patricia to her car. It had a large sliding panel door on the side. She got into the passenger side and waited on Mrs. Kline to walk around to the driver's side. When they pulled onto the circular road in front of their house, Mrs. Kline seemed to be driving very slowly. Majken decided to not comment and watch for things they passed to have something to converse about.

They followed a county road north into the town. Majken recognized her first donor's overpass as they entered the main street of Sumter. The post office was on their right. Majken asked Mrs. Kline if she could meet her at the downtown fountain in an hour. Patricia said she would visit friends at the boutique.

Inside the post office, Majken bought paper and penned a simple letter to Stefan in neat precise block lettering. She wrote the date at the top of the paper in European format.

Then the body of the letter:

Found American car running. *Thomas was alive.* Engine idles rough, may need work. *Thomas has symptoms, uncertain of his survival.* Told owner would make firm offer in three weeks. *He will live if he survives the next three weeks.* Expect delivery soon. *I will bring him if he survives the three week period.*

She signed her name in her usual stylish cursive script.

Majken held the photo of herself and Thomas and slipped it in the envelope. She addressed the first envelope to a courier service with a routing code. She placed the first sealed envelope in a second envelope and addressed it to one of her mail forwarding services. Stefan would get the letter delivered to him in person by courier once it passed the mail forwarder.

Satisfied, Majken crossed the street to the Kimbrell's store on the next block. She inquired about furniture delivery and asked to speak to the delivery boy directly. A rather clean-cut young man named Joey came from the back of the store.

She directed him to bring his truck to an address near where Thomas lived, "she who would not be named," and wait between nine and ten o'clock tonight. She paid Joey one hundred dollars in advance and promised four hundred more for a few hours work.

Majken left Kimbrell's and headed for the downtown fountain. Patricia's car was parked nearby but she was not there. She browsed several nearby stores waiting. Mrs. Kline came to her car within twenty minutes. Majken felt well satisfied with her travel arrangements. She intended to get Joey to take her and Thomas to the largest medical facility she could find in Columbia. Then she would pick a new city to the north.

The fountain clock time was almost noon.

Time, Majken thought. Now it was a race.

Early afternoon Donald returned from his meeting with the new client excited about the prospect of a new project. After a cursory kiss on Patricia standing next to the refrigerator, he went at once to his office to begin making notes and draft sketches.

Kimberly came down for sandwiches and leftovers.

When she stacked the platter with food, Majken smiled to herself. Her appetite meant she was recovering well.

Majken excused herself twice from Patricia, who was putting on a roast for the evening family meal, to see if Thomas was awake or not. He was sleeping both times. Kimberly took note that her brother was asleep and turned down her music.

To pass time, Majken told Patricia of her alleged family estate in Kensington and of her modest loft in Croydon. She spoke of the library where she allegedly worked and stayed deliberately vague on the details, aware that Kimberly could poke holes in virtually any cover story she came up with.

As dusk settled over the placid sky, Patricia invited Majken to her sanctuary, a rose garden outside the house to the north.

Majken stepped into paradise.

"They are beautiful!" she said. The different roses were all colors, from deep red to peach to vibrant yellow. Two rectangular patches of earth were bordered off. Between the plots, a lattice of rough wood formed an arbor where climbing roses made a canopy.

The different scents of the roses were heady. Patricia smiled at Majken's delight in her garden. There was a little wooden shed where her tools were kept. A stone bench was placed under the arbor. By morning's light, the little garden would be dazzling.

Majken leaned forward and drew in the scent of the hybrid English roses near the arbor. Patricia invited Majken to sit beside her on the stone bench. "Donald," she began, "doesn't see this."

Her smile and her eyes held a touch of bitterness.

"He comes out here with me when I drag him out here. But unless I purposely invite him, or Thomas, or Kimberly – they don't see what's right in front of them. I tried for years to get Kimberly to develop a green thumb, but she just doesn't have one. She's not inclined to work the blossoms and soil as I do. Thomas thinks they're pretty. He even picked one for his long-ago girlfriend. It's all in what people see and what they choose to see."

Majken nodded in agreement.

Patricia rested her hand over Majken's hand. "I know that my son loves you. We knew that every time he called us. All he could talk about was you. I can see that you deeply care for him as well. He's a good boy and Donald and I are very proud of him."

Her eyes were misting, Majken noticed.

"I know there's far more to you and him than you've said. I've seen the way he looks at you. I've seen the way Kimberly is taken with you – how she hangs on your every word. My daughter is brilliant in her way, but she's the best judge of character and spirit that I know. I only want to hear it from your own lips. Do you love my son and will you stay with him?"

Majken listened to Patricia's steady heartbeat. She could hear the light buzzing of insects nearby. The soft breeze stirred the leaves overhead. She smiled at Thomas' mother. "I love him," she replied. "I will do my best to take good care of him."

Patricia brushed the back of her hand gently across Majken's cheek. "It's all in what we see and what we choose to see," she said. She pulled Majken into a hug and embraced her for several moments before releasing her.

To Majken it felt like a literal release.

"Take care of each other," Patricia said. "That's the best advice I can give you."

Majken glanced up at the lattice of roses towering over

this stone bench. She wanted to remember this moment and the sweetness of the fragrance of the flowers and the trust imparted to her. She laid her hand atop Patricia's hand and gently squeezed Thomas' mother's hand.

"Thank you," Majken said.

The two women communed in silence as the night sky deepened around them.

Thomas awoke feeling groggy.

He became aware of his bedroom, sounds sifting through his consciousness. He'd slept much of the day. When he sat up, he did not hurt anywhere. He was only mildly thirsty and he felt like a hollowness – it was hard to describe – like a, ah, slight ebb in the pit of his stomach, sorta like nausea, but not queasy like he was sick. He clearly heard his bedside clock flick the next change of the minutes. When the little peg moved and the numbers rotated around like the numbers placed on a scoreboard. He'd never focused on his clock like this before.

Thomas listened around him.

Strains of music came from Kimberly's stereo. She was obviously in her bedroom 'cause she never played her music when she wasn't there. Majken's bedroom was silent. She must be downstairs somewhere.

Thomas stood and stretched.

He vaguely remembered Majken coming with him after his morning tea and putting him to bed.

He walked naked to his bureau and pulled on underwear, a long-sleeved pull over shirt, and he found a folded pair of jeans. An open suitcase lay on his desk. Majken had told him to pack only essential things – three changes of clothes and toiletry items. Two jars of her sunscreen and his new dark glasses lay on top of the case.

He went to his bathroom and gathered his toothbrush,

toothpaste, a few disposable razor blades and shaving cream. He tossed these into a travel bag and zipped it. He picked fingernail clipper and comb from his front desk drawer. He packed two changes of underwear and found several pull over shirts like he was wearing. Travel light, she had instructed him.

He tossed two pair of faded, well worn jeans and a dress shirt into his suitcase and put his sunscreen and dark glasses in the side. He pressed on the case and latched it shut.

He glanced up. The music in Kimberly's bedroom ceased.

She came out of her bedroom and bounced down the stairs a few seconds later. It was time for the family evening meal.

Never one for tradition before, he sought his family this time, especially tonight.

Thomas left his suitcase with Majken's in her borrowed bedroom. Her bed had been neatly made and she had left nothing amiss. It looked like she was never there. Looking at the room so neat made Thomas feel sad. She was a wanderer, living among humans – a part of, but forever apart from, them.

He tried to put on a brave smile for his Mom and Dad.

He was not struggling alone.

Whether he survived his Change or not, she would be with him to do whatever she could do. For her presence with him now, he was very, very grateful.

Thomas went down the stairs and met his Dad coming through the living room going toward the kitchen. Normally, his Mom's cooking would have him running to the table. But things have changed. Literally. His Dad smiled at him and playfully punched him on the arm like he did when Thomas came home from winning at a school game – years ago.

The little table in the kitchen was set with only three places to dine. Two extra place mats were together to the left with two large glasses filled with ice.

Majken's touch, Thomas assumed.

Patricia came out of the kitchen with her roast. She carried it with both hands and the large fireproof mittens he always said made her look exactly like Betty Crocker. Majken followed her carrying the other dishes from the stove. When the table was set, the family took their places.

Donald sat at the head of the table.

Patricia at his side to his left.

Kimberly sat at her place two seats down from Patricia.

Thomas took his place across from his father at the empty place mat. Majken sat next to him on his left at the other empty place mat. Surprisingly, Donald took Patricia's hand, who took Kimberly's hand. Kimberly reached for his hand. He automatically held Majken's hand. His father spoke to him.

"Thomas, would you say grace?"

Thomas sat there, stunned.

You mean pray? It had been years since Thomas had even thought about praying – here his father had put him on the spot – he stammered, "Uh." He couldn't even remember the little prayer he used to say as a child. God is good. God is great. Let us thank him … Kimberly was looking at him with expectancy and longing in her eyes. She closed her eyes and bowed her head.

Thomas bowed his head.

"Father God, we thank you for this meal. We ask that you bless it to the nourishment of our bodies and our souls to your service." He looked up.

Kimberly added, "Amen."

Majken smiled at him, then got up and poured ice water for everyone. She had hot tea steeping on the stove. She poured hot tea for herself and him.

They sipped hot tea while the family ate.

Kimberly dug into her roast with potatoes and carrots. She smashed her corn bread into the gravy and added the field peas Mom had gathered from the freezer.

Conversation centered on the weather, how Kimberly was feeling, and Donald's new project. Every once and a while, Thomas noticed Majken looking at his Mom and Patricia looking at her. Like they had a pact.

The meal soon ended.

When she had finished dining, Patricia got up and came around to Thomas. She hugged him from behind his chair. "I think I'm going to turn in a little early tonight," she said.

Donald got up and said he was going back to his office for a few more hours work.

Kimberly was left in the kitchen with Majken and Thomas. She picked up her plate and her Mom's and started cleaning the table. Majken looked knowingly at him. Thomas glanced at the little kitchen clock. It was almost eight thirty.

He choked. This was it. Time to leave.

Majken quietly got up and went upstairs to retrieve their luggage.

Kimberly made another trip to the table and stacked more dishes in the dishwasher. Thomas thought to kid her one more time. He thought to tell her she was the best brat any brother could have. None of these words came out of his mouth.

He choked on emotion and at all that he meant to say.

Majken walked quietly by him and took their luggage to the back porch. She left the porch light off. The blue-white cast of moonlight had illuminated the yard. In contrast with the arc white light from the street lamp at the corner of the house.

Thomas stood numbly. He automatically lifted his key ring from the key holder and slipped it into his pocket.

He got up and started toward Majken on the back porch.

Kimberly came into the kitchen and just stood at the empty table. Looking at him. Imploring him. Reaching for her lost brother with her eyes. He noticed her hair had been tied into a pony tail. No matter what, she was his baby sister.

He saw her, then turned to follow Majken outside.

Kimberly followed him.

Thomas stood at the back door. When Kimberly came outside, she looked crestfallen. She immediately flew into Majken's arms. Majken reached around Kimberly and cradled her face into her shoulder as his sister cried. Then she finally stopped crying. Her lips quivered as she looked at her brother.

This was it, Thomas thought.

He bent over and hugged Kimberly.

All the arguments and fights, all the spoiled Christmas presents, all the times she'd tried to embarrass him in front of his dates, all of her infernal snooping that drove him crazy – none of that mattered now. Her voice was shaky.

"I'll miss you," she breathed. She broke down and cried when he parted from her.

Thomas found his voice. "And I'll miss you, brat," he said lowly. Majken walked down the steps. Thomas followed her into the yard. Kimberly just stood, forlorn and lost at the back porch steps. The grass of their yard drank up the white light from the street lamp at the corner of the house. Thomas glanced at the hammock as he passed it.

He felt the bulge of his keys in his pocket.

"Wait," he told Majken. She paused.

Thomas took his keys from his pocket.

"Brat!" he called. Kimberly looked up.

He tossed his car keys to her. She caught them by reaching over the steps. Her face was awash with dismay.

Before Kimberly could run after him, before his heart broke, before he changed his mind, Thomas turned to Majken and walked into the night with her. He was surprised to find the transportation she had arranged for them. It seemed the height of irony that the last house he would see in his former home town would be the former home of "she who would not be named."

Chapter Ten

Thomas awoke cold and alone. Sharp pains caused him to curl into a fetal position. The narrow slice of street light through the window of his bedroom in the third-story loft illuminated the unfinished slab floor and his metal frame cot. Thomas tried to roll to a sitting position. Sometimes this helped.

He curled and hunched forward.

The dark gray concrete was cold and rough on his feet. He judged the distance to the doorway barely passable. Beyond was the bathroom to his right and the kitchenette to his left. He grimaced in a somber mood. The pantry was well stocked for a human. Since they had come to Charlotte, he had consumed nothing but blood for sustenance. At least the bloody coffee grounds discharge stopped. What was coming out of him now was a bright pink froth that quickly dissolved in water. Majken said this was normal.

Thomas gripped the edge of the thin cot he used as a bed and leveraged himself to a sitting position.

The pain lessened slightly.

He had no clock. By the look of the amber night skyline, he judged it was about two a.m., and Majken was still out securing their blood source for the evening. He'd seen the queen-sized bed and bureau across the room from him put to good use.

Thomas planted his feet firmly on the gritty concrete and stood shakily. His insides now felt less like a sieve and more like a kitchen strainer. He ambled forward and reached for the door frame to make his way to the kitchenette to get water. His huge thirst for water had subsided as well. He still drank as much as he could from years of athletic activity and habit. Their little refrigerator was small. It was the size a college student would keep in a dorm room. For an instant, he felt a pang of nostalgia for their school in Trenton. A million years ago. He knelt and reached for the plastic jug of water and stumbled to the cups on the shelf. He filled his cup and replaced the jug in the refrigerator. He sipped the ice cold water.

It was highly refreshing.

Thomas made his way to the living room from the kitchenette. The furniture was an all in one type of couch. It wrapped around the east corner of the room. The carpet was deep blue and highly stain resistant, according to the salesman. Thomas sat on the end of the couch and let himself sink into the cushion. He idly wondered what blood stains would look like on the blue carpet.

Thomas tapped the brushed stainless steel lamp base to make the lamp glow dimly and reached for the notebook on the end table. If he tapped the lamp base again, it would get brighter and brighter, then it would go off. He'd never known that lamps like this existed. The notebook had drawn squares representing a calendar. Majken had been taking his temperature in the morning after she had rested from feeding and evenings before she started hunting. She had him lie on their kitchen table with no shirt so she could feel of his abdomen. She looked into his eyes and felt of the glands at his throat.

When he peed she wanted to see it before he flushed the toilet. He'd noticed that his urine had gradually turned clear.

She wrote numbers down the side of the page, invisible calculations in her head, he assumed. He tried a few times to engage her or to catch her attention. She winced a few times, so he stopped trying to distract her. Thomas tossed the notebook on the glass table in front of the couch. The numbers themselves were meaningless to him. His body temperature had remained largely normal, or rather, slightly below standard human body temperature.

He propped his feet on the brass frame of the glass table. He was reminded of another table not so long ago. This table had no knife taped under it. Her knives had been secured in three places along the top cushion of the couch. They were about a handspan length from the back seam of the couch. The queen-sized bed had also been prepared for guests.

A wind chime tinkled in the west corner of the room. Majken's signal. Thomas rose to his feet and grabbed her notebook and his cup and rushed for kitchen and the large closet to the left of her bed. He put his cup in the sink, folded his cot and wrestled it into the closet, and pulled the closet doors shut.

Minutes later, Majken and this guy she had picked up staggered into the living room. She was in ditzy mode – generally acting like such a complete dope so that almost any male she encountered would appear like the most suave and debonair gentleman there was. She took off one of her long scarves and wrapped it around the back of this guy's head. He took a swig of whatever was in the bottle. Majken giggled like a silly strumpet.

She started unbuttoning this guy's shirt.

Thomas knew what was coming next.

She kept leading him toward the bed.

The guy collapsed backwards onto the bed. Majken caught the dropped bottle of whatever and set it on the floor before the guy realized he had let go of it.

Thomas' pillow lay midway from the closet to the living room. She kept kissing the guy and urging him. It was way too late to get his pillow. Majken began to pirouette and sashay around the bed where the guy was watching. Thomas noticed he only had on his underwear now. She would strip and twirl with the long scarves she had. Her dance made him think maybe she'd known Mata Hari.

When Thomas shifted, his foot rammed into the folded frame of his cot. He muffled a swear word. He parted the sea of her hunting clothes around him and tried to make himself comfortable. When he peeked again through the narrow crack of the closet doors, the guy was naked and Majken was on top of him.

Oh, joy, Thomas thought morosely.

Breakfast of champions, Thomas thought. Why on earth was he thinking of *cereal* at a time like this? The bed started rhythmically squeaking. Thomas looked away.

This was an aspect of her life he did not like, but he went along because she had to do what she had to do.

He could do nothing now but wait. His toes still smarted where he rammed the cot frame. He adjusted his stance and tried to prop on his other leg. This part generally took about twenty minutes. He remembered a pre-marital couples seminar he once went to with a classmate from school a few years ago. The counselors emphasized that a couple must have quality communication time.

Instead, he had quality closet time.

The guy moaned loudly from the bed.

Thomas glanced up before he could stop himself.

She was making progress. Thomas sighed quietly to himself and looked down again. Networking. That's the ticket, he thought. When they had arrived and she dressed to hunt the first time – her low-cut jeans and her skimpy loose blouse that would let a guy see everything when she danced – made him angry. She was ... his, wasn't she?

She didn't get mad.

She didn't look at him. She just stood quietly in front of her dresser mirror and bowed her head.

He'd learned. When she became so very still, he now knew he'd screwed up royally. That evening, she just walked out and did not speak to him for nearly three days, except to prod him to take his temperature and check his abdomen for swelling.

The third evening she asked him to come up to the roof with her at sunset. The red sun was bleeding into the horizon. She tucked wisps of hair over her left ear.

Little motions and habits she had.

She looked away from him toward the sun.

Her voice was low when she spoke, but her tone had an edge. "I don't have an answer why this happened to you. I only know that unless you choose to live you will die. I cannot be Mary Harris for you again. She does not exist. She never existed. You now know who and what I really am. I cannot be other than what I am. I chose to live when I Changed and this is part of what I must do to survive. I deeply regret that you were exposed to my blood, Thomas. I never wanted you to be hurt."

She turned to look him in the eyes.

"I love you," she said, "but the one thing in the whole world I wish I can give you, I do not have. It's because of me this terrible thing has happened to you. I cannot undo any of it. We are where we are and we must choose to go on. Please live, Thomas. I do not want to watch you die."

He remembered reaching around her. He drew her close and held her. She smiled at him when they parted and gave him a little kiss on the cheek.

Thomas adjusted his position again in the closet. Through the narrow crack in the door Thomas could see Majken riding the guy now with abandon. The guy climaxed quickly and went still. Majken, too, made the sounds like she climaxed also. Touching moment. She lay on top of the guy but not with her full body weight. From his vantage point, Thomas could see she was balanced on her toes and held herself aloft with one arm.

He saw Majken reach for the man's throat. When she

rendered him unconscious, she glanced in his direction for the first time and made a subtle nod of her head.

Thomas emerged from the closet. Majken unstraddled the guy and reached for a towel to clean him up. Then she found another towel to wipe her inner thighs and buttocks. She said nothing. She did not have to.

Majken retrieved an elastic band to fasten around the guy's right arm and found her puncture site. She sterilized the site and prepared her needle and tubing. Thomas came to her left side.

"Feed," she instructed him.

Thomas placed the tube to his lips and let the man's blood fill his mouth. He was patient. The smaller tube she used took longer to feed, but it did not allow a donor's blood to flow out too quickly either. Majken adjusted a pressure point at the man's biceps. She gently altered the bevel of the needle.

When Thomas finished, she moved to the right of the guy and started feeding as well. Majken took longer to feed. She had been doing all the work, Thomas reasoned. As they made their way from Columbia to Charlotte, she explained that a vampyric person's blood needs rise when they exert themselves. Thomas recognized his exertion at Dwight's house is probably what made him require Sassy's blood immediately.

She also told him when vampyric people are deprived of blood for a day or two, or if they are badly injured, then their blood needs go up dramatically.

Thomas tried as she was feeding to listen to the man's heartbeat. He was not yet able to hear it. When Majken finished feeding, she withdrew the needle, disposed of it, and checked the man's vital signs. He looked pale. He was a big guy, but still – he just made an unexpected double donation at the vampyr blood bank. Majken slid to the floor and started picking up her hunting clothes off the floor. She tossed them into a hamper for later cleaning and found normal clothing to put on.

Majken dressed.

Thomas slipped on surgical gloves, then cloth gloves.

She found the guy's keys in his discarded pants and tossed them to Thomas. "Red truck a block and a half to the north," she said. Majken began to dress their unconscious donor on the bed.

Thomas left. It took him a few minutes to find the guy's truck and move it out back. Majken brought the guy down in a fireman's carry and deposited him in his vehicle. Thomas didn't ask. He could see the guy was still breathing. Majken checked the guy's pulse at his throat a final time, then nodded to Thomas. He drove the truck several miles away and left the guy behind his wheel and locked the vehicle.

On an adjacent street, Majken followed in a hired cab and picked Thomas up.

Just four months ago, he couldn't spell vampyr.

Now he was one.

Before they returned to their loft, the sun had peeked over the horizon. Majken was likely eager to get back to bed so she could rest. She lay sideways against Thomas in the back seat of the cab. Thomas rested his arm across her front from her right shoulder.

She looked at him. "How do you feel?" she asked.

Thomas was aware of the black man in the cab driver's seat. He had been glancing in his mirror several times — apparently to watch them in the back seat.

Her question caught him by surprise.

How do I feel? he wondered to himself.

Her dark violet eyes were searching his brown eyes.

He didn't relish what he had become. God only knows

where he'll end up. When he was with Kimberly at the construction site, she begged him to stop and live. Because Majken had come for him, he was no longer hopeless.

Majken, herself, said choose life.

He believed he had moved beyond the point of absolute resignation at his fate. He was no longer angry – at least with himself and her over his condition. He knew she did not mean to expose him to her blood. These things just happen. And he trusted Majken.

What she'd said to him on their long ago camping trip came across his mind: *All whom it touches suffer.* How true! At that point, he did not yet have a clue as to who and what she really was. He now knew she was right. He sighed. "Okay," he replied.

She closed her eyes for a moment's respite.

Thomas could tell by holding her that she was tired and needed to rest. Her body forced her into a deep sleep after feeding. So far, he had not experienced this same phenomena.

The cab pulled around the corner to their stop. Thomas glanced at the charge on the meter and fished a ten from his wallet. He paid the cabbie and opened his door. Majken got out on his side of the cab into city traffic. The morning sky had brightened considerably. It was still just below his light tolerance level. Any brighter and he would need to put on his dark glasses.

Thomas placed his arm behind Majken's back and guided her around the rear of the cab. He'd put her to bed and give her time to rest. Yet he was wide awake. At this point, he couldn't sleep even if he wanted to.

As Thomas opened the door to their building, a young urban couple stepped out into the street. They were both dressed in business attire, and the young woman was carrying a Yorkshire Terrier in her arms and the young man with her carried a briefcase. They breezed past Thomas and Majken without even seeing them. Cute couple, Thomas thought.

He found himself thinking of how much blood a given person had in their body by sight. They were young and apparently in good health. The man looked to him to have about five and a half liters. The woman, uh, maybe four or four and a half liters at most. Thomas led Majken up the stairs to their third-floor loft. Once inside, she kicked off her shoes at the door and padded barefoot to their bed. She began undressing. Thomas stripped the soiled bedsheet off the bed and spread clean sheets on it.

Their loft could be as bright or as dim as needed. In the skylight above, he'd taped black construction paper across the window.

Her bed freshly made, Majken slipped between the sheets on the right side and Thomas pulled the comforter over her and tucked it around her shoulders. He smoothed her hair out of her face and kissed her on the side of her forehead.

Thomas went into the living room and kicked off his new work boots. He no longer wore socks. He tapped the lamp and made it glow dimly. He found yesterday's newspaper and scanned the entertainment section for events and happenings that involved crowds of people. The area called First Ward looked promising. Thomas knew when Majken went under it would be hours before she would be properly rested.

It goaded him to just sit and sit and sit.

Thomas got up and went to their little bathroom and applied his sunscreen. It was still early in the day. He'd be able to walk around for a little while before the high time of the day. He picked up his dark glasses as he went outside.

The air was brisk and fresh to his senses.

Thomas stepped into the hustle and bustle of Charlotte Uptown activity. The shadows of many taller buildings still covered the sidewalks to the north. Thomas walked on that side of the street and found a main thoroughfare in the city, Tryon Street.

Majken had told him, observe everything.

Behind dark glasses, Thomas practiced seeing and hearing.

He heard the compression of bus brakes from around the corner of the block before the bus appeared. He heard the rhythmic beat of a jackhammer splintering concrete several blocks away. Thomas overheard a heated argument between a man and woman from the second floor of a tenant dwelling. A man on the street ahead of him was hawking his wares to solicit buyers.

So many cacophonies around him.

Colorful flags streamed from the tops of traffic lights. Bright displays of fashionable women's clothing were in the store windows he passed. He admired the beautiful round stained-glass window of a brick church as he passed by.

People milled around him everywhere.

A young woman passed the sidewalk in front of him. Thomas noticed her because her shoulder-length hair was very curly and honey blonde. She was taller than Majken by a few inches, but slender. The young girl with her, probably her daughter, had dark brown hair and was talking animatedly.

Thomas watched as they crossed the street together and the young woman led the little girl into the church.

He continued his tour of Tryon Street and looped back to his building. The early morning sun was hot on his face as he opened the door to their building. He no longer listened to the weather forecasts. He'd left his new watch at home. Although the sky was clear with barely a hint of clouds, he felt the moisture stirring from the ground up and it would likely pour tonight.

The shaded corridor and ancient stairwell leading up was a blessed relief to the sunlight. Majken's sunscreen protected him from the radiant energy of the sun. He decided he would go to the library to research radiant energy while she hunted this evening.

He listened before he opened the door to their loft. He could hear nothing, but she urged him to always listen before you enter a room. Their loft apartment was still, cool, and dark. He could see a hint of Majken's outline on the bed. Thomas unlaced and quietly slid off his work boots at the door. He padded to the puffy couch and picked his pillow up off the floor and made himself a bed on the couch.

He stripped off his shirt and jeans and just lay there thinking. Some birds were making a nest in one of the alcoves on the roof. Majken was now sleeping normally. She would be up in a few hours. Then they could spend some time sitting in the kitchenette. He would tell her what new events and places to go he had found in the paper that day.

Thomas opened his eyes again. He was aware that a few hours had passed. He awoke thirsty and with an urgent need to pee. He quickly made his way to the bathroom, lifted the toilet seat, and used the bathroom.

When he finished, he felt a sharp pain under his ribcage – about where the pit of his stomach would be. He lurched and held to the wall for support.

The pain increased.

Thomas caught his breath and fell to his knees. It was like a burning hot knife had been thrust into his gut. He lay on the rough concrete floor barely aware of anything other than the pain.

He felt cool hands around him.

Majken picked him up as gently as his huge frame would allow and carried him to the bed. By the time she lay him on the left side of the bed, some of the pain had gone. She had touched one of the dimmer lamps next to the bed. Thomas opened his eyes. Her face was near his. She looked sympathetic. She adjusted his pillow and smiled.

"How am I doing, doc?" he asked.

She smoothed his hair out of his eyes.

"They say the pain in this part of your Change is greater than that of a woman having a baby. I was never blessed to give birth and my Change was gradual. So I do not know personally how you feel. It is, at least, for a mercifully brief time."

Majken went to their refrigerator and got him an ice cold cup of water. When they'd gone shopping a few days ago, she got the flexible straws like they keep in hospitals for patients. Thomas had questioned her on her choice. She got one of these straws and bent it for him so he could sip his water lying down.

"Gracias," he said. The pain gradually subsided.

Thomas sipped a little more water, then lay back like he was exhausted. His entire body felt numb and unresponsive. Majken turned off the lamp and lay on the opposite side of the bed from him. She lay curled facing his direction. Her feet were cold on his right leg. He tried to move and found he could not.

He pushed back a bolt of panic.

This was part of his Change. The entire metabolic mechanism inside his body was realigning to make him a blood drinker. From time to time, Majken explained, his voluntary muscles would put out a DO NOT DISTURB sign while the rest of his body did what it was doing on the inside.

Thomas closed his eyes.

He must have slept again. When he awoke, Majken was dressing quietly in her hunting clothes for the evening. It was Friday night and many more people would be on the street in search of tonight's prey. Thomas smiled in spite of the gravity of his situation. A man who picked Majken up may think he had preyed on a young woman, but in reality, she was the hunter.

Thomas sat up. His whole body felt out of sorts, like his skin no longer fit him.

Majken glanced at him and, seeing him now awake, smiled. She adjusted her top – a shimmering loose chemise that was lavender in color. It had sparkly glitter in the fabric so when she moved, it would catch the light.

She put her hands over her head and gyrated for him. She found his thermometer and her notebook and approached him.

Majken shook down the thermometer.

He met her at their kitchen table.

"Say, ahh," she instructed.

Thomas opened his mouth obediently.

She placed the thermometer under his tongue, then gently felt of the glands at his throat. He felt jittery and out of sorts. He thrummed his fingers on the table to have something to do with his hands. She glanced at him from the corners of her eyes.

He stopped thrumming the table.

She took the thermometer and read it, then recorded his temperature in the square that represented the day. He glanced at the numbers. His temperature tended to be just below standard normal human temperature.

She made a face when she read the numbers. Thomas

didn't know if he was doing well or poorly. Majken had him lie down. She always started on his right side and palpated to his left side. The upper left quadrant of his abdomen felt very tender.

He looked up at her. "Have I told you lately how beautiful you are?"

Majken smiled at him. "Eleven days ago," she replied. From the day they first met her dark violet eyes called to him. She helped him sit up on the table. She poured ice water for him and started heating water for their hot tea. The pain had subsided – for now.

"How much longer do I have, doc?"

She glanced at him. "Seven days."

Thomas looked again at her notebook and the squares drawn across the pages. She only had one more row at the bottom of the page. His very life would come down to a week, a mere span of seven days. It was a sobering thought.

She handed him a cup of hot tea and they sat at the kitchen table quietly communing. Majken told him she would be hunting at a bar this evening. The Mecklenburg County library was just across the street. Thomas dressed in jeans, shirt, and work boots and followed her into the street.

Thick clouds masked much of the gorgeous sunset. Like he thought that morning, rain was certainly on the way. He told her of a new dance club he'd found in the newspaper. It was in the city epicenter.

Majken went hunting. Thomas went into the library.

Scholarly people, many of them middle-aged or older, huddled around the stacks and tables and chairs. It seemed anyone his age or younger was already out partying.

He stepped up to a terminal and entered several inquiries. He jotted down several call numbers and went hunting on the second and third floors. The hour and a half until the library was closing passed quickly. Patrons were milling toward the exit at ten 'til seven. Rows of lights were turned out by the patient library staff that wanted to get off for the weekend. A woman spoke to him and said the library was closing.

Thomas found himself sitting on the steps outside the darkened library after everyone had gone.

The bar was across the street.

He considered for a moment going in, but his presence among the people in there would not help her hunt any quicker. Majken had warned him to not consume alcohol right now. He wasn't much of a beer drinker anyway.

He walked across the street and milled up and down the sidewalk in front of the place.

Well, he was either going in or he wasn't.

Thomas turned and walked up the street away from the bar. He would only distract her by going in there. Majken had assured him she could find him anywhere in the city. It weirded him out when she said things like that. As he walked, his hands and feet felt numb. He caught himself on the rough cold brick of the building next to him. His breath came in short gasps.

Then the sharp pains began.

His vision blurred and he felt himself double over. He was a body length from the corner and there appeared to be a lounge in front of him. Two men and two ladies passed him as they came out of the place. His ears burned as he overheard what one of the men called him as they walked by.

Behind him, they got into their BMW and laughed as they pulled into the street. Thomas felt his back slide down the rough wall. He could do nothing else but endure this episode.

He closed his eyes and grimaced.

A female voice called to him. "Are you all right?"

A young woman was kneeling over him. Her shoulder-length curly blonde hair framed her sweet face and hazel green eyes. She spoke to him again. Thomas heard her as if she was in a long dark tunnel far away. Between the stabbing pains, he gasped, "I'll be okay – when – this stops."

She knelt on her knees in front of him.

A pretty girl, he noticed. She helped him sit up.

He remained curled with his back to the rough brick. Several more people from the street entered the lounge and stared at them as they passed.

From the distance he heard the wailing of a siren, then another siren. A fire truck and a paramedic truck sped by. He held his hands over his ears. More sirens split the night with banshee screams. The girl in front of him also had her hands firmly over her ears. He could not detect the scent of smoke, or of burning, but the wind could be carrying any flame another way. Whatever it was, people in the lounge on the corner started pouring out of the place and staring down the street.

A man stepped on Thomas' leg and nearly tripped. Several people cursed as they stumbled over him.

The girl said, "You can't stay here. My place is nearby. Can you walk?"

Thomas managed to nod yes – all of the breath had been wrung out of his body. The spirit was willing, but the flesh was weak. He held his abdomen tightly. The sharpest pains seemed to come a little farther apart, giving him a chance to catch his breath. The girl knelt along side of him next to the building and lifted him up. She placed his arm over her shoulder and pulled him through the masses of people gathering in the street.

His feet did not wish to cooperate.

He stumbled at the curb. She guided him into the street.

When Thomas looked up, a young woman dressed in black was pointing a camera in their direction. By the time they crossed the street, the photographer had moved across the adjacent street toward the sounds of the sirens. The girl pulling him along held his right arm over her shoulder. Her left arm was around his back and firmly gripped the waist band of his jeans. Thomas felt dizzy for the next few blocks.

He lapsed in and out of awareness.

They came to an older apartment in the center of the block. Less traffic here. The sounds of the sirens were diminished. She led him into the cooler corridors. The wash of cooler air over him made him feel more alert. She stopped in front of an elevator and punched the up button.

"My apartment's on the top floor," she said.

Thomas did not argue. His insides were plastered to his abdominal cavity. Maybe she would have cold water for him to drink. That would be heavenly.

The elevator creaked and wheezed to a stop. It was empty. They got on. She punched a button for the fifth floor. He noticed another unmarked button above the fifth floor button. He wondered if you pressed this one, would you end up on the roof.

The girl led him into the corridor of the fifth floor. She stopped at the third room on the right. She pulled a chain from around her neck and unlocked the door.

Thomas' legs gave away as they crossed the threshold.

A young girl bound forward. "Jennie!"

She seemed to become instantly shy when she noticed they had company.

The young woman helping him somehow held him up

and guided him into their living room. It looked like a small cozy den you might see in a fifties show. A half-finished jigsaw puzzle lay in the floor. Their couch was barely big enough for his six foot frame. Thomas lay with his calves over one armrest and his head on the other armrest. The little girl disappeared for a moment and came back with a blanket to cover him. Apparently, Mommy came home with strangers often enough.

The world spun around him.

The face of the young woman who had rescued him blurred. When the little girl stood beside her, they seemed familiar. She loosened the collar of his shirt and unbuttoned a few buttons. He didn't have on a belt and his jeans were not tight. Thomas phased out for a moment. When he came to himself, she was removing his second boot. "Wa–" he made a sound.

Thomas heard her say, "Baby girl, get me ice water from the refrigerator." The little girl ran to get it. She returned with two Kerr glass jars of water.

The young woman opened the first jar and turned him and placed the rim where he could put his mouth against it. She poured slowly. Water dribbled on her couch. "Easy," she said. "A little at a time." The little girl was standing back from her mother. She was a cute little thing, Thomas judged. Maybe seven. The young woman and the girl were speaking, but Thomas could not discern what was being said. Sounds were like muffled droning. He faded from consciousness.

When he opened his eyes again, the little girl was lying on the floor working on her jigsaw puzzle and the young woman who had rescued him was elsewhere. Thomas tried to listen like Majken told him to, but he could not discern his rescuer's whereabouts. The sharp pains had faded to a dull ebb.

He closed his eyes.

Their couch was certainly far more comfortable than the sidewalk. They did not look like they had much, but the little girl certainly hovered around her Mommy. Then Thomas remembered the pair he saw going into the church that morning. It was them.

He felt exhausted. Thomas allowed himself to fall asleep.

In a dream state, he saw the young woman come into the room with two bowls. The little girl had gone to her bedroom, Thomas presumed. The young woman bared his arm below his elbow and held his arm firmly. She produced a razor blade and made two parallel cuts on his forearm.

As he bled, his blood trickled down to his wrist and dripped into the bowl on the floor. Thomas knew he was not dreaming this – she drank the blood from the first bowl and started filling the second.

She was a vampyric girl or a loon.

If he was asleep, how did he know what she was doing with his eyes closed? He wanted to stir to consciousness, but he found his muscles were not cooperating right now. She was done. From the far reaches of his consciousness, he was aware that the young woman was in her bathroom dry heaving over her toilet.

He slept.

When he awoke, he found a tight bandage on his forearm. Their little home was quiet except for the ticking of a mechanical clock on a fireplace mantle. Thomas could move. He sat up. Wind blew loose weather stripping against the glass pane. It was only a few minutes past ten.

When he stood the floor creaked. Thomas searched for his boots. A bedroom door opened. Thomas faced the young woman. She was wrapping a housecoat over a tiny slip.

"Good. You're awake. How do you feel?"

"Okay," Thomas replied.

The next moment, another bedroom door opened and the little girl poked her head out. Her mother reached for her and she slid into her arms.

"Who are you?" Thomas asked.

His rescuer smiled. "My name is Jeanine Jones. This is my daughter Alecia." Thomas extended his hand. The young woman shook his hand first, then the little girl.

Thomas smiled. "My name is Thomas Smith," he said. Thomas looked for a way to open the conversation without the little girl present, but he finally had to say what he had to say.

He looked her in the eyes.

"You drank my blood while I was out. I saw you cut my forearm and drain it into bowls. Then I heard you throw up. You're vampyric, aren't you?"

The young woman was nonplussed.

The little girl looked up at her mother and said, "He knows what you are." The young woman seemed to catch her breath.

She finally said, "I'm sanguine."

"What?" Thomas said. "What's sanguine?"

Jeanine replied, "Latin – for *blood*."

Thomas persisted. "You are a literal blood drinker, though. You've gone through the Change?"

Jeanine stammered, "Yes – but how did you know?"

"How long ago?" Thomas asked. He was on a roll.

"Twenty-five years ago," she said.

Made perfect sense, Thomas thought.

"I'm going through my Change now. When I was out, I saw you. Although I was dreaming, I knew what you were doing. I don't know how I knew it." Jeanine offered they should go into the living room and have a chat. Thomas took the couch. Jeanine and her daughter sat in a padded chair covered with the same twilled upholstery as the couch. Alecia sat on Jeanine's knee.

Thomas judged Jeanine's appearance.

If she had been vampyric for twenty-five years, then the little girl with her could not be her own biological child. Thomas decided to tiptoe softly over this point. The little girl and her mother seemed inseparable.

"What happened to you?" Thomas asked.

Jeanine cleared her throat.

"I'm from Charlotte originally. My boyfriend at the time persuaded me to go to California with him. We landed in a blood cult – in essence, he died and I did not." She made a gesture with her hands. "I've been this way for twenty-four years. Alecia is the daughter of the fourth blood cult leader. I discovered he wants to sacrifice her so he can become a vampire himself. I doubt if it would work for him. He's been drinking my blood for years and he has aged. To save Alecia's life, I ran with her, and we found ourselves here."

Thomas recalled what Majken had said.

"You drank blood as a human being and became vampyric?" Thomas clarified.

"What do you mean 'vampiric'?" she asked.

Thomas found a scratch pad and the stub of a pencil and wrote the word for her.

"Vampyric," Thomas explained.

"Your body has a vampyric medical condition that forces you to only consume blood for sustenance. It is marked by a profound Change and, from that time on, the person does not appear to age at the same normal rate. We do age, just like everybody else, but the effect on our bodies is not the same as normal people. We are human, yet not human; forced to live by blood alone."

Jeanine nodded numbly in agreement.

"Your Change was mutagenic. This is when a normal human consumes blood and becomes vampyric in the true sense. The survival rate is very low."

"What about you?" Alecia asked boldly.

Alecia was wiggling her legs as she rested on Jeanine's knee.

"I met and fell in love with a coed from school up north. But she was a vampyric girl. I was caught in a fight between her and a vampyric killer. I was exposed to her blood – and," he said with a flourish, "here we are."

"How many times were you exposed to her blood?" Jeanine asked.

"Once," Thomas answered.

Jeanine exclaimed, "Once?!"

She set Alecia off her knee, but wrapped her arms protectively around her charge.

"Nolan, her Daddy, did everything but bathe in my blood for six years. He started when he was twenty-two – now he's twenty-eight. He's already aging. I don't doubt what you're saying, but I don't see how you can be exposed once and get it and someone like Nolan and the blood cult members not get it, even after trying to get it for years."

Thomas held up his hands in defense.

"Hey," Thomas said, "I'm new at this. I only know what my girlfriend told me about the vampyric condition less than two weeks ago. If you're going to ask hard questions, better ask Majken."

"Who?" Jeanine asked.

"My girlfriend – well, she's not Mary Harris anymore. Her real name is Majken." Thomas wrote Majken's name on the little slip of paper also. Then he ripped the note into little bits. Jeanine repeated Majken's name.

"Who is Mary Harris?" Jeanine asked.

"Majken was Mary Harris. That was her student alias," Thomas replied.

Thomas further explained. "I met her as Mary Harris in Trenton. We were at the same college. We dated and became very close. I didn't know she was vampyric. I thought she was promiscuous or had emotional problems. I still cared for her and wanted to be with her. One of the professors was putting pressure on her because his son died – I found out she was vampyric the night I went with her after an award's program the school does annually. She kept disappearing, even more than usual. I didn't find out until later that she was trying to get rid of a killer vampyr in the city. I was exposed to her blood in that fight."

Jeanine and Alecia exchanged glances.

"She had another name," Alecia said.

"Yes," Jeanine added, "we have a problem with our identities. We need a way to get new names so Nolan can't track us. My driver's license from California is known by the blood cult. I can't enroll Alecia in public schools here because her former school records are traceable. Do you think your girlfriend would help us? At least tell us what to do."

Thomas considered. "I don't see why she wouldn't."

Jeanine slipped off the chair and knelt in the floor before Alecia. "Baby girl, will you be all right here alone for a while? This is our chance to be totally free."

"Yes, Jennie," Alecia said.

"May I come with you?" Jeanine asked Thomas.

Thomas shrugged. "I guess she wouldn't mind." He found his boots and sat on the couch to put them on. Jeanine went to her room to get dressed. He then noticed the jigsaw puzzle on the floor was missing. He spoke to the little girl.

"Got tired of your puzzle?"

"Finished it," Alecia replied.

Sure enough, on the wall, the puzzle had been covered with a thin plastic. It was hung on the wall next to the little girl's bedroom. It was a harbor, with colorful boats and a dock. It must have had a thousand pieces. Thomas was impressed.

"You need to meet my sister. You and her would get along great together."

He finished lacing his boots and stood. A moment later, Jeanine came out of her bedroom wearing a simple cotton blouse, jeans, and sandals.

Jeanine knelt before Alecia and Alecia gave her a hug. She held her daughter and seemed to relish each moment of their time together. "I'll be back soon," she promised. Alecia went to her bedroom door and waited there until Jeanine followed Thomas into the hallway. She lifted her key from the chain around her neck and locked the door from the outside.

They made their way to the rickety elevator and it slowly wheezed down five floors. Thomas judged it was not too late, not past eleven, but the building seemed deserted. Jeanine said the building, once commercial, had been converted to apartments. She commented that many of the tenants were elderly and only lived on the first two floors. Gusts of wind blew around them as they stepped into the nearly deserted street.

Thomas noticed that Jeanine held back to let him lead. Twenty-five years, he mused. Depending on her age when she became vampyric – at least less than twenty, he was sure, Jeanine would be about the actual age of his Mom! He paused for a moment at a street corner, then the light changed. Whatever the pandemonium from the sirens earlier, the sidewalks were now largely deserted.

The little bar in the middle of the city block was still in high swing. Thomas and Jeanine stepped into the door and was met by a little man, backed up by a bouncer.

"ID please," he said in a tiny voice.

Thomas reached for his wallet and produced his license. The man nodded for him to pass.

Jeanine had her license in a skirt pocket. When she held her license for the man to read it, he held up his hand. Thomas thought he saw Jeanine recoil in fear. The little man adjusted his position to better view her, then nodded for her to pass also.

The little bar was dark and noisy. The band on stage was trying, but the enthusiasm of the crowd registered barely above conscious. Jeanine waited near the entrance while Thomas made a circuit through the room and back. He shrugged when he returned to his new friend. "She's not here."

It was actually a relief to step out of the bar back onto the street. Thomas looked over the darkened library.

"She may be at the dance place." Thomas led the way upstreet. From two blocks away a reverberating pounding beat could be heard.

The dance club was swathed in bright neon. You entered on the third floor looking down. People thronged around the banisters over the dance floor. The dance floor itself had lighted squares that pulsated with the beat. Thomas spotted Majken immediately on the dance floor below dancing with some guy.

"There she is," Thomas shouted over the din. He pointed. Jeanine leaned over the rail and looked down his arm.

"Her?" Jeanine shouted back. She pointed. "The girl in the lavender top?" Thomas shook his head affirmative. She motioned Thomas back. She led him to a less populated area overlooking the floor.

"Why, Thomas. She's lovely!"

A waitress carrying a tray passed by and asked if they wanted anything to drink. They politely declined.

Thomas leaned close to Jeanine's ear and said, "She's two hundred and ninety four years old." Jeanine exclaimed disbelief. He gestured to her again. "I told her she didn't look a day over two hundred."

Another waitress stopped by to ask if they wanted to buy drinks. The dance place had a mandatory tab – everyone who entered was required to buy some alcoholic drink. Thomas waved the waitress by.

"I can't stay here – during my Change I can't drink. We'd better go. No telling how long she'll be before she gets a guy to come with her to our loft."

He motioned toward the door. "C'mon," he said.

Jeanine took his hand and followed him through the throngs of people pulsating with the rhythmic beat. Several blocks away, on the street, his head was still pounding.

The sky opened and torrents of rain filled the city night. Thomas held Jeanine as they made their way to the loft apartment. They were drenched and freezing cold by the time they got into the building.

Not yet eleven, Thomas led Jeanine to the loft and unlocked the door. The studio was spacious compared to Jeanine and Alecia's small apartment. Jeanine stood just inside the door dripping on the floor.

Thomas unlaced his boots and left them in the kitchenette. Jeanine left her sandals by the couch. Thomas went into the bathroom and found towels. A few moments later Jeanine used their bathroom and came into the living area. She held her towel over her front. Thomas noticed her cotton blouse was literally transparent. She was shivering.

"You're still cold," he said.

"I'm always cold," she replied.

When Thomas moved, his jeans and long-sleeved shirt were heavy on his body. The cold wet garments clung to him. He led Jeanine to the bed. "We'd better get out of these wet clothes," he said, as he found two dry blankets for them to wrap in. He drew down the cover of the bed. He turned on the dimmer lamp.

Thomas pulled two chairs from the kitchenette into the bedroom. He undressed to his underwear and placed his sodden shirt and jeans over the back of the chair. Jeanine did likewise.

Nude to her panties only, Thomas wrapped Jeanine in a blanket and led her to the bed. She continued to shiver. He noticed her eyes distinctly for the first time. A lovely hazel green. Jeanine's pale alabaster skin was beautiful and unflawed. She was taller than Majken by a few inches.

Remembering his manners, he asked her if she could drink hot tea. Jeanine said yes. Thomas got up and went into the kitchenette to make them both a cup of hot tea. She accepted the cup of hot tea gratefully and took a sip.

Thomas rewrapped himself in his blanket and curled next to Jeanine.

"She's two hundred and ninety four," Jeanine repeated with dismay. "That doesn't seem possible. Are you sure she wasn't just teasing you?"

Thomas recalled his rooftop conversation with her and the wry smile on her face just before she told him how old she really was. It was all to her a matter of respect. When he'd implied the first time in Trenton how old she was, she got angry at his sarcasm. This time, he believed she was truthful.

"She told me she was born in the winter of 1698 and I believe her. I overheard her singing at my parent's home in Norwegian. Her mother was from Norway, she said.

God only knows how she survived for so long and how she got to this country."

Thomas laughed self consciously. "Majken really is a remarkable girl," he commented.

Jeanine sipped her tea. "What did she tell you about this vampyric condition? When you recognized me and what I was, I thought you were the smartest man on the planet."

Thomas briefly flushed at her flattery.

It was sincere, but highly undeserved.

If Majken had not come for him ...

"I only know what I know because of her. I can't wait for you to meet her. Alecia's so bright. She'd get along great with my sister Kimberly. I just know it."

Jeanine confessed shyly, "Our last name is not Jones."

Thomas chuckled, and said, "My last name is not Smith." Thomas smiled at Jeanine. She was a very pretty girl when she smiled. Thomas sipped his hot tea and stayed on the topic at hand and described for Jeanine what Majken had told him about the ways to Change and the types of people, other than vampyric people, who drank blood also.

He'd never heard of a blood cult before.

"He's obsessed with his lifespan," Jeanine remarked of Nolan. "My boyfriend led me into this wretched existence. I never wanted it, but these people – it's all they want."

Thomas shivered in spite of the bitter hot tea he drank. These people were evil, and it was good that Jeanine had finally gotten away from them. He'd seen sadness in Majken's eyes and now he noticed the same hollow ache of loneliness in Jeanine's eyes. He recalled what Majken once told him on their long ago camping trip.

"All whom it touches, suffer," Thomas remarked. "She said that to me before I knew exactly what she was."

"Oh, how true!" Jeanine exclaimed.

Thomas paused, then said, "That's why it won't stick to these blood cult zombies. They wouldn't suffer. They would enjoy it."

Jeanine looked up sharply. "Oh, God."

When Jeanine finished her tea, Thomas set her cup and his empty cup on the bedside table. He saw her bared pert breasts as she gave him the cup. Then he noticed a little circular mark on her left shoulder. It was like tiny pin pricks in her skin.

"What's that?" Thomas asked.

Jeanine looked at her shoulder.

"Uh," she said, "smallpox vaccination."

Thomas noticed the way her tangled hair hung in dishabille around her sweet pretty face. The little loft apartment was becoming uncommonly warm to him as he sat on the bed with Jeanine. He suddenly wished Majken would hurry up and get here. "Tell me more about this reactive Change of yours," Jeanine prompted.

Thomas said, "She said she knew my Change would be reactive based on how old I was when I was exposed to her blood. I'm twenty-four and, she said, the oldest person she knows to have survived a reactive Change is twenty-two." He sighed. "If I survive the next week, she said, then I should live."

Jeanine gently placed her hand over his. "You'll live," she said in faith.

Thomas spoke somberly. "Thanks."

He continued to explain: "If a person is too old, they will die of hemorrhaging. When a child is exposed to vampyric blood, she said, their immune system collapses, their brain swells, and their temperature goes through the roof. She said it was very brutal."

Jeanine's eyes were wide.

She seemed in shock, Thomas thought.

"Oh, God, no. Alecia!" she exclaimed.

Jeanine climbed out of her blanket and stood next to the bed looking to the north, in the direction of her and Alecia's apartment. The look on her face was total shock. Thomas heard the rain outside pounding the skylight and maybe the crash of thunder. Jeanine scrambled for her still wet clothing.

He could tell by her face, something was bad wrong.

Thomas jumped out of the bed and began dressing also. He heard her speaking under her breath, "Oh, God, no, no," over and over again. His boots squished when he pulled them on.

Jeanine pulled on her sandals and raced for the door. Thomas followed her down and down and down the stairwell. Before she disappeared into the deluge outside, tears were in her eyes. She viciously shoved the outside doors apart.

She ran down the nearly deserted streets.

The blinding heavy rain pounded the earth. Thick night clouds obliterated all moonlight in its path. Peals of thunder resounded and flashes of lightning could be seen and literally felt.

The sky was on fire in blind rage.

Thomas barely managed to keep up with her. Blue flashing lights were visible two blocks away from her apartment.

As they approached a block away, Thomas dragged Jeanine into a copse of trees between the buildings as a police officer with a woman emerged from Jeanine's apartment building with Alecia. The woman, probably a social worker, forcibly pulled Alecia along and put her in the back of the police car.

"My baby girl!" Jeanine reached for Alecia.

Thomas barely held her.

"No, wait. They'll get you too. Stop!"

He pulled her into the shadows as the blue and white cruiser passed them. Jeanine fell to her knees crying as the Charlotte police car disappeared around the block. Thomas knelt next to her. "C'mon," he urged. "Majken will know what to do."

The blinding rain made the night city streets that much darker. He got her to finally stand. Jeanine was shaking badly as he guided her down the streets toward the bar and dance club.

They had to find Majken quickly.

Behind him, Thomas noticed a white van with oddly unmatching headlights slowly pull from an adjacent street and shadow them. He could not see the driver. The windows were mirrored. Thomas took an abrupt left hand turn around the city block and the van followed them. Jeanine saw the van for the first time. She stood and backed against the nearest building. Her eyes went wide. Jeanine was clearly afraid.

She started running down the deserted city block.

The van sped across the empty lane of traffic and stopped just in front of her. A man came at her out of the driver's door. Thomas saw a flash – Jeanine fell on the sidewalk.

Her body was spasming and writhing.

Thomas saw the cruelest visage he had ever seen in the man's face towering over Jeanine's twitching body. He barely saw another flash before his body exploded and convulsed from the inside out.

Darkness closed around Thomas.

* * *

"Where's the party?" the man with Majken said as he nuzzled her earlobe.

She stood numbly before rumpled bed sheets in her deserted loft apartment. The searing white hot flash of pain in her heart obliterated everything else. Rumpled bed sheets. Blankets in the floor. *Thomas' scent with a young vampyric girl's scent on my bed*, she thought. Her empty cup was on the bedside table next to his. It was still warm to touch.

The man behind her was pulling at her skimpy blouse and lifted it over her head. He cupped her breasts with both hands.

The female's scent was in their bathroom too.

The slightly sweeter scent of the vampyric girl's urine was the telltale give away.

Majken stood numbly as the guy turned her around and placed his mouth over her nipple. He unzipped her skirt and pawed her body. Majken alone would get blood tonight. Thomas' scent was strong as the man led her toward the bed. Majken stopped the man and pushed him toward her couch. The times she and Thomas had laid curled lovingly on this couch started breaking her heart.

Thomas awoke with his face against cold hard metal. Water dripped nearby. When he opened his mouth, his lower jaw hurt and his tongue felt swollen in his mouth. He felt a sting under his chin. He couldn't speak. His throat was completely numb. All he could do was breathe heavily. No sound at all came out of his mouth.

Cold shackles bound his hands and feet.

It was still raining, but the sound of the rain was distant, like he was in an aircraft hanger or something. A heavy hydraulic door opened and the rain outside became louder.

Jeanine lay unconscious across from him.

She had been placed in a straitjacket and heavy metal bands bolted her neck, waist, and legs to the van floor. Some type of electrodes had been placed around her head. Thomas felt a rhythmic pulsing in the air.

The back of the van jerked open.

A man dressed entirely in black stood in the yellow-orange glow of sodium street lights. Beyond him, what looked like rows and rows of surveillance monitors. Thomas judged they were in an abandoned factory of some sort. Boarded windows made the inside of the old place dark to human eyes, but Thomas could still discern details in the shadows.

A police car pulled into view with lights off. Thomas wanted to scream, but could not make a sound.

His vocal cords were frozen.

The police officer and woman they had seen earlier stepped out of the vehicle. The woman proudly retrieved Alecia from the back of the patrol car.

The little girl was crying heavily.

Her dark brown hair had been tightly braided out of the way. She wore only the little jumper she slept in. Her tiny body had been wrapped neck to knees in clear plastic.

The woman handed the little girl over.

The only part of her body Alecia could move was her head and her little kicking feet.

She whimpered, "Daddy, no," when the man reached for her.

Nolan! The blood cult leader.

Thomas felt cold fear spread through his entire body.

The sound of his own racing heartbeat was loud in his ears.

They were on their way to hell.

PART III

THE WOLF AT NIGHT

Chapter Eleven

Jeanine awoke in darkness alone. She hated it when Bobby did this to her. She turned over on the small cot that had become their bed and pulled the quilt tighter around her bare shoulders. They shared a rented flat on the second floor of a Victorian house in The Haight of San Francisco. Nearly a month away from home, her love was on a quest to "find himself." To her, that meant sleeping on the floor on a cot that was barely better than sleeping on the floor itself. It was a bohemian existence.

She sighed.

If this was what he needed, she'd already decided to endure it. He seemed to want to divorce himself from his family's wealth, but he held on to the purse strings. She knew he could get money anywhere if he wanted it.

He still drove his Mustang – the envy of just about everyone they met. How do you picture him being a poor hippie, but driving a car like that?

The door creaked.

Jeanine squinted and tried to make out what he was carrying. Bobby entered with a huge hoagie sandwich and pop. Raiding the refrigerator downstairs again. He was outlined from behind by the thin sliver of moonlight and streetlight penetrating the hallway.

He was naked, too. Jeanine pursed her lips in disgust. Lately, he'd acquired a lot of new traits – like parading himself deliberately in front of the others, even in daytime. She didn't like it when the others saw him that way, especially the girls. Barb in particular. He sauntered over and used his foot to flip the quilt out of his way on his side. He sat on the little cot.

Bobby kept eating.

Jeanine rolled on her left side and propped her head in her hand. It took him a minute to notice her.

"Wanna bite?" he said with a mouth full.

She felt the corners of her mouth turn up in a smile, even at his brusqueness. She'd seen a great deal of good in him. If only he would trust himself more.

"No, thank you," she replied.

With her free hand, she started toying idly with his leg. When he sat in a lotus position, she could just wander to a lot of interesting places. Since she was up anyway … By the time he had drained the last of his pop, she finally got his attention. The glass bottle rolled empty across the hardwood floor and he turned to embrace her.

Thank God for The Pill.

Jeanine squelched her guilt and shoved thoughts of condemnation out of her mind. Since they had become lovers, all she ever thought about was holding him close and pulling him into her heart.

She cried when he got on top of her.

Jeanine awoke when bright sunlight was streaming down the hallway. Bobby was already up and out. It must have been mid-morning by now. He'd left their bedroom door open again. She flipped the end of the quilt over her upper body and scrunched to a sitting position.

Her face burned with embarrassment. Anyone coming by could see her naked. He may like to show off, but she did not!

Jeanine dressed in bell-bottom jeans and her quilted sweater. The weather was mild for August. She did not wish to get too cold. Before she went downstairs she retrieved Bobby's heart necklace from her hiding place behind an old loose board and placed it around her neck. She examined it in the little mirror taped to her inner closet door.

Each time she touched it and felt it on her skin, her heart soared. It was her own part of him that no one could ever take away. He belonged to her, and she intended that it stay that way.

Jeanine slipped on her sandals and went downstairs to see what's happening. She met Stacy coming up the stairs as she was going down. "Where's Bobby?" she asked.

Stacy smiled and pointed to the front door. "Follow the extension cords."

Jeanine found the front door ajar and an extension cord going outside. She tipped the door open and looked out. Across the front yard to the street, Bobby had wired together five extension cords to reach to his Mustang. It was a beautiful clear sunny day. She went out to see what Bobby was up to.

Bobby knelt on the passenger-side half in and half out of the car. He wore jeans, his tie-died shirt, and a leather vest with beads laced in the hem. She came up behind him. He was holding something in his hand. Then she smelled burning.

He'd taken Montel's soldering iron and was burning the black dash of their car. He was etching neat block letters using the silver solder their initials BB/JB. Bobby must have "borrowed" Monty's tools from his work bench.

Jeanine smiled. He had not noticed her yet. This was another endearment. She cleared her throat just behind him. He was startled for a second, then grinned back at her. He lay the soldering iron on the street, sat cattycorner in the passenger's seat, and patted his lap for her to sit.

She sat in his lap. He reached around her.

"This is you and me, Jen, forever."

Her heart necklace glinted golden in the morning light. Even the things he did that made her angry seemed to vaporize into nothing when he smiled at her. That look turned her insides into mush every time.

"I love you," she said, as she kissed his nose.

"And I love you," he responded.

Bobby gently prompted her to stand. He stood beside his car and took her full into his arms. She loved it when he did stuff like this. The whole world knew that she belonged to him and he belonged to her. He was right, though. She would love him whether he was rich or poor, in sickness or in health, until death do us part.

The warmth of his kiss reached from the crown of her head to her toes. Her whole body tingled and her breath came hot and heavy. Maybe they could go inside for a little more rest and recreation – like they had last night! He parted from her, let his fingers drop away from her's, and turned to pick up his tools. She guessed he had indeed "borrowed" Monty's soldering iron without asking and he likely wanted to put it back before the owner noticed it was missing.

She followed him into the house.

Joanie, the eldest of the group at thirty-one, came out as Bobby was entering. Her hair was the color of sand and wavy. Her face was deeply tanned, with the beginning of wrinkles around her eyes. She'd taken, lately, to wearing reading glasses at night when she skimmed the evening newspaper.

Jeanine was thankful she'd never been out in the sunlight much. She had a very lovely and pale complexion, just like her Mamă.

"Hi, Jeanine," she said as Jeanine walked up.

"Good morning," Jeanine replied.

"There's some fruit left in the kitchen if you want some. I put on a fresh pot of coffee, too. Our kitty's getting low on funds. We're going to have to hit the streets this weekend."

Jeanine nodded. Pan handling was the group's major source of income. Bobby kept over three thousand dollars locked in their Mustang. Yet it was important to him to be accepted by the group. That is, be poorer than a church mouse. No one was in the kitchen. The fruit had been smashed and picked over. Jeanine put it back into the refrigerator. The coffee was not too appealing either. She heated water to make herself a cup of hot tea.

In her mind, Jeanine rehearsed what she and Bobby would likely do that day. He liked to hang out at a bistro where street people from Uptown and Downtown met, a mixture of whites, blacks, wealthy urbanites, and poorer families. She could listen to Bobby talk for hours about the Vietnam war, the injustice of segregation, and the needs of people whatever their race or ethnic group. His passion and credo was that all people should be treated fairly.

She couldn't be certain, but the old guitar-playing man who begged on the street – she thought she saw Bobby press his palm to the man's empty palm last week. Like he secretly gave the man over a hundred dollars. The other thing she admired about Bobby. He had a generous heart. This was so unlike the stereotypical rich person who hoarded his wealth. And when he gave, he did not look down on the other person for not having. This sense of humility in him would make him a great man, if he would only come to the place where he trusted God and himself to just be – himself. Bobby came quietly into the kitchen, followed by Barb.

Oh, joy, Jeanine thought.

Darker skinned with long black hair that hung straight to the middle of her back, Barb had her hands on Bobby's hips dancing the cha-cha-cha behind him. She had a pretty pixie face with smouldering dark brown eyes and a come hither grin that made everyone think she was always up to no good.

She claimed to be from Romani stock, her family originally from Czechoslovakia. That, in Jeanine's mind, made her a near cousin. However hard she tried to like her and be a friend, Barb's problem was – she wanted my man!

And not just mine, she thought, *but any man that wasn't already hers*. Jeanine sauntered over and removed Barb's hands from Bobby. Barb, known as Barbara to her enemies, paced to the sink and poured herself a glass of water.

Bobby was watching her. The petite girl exuded sex appeal just by drinking tap water for goodness sake! The telephone rang and Barb picked up. Jeanine guessed it must have been a man calling. Barb went into overdrive by ohhing and ahhing.

Well, Barb had to be tolerated.

Barb's boyfriend, Ivan, had become a friend to Bobby two months ago. Ivan had the typical look of a German man, blonde hair, blue eyes, and very, very well built. About two years older than Bobby, the guy worked out. Ivan let Barb do most of his talking. He was the strong silent type, except when he and Barb went to bed. Their bedroom next to hers and Bobby's, everyone in the house knew it when Ivan and Barb were making love.

The chandelier in the living room shook.

Jeanine pushed thoughts of Ivan and Barb out of her mind. She wanted Bobby to hold her. He poured himself a cup of coffee and drank it black. Bobby got a half eaten croissant.

Who ate the other half? Jeanine wondered.

Barb's presence and high-pitched chatter ruined her appetite. When Barb laughed, Jeanine felt icicles run down her spine. She finished her conversation with her customary, "Toodaloo!" and hung up the phone.

She had a smirk on her pixie face.

Mischief was at hand.

"Tonight's the big night," she announced.

Bobby looked up with a start. Jeanine noticed he went from casual to tense in about three seconds.

Barb walked past him, pointing her forefinger and raking it across his chest as she passed, "Oh, I wasn't supposed to say that," she cooed. She laughed and swayed into the back part of the house – damage done.

Jeanine eyed Bobby standing with his arms propped behind him on the sink.

"What did she mean, Tonight's the night?"

Bobby looked guilty to her. Like she'd caught him doing something he wasn't supposed to be doing. His eyes became very intense again, like she remembered from the night of their prom.

"I told you I met some guys that have some cool things goin' down in San Mateo. We're going to one of their meetings tonight. It's a private party by invitation only. No one knows where and when this group meets, and we're very lucky to even know about it." He was scaring her.

"What group? What meeting?" Jeanine insisted.

"You'll see. Ivan and Barb will be there. Whether you go with me or not, I'm going."

Jeanine felt belittled. Bobby had never been secretive with her except for a few minor instances when they first started dating. Most of the time he was so even keeled and open. But this – this was not the man she knew and loved.

She'd find out tonight.

Bobby went out with a couple of the guys, Ivan included, and came back an hour or two later. He was his sweet self again. Jeanine could not tell that he had ever been closed.

Ivan and Barb disappeared around two in the afternoon.

Less than an hour to sunset, Bobby said, "Let's go." Jeanine felt some queasiness in the pit of her stomach. They drove down Junipero Serra Boulevard past Dara into San Mateo.

Bobby drove through San Mateo like he knew the place very well. To her knowledge, he'd never been there. He pulled off the expressway and found a shoreline road that led to a ridge overlooking San Francisco bay.

It was nearing sunset.

The view was simply beautiful!

Bobby parked over the water below.

Jeanine started to open her door, but Bobby waved her off. He quickly got out of his door and ran around to her door to open it for her. He'd first opened doors for her when they first started dating, but after the first six months he had become so familiar, she tended to open her own doors.

She stepped into his embrace.

He wrapped his arms around her.

The sun was golden in their eyes. The water glistened amber, red, turquoise, deep blue, and silver from the darkening sky. Bobby pulled Jeanine's head close.

"Jen, I love you so much," he whispered in her ear.

Jeanine drew his face to hers and kissed him. He seemed to melt into her. Such was the intimacy that she never wanted to let him go. The blue of the water seemed to match his blue eyes. She'd known from the moment they met she would fall into those blue eyes. She searched his eyes, looking for the man she loved.

"I want to tell you something I've had on my mind for quite a while," he started. Bobby took both of her hands. "You've been with me through it all, through everything my family threw at me, through all my doubts in my abilities and questioning who I am, to loving me even if I had nothing – I want you to know I would not be here today if it were not for you."

Jeanine hushed him. "I love you."

Bobby moved behind her and pointed to the setting sun. The seemingly limitless expanse of water in the bay made dreaming the impossible seem possible.

"There's our future," he said. "Forever."

His fingers lingered at her earlobe and traced the gentle curve of her neck. His breath was hot on her ear. He kissed her earlobe and nibbled downward. His hands made a brand on her soul by tracing the golden heart necklace he gave her.

His heart to her heart, forever.

She swayed gently with him.

"I'll be with you forever," he promised.

Jeanine smiled sweetly at him.

His face was achingly handsome.

"Bobby, no one lives forever. What we have is time given by God to live the fullest life we can while we are here." He seemed to draw back from her.

"What if I tell you, there's a way."

His eyes became intense again, feverish. "I – I know it sounds impossible, it sounds mad, but I believe them." He held his wrist up. "The key has been in our bodies all along. The magick serum that leads to a greatly extended lifespan. It may not be forever, but it will increase our life expectancy and potency for years and years to come. We will not age at the same rate as everyone else. We can still be standing here looking as young as we do now, feeling as young as we do right now a hundred years from now. Two hundred years from now. Who knows, by the time we reach the two hundred year mark – death would have been abolished by medical science and everyone will be driving cars that fly!"

Jeanine stared at Bobby.

"What are you talking about?"

He seemed to sense her hesitancy.

"Just try it with me, Jen. We have nothing to lose. They'll explain it in the meeting tonight. I think it's something we have to do. Trust me, baby, on this one."

He smoothed the worry from her brow.

When he drew her into a kiss, the world went into oblivion anyway. She'd said she would stay with him no matter what.

She wanted to just hold him there – forever.

The sky drew darker around them.

Bobby told her it was time.

When she got into their car, her gaze lingered on their initials etched in the dash: BB/JB. The neat silver inscription was such a permanent mark. Forever.

He drove off the ridge into the residential district of San Mateo. The houses were white frame wooden houses. Nothing really distinguished one house from the other. He parked on a street, then got out and opened Jeanine's door again.

"We walk," he answered her silent inquiry.

The house they eventually went into was not nearby. Cutting across yards, picket fences, encountering barking dogs, and ducking behind people's houses, they found an insignificant white framed house. Jeanine did note one characteristic. The back door had been painted blood red.

Ivan opened the door and let them in.

They followed a young man to the front of the house, the living room, where people of all types were gathering. Jeanine noticed some of the hippie crowd, some suits, two young guys from the military, mostly men but quite a few women. Barb was seated near the front. She was sitting with her eyes closed, her limber legs folded in lotus position.

The place was eerie creepy. Jeanine shivered although the room itself was a bit warm with all the people.

She took a seat on the floor next to Bobby.

He reached across and held her hand as they sat. His touch settled her nerves a bit. A tiny bell rang. The tinkling sound ended. All occupants seated in the living room became deathly silent and still. The anticipation was so thick you could cut it with a knife. A man came from the passage beyond.

Jeanine immediately noticed his jet black hair and black eyes. His face held scars from some accident, she assumed, and his skin was very pale. When he extended his hands over the group, Jeanine judged that his knuckles were larger than a normal man's. "Friends," he began with a deep voice, "welcome to this gathering of the Illuminati. What you will see and hear tonight must be kept in the strictest confidence. You are here because you have been hand picked and chosen. None of you are present by accident. It is your destiny to be here."

Jeanine noted the people around her. They were in rapt attention, following this looney's every syllable. Bobby, just in front of her, was seeing only the charismatic man before them.

"We follow the path laid out for us by the ancients, even from Babylon and mystics that have sought the true path that results in the fullest, most satisfying life possible. We do humbly bequeath this our knowledge to you. If you are bold enough to believe what we tell you and act on it, the benefits could work for you for centuries to come."

He rambled on for twenty or so minutes.

Jeanine really was bored. For the life of her she couldn't see what Bobby saw in all of this mumbo jumbo. The man speaking never really gave his name, except call him Leader. In her mind, Jeanine named him Anton.

Anton droned on and on.

Finally, in a crescendo, he gestured to Ivan and Barb, who were now standing to his right.

"What do you see, my friends? Two beautiful young people who are not yet even in their twenties? Nay. Study them closely. They have lived far longer than they appear. Ivan was born, in fact, before the Great Depression. Barb was born, in fact, before the outbreak of World War II."

The people seated around Jeanine started to murmur. So, Jeanine thought, they're forty and not twenty. A lot of people look younger than their age, especially if they're physically fit. She watched Bobby watching them.

Four girls dressed in black robes appeared with trays of chalices for everyone. Ivan and Barb took the first cups. The young barefoot girls sauntered through the sitting people, letting everyone lift a chalice from the trays. The girls were naked under those robes, she was sure of it. Every male seemed acutely aware of this also. When the blonde girl before her offered her the tray, she lifted a chalice from her. It was heavy and golden.

The light in the room had somehow gotten dimmer. Jeanine swirled her chalice. Some dark liquid was in the cup. When no one was paying her attention, she dipped two fingers into the cup – they came up bloody.

Her heart started racing.

Blood. They had served them blood!

The Leader took a chalice for himself and held it aloft. He spoke boldly in Latin, "*anima carnis in sanguine est.* The life of the flesh is in the blood."

"Drink, my friends," the Leader commanded.

Everyone around her lifted their chalices.

Bobby held his with both hands and put it to his lips.

Oh, God, Jeanine prayed. Ivan and Barb drank before the masses. The Leader drank. Bobby drank.

Jeanine hesitated.

Strains of psychedelic music began low in the background. Some type of smoke, like reefer smoke, came from pipes along the wall. When the masses finished their drinks, they laid their chalices down at their feet. Jeanine laid her's down also.

The Leader's eyes were riveted on her.

"We welcome you who are worthy and bold to join us. Any who are not worthy will be cast out as dung." He pointed his long bony finger directly at her. Bobby glanced around for the first time since they'd come inside. He seemed afraid. He knelt before Jeanine. Her chalice was still full.

"Jen, you have to drink it. To refuse is to dishonor the group. It's punishable by death. If you don't drink, we both die."

He picked up her chalice and handed it back to her.

This wasn't the Middle Ages, she thought. People can't just kill you and get away with it. The eyes of the group turned to her.

She was acutely aware that no one, not her Papa, no one knew where she was.

"Drink it," Bobby urged her.

Jeanine lifted the chalice to her lips.

Oh, God! What choice did she have?

She drank the blood. It was warm and had a strange taste. She swallowed it quickly and tried not to think about what she was doing. She just did what she had to do.

The group seated around her seemed to become content little blood cult zombies again after Jeanine drank the chalice of blood given to her. All eyes turned to the front.

Oh, God, she thought. What did I just do?

People began getting up by twos and threes to leave

quietly. The Leader left the room of stupefied blood worshipers.

The remaining people in the room started hugging and laughing. The mood was jovial and friendly. Jeanine wanted none of this. She intended to have words with Bobby when they got out of this house alive. Bobby got up. He held his hand down to guide her to her feet. She reached for his hand and he picked her up. Normally, when she stood next to him she always wanted to be in his arms. Not this time.

His achingly handsome face was strange to her.

When they got outside, she wanted to throw up, but could not make it happen. Bobby was silent. In the sky, the August moon was full and bright over the bay.

They drove in silence back to The Haight.

This was not the man she fell in love with.

This man was now a total stranger to her.

He said to her before they slept, "We're going back."

Jeanine slept next to him, but curled in the opposite direction. She was aware when he got up and went to the common bathroom down the hallway, and returned. He tried to touch her but she remained very still.

Bobby got up and went out before she arose. According to Joanie, Ivan took him with him to do some quality pan handling. Two sisters, Stacy and Brenda, left about nine in the morning. Jeanine was left alone with Barb in the kitchen. The old Victorian house was silent. Jeanine looked for signs of Barb's age, like any telltale mark or wrinkle. Her petite body was perfect. She paraded around naked often enough for everyone to know it.

Barb toyed with a large cutting knife and a cutting block on the table. The large knife made Jeanine a little nervous.

Her eyes were smouldering and mean.

"Did you like our party last night?"

Jeanine did not wish to be intimidated.

"No, I didn't. You people are weirdos."

Surprisingly, Barb smiled.

She arose to her feet and pressed her fingers into Jeanine's cheeks. "Don't worry your pretty head about it. We've seen them come and we've seen them go."

Jeanine pushed Barb's hand away from her face. Barb continued, "Why don't you go home to Papa? Leave Bobby to me. From what I've seen, he likes me well enough. I'll take very good care of him. Ivan won't mind. He likes to watch." Jeanine thought to slap the smirk off her face, but restrained herself. Barb was just trying to get under her skin.

Trouble was, it was working.

"He'll never choose you," Jeanine insisted.

Barb laughed her shrill high-pitched laugh. Jeanine felt the icicles down her spine again. "Well, aren't we the tigress today? You weren't so brave last night. Remember this, sweet cheeks. If you tell anyone, we'll kill you both. If you leave Bobby here, we'll kill him. If you try to run with him somewhere else, we'll come after you. At the time and place of our choosing, we'll take you and bring you back. If that happens, you'll beg to die a million times before we let you." Jeanine stiffened her resolve.

Oh, God, she thought. What did Bobby get them into?

Barb picked up the large knife and waved it in front of Jeanine's face, then made a cut across her own forearm with the knife and watched her own blood drip onto the table. She lay down the knife and licked her own forearm. The blood was visible on her tongue before she smacked her lips to savor it.

Jeanine felt sickened, but she tried not to show how she felt. She couldn't afford to show weakness. She needed time to think.

"Remember this lesson well, sweet cheeks. It's the only warning you'll get. When we see you and Bobby again, you'd better be made up and madly in love with each other. Ivan and I will be watching, and we have far more people helping than you can even imagine. When you're in, you're in for life. No one leaves, no one talks — and survives, and no one retires."

Barb picked up the large knife and threw it into the far wall. It embedded into the old plaster wall almost up to the hilt. Didn't someone say she used to do a circus act with throwing knives?

Barb left Jeanine alone in the kitchen. Moments later she heard the front door slam. She was probably going to find where the guys were pan handling today.

Dark drops of blood remained on the breakfast table.

Jeanine was sure she would never eat in this kitchen again. She got up and went to her's and Bobby's bedroom. She found in her closet her silver crucifix – the one her Mamă once wore, her rosary, and prayer book. She wrapped her rosary and crucifix in her palm. Her prayer book was given to her years ago by Mother Rosalind. Somehow she had to get Bobby away from these people.

Jeanine made her way out of the house on Masonic Avenue down Page Street, due west to the wooded area apart from the group. She and Bobby had come a few times to this park to watch the children play. Now she sought solitude to pray and think. She felt in her gut that Barb meant everything she said. These blood cult zombies were nothing to mess with. Every time she tried to pray, she kept seeing the knife embedded in the wall and imagined it was Bobby's back. Disheartened by two hours or so of trying to think of an answer, Jeanine made her way to the Pan Handle area to find the guys and try to get Bobby alone long enough to find out what he was going to do.

He waved to her when he saw her. He seemed again the carefree young man she had fallen in love with. His smile was kind and gentle again. She wanted and needed him to hold her. He made a tentative reach for her. She melted into his arms. If only she could get him to listen to her.

However, he refused to listen to her. He firmly believed what they told him about greatly extending your lifespan by drinking blood. After all, he argued, Aren't myths about vampires all over the world bound to have some basis in reality?

They found themselves back at a different house in San Mateo the next full moon. By this time, Jeanine had figured out they drank blood each time the moon was full.

Barb made it clear that if Bobby came alone to the meeting, he would not be coming back to her alive. She reluctantly drank from the chalice given her again.

The weather changed in September. It was rainy and overcast more days than sunny. The darkened sky seemed to make her mood somber and gray. Bobby was his usual happy self. She'd noticed he seemed to be spending a lot of time with Joanie, just the two of them walking and talking. Jeanine judged that Joanie had a good soul. Maybe if Bobby talked to Joanie enough, she would make him see the lunacy of this whole blood drinking idea. Her hopes were dashed when Bobby came home just as determined as he was from the first to see this through. Jeanine waited with dread for the next full moon in October.

This time, Bobby left early and took her north across the Golden Gate Bridge toward San Rafael. They entered the woodlands. This time, Bobby had a map of sorts. He made his way to the inner reaches to the ridge east of

Route 1 to a thickly shaded area of woods. He led her to
a pavilion. They were to undress and put on robes this
time. Nothing but the sacred clothing was allowed. Jeanine had to leave her gold heart necklace, her crucifix, and
everything else in Bobby's car.

Their robes were blood red. Two men appeared that
Jeanine had not seen before wearing black robes. They
carried staves and blindfolds for Bobby and Jeanine. Bobby was blindfolded by one man and Jeanine was blindfolded by the other.

They led the pair away. Bobby was allowed to keep
on his sneakers and Jeanine was allowed to keep on her
sandals. It seemed like they were walking for hours. The
trails were treacherous when you could not see. Jeanine
made a few moves to loosen her blindfold just a little, but
the man with her hit her on the head with his staff.

She fell. Jeanine heard Bobby make a move to take
the man who hit her, but his guardian expertly wielded
his staff to hit Bobby were it would hurt the most. He
fell to his knees. When Jeanine touched his face, she felt
blood on his lower lip.

They walked in stony silence.

Finally atop a ridge they were forced to abandon their
footwear. When the blindfolds came off, they were standing in the center of a circle. Only a few of the people
around them wore blood red. Most wore black.

One man in the shadows had a gold sash around his
waist. Jeanine judged this must be the Leader.

Jeanine and Bobby were told to kneel in the center-
most part of the ring. There were only six people in blood
red robes. All others wore black. It was fully night. Those
in black robes lit torches and made a circle around the
initiatees. The circle had been cleared of foliage, but the
rocks in the ground made Jeanine's knees and toes hurt.

A sweet spicy smoke came from burning pyres outside the group. Incense of some type. The aroma was thick and heady.

Jeanine prayed in silence. All she could do was kneel there. She wasn't even allowed to touch Bobby to her left. She glanced at the unfamiliar faces in the circle with her. Male and female, she noticed. The young pair to her immediate right, she'd seen in the first meeting. The other couple she did not know. The moon rose. Silver-white light spilled like blood over the remote forest. Jeanine felt like she had fallen off the face of civilization itself.

They were told to stand when the moon rose above the tree line. The Leader stepped forward. The circle became deathly quiet. Even the normal sounds of the forest itself seemed to hush. The Leader spoke in hushed tones. She recognized the phrase, The life of the flesh is in the blood, as spoken in Latin.

Jeanine shivered, unexpectedly cold.

The black robed people behind her began to hum. Ethereal light seemed to come from the torches held by the blood cult members. Jeanine felt a wave of dizziness. It must have been the smoke of the incense.

One by one, the initiatee's were placed in a single line – Bobby was in front of her and she was last in line.

A single mangled cry, a male's scream, pierced the night.

Jeanine shuddered. Her entire body felt strange to her.

Moments later a large chalice was brought into the circle. The Leader stood with the chalice lifted high. He spoke in Latin and his voice rose louder.

Apparently, he was blessing the offering.

The young initiatee, the other young man Jeanine remembered from the first meeting, one of the suits, was pushed forward. The two men next to him forcibly removed his blood red robe. He was left standing before the Leader completely naked. He was made to kneel before the Leader.

The Leader instructed the initiatee.

"Say '*anima carnis in sanguine est*'."

The young man's voice was strained and barely audible. He managed to say it. The Leader dipped the large chalice for him to drink. Jeanine couldn't see clearly. The young woman initiatee was next, then the couple Jeanine did not know, then Bobby.

Bobby turned slightly when he had finished drinking his offering. Blood ran down his chin and had spilled onto his chest.

Her turn.

The man behind her pushed her forward and pulled at her robe at the same time. She wanted to use her hands to cover her shame, but this was not allowed. The sharp rocks in the path hurt and cut her feet. This was probably by design.

She ambled forward painfully.

"Speak," the Leader commanded her.

Jeanine found her voice.

In Latin, she repeated the phrase, The life of the flesh is in the blood. When she looked up, the full moon over her shoulder appeared red, like blood. She blinked. It must have been the incense. The face of the Leader before her was cruel and without compassion at all. This was their worship and she was compelled to participate.

She looked up at the Leader with wanting eyes. Wanting to be anywhere but here now. Wanting to be home with her Papa. Wanting to be safe and loved again. When she lifted her face to drink from the chalice, the stones of the rough path cut her knees as she shifted.

The blood was very warm.

She drank. The strange taste was familiar now. She drank and felt utterly desolate and alone. She didn't think of Bobby at all. The Leader continued to pour from the chalice. She was the last. He kept pouring. She gulped and kept drinking. Anything for this to be over.

Blood dripped on her breasts and she felt blood streaming down her chin, across her shoulders, and down both arms.

Finally he stopped and she was allowed to stand.

The Leader dropped his robe and lifted the chalice to drink also. The other members, those robed in black, dropped their robes and circled the frightened initiatees. Unknown to Jeanine at the time, the established members had been given each a golden chalice from which to drink. They joined their Leader and spoke the phrase in Latin together.

Ivan and Barb were at the Leader's immediate right. Those in black were paired male and female. Without exception, the men were aroused and ready to mate. Most of the couples paired off, even the initiatee's.

Ivan came directly to Jeanine. Barb stood before Bobby. When Barbara reached for Bobby, he stumbled backwards out of her reach. Ivan stood before her and looked down on her. He was a good foot taller than her, and massively built. He pulled her shoulders to him and said deeply, "I will have you."

Jeanine pushed her hands onto Ivan's muscular chest to give herself space. Where was Bobby? He had eluded Barb for the moment. Bobby was crouched beyond Barb's reach. Jeanine implored him with her eyes. He got up and moved between Ivan and Jeanine. Ivan sneered at him, but Bobby did not move away from Jeanine.

Barb took Ivan's arm and led him away from Bobby

and Jeanine. They would have their fun later. Bobby's blue eyes were wide and afraid as he looked into Jeanine's hazel green eyes.

He was shivering under Jeanine's embrace. All around them, the couples were mating. Sounds of passion filled the forest night. Bobby held tightly to Jeanine.

He placed his face close to her ear and whispered, "I'm sorry I got us into this."

When she looked into his eyes, by the cast of moonlight, he had again become the man she loved instead of a stranger. But he was afraid and they were naked, alone, and far from home with these dangerous people. Jeanine glanced out of the corner of her eye. The Leader was watching them. They were expected to mate. She didn't want to know what would happen if they failed to do so.

Jeanine held to him and kissed him to urge him on. He was shaking so badly. She tried to touch him to arouse him, but nothing worked. He seemed cold to her touch.

His face had become a mirror of misery.

She tried to get on top of him and make sounds like they were having a grand time. She kept praying, Oh, God, oh God, oh God. When he reached up for her, tears were in his blue eyes. She had fallen into those eyes even three short years ago. Now she whispered, "Help me, help me, help me."

Jeanine did all she could do, but it was not going to happen. So she just held on to Bobby while she could. Two of the blood cult men started toward them.

Oh, God, she prayed.

The Leader made a gesture and the pair stopped short.

His face was a mask of hatred.

His coal black eyes seemed to say, Let them stay together for now. It serves our higher purpose.

The love-making grew to a crescendo as the moon reached the highest point in the sky. It was nearly dawn before Jeanine, Bobby, and the other initiatee's were allowed to dress and embark to civilization again. The black robed people just seemed to disappear. They left by a different route, she guessed.

Every part of her ached as they stumbled into their bedroom. Jeanine had secreted her silver crucifix in her palm and Bobby clung to her hand. His eyes were desolate and sad, but his gaze said he was with her again.

She held her crucifix and Bobby gripped her hands as they slept. She gathered her courage. Bobby was with her now.

The weather grew blustery and cold by November. Jeanine prayed and prayed and prayed, but silently, and tried to give their captors the impression that all was exactly like it was before. With her whispered encouragement in the night, Bobby continued to voice publicly the same opinions of drinking blood to extend lifespan.

For some reason, there was no blood cult meeting in November. Jeanine was elated. By the second week in November, she was allowed to call her Papa. The line was a little scratchy, but she waited with anticipation. There was a three hour difference in the time zones between them. He should be home between the hours of seven and eight. The line rang. Jeanine scarcely breathed. Her Papa picked up.

Warmth flooded her entire body when she heard her Papa's voice. She assured him they were okay and everything was doing well. Barb was in the next room listening. They may have been listening on another line also. Jeanine was careful to say nothing that would give away the predicament they were in.

Her Papa said he missed her and expressed his desire that they come home for Christmas. Jeanine realized that Bobby's family would surely want him home for his birthday in December also. This became her goal and plan. Surely the blood cult could not keep them from going home at Christmas. It would attract the wrong kind of attention.

Jeanine got sick several mornings in a row. Her insides didn't feel right. A stringy black tar came out of her with diarrhea-like symptoms. When this kept up for weeks, she convinced Joanie she needed to go to a doctor to see if she was pregnant. She was not pregnant.

Jeanine seemed to have a mild infection and that was all. He prescribed antibiotics and bed rest. Bobby did not wish to leave her side, not to go pan handling, or especially to leave her alone in the house with either Ivan or Barb. They made it through Thanksgiving with a quasi-traditional meal of roast duck and cream of celery soup. Joanie even splurged and threw in a bag of oyster crackers for the soup.

By this time Jeanine could barely hold food down. She sipped hot tea and kept a heating pad pressed over her abdomen. The group got her a rocking chair to sit in. They teased her mercilessly about being a granny.

She ignored their taunts. She set her gaze beyond the next full moon early in December so she and Bobby could leave.

She'd missed her period also. Normally a heavy bleeder, her menstrual flow was very spotty and greatly diminished. She worried about this. The doctor tested her again. She was not pregnant.

With everything else on her mind, it was three weeks before she noticed that Monty was gone. His tools were present at the table next to the window where he worked repairing radios, but his clothes were gone.

Brenda said he'd just left without a word.

Cold rainfall soaked the ground when the time for the full moon came in December.

Bobby was told to follow a black van out of the city at near dusk. Jeanine held her silver crucifix in her palm, prayed, then locked it in the glove compartment with her rosary and prayer book. When the black van appeared, Bobby followed. They left the city to the west across the Bay bridge and headed north into Berkley. They circled into the residential area around the University of California, and reached the hilly part of town were the wealthier homes were. Jeanine took note of streets they passed so she knew exactly where they were. Under the thick shade of cedar and cypress trees, they found a adobe white stucco home with an orange tile roof. The black van parked.

A man in standard street dress came out to escort them inside. The van that led them there drove away. Jeanine noted the intricate landscaping and work done to make the estate attractive.

She quickly squelched her ideas.

Since she and Bobby had fallen into the blood cult, she was now acutely aware that things were not always what they appeared to be. The inside was hardwood and very well appointed. The furniture was all leather. Murals hung on the walls. Pretty things to turn our head, she wondered.

For all appearances, this was a normal home. They were led through a kitchen area into a common room. Here they were allowed to wait for the evening festivities. Except for the man who escorted them in, they were left on their own. Jeanine paced back to the kitchen a few times to get water. Bobby wanted pop and crackers and cheese. Jeanine, herself, was not hungry. It hurt to walk and stand upright, but she wasn't about to show weakness to these people.

She knew when the full moon arose by the slight silver cast to the light in the estate garden out back.

Blood red robes were brought to them by the man before eight o'clock. They were told to don them and follow him downstairs.

They slipped them on over street clothes because it was cold. The man took a burning torch and led the way down, below the level of a basement, farther down than Jeanine would have thought possible. There appeared to be catacombs cut into the hillside. The walls of the tunnel were dusty, but torches lit every ten feet. Jeanine heard mice scurrying around in the dark. A huge cavern was before them. Four people waited in black robes before an altar that was covered with a tapestry.

A table with knives was set before them.

Barb pushed back the cowl of her robe.

"What do you think of my estate?" Barb asked.

"This is *your* place?" Bobby asked. His voice held wonder and awe, but he squeezed Jeanine's hand. Coming from a wealthy family himself, he was not so easily swayed.

Barb seemed smug that she had surprised them. She looked at Jeanine.

"It's beautiful," Jeanine admitted.

Barb picked up a knife from the table and twirled the point into the wood. By torchlight, her dark eyes appeared black.

"Tonight we have a special treat for you both." She made a gesture. Ivan lifted his cowl off and came forward. The two others stepped forward. One was Joanie! The man Jeanine did not know. Joanie seemed to relish the shock value of her appearance.

The tapestry started moving around the altar. Jeanine thought she could hear some type of mechanism in the floor. Two naked girls were bound and ready to be sacrificed.

Barb went to the victims and lifted the masks from their heads.

Jeanine gasped. Brenda and Stacy!

Bobby went extremely pale.

"Why?" Jeanine asked. "What harm could they have ever done to you?"

Joanie answered, "They were asking on the street about Monty's disappearance. We have people everywhere and word came back to me. You're ready to take the next step, and who better to offer their lives for yours."

Ivan picked up a curved knife and came behind Bobby. Barb picked up a similar curved blade and grabbed Jeanine's arm and dragged her toward the altar.

Barb pulled up Jeanine's robe to expose her arm. "All of these blades are deadly. Some are dipped in poison." She made a sudden slice down Jeanine's arm. The cut was not too deep, but it bled freely. "Oh, not this one." Her face had a little pout, like she was playing a game only she could see.

"You will kill the sacrifice tonight," Ivan intoned.

Bobby and Jeanine exchanged glances. He reached for the hilt of the blade Ivan carried. He grasped the blade in his right hand and held it up before his face.

What was he doing? Jeanine thought.

Barb came beside Jeanine, her breath hot in her ear. "Remember what I told you, sweet cheeks." Jeanine caught Bobby's eye for a brief second, then reluctantly took the curved blade from Barb.

Ivan stood to Bobby's left. Barb stood to Jeanine's right. The air in the little cavern became still. Dripping water could be heard in the distance. Brenda and Stacy were whimpering. Joanie and the man with her went around to the opposite side of the altar so they could watch the sacrifice.

All was ready. All became deathly still.

With a bitter cry, Bobby lunged for Ivan with the curved blade. He grazed him on his shoulder and he fell. Jeanine jabbed at Barb but she was too quick and jumped to safety.

"Run, baby," Bobby told Jeanine.

He guarded her back as she ran for the tunnel that would lead to safety. He was swinging the curved blade from side to side to keep the two men at bay. Jeanine wrestled the man guarding the tunnel entrance. He was strong, but surges of adrenaline pumped in her body. They had to escape or die. She put her head down and rammed into the man.

Pain wrenched her gut but she kept going anyway. Bobby had cut one of the men on the leg. This man fell to the floor. The other man had been stabbed in the arm. When Bobby ran for the exit, Jeanine reached for him. He suddenly stumbled and swayed uneasily and reached behind his right leg.

It ended here. It ended now.

Jeanine pulled Bobby along the tunnel. He was limping. When they reached the basement of the home above, Bobby jammed a piece of wood over the trapdoor so the people below could not easily get out. Jeanine ripped off her blood red robe and helped Bobby out of his. They ran through the upper floors of the estate, out into the drizzling rain, and made their escape into darkness. No going back.

The full moon was hidden by cloud cover.

Jeanine doubled over in the car seat.

She could scarcely breathe.

Bobby drove east, then north. They ran.

As Bobby drove, he clutched his right thigh. Blood trickled through his fingers. He swerved in the road apparently unable to see clearly. He said his vision was blurred.

Jeanine held to her seat belt as they took a northern path. The landscape became mountainous and snowy. Too many places to get stopped if they tried to drive east, he said. His plan was to go north to Seattle, then fly home. They took a winding route north for nearly two days, ending in Helena Montana where Bobby could drive no longer.

He was unable to walk. At his direction, he told Jeanine to take what money they had in reserve and buy the third trailer in the little trailer park next to the lodge.

Jeanine pulled and dragged him into the little bedroom at the back. Bobby fell on the bed and lay shivering. He had chills, but he was sweating. Nausea and vomiting. Purple splotches appeared on his ankles and along his arms. Jeanine lay next to him, herself barely able to move. Her body felt completely numb and she was no longer able to keep any food down. Tears spilled down her face.

Snowfall obscured their white Mustang.

Bobby would shake and convulse, then lay so still. His breathing became so shallow, Jeanine was uncertain whether he was alive or not. She held her rosary and silver crucifix in her hands as she prayed and prayed.

The only sound in the little trailer most nights was of her crying alone in the dark.

Something was bad wrong with her.

She would wake up in the night thinking of drinking blood.

Food of any type would not stay down.

Bobby lapsed in and out of awareness. Sometimes he

was delusional. He would fight her and other times he knew her. By the look in his eyes, he was far, far away.

She started writing in a journal.

Christmas came and went.

His birthday three days after Christmas came and went. New Year's Eve and New Year's Day came and went. The night before the full moon in the month of January 1969, Jeanine held him in her arms.

She just knew. He was going to die.

Jeanine gently caressed his darling face. Sometimes his eyelids would flicker like he was trying to arouse himself to consciousness. She wanted to hear him tell her he loved her. She ached and ached for him to speak to her just one more time. Until death do us part.

I'll be with you forever, she remembered.

She cradled him all day. Then night fell.

Perhaps the full moon on the third of January 1969 would have been beautiful for lovers to stroll under and gaze breathlessly at its wonder. He was gone and she knew it.

The next day she managed to drag herself to the lounge nearby to call home. Her Papa would come and get her. She dialed the number, but the operator said the line had been disconnected. She tried again and the call would not go through. Then she dialed the house in San Francisco. Ivan picked up.

She needed blood and knew it.

They found her on the living room floor of her trailer. How she got there and how long she lay there before they came, she did not know. They got fresh blood from someone and gave it to her. Two women and a man she did not know took her to a motel nearby for a week. She knew. Her insides were changing.

Little by little, Jeanine came back to awareness. They

nursed her by cutting themselves, one by one on a different day, and feeding her blood. After ten days, she could sit up in bed. She could hear men talking outside her motel room. Jeanine no longer cared. She walked into her trailer alone fifteen days after Bobby died. His body was gone. Everything he had, his clothes, her necklace, gone – as if he'd never existed.

The blood cult would come to her.

When Jeanine got her shower that first day in her tiny bathroom, she turned the water as hot as it would go. Yet, she still felt cold. Before her seventeenth birthday on the eighth of March, 1969, the vampyric condition in her body set permanently. She cried alone.

She had no where else to go.

Chapter Twelve

Kimberly lay sideways on her bed looking at a magazine she was not really interested in. After supper on Sunday night, what was there to do? Television was boring. Movies were boring. Music was boring. Well, not Bon Jovi, but everyone else. It had been over two weeks since Thomas left with Majken.

Mom cried all the next day. Dad really didn't seem to change except at supper. Kim noticed he kept looking at Thomas' seat, like he wished Thomas would reappear. Kim had to watch it with Mom. She'd almost mentioned Majken by name instead of her nom de guerre Mirriam.

Yesterday, just to see what they saw in it, Kimberly pushed open her bedroom window and climbed onto the roof and sat under the night sky. So, it was a roof. What was the big deal?

She flipped a few more pages of the old magazine, then dropped it in the basket at the foot of her bed.

She sighed. She really missed Thomas.

It wasn't like he was away at school or anywhere else. When Majken took him with her, he was going into the unknown. Thomas had to be at least a little scared. Whatever was wrong with him, Kimberly was firmly convinced that Majken was the only person who could help him.

The cut on her forearm had scarred.

Something to remember your brother by.

Kimberly rolled over and considered going to the den to watch some television when her Mom called. Kim got up and replied from the top of the stairs.

"It's Marsy," Patricia called. Kimberly perked up.

Marsy, her photographer friend from Charlotte! Kim quickly bounced down the stairs and took the call in the seldom used living room. "Hi, Tea," Kim began.

Tea, for the oolong tea she drank. Kim could visualize her dear half American half Vietnamese friend as she talked. "Why didn't you tell me Thomas was coming to Charlotte? I would've liked to have known so I could have stalked him properly."

"Tea," Kim whispered, "are you sure?"

Kimberly quickly covered the receiver and looked to make sure Mom was not where she could overhear this conversation.

"Oh, it's him. He's gotten taller than I remember, but even with the start of a beard, it's him. I'm looking at the photo now. He's with this girl. She's literally holding him up and pulling him across the street, by the look of it. I wish I knew what gym she works out at. I'd love to have her muscles."

Kimberly grinned at that. Marsy was in superb condition, what with all the running, jujutsu classes, and bo training.

"What street?" Kim asked.

"East Sixth, next to Bank of America."

What she remembered of Majken. Lithe and very strong. The times Kimberly reached around her, she was all muscle. Kimberly hunched forward and whispered into the receiver. "No one's supposed to know where Thomas is right now."

Marsy said, "Why are you whispering?"

Kimberly glanced into the kitchen area. All clear. Dad apparently went to his office and Mom probably went to her garden. "Sorry," Kim said in a normal voice. Yet she spoke lowly. "No one's supposed to know where Thomas is. It's complicated. A lot has happened this summer."

Marsy seemed suspicious and interested. "What's going on Kimberly? Anything that concerns your brother concerns me."

Kimberly considered her long-time friend. From the summer they spend together when Marsy had just graduated and Kim was just a teen, she was very smitten with Thomas. But he was twenty-one at the time and didn't have eyes for a high school girl.

Bad timing, really. Julie had just broken his heart by marrying someone else and, at the time, Thomas was not interested in any relationship. But Marsy had filled out well from the lanky tall high school girl into a beautiful confident young lady. At twenty, barely four years older than Kimberly, she would be a catch for any man.

Other than her now spoken for brother.

Kimberly softened her voice. She was about to step on her friend's very tender feelings for Thomas. She'd had a crush on him since she was seventeen.

"Marsy, I have to tell you something you don't yet know." Kimberly paused. "Thomas found a girlfriend in Trenton this summer." Kimberly heard the sharp intake of her breath.

"Oh, God," Marsy retorted. "You're not saying he's married or something?"

Or something, Kim thought.

"Marsy, we just met her. Thomas came home in August and – Mirriam visited with us just a few weeks ago. She took Thomas with her to parts unknown. No one is supposed to know where they are."

The telephone receiver was silent for a moment. Kimberly overheard Marsy flip the photo she was obviously holding. This was hard. Kimberly did not wish to break her best friend's heart. Yet she had to know. "Why is no one supposed to know where they're at? And what's wrong with him? He looks like he's half unconscious."

Kimberly reviewed in her mind everything Thomas had told her and everything Majken did not tell her. Quite a bit was wrong with him, in her opinion. Once her friend caught a whiff of a story, she'd follow it until satisfied. Marsy cared for Thomas a great deal. But Kimberly promised Majken she would keep their secret. That was the clincher. "I can't tell you, Tea. I have to ask you not to tell anyone else, particularly Mom or Dad, where he is."

Marsy sighed for a moment, then said, "She really is a pretty girl."

"Yes," Kim replied, "she's got the loveliest long chestnut hair I've ever seen. And her eyes are a rare deep violet color."

"Ah, Kimberly," Marsy said, "that's not the girl in my photo. The girl I'm looking at has shoulder-length medium blonde hair."

"What!" Kimberly exclaimed.

She spoke much louder than she intended. She held her hand over the receiver again and checked to see if either of her parents had heard her. Then Kimberly said, "That's not his girlfriend." Marsy seemed to become very suspicious.

"Out with it, Kimberly. You've never kept secrets from me before. I hesitate to remind you, that you owe me for getting you that intern opportunity last summer. Not to mention that you lived with us all summer."

"Yes, I do owe you, but I still can't tell you." Kimberly hesitated. This was wrong. Whoever this other girl is, it did not sit right in Kim's mind. She made her decision in an instant. "Hey, Tea. Do you and your Dad have room for an unexpected guest? If I come up will you let me stay with you again?"

"Father is having new skin grafts to his nose. He stays at the VA a lot and he's in more pain. Now wouldn't be a good time." Kim liked Tea's father, a Vietnam veteran who had been badly burned and honorably discharged. Too bad Tea's mom didn't stay.

"Tea, you're the only person I can trust. I don't know

who the girl in the photo is, but Thomas has changed from the person you knew. He nearly died this summer, and his girlfriend saved his life. I have a bad feeling about this – he should be with Maj– Mirriam. Please help me. I need to come up there so I can make sure he's okay. Just for a few days."

Kimberly waited, scarcely breathing.

Marsy relented. "You can sleep with me."

"Thanks, Tea. I owe you double for this."

"What about your carpentry job? What are you going to tell your boss?"

"My brother is more important than any job. I'll be up first thing in the morning. I'll meet you at the *Observer* and we'll go from there." Kimberly said goodbye to her friend and hung up the telephone. Logistics on her mind, she called her boss and said she had a family emergency and couldn't come to work the next week. She could tell he was not pleased, but he didn't fire her on the spot. Maybe she'd still have a job when she came back.

She didn't want to ask Mom or Dad for the money. She decided to raid her piggy bank. The money she'd been saving and saving and saving for a new stereo would just have to pay her way to Charlotte. More was going on here than was apparent. She admitted to herself; she wanted to see Thomas again. But this was not why she had to go. If Thomas was not with Majken, then the situation had changed, and she felt in her heart, not for the better.

Kimberly prepared for a trip in the morning. Wait to tell Mom and Dad after breakfast. *After* breakfast. Why ruin a perfectly good breakfast, Kim thought.

The bright morning sky was beautiful over the city of Charlotte Monday morning. Kim liked the hustle and bustle of the urban life. The city was infinitely more appealing than doldrums in the sleepy town she grew up in. Only Mom's pancakes made it bearable.

Kimberly parked Thomas', well – now, her Honda in a parking space across the street and made her way into the *Charlotte Observer* building. She wasn't sure working for a newspaper was what she really wanted to do, but just being inside the building inspired her.

She stopped at the receptionist's desk.

"My name is Kimberly Kline. I'm here to see Marsy Latham, please."

Kimberly pulled uncomfortably at her skirt and stood uneasily in heels. When her Dad saw that she actually wore a dress, he nearly fell out of his chair. Mom knew a gig was up. She just smiled at Kimberly when she said she needed to see Tea for a week. Mom's have a way of just knowing. Dad gave her a kiss on her cheek and told her to be safe.

The receptionist called Marsy and moments later her friend appeared. She was a little taller than Kimberly, and as long as Kim could remember, her friend usually wore black. She wore layered clothing, with a band of ivory visible just below her black jersey and a subtle turquoise necklace at her throat.

Marsy smiled and hugged Kimberly.

She signed Kimberly in and got her a visitor's badge, and the two made their way to the second floor far west corner of the building where Marsy worked with the other two staff photographers. Her cubicle was littered with photos of candid shots she'd made through her two years with the newspaper.

Kimberly borrowed a chair from the empty cubicle next to Marsy's and made herself at home. Marsy's telephone rang and Kim had to wait a few moments for the conversation to end. Her friend turned to her.

"Let's see it," Kimberly said.

Marsy opened her lap drawer and pulled out the original and an enlarged print she had made. Yep, Kim thought, it was certainly her brother. The blonde girl with him was slender but taller than Majken. Kim judged she would be about five foot seven. The mystery girl held Thomas' arm over one shoulder and visibly supported him with her arm wrapped around his back. Pretty face. With all the effort required to actually carry her brother, she was not straining. Kim agreed with Tea. This girl was at least as strong as a man.

She studied the enlargement photo also.

Kimberly let the images in the two photos soak into her awareness. The trick was to let the crime scene talk to you. Let details in the photo tell the story about what happened.

Marsy let Kimberly peruse the photos.

Thomas was clearly not with it. In fact, now that Kimberly saw the photo, she could tell he was obviously in pain and unable to walk unassisted. The girl was helping him. Crowds of people milled on the sidewalk and street behind them. Everyone seemed to be looking north. Toward the sounds of sirens in the distance, Marsy explained.

"Who is she?" Marsy asked.

Kimberly slipped the photos into Marsy's camera backpack. "I don't know. This isn't his girlfriend. Maj– Thomas' girlfriend would never leave him unattended. Can you take me to this street?" Marsy grabbed her backpack.

"Let's go," she said.

Jeanine came to consciousness gradually. The entire front of her body hurt, and she found she could not move her arms or her legs. The last thing she remembered was Nolan coming at her from the van. Everything from there was blank.

Her mouth was dry. She was thirsty.

A deeper hollowness inside of her body signaled her need for blood. The rough wall behind her back felt like hewn timbers. Jeanine felt a distinct cold awareness course through her body. Nolan's cabin. He brought her back to Helena!

She looked around. She felt a heavy cloth tied around her face. Nolan had blindfolded her. She licked her parched dry lips.

"Nolan," she croaked.

He did not respond, if he heard her at all.

"Nolan," she called louder.

Nearby she heard a chain rattle against the rock floor, movement close to her.

"Who's there?" she asked warily.

A young man's voice replied, "It's me Jeanine. Nolan got me too." The young man with her when she saw Nolan's van. Thomas. Nolan had captured him with her.

Oh, God, Jeanine thought.

"Thomas," she said weakly, "are you all right? Can you see where we are?"

The chains moved some more.

"I'm okay. We're in a root cellar, I think. Nolan shocked me after he shocked you. I came to in the van while we were still in Charlotte. He got Alecia. I saw a police officer and this woman hand her over."

Jeanine struggled against her bonds.

She could not move.

"Nolan!" she shouted. "If you even so much as touch Alecia, I'll kill you! I swear I will!" From above, Jeanine heard the creak of a trapdoor above being raised. Jeanine could imagine him kneeling above them with a very satisfied smirk on his face.

"Well, well," Nolan said, "the prodigal daughter has returned. I trust you slept well."

Jeanine struggled to move her arms. They had been wrapped around her. She had been shackled with her arms crossed around the front of her body. The bands holding her wrists were metal and cut into her flesh. She heard him come down the rusty metal rungs embedded in the floor joists beneath his cabin.

When Nolan stood before her, she knew his exact position because the grit on the floor made a grinding sound as he moved. She wanted to kick him, but her legs would not move either. Her jeans were gone. Her legs had been secured to the rock floor spread apart. Fuck! she swore under her breath.

"What have you done with Alecia?" she asked.

She heard Nolan kneel directly in front of her. Never had she loathed another human being as much as she loathed this man now. He replied, "Why, nothing – yet. She's locked safely in her bedroom."

Jeanine wanted water, but knew not to ask Nolan for it. She needed blood badly. If Thomas was in his Change, he would need blood as well.

"Nolan, listen to me. Taking Alecia's life will not make you vampyric. Nothing will. You've already begun to age." Her throat was hoarse. She could barely speak. "Nolan, she's your daughter. Please let her go." Nolan pulled the blindfold off her face.

Jeanine blinked against the shaft of sunlight that showed above the cellar.

Nolan's cruel face, at first blurry, came into view. "You're in no position to make any demands or any threats. Running with Alecia was stupid. If you had run away on your own, I might have let you go. As it were, your running was a small inconvenience. Sacrifice will be in four days. Because this next full moon will be a harvest moon, and we've just passed the autumnal equinox, the power will be at the highest possible level."

Jeanine struggled against her bonds. Nolan ran his hands along both of her thighs. She cringed. She thought to spit in his face, but her mouth was completely dry.

"Give her water," Thomas demanded.

Nolan turned to regard his other prisoner.

"And give her blood – she's not fed since we left Charlotte."

Jeanine could see Thomas more clearly when Nolan moved from directly in front of her. Nolan had taken his boots and his shirt. At least he still had on his jeans. He had been shackled to the floor joist on the opposite side of the cellar.

When Nolan stood, he had to hunch to keep from hitting his head on the flooring above. He glanced at Jeanine and Thomas, then climbed up the rungs and slammed the trapdoor shut above them. Fifteen minutes or so, by Jeanine's sense, Nolan reopened the trapdoor and came down the rungs with a canteen and what looked like a wine bottle. From a nook in the side of the cellar, Nolan retrieved a gas lantern and turned it on. The lantern made white light glow in the dismal cellar.

Jeanine squinted. The brightness of the light hurt her eyes. She saw Nolan in a blur surrounded by a halo. She laughed bitterly at the imagery. He knelt before her again and swished water in the canteen.

"Want some?" he taunted Jeanine.

He unscrewed the cap and took a large drink of water in front of her. He swished the canteen some more and poured water on the rough stone floor.

"It's good and cold," he said mockingly.

Jeanine wanted the water, but she firmly resisted begging for it. She knew Nolan liked it too much when his victim's begged.

He seemed to tire of the sport if she would not play along. Nolan uncapped the canteen and brought it to her lips for her to drink. He poured cold water into her mouth, slowly and carefully. Jeanine wanted to cry when the cold water went down her throat.

He probably understood when her thirst was satisfied, her blood needs would hurt her.

Nolan had to have a reason for keeping her alive. If she let herself be seen as docile, he may overestimate her and make a fatal mistake. She answered humbly, saying something she thought she'd never say to the man.

"Thank you."

With that, Nolan capped the canteen and set it on the floor beside him. He lifted the wine bottle from the lantern shelf and pulled the cork with his teeth, then spit the cork out.

"Freshly drawn," Nolan said, "just for you." Nolan kept goats for occasions where Jeanine could not acquire blood any other way. He put the tip of the bottle to her lips and allowed her to taste and smell the blood.

She nodded. It seemed okay to her.

It was very warm. He poured the blood for her, allowing her to pause every few seconds. Her body began absorbing the blood immediately. She felt stronger.

When the bottle was empty, Nolan set it on the floor and took a napkin he'd stuck in his pocket and dabbed her lips with it. It was such an insanely nice thing for him to do, she laughed nervously. It was so out of character.

"Need more?" he asked.

Jeanine felt her body still absorbing the blood she had consumed. Right now, she was good. She shook her head no. When Nolan stood up, Jeanine called, "Feed Thomas.

He needs blood, too." Nolan turned from Jeanine and she could not see his expression.

He held the lantern over Thomas so he could see his new prisoner clearly. Around Nolan's legs, Jeanine could see Thomas trying to shield his eyes against the white bright light. When Nolan spoke, his voice was high with elation. "You may prove to be a greater gift to us than Jeanine has been."

With that, he doused the lantern, set it back on its shelf, took the canteen and wine bottle and left.

Nolan soon returned to give Thomas water and goat's blood as he did her. Jeanine had a sudden realization. Nolan was keeping them alive to die.

Kimberly stood on the corner of East Sixth Street and looked in four directions. A steady stream of mid-morning traffic and pedestrians made the scene a bustle of activity. In a little while it would be time for lunch. Later on she planned to treat Marsy at her favorite Hunan restaurant. Business first.

Marsy stood on the opposite street in the position she was when the photograph was taken. Kimberly waited for the red light to change, then walked across the street toward her friend – but stopped halfway and looked back at the corner restaurant.

A few people came in and out of the door as she watched. The picture was taken on a Friday night. Kimberly walked back to the corner where her brother was being carried from. The street at the time the photo was taken had been flooded with onlookers who had come outside to watch fire trucks go by.

Marsy came across the street to join her.

She waited silently while Kim pondered.

At this point, too little was known of what took place

that night. As she reviewed her store of knowledge, a few facts came to her remembrance. First, Thomas at home had gone to a clinic. Charges on her Dad's account meant he must have thought something was wrong with him physically. Second, she recalled Mom saying the day before they left together, Mirriam fussed over him and had to guide him back to his bedroom. He had stayed in bed most of the day. She, herself, had felt drained and had to rest all morning. Third, and most important, when she thought Thomas was going to jump into that endless dark pool he said, It's not stopping.

If her brother had an episode on the street and Majken happened to be elsewhere, she could see him lying close to the building and almost getting trampled by the masses.

So kind-hearted girl sees him and picks him up. Kimberly looked down the streets on the same block to try to discern from what direction her brother may have walked. She felt a brief pang of guilt for him having given her his car, but Majken took him with her and did not require him to bring his car.

She recalled what Thomas had said about Majken. That she had been cut deeply across her abdomen by the John suspect and lived. Kimberly imagined Thomas again drawing his finger across her own abdomen. Yet when Kimberly actually saw Majken and even hugged her, no evidence could be felt that she had ever been injured. She stepped into the shade on the northward side of the restaurant. Down the street, she noticed a library on the opposite side of the street. Kimberly stood with her back against the red brick wall. She wasn't sure why she thought of her brother living in shadows, except when he was in the hammock at home, he preferred the night.

So brother collapsed against this wall and kind-hearted girl, who happened to be so very strong like Majken, picked him up and carried him – where? Marsy stood next to her. People on the sidewalk continued to pass her going both ways. More people were going into the restaurant on the corner because lunch was getting closer. "He fell here," Kimberly announced. "The girl saw him and picked him up. I think she did it to keep him from being trampled on this side of the street by onlookers. She was moving him to safety."

Marsy picked a camera from her backpack and took several shots, to record Kimberly's observations. She stepped away from Kim and took photos of her friend leaning against the outer wall of the restaurant. Kimberly reached out her hand. "Lemme see the enlarged photo." Marsy retrieved the photo and gave it to her.

She entered the restaurant and asked around. Do you know these people? Have you seen them before? Most of the patrons said no. A bus boy recognized them. They were on the street that Friday when the sirens went off. And no, he didn't see them before that.

No other restaurant staff recognized Thomas and the mystery girl. The girl did not know Thomas beforehand and Thomas did not, likely, know the girl until they met on the street, she reasoned.

Kimberly treated Marsy to lunch at her favorite Hunan restaurant on The Plaza, then returned to the scene of the crime. As the pair searched all afternoon, Marsy kept records of observations and photographic evidence of what they discovered. Kim asked people if they had seen her brother or girl in the photo.

A woman on the second floor of the library remembered Thomas. When the library was closing, she had to prompt him to leave. The librarian nor any of the other library staff knew what Thomas was reading or searching for. When the library closed at seven, a manager who was the last to leave reported seeing Thomas allegedly sitting on the steps outside.

Kimberly inquired about his girlfriend, about five foot four, medium chestnut long hair, slender pretty girl. No one saw a girl like this. The pair went out and sat on the steps. Marsy took her camera and started taking pictures of the bar across the street. Kim was stymied for a moment.

When Marsy suggested they ask in the bar, Kimberly exclaimed, "Tea, you're a genius!"

The little bar did not open until five so they had an hour to wait. Kim suggested they walk down the path where the girl was leading Thomas to see if anything down the street caught their eye. Marsy took photos of their journey two-thirds of a mile and the return trip down adjacent streets.

Nothing substantial yet.

Both Kimberly and Marsy were too young to enter the bar itself. Kimberly took the enlarged photo and tried to ask the man about her brother. The little man in the booth rudely shut the door in her face. She had Marsy try next. The little man looked Marsy over, Kim noticed. He did not remember her brother, but the bouncer did. The little man remembered the mystery girl. Then Marsy described Thomas' girlfriend and hit paydirt. She had been there for a little while, but left early.

The pair returned to the *Observer* to allow Marsy to develop the photos she had taken that day. After hours, Kim did not need a visitor's badge. She browsed microfiche of news articles for the last two weeks just on the outside chance she would see something important. Marsy bundled the new photos in a large intradepartmental envelope and they left for Marsy and her father's home. They found Captain Jason Latham, Marsy's father, in his powered wheelchair.

Marsy bowed and kissed her father on his left hand, one of the few places he had not been so badly scarred.

Kimberly bowed respectfully to Marsy's father. When he smiled, the crease that was once his lips seemed to curl just a little. Yet his eyes were just as alive on the inside of the man as they ever were.

When Marsy and Kimberly prepared for bed, Marsy opened her bedroom window to the night air. The soft breeze stirred the bamboo wind chimes Tea kept there. It made a soft clacking sound that was very soothing.

Marsy sipped her oolong tea from a small round cup. Her dearest friend had been so patient all day. Now she wanted to know what was going on.

Kimberly balanced her cup in her palm.

"Before I tell you anything, I must have your word that this will be kept off the record. I think Thomas' life has now changed, and he cannot go back to being the brother that you or I remember. Tea, promise me you won't tell a soul anything that I tell you." Marsy promised. Kimberly felt guilty because she'd promised to keep Majken's secret, but she had a distinct impression all day that the situation had changed with the mystery girl and Thomas was in trouble.

Where to begin with all of this?

"When I searched the mainframe for news articles in Trenton during the summer, I found numerous headlines on a serial killer the press dubbed the *slasher*. From all accounts, he was believed to be a transient male suspect about thirty years old. Thomas came home injured in August. He claimed to have fallen out of his own car, but the cuts and bruises on his body didn't agree with what he said.

"This *slasher* suspect kidnapped Thomas and, according to my brother's own testimony, hurt him by pushing him repeatedly onto sharp rocks along the side of a cliff. He said his girlfriend saved his life by coming after him.

"Thomas was behaving so strangely that we, Mom Dad and myself, were all worried." Kimberly held up her scarred forearm.

"One night he came into my bedroom and cut me. I don't know why. I smacked him and hit him until he let me go. Then he ran out of the house and disappeared into the woods. His girlfriend showed up the next day. I don't know how, but she found him in the middle of nowhere in the woods south of Sumter."

Kim sipped her hot tea and continued.

"I liked her, Tea. I still do. Thomas trusts her. Thomas told me such a wild tale, that if even half of it took place, no one would believe us anyway. When Thomas met her in Trenton, she went by the name Mary Harris; when she arrived at the house, she said her name was Mirriam, and she was from England. Neither of these are right. Her real name is Majken. I almost said her real name twice today. You might as well know. We have to find her, Tea. She's the only one who can help my brother."

Marsy set her empty tea cup beside her bed on the little shelf next to the wind chimes. Kimberly watched her friend's eyes to see how she might react. She still cared for Thomas a great deal, but her strong feelings for him might get in the way if she considered his new girlfriend to be an obstacle.

Her friend sat cross-legged on the bed in a way that Kim found enviable. She was so limber. "Tell me everything you know. I'll help you sort through it when you're done." Kimberly told Marsy about burning mansions, serial killers who fall off cliffs but don't die, and Majken.

Her friend's pretty almond-shaped eyes narrowed a few times as she asked Kimberly to explain a few things again. Generally, she just listened. She was the best sounding board Kimberly ever had. The girls talked until nearly midnight.

Marsy agreed with Kimberly.

Majken had to be found if they were to help Thomas. Kimberly's conviction was contagious. Marsy told Kimberly she would put aside her personal feelings because, she, too, now believed Thomas' life was at stake again.

Kimberly slept soundly until sunlight streamed across Marsy's bed and her clock radio came on with the morning news.

Marsy had just showered and was getting dressed for the day. She smiled at Kimberly, who kicked her legs from under the covers and sat on the edge of Marsy's bed. Marsy said, "I'm scheduled to do two shoots today; one at the airport about eleven and another at a reception at BoA corporate after five. I'll not be able to help much today."

"I understand," Kim replied. Kimberly stretched in the long nightshirt she borrowed from Tea. She felt hungry and had a craving for a bagel and cream cheese.

Marsy commented as she finished dressing. "This girl-friend looks to me to be a very deliberate person. Nothing is left to chance. She came to your parent's house to find Thomas and she did. She followed Thomas and this killer in Trenton and rescued him. She was in that bar last Friday because she wanted to be or needed to be there."

Kimberly got up and stood next to her friend in her vanity mirror. "What if I'm wrong? What if all of this is just my wild imagination? We're not only coloring in the margins – this is off the page!"

Marsy crossed her arms.

"What if you're right?" she said quietly.

Kim pursed her lips.

"That's what I thought you'd say."

Marsy sat on her bed and started lacing her black sneakers.

"These people, Majken, this killer in Trenton, and now Thomas himself, are dual. They occupy two worlds. They live in the world that we all see every day and they live in their own world. To find Majken you must enter her world. You must think from her perspective."

"How, Tea?" Kimberly exclaimed. "She didn't give me any information."

Marsy stood up. "Yes, she did. What did sitting on your roof at night tell you? You said it was just a roof – no big deal."

"Yeah, all I could see was the moon and a few clouds and the wind stirring the limbs of the trees around the house a little bit. Quite frankly, it was boring."

Marsy stood behind Kimberly and held her shoulders. "You said Thomas collapsed on your deck during your cookout. He collapsed in the sunlight. Majken gave him sunscreen. Thomas started wearing dark glasses."

"Her world?" Kimberly repeated.

"Kimberly, my love, you won't find them out in the daytime."

Marsy gave her a hug, then left for work. Her father had gone back to the hospital before six for more surgery. Tea had given her a spare key. She had the house to herself. Kimberly got a quick shower, then laid out the photos Marsy had taken yesterday on their oval kitchen table.

Little things about Majken started making sense. She left with her brother at night, not the next morning. They sat on the roof at night – why? Well, she surmised, because it was night! Kim felt like a dunce. If sunlight bothered you, where else would you spend all your time? She sorted through the photos on the table until she got hungry.

Kimberly found wheat bread to make toast. She scrambled three eggs and made herself two egg sandwiches.

She washed her breakfast down with tomato juice she happened to find in the back of the refrigerator. She caught a reflection of herself as she drained her glass of tomato juice. Kimberly stopped drinking and stared at her reflection.

Oh, God! She set her glass down.

She rested her scarred forearm on the table. She just remembered Thomas having his mouth over the cut before she hit him the first time. The idea she was having boggled her mind! Thomas had allegedly cut her to drink her blood!

Kimberly paced the length of the kitchen and back. Her brother had been trying to drink her blood when she smacked him! This was ludicrous.

She knew Thomas wasn't crazy.

Only crazy whacko people actually drank blood. Vampires did not exist. All of that was myth and superstition.

Yet, the subtle connection in her mind had been made and refused to go away. Majken said of herself, John and I are sojourners. She said we exist in society where we can. Kimberly felt her heart racing.

Where we can find blood!

The *slasher* obviously killed for his blood. Why else cut a victim clean open? But what of Majken? She didn't feel like the killing type, at least not unless pushed into it. Kimberly recalled, when Majken hugged her and called her a snoop into everybody's business, like Thomas once told her, she was gentle.

Yet, her brother had fallen for Majken when he did not know who and what she really was – that much was apparent. That's why he nearly knocked her down when she wanted to put out a few stringers to find his Mary. He was protecting her because he well knew she was a blood drinking person.

Now her brother either is becoming or already was a blood drinker!

Majken had said, His life has changed and it cannot be reversed. Obviously, Thomas had been exposed to Majken's blood as she fought John to save his life. That was the so-called accident her brother came home with.

Oh, God, she thought. Oh, Lord, help me!

It all made sense now.

Why did Majken have to take her brother with her? Because he was changing into a blood drinker like herself and, in a little town like Sumter, people would notice. Yes, she thought. This was why he collapsed on their deck. His new condition includes sensitivity to sunlight, she reasoned. Now her brother and his love wore sunscreen and dark glasses. He was becoming like her! It all made sense now. Boy! Tea would get a hoot out of this theory. Kimberly thought to call her, but the hour was nearing eleven o'clock and, by now, Tea was likely at the airport preparing for her shoot for whatever was going on there today.

Kimberly wanted to race out and just go.

The urge to run out subsided quickly. She really didn't know if she was right, but key pieces of a puzzle bothering her for weeks suddenly snapped into place.

Her brother's life and Majken's life were now deeply interconnected.

Whatever affected Majken would affect Thomas – and whatever affected Thomas, like another girl similar to

Majken, would surely have an impact on Majken.

Majken loved her brother, she just knew it. Thomas' feelings when he only thought of her as Mary Harris were certainly strong enough, but finding out your girlfriend drinks blood was bound to put a damper on the romance. No wonder Thomas came home moody and not talking to anyone!

If she was right, this would explain a lot.

Kimberly put her brunch dishware and her fry pan in the sink and washed them. She cleaned up the photos from the kitchen table and stuffed them back into the envelope. What she needed was a plan. Tea said she had to enter Majken's world.

It wasn't clear at the moment, but it would come to her. She went into the living room to search through their entertainment center. Although it had room for a large television, it had been crammed stem to stern with books – most of them hardbound.

Kimberly searched the lower shelves and opened the wooden panel doors along the bottom. She remembered Marsy had a map of Charlotte in book form. It was soft bound, but had very detailed street information. Several drawers later Kimberly found the desired book of street maps and took it to the kitchen table to study. Several of the pages had been dog-eared from earlier exploits the summer before when she worked the intern position.

First things first. She found the section of the city around the Bank of America Plaza in the vicinity of the corner restaurant and took a bird's eye view of the situation. She found a yellow notepad under the small table with the telephone and went to Tea's bedroom to get a fountain pen.

Majken's world, she kept thinking.

Being an experienced blood drinker, she would know

how to do things for Thomas that he did not yet know how to do. The bar was part of the equation. She remembered some of the perpetual party scene from her senior trip and her face blushed.

She heard more pick up lines the four days they were in Miami than all of her life put together. Bars, in her view, were places to solicit members of the opposite sex for sex. Majken would need a larger city from which to search for people to get blood for Thomas. She circled the bar across from the library on her map. The local bingo place in Sumter would get old in a hurry.

Even if Majken came back to that same bar, which she considered unlikely for an experienced huntress like Majken, they would need an adult to get into the place to verify she was there or not. Neither she nor Marsy were old enough to get inside.

Since only Kimberly had actually seen Majken in person (now that Thomas' photo of them together had disappeared), she herself would be the only person to recognize Majken by sight. Enter Majken's world, she thought.

Kimberly expanded her premise.

Majken was likely finding one or more men to take home so that both her and Thomas could drink their blood. The notion of her own brother actually drinking anybody's blood, and seeing him do it, was kinda gross, but she'd seen far worse.

Everything boiled down to finding Majken.

Kim thumbed back to the beginning of the map book just to get some fresh ideas. In the front, an index of hospitals caught her eye. There were people in hospitals that drew blood for a living. She considered a hospital in the area a very likely place for Majken to go – especially since Thomas was not with her now. That certainty inside of her made her nervous and determined at the same time.

It was just past two in the afternoon.

Kimberly wrote the address of the nearest hospital to the downtown area and directions on her notepad. She stuffed the yellow paper and fountain pen in her back pocket, then made sure she had her license and spare key before she locked herself out of Marsy's home.

The Carolinas Medical Center was massive, like other big- city hospitals she had been in. She found a parking lot and entered the front of the sandstone brick and glass building. She sat near the front vestibule waiting area where she could see the main entrance. Her hunch was either right or it wasn't. Nothing to do now but wait.

Majken made a circuous route on the second and third floors of the medical center to find patients from whom to withdraw two or three Vacutainer tubes of blood each. One man said he had a daughter her age. He was being kind. Majken smiled at him, withdrew the blood she needed, and quietly left.

She found a place on the lowest level in a maintenance corridor to consume her blood meal. Pipes and huge HVAC conduits ran overhead. Standard incandescent bulbs hung from the high ceiling above in cages. The concrete floor had pooled water in places. Once she consumed her meal, she found an incinerator to dispose of her used Vacutainer tubes, and proceeded to leave the hospital complex.

Majken paused at the glass frontage to watch the golden sunset in the sky. Normally aware of her surroundings, she felt displaced. She could put on a brave front for a little while, but inside, her heart still ached.

She'd not been back to the loft since ...

As she started to exit the medical center, she was vaguely aware that someone was calling her name. She turned and saw Kimberly running toward her. In an instant Thomas' baby sister rushed into her arms. Majken breathed sandalwood soap.

It was Kimberly. Majken held her. She was clinging to her, crying, saying, "I had to find you, I had to find you."

"Kimberly," Majken said, "what are you doing here?" The teenager wiped at her eyes.

"Tea took a picture and Thomas is in it with this girl, who isn't you, and I came up here to see it. At first I just really wanted to see Thomas again, but I got a way bad wrong feeling about this whole situation because you weren't the one in the photo. It was someone else and he was supposed to be with you. I couldn't figure it out and Tea said you were dual and to enter your world. So I figured it out when I was drinking tomato juice. Then I came to the hospital hoping and praying you'd show up because if I didn't find you, I kept thinking I'd never see my brother again. I had to find you – oh, God. I know I promised but I had to have help. Please forgive me, Majken. Do you know where Thomas is?"

Majken processed all Kimberly just said. "Who is Tea?" she asked. Kimberly stood abashed in front of Majken still wiping tears from her eyes. They were in the main entrance to the hospital. Majken prompted her to go outside. A van was parked and a young man was loading his aged mother into a car, apparently to take home.

Majken walked toward the blood red sunset. Kimberly seemed to have settled down. "Who's Tea," she repeated, "and what is this about a photograph of Thomas?"

"My friend is a photographer for the *Observer*. Her name is Marsy Tam Latham, but I call her Tea because she drinks oolong tea so much."

"And this photographer took a photo of Thomas – When?" Majken asked.

"Last Friday night. Next to Bank of America on East Sixth." Kimberly reached into her back pocket for the folded enlarged picture. She took it out of the yellow notebook paper and held it before Majken.

Majken stiffened when she saw the photograph and the girl with Thomas. Kim rattled on. "This girl was with him and it wasn't you. When Marsy told me about it, I first thought it was you, but you obviously don't have blonde hair. I think Thomas collapsed and this girl was helping him not get trampled in the masses behind them."

Majken reached for the photo and forced herself to look at it. Yes, the girl was pulling him across the street. Majken paused to judge how to explain this to Kimberly. "Who is it?" Kimberly asked.

Majken studied the girl. Pretty girl, now that she had a face to go with her scent. It was obvious Thomas had collapsed on the sidewalk and this vampyric girl just happened by and picked him up. She handed the photo back to Kimberly.

"I do not know her," Majken replied.

"I was hoping you'd know. I've had this bad feeling about this photo. Not the girl herself. I think Thomas is in trouble. Do you know where he is?"

The white hot flash of pain in her heart blinded her to all else. A bit impatiently, she replied, "I do not know where he is – I don't care to know." Kimberly appeared crestfallen.

Then Kimberly stammered, "Why? What happened?"

Majken realized they were still standing in a public place. She gently guided Kimberly to cross the lane with her away from the flow of people. She decided to take Kimberly to the loft. It would be easier to explain if she could see it. "Did you drive?" Majken asked.

"Yes," Kim replied.

"I'll show you." She prompted Kimberly to lead the way to her car. Seeing Thomas' familiar Honda made her heart ache, but she got in without comment and gave Kimberly directions to their – excuse me, her loft.

Kim followed her up flights of stairs.

Majken unlocked the door and bade Thomas' sister enter.

Kimberly strode in without regard.

The loft apartment was dark and it was now late twilight outside. She thought to say something to Kimberly about just barging in, but she held her peace. In Thomas' sister was an innocence that was rare and priceless. Majken smiled behind the teenager and went to the dimmer lamp by the couch and turned the light on for her. The couch was as she left it. Her date had his fun, then she had hers. She did not wish to hurt the man, but she was so angry. His blood stained the carpet from the couch to the kitchen. The thickest blood stain on the floor was just in front of where Kimberly was standing.

It was a wonder she didn't kill him.

When the light came up, Kimberly noticed where she was about to step and backed up. Majken avoided commenting about the blood stains. Just pretend they do not exist. Kimberly looked around and took in the view. "Nice place," she said.

She looked up at the high vaulted ceiling and skylight now open to the night air. Thomas' scent and the young vampyric girl's scent had faded quite a bit, but it was still present on the bed. Suddenly, night birds overhead flew by the open skylight.

Kimberly was startled for a second, then laughed. The girl's light hearted laughter made Majken feel better. The teenager walked past the bed with rumpled bed sheets, past the fallen blankets in the floor, past two kitchen chairs in the middle of the floor, and made her way to the kitchen.

Majken considered it odd that the kitchen chairs had been moved next to her bed. She thought to make Kimberly a cup of hot tea. Her cup and the cup Thomas drank from was still on her bedside table. She started heating water to make the hot tea.

"Do you drink hot tea?" she asked Kimberly.

Her visitor nodded yes.

With some trepidation, Majken went to her bed and got the cups, and made hot tea for herself and Kimberly. It felt odd having her in her loft. She'd not expected to see Thomas' sister – especially so soon. When the hot tea had steeped a little while, she gave her Thomas' cup and she drank from her own cup. Kimberly just stood in the kitchen, likely expecting Majken to start talking. The ache, she felt, would only get worse.

She began. "I came home and found that Thomas had been here with the girl in the photo. I could clearly smell their scents on my bed together." Majken set her cup down and paced into her living room with her arms tightly crossed. Her head bowed. "I – I'm sorry Kimberly. You really should not be here."

Majken heard Kimberly set her cup on the sink next to the stove and approach her from behind.

"Thomas loves you. I know he does. He wouldn't just pick up a girl and bring her here. I can see you're upset, but this doesn't make sense." Majken turned and looked directly into Thomas' sister's light brown eyes. The same innocent eyes that looked into her's and trusted her to find her brother when none else could. Majken smiled bitterly.

"It was a mistake for me to come to him and try to reenter his life. I cannot be Mary Harris for him again. I cannot be other than what I am, but this isn't good enough for him – apparently."

Kimberly pulled the photo from her back pocket and looked at it. "This girl is like you. Isn't she?"

"What do you mean?" Majken asked.

"She drinks blood, like you. Like the *slasher*. Like my brother." Majken felt alarm stir in her mind, but let it quickly subside. If Kimberly knew, then she knew. What was the point in trying to deny it now with blood stains all over the floor?

Majken bowed her head and glanced at her bed.

"She is vampyric."

Kimberly looked a little confused.

Majken prompted her for the piece of yellow notebook paper and her fountain pen and wrote the word for her.

"We have a vampyric medical condition that forces us to only consume blood for sustenance. Thomas became this way when he was exposed to my blood during my fight with John. He is in his Change right now. This," Majken indicating the pretty blonde girl pulling Thomas across the road, "is a younger vampyric person – I would say, probably, less than fifty years old."

"You're stronger than a normal person? Faster?" Kimberly surmised.

Majken nodded.

"How did you figure all this out?" she asked Kimberly, now curious.

"I talked to my friend, Marsy, and told her all that Thomas had told me. Tea said you are dual; that is, you occupy two worlds. When I saw my reflection this morning drinking a glass of tomato juice, I remembered Thomas had his mouth over my forearm before I hit him. When I realized he was trying to *drink* my blood, all that I found out about John and you came together."

Majken smiled wistfully.

"Undone by a glass of tomato juice."

Kimberly slipped the photo into her back pocket. She walked between Majken and the couch. She appeared to be concentrating. "Tea said there came a frog strangler that night between ten-thirty and midnight. When did you get here and find the bed like it was?"

Majken said, "I got here just after one."

She felt her mind starting to open up.

Kimberly was clearly going somewhere with this. Thomas' sister rest her hands on the two kitchen chairs at the foot of her bed. "I don't know why he would bring the girl here, except she helped him, and he may've felt indebted to her. But let's say they got soaked on the way here. If they were wet and cold, Thomas would've put his clothes over a chair like this, and" – picking up a blanket – "he would've wrapped himself and her in a blanket to get warm again." Majken glanced from her bed to the blanket on the floor. She saw it as Kimberly described.

Majken's awareness of her surroundings rapidly expanded. Kimberly watched Majken as she paced in a circle around her.

"Do you know where he is?"

Majken closed her eyes.

"No. He is not nearby. I do not feel him anywhere nearby."

Kimberly dropped the blanket.

"What do you need in order to find him?"

Majken replied, "It would help if I could get to a high place. The top of an office building would do."

Kimberly clapped her hands and pulled Majken's arm. "I know just the place," she said. By the time they reached Uptown and the new Bank of America building it was seven thirty. Majken and Kimberly went in just as Marsy was leaving. Kimberly's friend left her camera gear in the lobby with a guard and raced into the elevator with them.

Majken used a key, she said a friend had given her, to override the elevator controls and go directly to the highest floor. In the elevator, Kimberly introduced them.

"Majken, Marsy. Tea, Majken."

Thankfully, the upper floor suites were deserted. Majken sought a window. It was sealed. "Can't get out here," Kimberly said.

Majken placed her right forearm against the frame and pushed with her body weight. The metal buckled and warped. She pushed the entire window outward. Cooler night air spilled into the silent office. Majken lay the window sideways against the exterior wall and stepped outside. The lights of the city below were dazzling at this height. Kimberly hushed her friend from saying a single word. Just watch.

Majken walked from the north corner, to west, to south, to east, and back to north. The girls paced her. No one spoke. She made the circuit again. "Thomas is not in the city," Majken announced. "He is not anywhere nearby." Majken narrowed her eyes and walked to the ledge of the westward corner of the bank. She felt a slight tugging from far west. She knew he had been pulled from east to west.

"We have a problem," Kimberly said.

Thomas crouched in darkness.

A cry escaped his lips as intense pain swept through his body. The little blood that their captor had given them had to be enough. Jeanine struggled to get free. It was no use. The sounds of wolves howling replayed in his mind.

Thomas closed his eyes and set his face to endure.

Chapter Thirteen

Jeanine felt blood trickle down her hands from her bound wrists. She had tried to break free, but the metal bands were too tight and unforgiving. Even where the sharpened edge of the cuffs dug into the flesh of her hands, she thought to make her hands slippery enough with her own blood to pull her hands free, but this failed miserably.

Thomas had not moved for several hours. He cried out loudly early that morning then lay still. She could still hear him breathing, but he lay motionless in the scant light that penetrated the gloomy cracks in the wooden flooring above. He was alive.

Through the night she was sure she heard people walking above. Nolan's footsteps she knew by his size and gait. She heard smaller shorter footsteps as well. And a clomping sound she did not recognize.

Now all was silent above her.

Jeanine bowed her head. She failed to protect Alecia. She failed Thomas by letting him get captured with her.

She failed her Papa by leaving with Bobby in the first place. She failed Bobby by not recognizing the danger from these blood cult zombies before they were entangled and trapped.

The only bright spot in her life that she could see was Alecia. Now, if Nolan had his way, Alecia would be sacrificed to a false god to satisfy his lust for immortality – which would not work for him anyway. The irony and futility of Nolan's quest struck her like a blow to the face.

He will kill Alecia, and likely her, just because he can.

What of Thomas? she wondered.

He had told her more of the vampyric condition in a half hour than she had learned on her own in a lifetime. Although the blood cult held the upper hand by controlling her life all these years, it was now clear that they did not know everything.

Thomas' girlfriend, Majken, was two hundred ninety four years old. She'd heard rumors through the blood cult underground of other similar vampyric people like her held in captivity. None yet over one hundred twenty.

She smiled in grim satisfaction.

Nolan and the likes of the blood cult had a little surprise coming. The longer Nolan kept Thomas alive in captivity, as they kept her, the greater chance his girlfriend would find him.

Jeanine closed her eyes and tried to conserve her strength. She was very thirsty again. Her blood needs caused her awareness to ebb. So far Nolan had brought no fresh blood since yesterday. The morning droned on and on.

Finally Thomas moved and stirred to consciousness. The chains binding his legs moved. His left arm moved.

"Thomas," she said lowly. "How are you doing?"

He sat up on hearing her voice. "Okay," he replied.

Jeanine could tell he was gasping for breath. Then his voice modulated. "I'm okay." Far above, Jeanine heard the front door open and slam shut. Nolan entered. She knew by the sound of his walk. She heard him go up the stairs to their loft bedroom.

Jeanine bowed her head.

"I'm sorry you got captured with me," she said. "This was not your concern and you were dragged into it."

"Who are these people? What gives them the right to do this to us?" His voice was agitated. Perhaps the reality of blood cult life through the years had made her callous, but Jeanine did not see much hope at this point. Yet for Thomas' sake, she tried to think of something positive.

"I told you. They're obsessed weirdos that will do anything for an extended lifespan. They have money, connections, and they are ruthless. They will kill whomever they wish to satisfy their agenda." Jeanine heard Thomas' chains snap hard. She suspected he was grasping the chains with his hands and attempting to pull them free from the floor joist. Finally, he settled down again.

"Ahhh!" Thomas exclaimed, then curled on his left side. He lay on the cold rock as far down as the chain around his neck would let him. He spoke low, but Jeanine heard him clearly. "I know not to try that again."

Upstairs, Jeanine heard Nolan come down from the loft bedroom. He walked toward the kitchen, then left to Alecia's bedroom. When he opened her bedroom door, Jeanine thought she heard the scampering of little feet.

Run, baby!

Jeanine stopped breathing to listen.

Nolan's heavy footfalls pursued Alecia across the common room. It sounded like Alecia was trying to unlatch the door, but was unable to open it in time.

A heavy clumping sound was heard.

Nolan chased Alecia across the floor.

Alecia screamed.

Jeanine thought she heard Nolan slap her.

"Nolan, leave her alone!"

Jeanine shouted, but her voice came out cracked and broken. She started sobbing. Alecia was crying, and it sounded like Nolan was shaking her.

Several more seconds of tense silence, then Nolan clomped across the floor to the trapdoor and jerked it open. Jeanine looked up and squinted against the mid-morning light. Nolan held Alecia under his left arm. Blood trickled down Nolan's right forearm.

Alecia had bitten him. Enough to draw blood. Good girl, Jeanine thought.

"There she is," Nolan said, pointing down.

When Alecia looked down, she started screaming and reaching for Jeanine. Nolan held her bodily over the trapdoor like he might drop her. She was clenching her little fists and hitting him. Jeanine called up to Alecia. "Baby, I'm all right. Don't fight him. He'll hurt you if you keep on."

Alecia stopped struggling but kept whimpering.

Nolan left the trapdoor open and walked toward the kitchen with Alecia under his arm. She was no longer screaming. Nolan returned pulling Alecia along and carrying a large kitchen knife and a canteen with water. He set Alecia on the floor and told her to climb down. Alecia's tiny feet curled on the rusty rungs embedded in the timber. She stepped down a step – it was a huge stretch for her each step. Jeanine could not see her baby's face because of the height, but she prayed as Alecia came down.

When she was beyond halfway down, Nolan followed Alecia.

To make the last step to the floor Alecia had to hold to the second rung and let her legs stretch as far as she could toward the floor – then she dropped the remainder.

She fell with a thunk, but Alecia quickly recovered and ran to Jeanine.

Jeanine remembered what exposure to vampyric blood does to children. Alecia reached for her. "Move between my legs, honey. Don't step where I've bled. Don't get my blood on you anywhere." Alecia knelt between Jeanine's spread legs and would have wrapped her arms around her waist, but Nolan stepped down on the gritty rock subfloor and pulled Alecia by her arm away from Jeanine.

When Nolan stood over Jeanine, he blocked the light from above. He unslung the canteen from his shoulder and let it fall.

Jeanine stared at Nolan. He held the blade poised in

his right fist. She refused to be afraid of him. Nolan knelt in front of Jeanine and brandished the knife in her face. He turned to Alecia, now huddling in the far corner.

"I'll show you what she is," he said coldly.

With that he made a slice down his left forearm and let his blood ooze on his rolled-up sleeve. He embedded the knife in the wood beside Jeanine's head and reached for Alecia with his right hand. Jeanine saw his blood dripping on the rock subfloor. She *needed* the blood. Yet this was just another game Nolan was playing. Alecia was afraid of her father. He had to wrap his right arm around her body and hold her next to him. Jeanine closed her eyes in respite.

Waves of vertigo passed through Jeanine's body – the hollowness inside her that made her require blood would not be silent.

Nolan held his bleeding arm before Jeanine's mouth. She could smell the blood. She could almost taste the blood. The life of the flesh is in the blood. She gazed directly into Nolan's coal black eyes. All she saw was a seething hatred of all life. His very essence had become the thick darkness he had pursued and wished for all these years. Nothing was left of the man himself.

Jeanine found her voice. "She knows, Nolan. I told her what I was before we ran from you." Only darkness remained in him.

He jerked her hair with his left hand. "You have been a precious little pet," he cooed, "but we now have another to play with thanks to you. There was no way for you to escape. What made you even try to run?"

Jeanine shifted her gaze from his eyes burning with hatred to Alecia's bright, clear, trusting eyes. Her throat was very dry. It hurt to talk. She was very thirsty.

She *needed* blood.

In the face of death, peace welled up from inside her deepest place. "Something you'll never understand," she replied sadly.

Nolan shoved his bleeding forearm into her mouth. She drank his blood. It was only a little, but her body began absorbing the blood offered to her. He gave her and Thomas water then left Alecia down there to get goat's blood for his captives. Alecia did not cry when Nolan left her alone. Jeanine felt so proud of the beautiful confident young lady Alecia would surely become. Tiny hands reached around her neck. Jeanine knew. Nolan intended to sacrifice them all with the next full moon.

Kimberly read through sheaves of paper while sitting in the second-floor break area of the *Observer*. What she wanted to find was right in front of her.

She need only see it!

No one paid her any attention.

Scores of journalists, real journalists, and none of them seemed even remotely interested in what she and Marsy were doing. Majken was sure that Thomas had been taken. After three fruitless days of searching Kimberly was ready to believe her.

Kimberly folded their book of maps closed.

Marsy came into the break area.

"What do you say to me treating you to Italian tonight? Father will be at the hospital until Friday. Until then, we can do whatever we want."

"Thanks, Tea, but I'll take a rain check."

Marsy sat beside her.

"You've been at this all day. We only have her word that Thomas is not in the city. He could be here a few blocks away with that girl in the photo and everything is fine. Why are you going on like this?"

Kimberly rubbed her eyes and glanced at the clock. It was just past three-thirty. "You didn't see her bring your brother out of the wilderness when no one else had a clue where he was. I believe her, Tea. She knows things – just because she knows!"

Marsy pushed her chair back and leaned forward. Kimberly started stuffing yellow notebook pages into a binder.

"Look, I said I would go along with this, my feelings and opinions aside, just because you want to make sure Thomas is safe. I want to know that he's safe, too. But this looks more and more like a lover's quarrel, and he's likely gone off with this blonde girl regardless of what his new girlfriend says."

Kimberly avoided saying anything at that point. Life was generally simpler before she deduced that her brother now drank blood to live. It was the one little thing that she didn't tell her best friend. She looked into Tea's almond-shaped black eyes.

"Tea, a lot has gone on between Thomas and Majken. They're somehow connected now. If she says he's a thousand miles away, then he's a thousand miles away."

"If he's missing, then why don't we call the police? If she's so sure he's been taken across state lines, then it's in the jurisdiction of the FBI." Kimberly finished stuffing the binder with her notes, handed the binder to Marsy, and followed her friend around the corner to her cubicle.

Kim put her hand on her hip.

"We can't. Majken said no."

Marsy dropped the stuffed binder in the lowest drawer of her desk. "Listen to yourself, love. Just listen to what you're saying."

Kimberly glanced at the clock on the far side of the wall. It was twenty minutes until the hour. She picked up a copy of the enlarged photo of her brother and the mystery girl.

"Trust me, Tea. I still have this bad feeling about this. We have to find out who this girl is to even have a clue as to what really happened last Friday night."

She left the book of maps on Tea's desk.

"Are you with me?" she asked.

Marsy was still for a moment, then picked up her camera backpack. Kimberly drove.

Majken's loft apartment in South End was actually less than a half-mile from Marsy's home. She led Marsy up the flights of stairs. Majken waited for them in the now scrupulously clean loft apartment. Every time Kimberly saw Majken, she wanted to rush into her arms. Majken was dressed in jeans and a long-sleeved black blouse. She'd woven her long chestnut hair into a braid. Marsy seemed to eye her up as she approached from the kitchen. "Any new leads?" Kimberly asked.

"I found a man that saw them going up Church Street just before he got off work at midnight. He said it was pouring rain and they were running. The girl was in the lead and Thomas was following her."

Kimberly glanced at Marsy.

Marsy pointed toward Uptown. "That way," she said.

"Let's go," Kimberly said. "Show me."

With that, Majken led them to the hallway, locked her loft door and let Kimberly lead the way to her car. Marsy opened the passenger door and pulled the seat so she could climb into the Honda's little back seat. Her long legs folded into the cramped space. Kimberly tried to imagine Thomas rushing in torrential rainfall with the mystery girl. Why? The girl was the key. She was sure the girl lived somewhere in Fourth Ward.

The spires of Bank of America lay ahead.

Once they crossed the interstate, the dividing line between South End and the First Ward, Majken stopped Kimberly at a parking lot. The attendant stepped forward as they pulled in, but smiled and waved them through when he saw Majken was with them. Kimberly parked.

They got out and met the man beside his booth. Kimberly judged he was young, but his jaw was larger than normal and his teeth had been misshapen and protruded. His hands were gnarled. Likely, a genetic defect.

Majken spoke to the attendant in Spanish.

He began an animated description of what he saw, including gestures and pointing to the sidewalk across the street. When he finished Majken translated his discourse. "He saw them running, the woman in the lead, and the young man chasing her. The rain was very heavy. I saw them clearly because the lightning flashed as they ran beside here."

Kimberly stood where the attendant was likely standing that night and visualized her brother and mystery girl running – where? Obviously back to wherever the girl lived.

It looked like a dime store romance plot.

Girl picks up boy. Girl takes boy home. Boy recovers and thanks girl. Boy brings girl to his home. Boy and girl get soaked on the way. Boy and girl sit on Majken's bed wrapped in blankets. Then, unexpectedly, girl gets up and runs home. Girl runs and boy chases girl down street in pouring rain. Boy and girl disappear.

The 'unexpectedly' nagged Kimberly's mind. Why run home with such urgency? Someone else was in this equation. Someone precious to the vampyric girl who picked up her brother. She remembered seeing in her mind Thomas as he collapsed on the deck during their Labor Day cookout. Mom had literally jumped across the space to her son and held him as he rolled over.

"A child," Kimberly said. She stared at the empty street, and repeated, "her child."

Majken thanked the attendant in Spanish. He returned to his booth to get a token from a car leaving the lot. Kimberly went to her car and locked it. Marsy got her camera pack.

Majken held her copy of the enlarged photo of Thomas and the girl.

"What now?" Marsy asked.

"We follow," Kimberly stated as she led them across the street. Traffic picked up and many more pedestrians were on the sidewalks as they entered the heart of Charlotte. Majken crossed back to the opposite side of the street and maintained her pace with Kimberly. They walked the circuit several times to Ninth, and back to Fourth.

Long shadows reached across the streets.

Several times Majken halted, Kimberly noted. When Majken stopped and looked down West Fifth street, Kimberly felt a shiver. The little street looked fine in the daytime, but the stretch of long building to the right and empty storefronts to the left would make this a desolate place in the middle of a storm.

Marsy took photos as they walked.

Majken motioned for Kimberly and Marsy to come to her.

She pointed toward Tryon Street.

"This way," Majken said. About half a block down, they stood before the vestibule of a brick church. The frontage had circular glass in a half moon shape.

Majken drew the folded photo of Thomas and girl and went into the building. A young woman with auburn hair and blonde streaks was getting up from a receptionist counter. The receptionist retrieved her purse from the lowest drawer of a cabinet and locked it.

Majken showed the woman the photo.

"Have you ever seen either of these two people?" The woman stepped into the hallway light and held the photo.

"Why, yes," she said. She pointed to the mystery girl. "She looks like the mother of one of our former students."

Kimberly and Marsy exchanged glances.

The receptionist went to her phone and dialed an extension. She spoke to the person on the phone for a moment, then she hung up and turned to Kimberly, Marsy, and Majken.

"Ms. York will be down directly to speak with you."

The receptionist left them standing next to the counter. In a moment, another woman came from the hallway to their far left. She extended her hand to the trio.

"My name is Rebecca York. How can I help you?"

When Majken showed her the photo her face brightened with recognition immediately.

"Why, yes. This is Jeanine Baker, the mother of one of our former students. Her daughter's name is Alecia. I met them in a city park less than a month ago. We had Alecia registered as Alecia Baker, but a police officer came by with a social worker and said this precious little girl had been kidnapped from her father. Of course, we gave them her address and telephone number."

Kimberly reached for the photo and pointed to Thomas. "This is my brother. We're trying to find him. No one has seen or heard from him since last Friday. Can you tell us where Ms. Baker lives?"

Rebecca seemed reluctant. "The police officer said if anyone comes asking about this student to contact him.

We wouldn't want to stand in the way of an investigation."

Marsy stepped forward, and indicating Kimberly, said, "Her brother is missing."

Kimberly persisted, "Please tell us where Ms. Baker lives. We just want to talk to the people that live near her to see if anyone has seen my brother."

Rebecca paused for a moment, then stepped into the receptionist counter and dialed a number. She got Ms. Baker's address for them. Majken handed the paper to Marsy. "I know where this is," she said.

"Who is the officer working on this case?" Majken asked.

Rebecca said, "I have his card right here." She reached into the receptionist counter and opened a drawer. Majken took the card from her and said, "I'll contact the officer. How long ago did the police come here looking for Ms. Baker's address?"

"Last Tuesday," Rebecca said. "I mean, we were so shocked. Jeanine seemed like such a good person when I met her. I guess you never know about people. We even took Alecia into our home. They said Jeanine had a mental condition where she really believed she was Alecia's mother. She'd stolen Alecia from her home. The social worker thanked us for restoring this little girl to her father." Majken thanked Rebecca for her help and quietly urged Kimberly and Marsy to leave.

Once outside Kimberly thought to ask why Majken insisted they leave so quickly.

Marsy had the address. "That way."

They found the building in the center of a block. It had been converted from commercial use to apartments. Kimberly took a second to glance at the entire floor plan mounted next to the elevator before she followed Majken and Marsy up. They found the apartment.

Police tape stretched across the door.

The door had been sealed.

"What do we do?" Kimberly asked.

Majken placed her palm over the massive brass lock that had secured the door. She tightened her fingers over the fixture and ripped it off the door frame.

The door swung open.

Majken ducked under the police tape.

"We enter," she said.

Marsy stood there with wide eyes.

Kimberly shrugged and followed her. Then Marsy followed. The little apartment was modest. Two bedrooms, a bath, kitchen, and living room.

Nothing much in the way of possessions.

Kimberly took the bedroom on the left, which turned out to be Ms. Baker's room. Marsy took the bedroom next to it, which was the little girl's room. Majken searched the living room, kitchen, and bathroom.

Kimberly rehearsed forensic procedure in her mind as she glanced around Jeanine's bedroom. First rule of searching a crime scene: touch nothing you do not have to. Second rule of searching a crime scene: see without trying to see. Third rule of searching a crime scene: keep things arranged like you found them.

She glanced into the closet and found a young woman's clothing. Mostly jeans, but a few pretty blouses and dark skirts. The few shoes there were feminine. Two black aprons, like what waitresses wear, were hung on a nail. There were no boxes on the top shelf. When Kimberly reached to the back of the top shelf, she touched a glass jar partially filled with some coinage and bills. Jeanine was putting money away for a rainy day.

Meant she had a middle class upbringing.

Because there was so little clutter in the closet, Jeanine and her daughter did not live in this apartment very long.

Kimberly knelt and looked under the bed.

Nothing there. Not even shoes.

Jeanine had little disposable income.

What woman doesn't have a closet full of shoes?

Kimberly left the closet door like she found it and turned to the little bureau. There were some porcelain nick knacks, like you'd find at a thrift store. The bureau had three sets of drawers. The knob on the left top drawer had been broken in half. This meant the furniture was likely used.

Top drawers, underwear, bras, slips.

She did find boxes of fresh razor blades under Jeanine's panties. Jeanine was like Majken. She drank blood to live. Second drawer down, things like jeans and a warmer sweater. Third drawer down, several wool blankets, bedsheets, and pillow cases. When Kimberly pushed the bottom drawer in she heard a clink as she shoved it closed. Reaching carefully for the drawer again, she pulled it out slowly and pulled it so the drawer itself tilted downward. The clink sound was heard from the front.

When she lifted up the blankets and sheets she found a large manila envelope with a rectangular metal object. Kimberly felt her heart beating faster.

She carefully lifted the envelope and opened it. It was a vehicle tag. Montana plates. February renewal month, likely for Baker. "Majken, Tea! I found something!" she called.

Marsy appeared first, then Majken.

"Look, a vehicle tag. This must have belonged to Ms. Baker."

Marsy winced painfully.

"I found something, too," she said softly.

They followed her into the little girl's bedroom. It had been turned upside down. The little twin bed had been pulled askew and contents of her little chest strewn across the floor. There were not a lot of clothes or toys, but what few things she did have had been pulled apart and destroyed.

Kimberly pursed her lips. "This looks deliberate," she said.

"Thomas has been here," Majken added. When Marsy gave her a sharp glance, she remarked, "I can tell by his residual scent. It's strongest over the couch. This is where they must have laid him." They stepped out of the bedrooms.

Pieces of broken wood frame and bits of sheared metal were in the floor. The original lock and deadbolt had been broken from the outside in. Police carry bludgeons that could break a door this way. Kimberly knelt and took her fountain pen out of her back pocket and picked at the broken deadbolt in the floor.

Majken added, "No one has been here for several days. The bathroom has the female's scent and the little girl's scent, but no other. There is only food suitable for the girl."

Kimberly stood with the Montana tag in her hand.

"What do we do with this?"

"We need an official who can search for its registration," Marsy said.

"I have someone," Majken said, as she reached for the tag. She found the telephone in the kitchen mounted on the wall.

Kimberly watched carefully the way Majken dialed: first an 800 number to dial out, then several codes, then another number dialed too fast for Kimberly to remember the keystroke sequence. Someone answered. "Hello, Christopher. It's Majken."

She listened a moment, then said, "I was hoping you would still be in the office. I have a Montana tag and I need to know to whom it belongs." Majken paused, then read the tag number. Kimberly imagined this person was typing into a computer screen an inquiry. They waited. Then Majken made a motion like needing a pen. Kimberly handed her the yellow notebook paper she carried in her back pocket and her fountain pen.

"Nolan Ciecuvich," she said. "Spell it."

Both Kimberly and Marsy stood over her.

She wrote this suspect's name down and an address in Helena Montana. Majken asked her caller to find out where Nolan Ciecuvich lived exactly, his background, and she gave him Ms. Baker's name. She asked him to call back at this number within an hour. Before she hung up, Marsy added, "Find out if he has a daughter named Alecia." Majken added that instruction, then said, "Thank you, Christopher," and hung up.

The trio went into the little living room. Marsy excused herself to use the bathroom, leaving Majken and Kimberly alone.

Kimberly waved Majken closer.

"I didn't tell her ... you know ..."

Majken glanced toward the bathroom. "I know," she said.

"Tea's had a crush on Thomas since she was seventeen. Thought you should know."

With the sound of the toilet flushing, Kimberly straightened up in the little chair . Majken resumed her restful pose on the couch. Marsy entered the room a few seconds later. She eyed Kimberly as she walked into the room. "Okay, love. What is it? What are you hiding?"

Kimberly did her best to feign wide-eyed innocence. "What do you mean, Tea?"

Marsy planted her hands on her hips.

"I know when you're hiding something," she said. "You get this guilty look on your face. And you" – she gestured to Majken – "you're unreadable." Majken made a place for Marsy to sit beside her on the couch.

"Please, Marsy. Sit with us. Kimberly is trying to protect you from potentially disturbing information she gleaned about Thomas. And about me."

Marsy crossed her arms like she was cold.

"What do you mean?"

Kimberly started crying. First slow tears spilled out of her eyes, then she covered her face with her hands. Between sobs, she said with a strained voice, "I'm sorry Tea. You are the best friend in my whole life. I felt so bad I couldn't keep Majken's promise. Now you can see right through me. I'll never be a secret agent at this rate." She wiped her runny nose with the palm of her hand.

"Nor any good at poker."

Marsy took the seat on the couch next to the cushioned chair. She took Kimberly's hands in hers.

"It's okay, love. It's okay."

Kimberly noticed that Majken leaned subtly forward. She laid her hand on Marsy's back. "You have to know the whole story now in order to protect yourself." She flipped the officer's card between two fingers and presented it to Marsy. "This officer and a social worker kidnapped Alecia from this apartment and took her to this man Nolan Ciecuvich. I do not think that a real missing person case has been filed for Alecia."

Kimberly's eyes opened really wide. She did not see that.

Marsy took the officer's card from Majken and took

note of the name. "I do not know him." She handed the card back to Majken. Majken put the card in her pocket.

"If you have a discrete source on the police department here, I believe you will find that no missing child report has been filed for her anywhere. The officer and social worker who were searching for Alecia at the church were working outside the law. From the looks of this door, I believe Alecia was forcibly taken from this apartment."

"Why?" Kimberly asked. "What harm could a little girl be to anyone?"

"What if Thomas and this girl were in here and the police took them?" Marsy added.

"That is possible," Majken said, "but I would have expected more signs of struggle. The only room that's greatly disturbed is the little girl's room. Jeanine registered Alecia with a false last name. Kimberly's premise that she is protecting her child fits well. When Thomas and Jeanine were taken, it was not from within this apartment."

"What do we do now?" Marsy asked.

Majken shifted her position on the couch. "Christopher has worked with me several years. He is diligent, thorough, and knows what to look for. I believe Kimberly is right. Thomas is in serious trouble. I have to get to Helena as quickly as possible."

Marsy stammered, "What is this thing you keep talking around? What's wrong with him now and what do you have to do with it?" Kimberly stiffened. This was it.

"Thomas has become vampyric because he was exposed to my blood in Trenton. He is undergoing a radical Change in his body and he must drink blood from now on to survive."

Marsy jumped up away from Majken and cringed in the opposite side of the living room. Kimberly bound up after her. She took her friend's hands in hers.

"It's okay, Tea. She won't hurt you."

Marsy's eyes were wide and stricken with fear. She kept looking from Kimberly to Majken and back. Kimberly pleaded with her eyes to her long-time friend. She needed her now. After all, where could she go and who could she tell now that she knows? Marsy seemed to settle a little bit.

She looked directly at Kimberly's face.

"You're telling the truth," she said lowly. "I see it in your eyes." Marsy staggered and Kimberly guided her friend toward the chair, then she herself took the empty seat next to Majken on the couch. Marsy held her head in her hands and leaned far forward. She kept muttering, "It can't be. It just can't be." It broke Kimberly's heart to see her friend so distraught.

Fall apart later, she urged mentally. We have to get to Thomas first. Kimberly noticed that Majken kept her movements very measured and slow.

"Marsy, listen to me," Majken instructed.

Her voice was calm and even, but had a commanding tone. Marsy looked up. She looked directly into Majken's deep violet eyes. It may have been the first time that Marsy let herself really look at Majken. "I need your help. Thomas needs your help. I believe he was taken from this city by the same people that took Alecia. Right now I can only guess, but Christopher will find out who these people are and what they want with Thomas, Jeanine, and Alecia."

Marsy took a deep breath and seemed to collect herself. She did not volunteer to sit beside Majken again, but she was not running out the door either. Kimberly considered this a triumph of sorts. "What do you need me to do?" Marsy asked.

"Right now, all we can do is wait."

Kimberly sprang up and went to see if anything good was in the refrigerator. She had not eaten since breakfast. Majken joined her in the kitchen and began heating water for hot tea. She had not thought of it before, but apparently most vampyric people could drink hot tea. Marsy came to the kitchen archway. Majken selected three cups and set out the tea bags once the water boiled.

Kimberly exclaimed joyfully.

In the meat drawer, there were packages of sealed cold cuts. The sliced cheese had been opened, but the wrapped slices were still good. They did not have bread, but she rolled the meat and cheese together to make snack rolls, then found olives and toothpicks to fasten her creation together.

Marsy set herself to find condiments and found honey, packets of sugar, and lemons.

Soon Kimberly had several plates of rolled snacks. There were only two chairs in the little kitchen. She was hungrier than she thought. Majken stood with her cup of hot tea and let Kimberly and Marsy have the chairs so they could enjoy their dinner. Kimberly glanced at Majken a few times as they were eating. It was painfully obvious that Majken was not eating. After all these years, watching people eat did not bother her, but she wondered what Majken thought about and how she felt being the person she was.

Majken paced to the living room and looked out the window to the street below. To Kimberly, her pose struck her as lonely. Sojourner's existence. But at least Majken and Thomas had each other. He was not struggling alone. Kimberly saw grace in that arrangement.

The telephone rang. Majken returned immediately to the kitchen and answered. By what she said and how she listened, Kimberly reasoned it was Christopher calling back.

Then she asked, "Marsy, what is the closest airport here?"

"Charlotte Douglas International."

Majken relayed this information.

She listened for a few more seconds, then asked, "What did you find on Alecia?"

Kimberly noticed she was shredding her paper napkin. She wanted so much to listen in on this conversation.

Majken looked downcast.

That wasn't good, Kimberly thought.

"When is the full moon?" she asked.

Apparently Christopher told her. "Tonight!"

She stooped down to look out the window at the fading daylight. Kimberly judged she was guessing the time.

"I need a mid-range jet to take me from Charlotte Douglas International airport to Helena Montana – and quickly, Christopher." Majken held the line and prompted Kimberly for her paper and pen again. Kimberly caught words as she wrote.

Atlanta. Flight. Concourse C. Within the hour. Majken thanked her helper and hung up. "What is it?" Kimberly asked.

Majken replied. "We have to hurry."

The trio raced out the apartment.

Thomas slept, but was jolted awake by the creaking of the trapdoor above and a heavy chain being dropped from the cabin above. Nolan came down the rusty metal rungs and dropped to the rock base subfloor. By the hot slant of sunlight above, it was probably mid-afternoon.

Thomas squinted against the bright light.

Jeanine had not moved even with the jarring sound. Nolan had not given her blood yesterday and so far today. He carried a plastic bag and some type of prod in his free hand. Her lip was bleeding where Nolan had hit her over and over again the night before. Nolan was standing in front of Jeanine, likely regarding her. The shadow of the man obscured the light from above.

He knelt in front of her and twisted her head from side to side. Thomas could see the left side of her face. Her eyes barely opened. Thomas felt relieved that Jeanine looked at Nolan. She must have been very weak.

She closed her eyes.

Nolan pushed the prod against Jeanine's open thigh and the device sparked.

Her thigh twitched, but Jeanine lay still.

Thomas saw the chain that Nolan had dropped was actually a set of manacles. He could not see Nolan's face from his position, but he envisioned a sneer and lips curled in contempt.

Nolan set down the prod device and unwrapped the plastic bag and placed it over Jeanine's head. Immediately, her breath caused the clear plastic to mist inside. Jeanine opened her eyes wide and struggled, but Nolan held the bag firmly against her neck to cut off her air.

Thomas could not see clearly.

Nolan would check Jeanine's pulse at her throat, then loosen the bag, then pull it tight around her throat again.

Thomas closed his eyes. In his mind he could hear Majken's instruction again.

Listen, she said.

Nolan's boots made a gritty sound on the subfloor. His own chains made a light chink sound as he shifted position. Below the level of human hearing, he could detect the rapid-fire beating of Nolan's heart and the slower rhythmic beating of Jeanine's heart.

Listen, Majken had told him.

Thomas almost cried. Jeanine's heart was beating slower and slower, but she was yet alive. Nolan pulled the plastic bag off her face and Thomas heard the jangle of a key ring clipped to Nolan's belt. Before he unfastened Jeanine from her bonds, he pushed the prod against her inner thighs and shocked her with a bright spark. She barely twitched.

Jeanine was likely unconscious.

As Nolan unfastened Jeanine, he glanced over his shoulder at Thomas.

"The gas won't work on her," he said.

Jeanine's bloody arms dropped to her sides.

"So far no anesthetic we've tried would work on her. So we have to use alternate methods of rendering her helpless."

Nolan worked to unfasten her secured legs beginning with her left leg closest to Thomas. Thomas could see when he moved her leg that she seemed to wince in pain. He turned and unfastened her right leg. When Jeanine rolled forward, Nolan pulled her by her arms and lay her prone lengthwise on the subfloor. From behind her, he ripped her blouse open from the back and pulled it off her.

As Nolan straddled her prone body, now lying face-down, Thomas could see the bruises along her back where she had tried to break free against the rough-hewn timbers. Nolan started whistling a mindless tune as he pulled Jeanine's elbows tight against her spine and fastened a new set of manacles just above her elbows and to her wrists. He took off his thick leather belt and pushed and rolled her until he had it around her waist. He fastened the looped end of the manacle chains into the belt behind her back.

"She said she'd kill me," Nolan said. He glanced over his shoulder at Thomas. He was smiling with a twisted grin. "I believe her," he said. "That's why I'm not going to give her the opportunity."

Nolan pulled and maneuvered Jeanine back to a sitting position against the timbers, then knelt in front of her, and pulled her body against his chest and allowed her to flop over his right shoulder. He grunted as he pulled Jeanine close and stood up with her.

Thomas didn't know how heavy Jeanine actually was. When he'd tried to lift Majken when he came up behind her in Charlotte, he could not lift her. You'd never know how heavy and dense her body actually was by how she looked or how gracefully she moved. Nolan left the cattle prod and plastic bag discarded on the cold subfloor and climbed with Jeanine's unconscious body to the cabin above. Thomas listened for Jeanine's slow steady heartbeat, but Nolan had moved her too far away for him to discern where she was.

As Nolan moved out of the trapdoor egress, the bright afternoon sunlight filtered from the cabin above. He squinted. He felt and heard furniture being dragged on the living room floor. He heard Nolan's boots scuff the wooden floor above.

Thomas heard the squeaking of springs as Nolan apparently dropped Jeanine onto a couch or bed somewhere upstairs.

The upstairs was still for a while, then Thomas heard Nolan approaching the trapdoor again. When his shadow again blocked the sunlight from above, Thomas thought he saw some type of canister with a hose attached in his right hand. He climbed down the rungs with one hand and dropped directly in front of Thomas.

"Today's your lucky day," he said as he knelt in front of Thomas.

Thomas' wrists and hands had long become numb in

the chains that secured him to the joist. The cold band around his throat forced him to sit upright. Nolan was just looking at him, staring really, as if he was an insect specimen in a jar for the collecting.

He remembered the ether a buddy from junior high school used to kill the insects he had collected before he stuck a pin through them and mounted them on a white board. Nolan opened a creaking metal panel at chest level behind him and slipped a gas mask over his own head. He tightened the straps and made sure the canisters were sealed. His faceplate misted.

He lifted the canister and pointed the hose directly at Thomas' face. A yellow gas came out and wafted around Thomas' nose. He tried to hold his breath, but it was no use. He eventually breathed the gas and felt his entire body grow numb and his vision faded to darkness. The last thing he saw was Nolan's nearly black eyes regarding him with hatred.

The Charlotte Douglas International airport was always a bustle of activity. People going and coming, people wishing friends and family goodbye, and occasional heartwarming greetings as lovers flew into each other's arms in the concourse. Kimberly parked in the closest parking space she could find on the inside of the airport loop. She did not care especially about parking. She only wanted to get Majken on a flight to her brother now that they had a direction to go.

She entered the terminal with Majken in the lead, Marsy just beside her, and looked up at the posted arrivals. Majken went into line to make arrangements for her private flight. Marsy seemed to know the airport especially well. Several flight attendants going by waved at her as they passed.

Kimberly watched the clock. It took twenty agonizing minutes for Majken to get up to the teller, then another five minutes to show her identification and get the boarding information she needed. She returned to the group and they headed down Concourse C. Fewer travelers were down this area. Several of the boarding lounges were abandoned.

Majken stood before the tinted glass overlooking the tarmac and a jetliner being prepped for boarding. Kimberly came to her right side and Marsy stood on her left.

She had said little about what she learned from Christopher about Thomas' situation.

The only other travelers in this section was a man who looked to be boarding a flight across the hallway and an older woman who was busy reading her magazine.

"How much longer?" Kimberly asked.

Marsy looked at her watch and replied, "About fifteen minutes."

The late afternoon sun was glowing red against the horizon. Kimberly glanced at the digital clock over the flight counter. Nearly six. Anxiety over what Majken had learned concerning Thomas made her feel queasy.

"What did you find out?" she asked.

Majken made sure they were standing alone, unobserved, then spoke lowly toward the thick glass in front of her.

"Nolan Ciecuvich lives in Helena, but he owns a security company originally formed in California. His daughter Alecia is seven years old. No information was available on Jeanine Baker, but an inquiry did return information about a Jeanine Brown living in the Helena area fourteen years ago. I think this is the same Jeanine and she is somehow associated with Nolan and his daughter."

Behind them, an attendant opened up the counter for

boarding and a middle-aged man started leafing through a clipboard of papers. The fluorescent lights in that area turned on.

"What's the deal with a full moon being tonight?" Marsy asked.

Majken looked in Marsy's eyes, then Kimberly's, and back again. "Certain groups drink blood ritually with each full moon. These people try to invoke the vampyric condition by drinking blood, most of the time with human sacrifice. Christopher found traces of travel arrangements made by Ciecuvich and a companion every few months ranging from Washington state to southern California over the last three years. These coincide with reports of missing women and a few lone travelers who did not arrive at their destinations."

Majken went silent to allow a man to walk past them. "If Thomas has fallen into a blood cult through Jeanine and Alecia, then they will sacrifice him tonight under the full moon." Kimberly felt her heart hammering in her chest. This was even worse than the *slasher* incident! Majken looked far afield as a smaller mid-sized jet taxied toward them.

"How are you going to stop them?" she asked. She looked into Kimberly's light brown eyes.

Majken's eyes were hard in a way she had not seen before. They seemed brighter in the fluorescent lights above. "If I get to within fifty miles of Thomas, I can find him by the voice of his blood and my directional sense of him. Helena is two hours behind us. I should get there by dusk local time. Once I arrive, I will get transportation to Nolan's ranch in western Helena. Christopher scanned topographical maps and the last known photograph of Mr. Ciecuvich. These will be on the aircraft."

Marsy pointed to the smaller jet.

"There it is! It's a Hawker 800."

Kimberly looked at the jet. To her one jet looked pretty much like any other jet. She wondered how much time her friend had been spending at the airport lately. Marsy followed the movement of the approaching jet.

"Take me with you!" Kimberly begged.

Majken's dark violet eyes softened for an instant. "I cannot," Majken replied. "I have to move quickly once I arrive. I must rescue Thomas before the full moon rises. I cannot protect you and search for him effectively at the same time."

Kimberly looked down.

She then noticed the fading bruise in the bend of her elbow.

She motioned Majken to lean close.

Kimberly whispered in her ear, "Won't you need blood before you search for him? I can help you out." She held her arm up before Majken – a very tempting offer, she thought.

Majken gently lowered Kimberly's arm.

"Christopher should have arranged for two flight attendants to be on this jet with the pilots. I can feed from them and rest while in transit before I go hunting Thomas."

Stymied, Kimberly felt frustrated.

The trio stepped to the counter behind the older woman arranging her boarding to the large jet to their right. Kimberly tugged on Majken's shoulder.

"How will I know you got him out?"

Majken smiled at the middle-aged man at the counter and presented her credentials. The man seemed to regard her with a bored expression.

Kimberly waited patiently until Majken had finished her transaction with the man at the counter.

The man at the counter frowned when he looked at his

computer. He held Majken's assumed passport up to the light and seemed to compare her face to the photograph in the travel document. The man asked to see her driver's license.

Majken produced her non-driver's license under her assumed name. Kimberly glanced at her likeness on the card. To her it looked very official and real. Now understanding that Majken had to slip between identities made it far easier to empathize when she had to endure close scrutiny like this.

The man behind the counter asked her to wait a moment as he called a supervisor, or someone in authority, to help him.

Kimberly started getting a bad feeling about this. It was taking far too long to gain entrance to the aircraft. When he hung up, he returned her credentials to her and instructed her to go to the service desk to get her boarding pass. He apologized for being unable to allow her to board.

Majken retrieved her documents with a smile and stepped away from the counter. In the middle of the hallway, Kimberly and Marsy gathered around her.

"What happened?" Marsy asked.

Majken pocketed her passport and non-driver's license.

"There is a discrepancy between my travel documents. He will not let me board until it is resolved." Kimberly glanced over her shoulder at the officious little man.

Majken started walking toward the central hub of the airport. Her plan to get to Thomas quickly appeared to be crumbling around her. Each step away from the jet that could get Majken to Helena within hours seemed like they were escorting a condemned prisoner down to the gas chamber. "What are we going to do?" Kimberly asked.

Majken looked at Kimberly. "When I had these credentials made, I did not anticipate having to travel through a
commercial portal."

The sheer number of travelers and passersby increased
as the trio made their way to the hub of the airport.

Marsy suddenly hooked her arm in Majken's arm and
pulled her toward a metal door to their immediate right.
The Asian girl entered a four-digit code into the door
latch, and the latch emitted a beep. When she pushed in,
the metal door opened and the loud sounds of wind and
jet engines roaring filled the hallway.

She pulled Majken and Kimberly with her and pushed
the outer access door shut. In front of them was a set of
metal stairs going down to the below airport facility, luggage handling and aircraft servicing. They followed her
quickly down the metal stairs. To Kimberly, this looked
like opportunity.

A man with one of those flat luggage carriers was approaching. She really couldn't tell much about the man
with the headphones, dark glasses, coveralls, and gloves
he wore. A dreamcatcher swayed from the carrier front
window. When he stopped Kimberly noticed he was probably thirty. His face was clearly Native American, she
guessed, maybe Navajo or Apache. His light grey coveralls had been splashed with what looked like grease.
When he lifted off his earmuffs, hat, and goggles, his hair
was long, jet black, and braided.

He smiled at Marsy and stepped out of the carrier to
greet her. The last name SANSHIE had been embroi-
dered into his coveralls over his lapel.

"Gordon," she said, "you know Kimberly. This is her
friend from Europe. She needs to get on that jet over there,
but the official won't let her board. Can you help us?"

The luggage handler regarded Majken, standing next

to Kimberly, and asked, "Why won't he let her board?"

Marsy took his arm.

"I think it's a computer glitch. But Kimberly knows her personally and I can vouch for her too. Please help us."

She had to speak loudly to be heard over the persistent whine of jet engines. The heat of aircraft rose from the tarmac. A large jetliner made a landing and another jetliner took off from an adjacent runway.

Sanshie seemed to regard Majken for a second, then turned to his luggage carrier and pulled another set of light grey coveralls out of a bin and tossed them to Majken. "Put these on," he said.

Kimberly glanced around. The other airport workers were busy with two aircraft that had just landed at the western end of the airport.

Majken quickly slipped into the too large coveralls. The long legs bunched around her ankles and the arms extended past her fingertips. Kimberly helped her stuff her long braided hair down the back of her coveralls and into the hat. She helped Majken place the ear protectors around her neck. From above, Majken should look just like any other airport field worker.

Majken went to Marsy and drew her into a hug. Marsy seemed relieved when Majken released her.

Over the din, she shouted in Marsy's ear.

"Marsy, have you considered Gordon? How long have you known him?"

"Two years," Marsy called back.

Kimberly kept her head close to hear what was being said.

Majken leaned again into Marsy's ear.

"He's in love with you," she called.

Marsy's eyes became wide and she glanced at her friend and back at Majken.

When Majken looked at Kimberly, she rushed into her arms without being prompted. She felt the misting of her eyes. It seemed she was saying goodbye a lot lately.

With everything that had happened, she was so thankful. Majken would get to her brother in time. She just knew it. Then her thought at the flight boarding counter came to her mind. She pulled Majken's head close and shouted, "How will I know you found him and he's safe?"

Majken held Kimberly's face and called back, "I will contact you or I will have him contact you."

Kimberly released Majken.

Time was of the essence. Marsy's friend dove behind the wheel of his luggage carrier and drove directly to the waiting small jet. A set of portable stairs had been wheeled to the front cockpit of the jet and what appeared to be a male flight attendant and a pilot were standing in the open hatch of the aircraft.

Kimberly watched from the shadows.

Sanshie drove under the craft to the opposite luggage compartment of the aircraft, and made a thumbs-up motion to Majken. Within thirty seconds, she had hopped out of the luggage carrier, made her way under and behind the portable stairs, and up to the open hatch of the aircraft. She stood a moment exposed on the stairs before the pilot stepped aside and let her on board.

Kimberly let out the breath she had been holding. Marsy grabbed her arm in relief. They had done it!

Marsy's friend drove the luggage carrier and stopped behind them. When he got out, he pulled off the hat and earmuffs and stood behind Marsy. When Marsy turned and saw him, she smiled and extended her hand. Sanshie reached his right hand and took her left hand. They stood there together in shadows as the smaller aircraft powered up and taxied to the runway. The sun was now a golden-red globe just above the horizon.

Kimberly prayed for God to help Majken find her brother. She'd done all she could do.

The rest was up to Majken.

Jeanine awoke in billowing white and the face of an angel before her face.

Was this heaven?

As soon as she tried to move, a sharp jabbing pain in her shoulder and throbbing lower lip told her she was still present in her body on the earth.

She squinted. Her vision was hazy. Blurry images hovered before her. She heard sounds like from a long dark tunnel. She blinked several times to clear her vision. A form hovered over her.

A cherubic face smiled at her.

"She's coming to," a dear sweet voice said.

Another shape came into her field of vision, taller, darker, the devil himself.

Jeanine finally focused.

Before her Momma Lillian stood wearing a white knitted sweater, long gray woolen dress, thick orthopedic shoes, and a three-prong walking cane that went clump-clump when she moved it as she walked. "Momma," Jeanine breathed.

Her former landlady smiled at her and brushed her hand gently across her face.

"How are you feeling dear?" she asked.

"I've felt better," she replied.

She was very thirsty and felt a distinct hollowness from two days of blood withdrawal.

Jeanine finally focused on just who was standing behind Momma Lillian. Nolan stood with his arms crossed – watching her closely. Her right shoulder hurt. When she tried to move either arm, she found she could not. From her elbows to her wrists, her arms had been bound behind her back. She flexed her hands to try to work up some circulation.

She took stock of her surroundings.

She was in the family room on a cot just down from the fireplace. It was dusk and quickly getting darker. This was the night of the full moon. Against the foyer, Thomas had been secured to a gurney for transport to the sacrifice site. Nolan had placed a black mask over his face, but Jeanine guessed he was unconscious from the tilt of his head. Nolan had probably gassed him. Jeanine struggled to sit up.

"Where's Alecia?" she asked sharply.

Momma Lillian hobbled back a few steps and Nolan filled her field of vision.

"She's in her room," Nolan replied.

Jeanine glanced at the closed door of Alecia's bedroom. She tried to hear within the room, but Alecia was not moving around. She may even be at the door listening.

"I wanted to make sure you were awake before I brought her out. I couldn't deprive you of saying goodbye to her. Ms. Daugherty wanted to be here to say goodbye in person."

Jeanine glanced at Momma Lillian.

Her cherubic smile became utterly cold and void. Her gray eyes held a glint of hardness she had never perceived in her friend before. Jeanine moved as Momma Lillian came near again. She looked down. Her legs were free. She flexed her left knee and swung to a sitting position on the cot.

Her right foot touched the hardwood floor and found purchase. She unfurled her left leg and lowered it to the floor. Her center of gravity was behind her with her arms bound as they were, but if she rolled forward enough, she thought she could stand. Nolan went to Alecia's bedroom and unlocked the padlock.

As soon as the door was ajar, he thrust his right arm in and pulled Alecia out by her hair.

"Jennie!" Alecia cried.

The little girl started struggling, pulling her head away from her Daddy. Nolan took her by the arm and shoved her toward Jeanine. Alecia slid on the hardwood floor. She bumped Momma Lillian's walking cane.

Momma Lillian picked up her cane and set it squarely in the middle of Alecia's back. She pushed down with two frail little hands to pin Alecia to the floor. Alecia started crying.

"Leave her alone," Jeanine cried.

She rocked forward and tried to get up.

Nolan stepped around Momma Lillian and over Alecia to backhand Jeanine on the mouth. Her lower lip started bleeding again, but the blow was really nothing to Jeanine. He'd hit her a lot harder through the years.

Momma Lillian lifted her cane and allowed Alecia to scramble forward on her hands and knees.

Jeanine caught the look of utter disgust in Nolan's eyes as he watched his baby try to crawl to her. Alecia quickly pulled herself next to Jeanine and hugged her left leg.

How could he not love his baby girl?

Alecia was no longer crying. She was just looking at Momma Lillian and her Daddy with calm detachment. "Baby," she called, "are you all right?" Alecia smiled at her. As soon as Alecia looked up into Jeanine's eyes, she felt peace flood her being.

Whatever Nolan did to her, it was going to be all right for her baby girl.

"Look at her," Nolan complained to Momma Lillian, "the brat never looked at me that way – and I'm her father." He seemed to throw up his hands in disgust. He

paced to the kitchen. Momma Lillian clomped to the fireplace and seemed to be more interested in the fire than
Jeanine. Jeanine whispered, "Baby, climb up here."

Alecia climbed on the cot and sat next to Jeanine. She
reached around Jeanine's bare waist. Nolan returned
from the kitchen with a large serrated hunting knife.

Momma Lillian hobbled to his side and took the knife
from him and started toward Jeanine. She'd seen that
same look many, many times before – each time Nolan
killed the sacrifice. Jeanine quickly said, "Baby girl, get
behind me." Alecia crouched behind her. Momma Lillian
struck Jeanine in the chest with the hunting knife. She
felt the knife lacerate her lung.

Her blood spurted on the floor.

Alecia slid down behind her on the cot.

Jeanine held Alecia with her free hands as Momma
Lillian struck her again. This time in the left shoulder.
Jeanine used her foot to kick Momma Lillian's walking
cane away. The elderly woman toddled but continued her
attack.

A deep penetrating blow below her ribcage caused her
entire body to go numb.

Jeanine got to her feet, crouched and used her body
to knock Momma Lillian backwards. The knife flew from
her hand and the elderly woman fell onto the fireplace
mantle. When Momma Lillian's head struck the rock
ledge, her fragile skull collapsed. She died instantly. Jeanine fell facedown in her own blood.

Nolan stepped over Jeanine's body to pull Alecia away.
Alecia started screaming for her and continued to struggle as Nolan fastened her with Thomas on the gurney.
As the time of sacrifice was approaching, Nolan pushed
them both outside. She heard his van leaving.

Jeanine slowly faded from consciousness.

Chapter Fourteen

Outside the mountain sunset was brilliant hues of burnt sienna, red, purple, and blue. The Hawker jet circled for its final approach to Helena Regional Airport. While she was well elevated, Majken closed her eyes against the glare of the dying sun and tried to sense Thomas' direction. He was close enough that she knew he was here. It was still too soon for her directional sense of him to filter out the distractions of this place.

Just like the blood-soaked ground in Sumter, this ground also screamed from a great distance. She had not been out west except for a brief sojourn in Seattle twenty-five years ago.

The pilot notified her they were about to begin their final descent. Majken folded the topographical map she had been studying. Her eyes narrowed on the copy of the grainy newspaper photograph of Nolan Ciecuvich as taken four years before. Once she was on the ground, she would destroy any materials that Christopher had provided her.

In the two lounge seats behind her, the two air attendants slept. Majken was able to feed well from the male attendant, then rest two hours. She had to rouse herself sooner than she would have liked, but she had no choice. The jet set down smoothly and taxied to a squat white metal building.

While Majken waited for the aircraft stairs to be wheeled to the front hatch, the copilot came to the passenger section of the craft and asked her where the two flight attendants were. She directed him to the plush seats behind her's as the pilot opened the front hatch and let her depart.

Far afield, the full moon rose just above the horizon. The moon was glowing red, a full harvest moon.

Few other travelers were in the Helena Regional Airport at this time of evening. She asked several workers behind the counters and discovered that no transportation services existed in Helena except public transportation that closed down at five thirty. She spotted a dark-skinned slender man, likely from Egypt, holding a piece of cardboard with the word "Taxi" written in black marker.

She hailed the man.

"My name is Hassan," he said with halting English and a thick Arabic accent.

He bowed slightly and asked where he could take her. Majken asked to be taken to the western part of Helena. He led her to a maroon sedan with darkly tinted windows. She described where she wanted to go and he quoted a price. She agreed and let him open the car door for her. Majken rolled down the window to feel the dry air outside.

Inside the car, over his rear view mirror, three pictures were suspended in a sparkling iridescent frame. Himself, a woman near his age, and a young girl who appeared to be a preteen. When he got behind the wheel, he picked up a clipboard and wrote his mileage on the chart.

They quickly left the airport, crossed the expressway, and headed due west. Majken felt a distinct tug from that direction when the car faced west. Ahead of them, next to a gas station and a local restaurant, a snarling mass of bikers had filled the road and were criss-crossing over all the lanes of traffic. The bikers had stopped traffic.

The cars behind them started blowing horns at the bikers. Majken watched them. They would hoot and jeer and make rude gestures at the drivers who wished to pass. Most of the bikers had long unruly hair and several sported spiked collars.

They wore black leather jackets with their gang emblem on the back. A man riding a motorcycle with a woman on the back stuck out his tongue at her. The silver haired woman with him laughed. The rider behind this one swung a chain around and around over his head.

Hassan steered to the far right to try to get around the bikers. The rider with the chain and another biker with a stout club of sorts charged the sedan and smashed the front windshield.

Her little driver went pale.

The other biker hit the back of the car with the club he wielded. The back tire on the passenger side blew out. The vehicle lurched to the right and started riding the rim, metal against the roadway. Hassan pulled the crippled vehicle off the road into the parking lot to their right, watched for a clearing in the buzzing bikers, then abandoned Majken in his vehicle. She saw him make his way on foot back toward the airport.

Majken got out of the car and stood next to it. The bikers were circling her and the car, as well as darting in and out of traffic trying to cross the interstate. Most of the bikers had congregated at the convenience store and restaurant across the street. In the east above the airport behind her, the full moon had risen a good handspan above the horizon.

In the melee of bikers, she crossed the street and made her way to the restaurant where most of the bikers had gathered.

Territorial law prevailed.

Tribal customs prevailed.

She was allowed to enter the restaurant by the two burly men standing at the door. Good so far. Inside, she spotted the largest group massed at a circular table. Other bikers, and the women with them, partied with the beer likely purchased or taken from the convenience store. A waiter and waitress were huddled against the serving counter.

Majken pressed through the sea of people gathered at the circular table. Some type of wager and card game was in progress. She noted the two largest men, each with loud cheering supporters at opposite ends of the table.

She made her way to the table and stood between the two leaders where either biker could see and acknowledge her. She waited. A fight or disturbance of some kind broke out behind her next to the door. She ignored it. The two gamblers were drawing playing cards from a central deck.

A drinking man stumbled into Majken and tried to put his arm around her.

Majken lifted him bodily and dropped him into the center of the table. The card game abruptly stopped. The lively banter, cheering, and playing in the restaurant ceased.

Everything became still as all eyes turned to her. The biker Majken had deposited on the table scrambled to get out of the way. She leaned forward and propped both arms on the table. She looked at the leaders and quietly asked, "I need a ride. Will you allow one of your men to take me to western Helena?"

Nothing moved for a few seconds.

Then the biker to her near left started laughing. The other men and women at the table joined in. The jovial atmosphere in the crowd resumed at high pitch.

Majken assumed that meant no.

She turned to make her way out. In the press of people where one man was trying to stab another with a hunting knife, she quietly broke the man's wrist as she passed.

He howled and dropped the knife.

It embedded into the wooden floor.

A huge toothless bald man blocked her exit. He sneered at her. It was an obvious dare. The man and woman beside her started groping each other. Majken abruptly knelt, and reached for the large biker's boots. She pressed both of his feet together at the ankles and jerked his legs out from under him. He fell with a crash. Other party goers cheered her on. She stepped over the belly of the fallen man and made her way outside.

Many of the bikers had stopped blocking traffic. They had gathered at the nearby gas station. She made her way to the department store across the street to find another ride.

The department store parking lot was largely deserted. The sounds of motorcycles racing in the background pelted the barren lot like gunfire.

Majken considered the few shoppers remaining in the store. A woman and a child approached her on their way to their vehicle. She knew from the closed look in the woman's eyes and her wary glance at the stranger, that she would not help her. Another older man approached, likewise, ignoring her.

Then a young man left the store with a few groceries in a plastic sack. He had neatly trimmed blonde hair and a small moustache. He looked at her, then seemed to bow his head and pay attention to his keys to open his small truck. Majken approached him. "Sir, will you help me?" she asked.

The man regarded her, then said, "I don't have money to spare, ma'am." He fumbled for his keys and unlocked his truck.

"I don't need money. I need a ride. I'm trying to find the address of an old classmate. I've just arrived in Helena and I do not know the area. I will be happy to pay you for your time. I promise it will not take long."

The young man seemed to consider.

He looked inside his truck and stuck his groceries in the carrier behind the cab. "Sure, I'll be happy to help you." he said. "Where do you need to go?"

Majken smiled at him and glanced toward the west. She knew Thomas was generally in that direction, although not exactly where. Nolan Ciecuvich's ranch was in that direction as well. It was the most likely place where Thomas would be.

"My friend's name is Nolan Ciecuvich. He has a ranch somewhere in western Helena. I found out from another classmate he lives here, and I want to surprise him."

She extended her hand and shook the young man's hand.

"Oh," she added, "my name is Marie."

The young man seemed abashed.

"My name is Jeremy." He unlocked the passenger-side door of his truck and opened the door for her. Majken slid into the seat and fastened her seat belt. As he got into the driver's seat, he said, "I've seen your friend at the school a few times with his daughter. He's not really the friendly type, I would say. His live in is far more the sociable one."

Majken took a stab in the dark.

"Oh," she remarked, "I haven't seen Alecia since she was a little baby. His friend's name – I think her name is Jeanine, uh, Jeanine ..."

"Jeanine Bishop," Jeremy remarked.

Majken smiled at him, "Yes, Jeanine Bishop."

They drove to the far western end of the parking lot and slipped into evening traffic. Majken asked Jeremy if she could roll down her window. He said yes. It was fully night now. The dry air circulated in the cab of the truck. Jeremy rolled his window down as well and propped his elbow outside. He shifted gears easily with his right hand while steering by using his fingertips.

"Which school did you see Alecia at?" she asked.

"Smith Elementary," he answered. "I'm a fifth grade

teacher there. It'll be a few more years before Alecia will be in my class. From all I've seen, she's a bright little girl."

"Nolan's smart," Majken offered. "He would have to be to run a security company."

Jeremy nodded in agreement. They were leaving the main section of Helena and entering the mountainous region on Euclid. The traffic got lighter. Majken looked back at the rising full moon. She mentally urged this young man to hurry. "Where do you know Mr. Ciecuvich from?" Jeremy asked suddenly.

She recalled a few things Christopher had found in Nolan's background. "We had classes together at Caltech. I was only there a year before my Momma got sick and I had to drop out of school. I lost track of Nolan completely since then."

Jeremy seemed satisfied at that.

They were approaching storage buildings to her left and mobile homes for sale on her right. Majken pointed to the lodge ahead. "Can we stop here please?"

Jeremy slowed and pulled off into the parking lot in front of the lodge. Majken got out of the truck and looked around. Nothing was here. Thomas was not here, she was certain of it. She looked over the little white trailers then got back into Jeremy's truck. "What was it?" he asked.

Majken shrugged. "Just a feeling," she said.

As Jeremy pulled back on Euclid, Majken felt Thomas nearer, to the west and north of her position. It was highly obvious to her that Ciecuvich was involved in a blood cult and they had actively sacrificed in this area for many years. Her head literally throbbed with the silent screams and the blood-soaked ground to the northwest.

They would sacrifice somewhere in the woodlands ahead.

As Euclid became US Highway 12, the passage of the

road became mountainous. Majken asked Jeremy to drive slower. She shielded her eyes from oncoming headlight glare and concentrated on the approaching Helena West Side.

She scanned the roadway for signs that would lead her to Nolan's ranch. By now, the full moon had risen above the treeline and cast blue-white light across the darkened landscape. She looked for a trail marked with the Algonquin term for wolf: *mahingan*. If they made it to MacDonald Pass she came too far and missed her trail. Jeremy drove in silence. Majken was thankful he did not try to distract her with banter. She needed to concentrate right now. The roadway dipped and looped a few more miles, then – ahead, she saw the trail she had been looking for. She asked him to pull off the road to her right. Jeremy stopped for her. The little crease in the road was barely wide enough to park. A large truck passed them, then the roadway became dark. Majken asked him to douse his headlights.

He did so and she got out of his vehicle. She stood looking up the trail. Jeremy got out and came to her side of his truck. Her dark adapted eyes easily picked out the features of the forest trail before her. Jeremy stuck both hands in his front pockets. "Hey, if you're going to be in town a while, I'll be happy to show you around if you want to see the sights with a local." Majken thanked him and said yes. He wrote his name and phone number on his store receipt. He generously refused to take payment for bringing her out here. She gave him a hug, then watched him drive away. Nolan's ranch was just over the rise.

Majken ran to the top of the ridge and peered into the valley before her. By the climbing bright moonlight, she easily picked out detail in the cabin and barnyard below. Thomas had been brought this way. She felt him. He had bled in that cabin. Whether he was there now or not, his blood called to her.

Far into the mountainous passage nearby, wolves howled.

She approached the cabin.

Alert for movement within, and signs of habitation, she ran to the edge of Nolan's barnyard wooden fence. She detected the distinct smell of a small herd of domesticated goats. The scent of goat's blood was mixed with the dry dirt of the yard.

She listened within the cabin. The yellowish glow from the main room cast a golden pool on the hewn timbers that made the porch. No sounds yet within. Maybe the soft crackling of a fire in the fireplace. Majken moved to the front door and softly pulled the latch open. It slid open with a clink and the door creaked open wide. She found two bodies on the floor.

Before she committed herself, she listened within the entire cabin and assured herself that no other person was there. The young girl in the center of the floor, fallen into a pool of thick blood, was wheezing and laboring to breathe. The older woman above her was clearly dead. Her skull had been broken in her fall against the fireplace mantle.

Majken knelt next to the young woman's body. Every few seconds, her body would heave and she would take a labored breath. This was the vampyric girl Jeanine, she realized.

The girl's arms had been manacled behind her back. A blood stained hunting knife lay beyond the old woman's outstretched hand. Majken hooked her fingers into the manacle above Jeanine's right elbow and pulled the lock apart. She broke the other locks as well. When Jeanine's arms were free, she coughed heavily and spit up blood.

Majken knelt beside her and reached under her chest to lift her over. Jeanine was naked and had been stabbed several times in the chest, once in her left shoulder, and deep in her abdomen just below her ribcage.

Her eyes fluttered open in the soft yellow glow of the cabin. Her lips were pale. Majken knew that she was bleeding internally. The rhythm of her heartbeat was very, very slow.

Pretty hazel green eyes regarded her.

Majken's dark violet eyes softened as she looked into Jeanine's eyes. She knew Jeanine was dying. No way to prevent that now.

"*sorōris*," Majken whispered.

Latin, for sister.

She held Jeanine gently propped in her lap. Jeanine's lips moved. Majken bowed her head to better hear.

Her voice was weak and broken.

"He ... took them ..." she said.

Majken cradled the young vampyric girl in her arms.

"Which way?" Majken asked.

Jeanine labored to take a deep breath. Her body convulsed and she lay still. She looked into Majken's eyes.

Her breathing came easier.

"Stone ... east ... where US 12 loops ... north ... ravine ... he has Alecia ... Thomas." She closed her eyes for a second, then reached for Majken's hand with her bloody hand.

Her heart was beating erratically.

Majken bent low over Jeanine.

Jeanine seemed to rally, and spoke softly. "Promise ... you'll ... get her away ... from him. Promise ... Take her ... her ... to her mother ... Sarah Ciecuvich ... lives in Van Nuys ... California ... find her mother ... save ... Alecia ... baby girl."

Majken touched the slow pooling tears in Jeanine's eyes. Tears from her dark violet eyes splashed on Jeanine's cheek.

She squeezed Jeanine's hand.

"I promise," she said.

Jeanine smiled up at her. Her pale lips quivered, and she winced in pain. Her breaths came in labored gasps. Her body convulsed again. She drew several deep breaths, then lay still.

Her face was peaceful. Tranquil.

"I knew you ... would come ... knew Alecia ... saved." She closed and reopened her lovely hazel green eyes. She looked up.

"I'm finally ... warm," she said with great wonderment. Jeanine's body went slack in Majken's arms. Her eyes set in death.

Majken gently closed her eyes.

The only sound in the cabin was the faint crackling of the fireplace. A crumbling log fell into the ashes, stirring sparks and gray dust. Majken lay Jeanine's body on the hardwood floor. She had to get going. Yet she just sat numb, staring into the fire.

Her heart ached for Jeanine.

Yet, even in death, she was at peace.

Whatever suffering Nolan and the likes of the blood cult had put her through, none of that could touch her now.

Majken gathered herself. She stood and found a white bedsheet under the cot where Jeanine had been stabbed. She knelt and spread the white sheet over Jeanine's body, then rolled her in the sheet. Her blood quickly stained through the fabric. Majken searched and found a blue grey woolen blanket. She wrapped Jeanine's body in the blanket, tucked the ends to make sure her blood was no longer dripping on the floor, then carried her outside.

Beyond the barnyard, she spotted an old freezer with rusty engine parts piled on it. Majken swept off the freezer and opened it. She lay Jeanine's body gently in the freezer.

She turned to face a pack of wolves.

Thomas felt cold in spite of the dry air stirring the spruce trees around him. The full moon cast blue-white glow high in the sky. He opened his mouth, but no sounds came out. His jaw hurt. His tongue felt swollen and he could not speak. When he tried to move, he found he could not. His wrists and feet had been bound with tight leather thongs. He was naked and strapped spread-eagle. His heels and elbows bumped into a rough stone surface. Pressure was on his chest. He heard a little girl crying.

Thomas looked toward his feet.

Alecia lay across him face up. She was naked. Her tiny hands were tied at one end and her little feet had been tied together at the other end.

A black cloaked figure came into view. Nolan pushed back the cowl of his robe and lay the golden chalice beside Thomas' face. He unsheathed a curved blade and held it where Thomas could easily see it. Thomas tightened his fists and pulled at the thongs binding him, but they only tightened and cut off his circulation in his hands. Nolan resheathed the blade, then raised the chalice to the moon and began to chant in Latin.

Thomas listened. He heard the light fast beating of Alecia's heart. He heard the slower powerful beating of his own heart. He heard the rapid beating of the blood cult leader.

Thomas closed his eyes.

In his mind, he pictured his mom's face. His dad. Kimberly. Army brat. He saw his girlfriend as he knew her at school, Mary Harris. He then saw her the night he learned she was vampyric, when she lay on top of him after they had made love. She whispered her real name – Majken. He saw Jeanine as he awoke on her couch after she had rescued him. He remembered Jeanine's pretty smile as she drank hot tea with him and Alecia's bubbly charm. Live, Majken had begged him.

Choose life. Live.

Darkness tried to close around his mind.

Majken's dark violet eyes called him.

Only love remained. Nolan may take his life, but he vowed never to just give it away. He opened his eyes.

In the midst of death Thomas chose life.

Chapter Fifteen

The large gray black timber wolf regarded Majken with yellow-gold eyes. The largest wolf, a dominant male, approached from the edge of the forest that intruded into the barnyard. The other wolves held back to the shadows. By the cast of blue-white moonlight, the encounter was eerie. Jeanine's blood was still on Majken's hands and arms. Majken knelt and picked up the box of engine parts she had put off the freezer and placed it back on the top. She picked up handfuls of dirt and bramble and spread it over the freezer and nearby ground to cover where she had hidden Jeanine's body.

Majken looked up. The full moon was high in the sky. Thomas' blood called to her. East, Jeanine had said. The ridge to the east was split. The large male wolf sniffed at her as she passed. The pack followed her.

As she walked, she could almost hear a tribal drum beating. In her mind, she visualized the topographical map Christopher had made for her. She picked up her pace. From the opposite ridge, she got a glimpse of the mountainous valley and adjacent ridges. Majken moved steadily over the broken rock into the forest passage. When she stepped into the thickest of the forest growth, the moonlight above was shielded.

She now knew exactly where she was going. The drumming sound continued in her mind. Thomas' heartbeat.

The wolves behind her kept pace.

She saw a reflective surface in the ravine before her. The moonlight was reflecting off the windshield of a commercial van.

Majken knelt on the ridge top.

The large wolf approached her. The other wolves approached more cautiously.

She listened. A man was chanting in the center of the hidden ravine below. Although Majken could not see him, she knew exactly where he was. Majken touched two of the wolves on the back. They sat and stayed in place. One wolf was a male only slightly smaller than the dominant male. The other wolf was female and likely his mate.

She moved due north. The rest of the pack followed.

From the opposite ridge to the north, she could peer into the ravine itself. She could not see the face of the man holding the goblet up to the moon and chanting, but this was most certainly Nolan Ciecuvich. Before him a massive stone altar had been erected on four half-buried boulders.

Thomas had been bound to the slab.

A little girl was tied above him at his chest level.

The barrel of a high-powered rifle propped against the stone altar reflected the moon glow. Majken touched the two female wolves and they stayed on the north ridge. She continued southeast. The dominant male wolf followed her.

Majken listened. The man stopped chanting.

He lay the goblet at the head end of the stone altar. He pulled the scabbard of a curved blade from around his neck and unsheathed a jeweled scimitar. Majken moved silently to the ridge directly before the blood cult leader. The large male wolf sat beside her. She pursed her lips and whistled low.

The large wolf lifted his head and started howling. The mournful cry pierced the night. The other wolves began to howl in unison. She moved quickly down the ravine embankment.

Hidden in deep shadows, she could easily watch the man lay down the blade and pick up his weapon.

Majken moved silently into striking position.

The mournful howling of the wolves reverberated in the secluded ravine. The man jerked to the left, and then the right, to try to determine the source of the sounds.

Majken eased from the fallen tree to the boulder about twenty feet from the man.

She tensed, then calmed herself.

Majken held herself ready, waiting on him to turn the other way. The wolves continued howling. When the man turned, she sprang from her hiding place and covered the ground to him in a few seconds. She gripped his rifle first and wrenched it from his hands. Taking the barrel in both hands, she smashed the rifle stock and mechanism on the cold stone slab. It shattered.

The man before her fell backwards on the ground. The cowl of his robe fell from his face and the skirt part rode above his knees. Nolan Ciecuvich.

Majken jerked him from the ground and held him aloft by his robe. He hung limp and suspended by his flailing arms. From the undergrowth, the wolves approached from the three sides west, north, and east. From the corner of her eye, she saw Thomas looking at her. His expression was one of bliss and dismay. His mouth was moving, but no sound came out.

When the wolves formed a circle at the entrance of the ravine, Majken dropped the blood cult leader on the ground. Keeping her eyes on this man, she reached for the scimitar and sliced the leather bands holding Alecia's hands and Thomas' hands. When he sat up, she slid the blade handle into his hand so he could finish cutting himself and the girl free.

The man on the ground cowered before her. Thomas knelt on the carved stone surface and tried to get the little girl to look at him. She just sat numbly on the rough stone.

The wolves started snarling.

Majken reached for Ciecuvich again and pushed him hard into the stone altar. He turned to her with a murderous look in his eyes. He was getting angry. Ciecuvich charged her.

Majken easily sidestepped and hit a solid blow to his abdomen. He doubled over and fell at her feet. He coughed up blood. "Who are you?" he wailed.

Majken wanted to break his neck, but she restrained herself. She picked him up bodily and slammed him face-down on the stone altar. She ripped the black robe off his body and turned him face up so he was in the same position Thomas was originally.

Thomas had moved Alecia to the right side of the stone slab surface. She sat unmoving.

Fresh leather ties were coiled under the slab. Majken held Ciecuvich's arm with one hand while she made a loop with the other and secured his left arm. She hopped up on the slab itself and straddled the man and tied his right arm, then both legs far apart as Thomas had been bound. His nose and chin were bleeding where he had struck the stone altar. She straddled him with her full body weight. Nolan gasped to breathe as Majken sat on his chest. She eased up a little, then lay on him again with her face close to his. When his body shuddered with lack of oxygen, she rose up and let him breathe.

She took a handful of his hair in her left hand and made sure he looked into her eyes.

She spoke in his right ear.

"I'm Jeanine's sister," she whispered lowly. His eyes grew wide and frantic. He started struggling to get free, but the leather straps only tightened. Majken crouched next to Ciecuvich.

The little girl was just sitting on her knees staring at her father. Her expression was completely void. Thomas did what he could to comfort her. He held her from behind. She did not appear to know he was there.

"So, Mr. Ciecuvich. I have it on reliable authority that you wish to become vampyric." She motioned Thomas to join her. She smiled grimly at her captive. "Well, let me explain how your miserable life will Change if this happens." She used the discarded blade to cut his arm above his wrist.

Blood seeped like black tar on the stone.

Majken made another cut on his opposite arm where Thomas was kneeling. She knelt over and started feeding. Thomas joined her. After several minutes of drinking his blood, Majken paused. "If you become vampyric, you will need to drink blood just to live."

Ciecuvich responded angrily, "What gives you the right to judge me? We, too, have the power to take life. We are far less a parasite than you." Majken pressed her fingers into this man's jaw and directed his gaze her way. Her smile did not reach her eyes.

"I did not come here to kill you," she said.

Ciecuvich laughed a hard shrill sound.

She told Thomas, "Feed as much as you are able." Thomas held the man's right arm and continued feeding. His little girl was just staring in the blue-white cast of moonlight.

Majken finished feeding and climbed off the stone dais. The wolves were waiting beyond the ravine. She looked into the large dominant male's yellow-gold eyes.

It ended here. It ended now.

Thomas finished feeding. He backed away from Ciecuvich. Other than the fact that he did not have any clothing, he appeared fine. Alecia stared motionless at her father. Her expression was void and empty. Majken approached her slowly.

"Alecia," she said gently.

The little girl's head turned toward her.

Majken extended her arms to her to beckon her to come, and said, "Jeanine sent me to get you." She reached for Alecia.

The little girl's eyes snapped wide open and she started crawling toward Majken.

Majken lifted the little girl off the stone altar and allowed her to wrap her arms around her neck. Her legs automatically wrapped around her torso.

Thomas hopped off the dais stone as well.

He spoke very faintly, straining to speak.

"We have to go back to Nolan's cabin. He left Jeanine there. He was holding us in a subfloor cellar. Nolan took Jeanine up before me —" Majken warned him with a glance. He seemed a little confounded at her wary expression, then he got it. "Oh, no," he stammered. "Oh, God, no!"

Thomas winced a little walking over the rocks and bramble on the trail. After years of camping, at least he was not a tenderfoot. Majken brushed Alecia's dark brown hair out of her eyes and smiled at her. Her heartbeat was slow for a little girl. She was very pale and likely in shock. Thomas opened the back of Ciecuvich's van and found the clothes his former captor wore.

He slipped on the trousers gratefully. They were a little big on him. The hiking boots were tight, but they fit. Thomas took the flannel shirt and slipped it around Alecia. Then Thomas pulled on Ciecuvich's coat.

The large dominant wolf approached Thomas. Thomas backed against the van. He cast a glance at Majken, who appeared calm.

Majken handed Alecia to Thomas and knelt before the wolf. She brushed her hand down the sleek muzzle, past the thick hair at his head and throat, onto his flanks. Feral predator to feral predator, the wolf howled.

With a final glance upward at the harvest moon, Majken returned to the sacrificial stone altar. Occultic runes and glyphs had been delicately carved into the stone surface. She went to the base of the altar, at the sacrifice's feet. She realized that this was where Jeanine probably stood during the sacrifice rituals. Majken pressed both hands on the edge of the thick stone platform and dug her heels into the ground.

She pushed hard, then harder.

The stone altar rocked slightly.

The silent screams of the damned in this place, dying sacrifice after dying sacrifice, echoed in her mind. Her muscles bunched and she pushed even harder. Her feet made a deep indentation in the earth.

With the sound of grinding and broken concrete, the sacrificial stone slid off the four rock pedestals; it fell into the ravine floor. Majken panted in the center of the boulders that had formed the base. Ciecuvich lay even with the pack of wolves gathering around him.

"You can't leave me here like this!" he screamed, unable to get free. Majken took Alecia from Thomas and walked uphill.

Her sensitive hearing clearly heard the ripping of flesh as the wolves attacked the blood cult leader. Alecia started crying as they topped the northern ridge.

Majken and Thomas walked hours along the desolate US highway back to Helena. They exited from the forest at the tip of the northern loop, crossed the road, and continued until the moon had passed its zenith and was descending behind them.

The sound of motorcycles filled the air.

Majken heard them coming long before they were visible as a mirage ahead. At the convenience store she remembered about thirty motorcycles. The pack approaching were roughly half. When the first two gang members saw her holding Alecia and Thomas standing with her on the highway, they made a whoop cry and circled back.

Thomas tensed.

Majken remembered some of the faces.

A man with long silver locks and huge belly stopped before her. He rode a chopper with a gondola car. The blonde woman with him was very thin. Her flaxen hair had streaks of silver-gray. When the man held his fist up, the motorcycle roar stopped. "Need your ride now?" he asked. The other men with him, ten in all, sneered at her. Five women watched.

Majken regarded the outlaw biker.

The faint glow of Helena was just over the rise in front of them. Less than an hour's walk away.

"No, thank you," she replied.

Two of the bikers got off their motorcycles and approached her and Thomas. Thomas backed up warily.

The huge man in front of her ambled off his motorcycle. The thin blonde woman with him climbed out of the gondola. "Oh," she said, and tried to touch Alecia's face. Majken subtly changed her posture to keep Alecia out of the woman's reach.

The biker in front of her made a motion to his chest. "Me and the guys feel bad that we didn't give you a ride back in town. We don't just pick up everybody we meet. Now, we'll be greatly insulted if you refuse our company."

Three other bikers dismounted from their motorcycles. Two of the men dragged lengths of chain that scraped the roadway.

Alecia was staring at the bikers. Her face was expressionless. Majken's eyes softened in Alecia's face, then turned neutral to address the biker huffing and puffing in front of her. Majken commented, "If you will take us to Helena, we will be most grateful."

By the fading moonlight, Jeanine's dried blood was still visible on her hands and arms. The biker in front of her seemed to notice the telltale signs of a serious fight and bloodshed.

He smiled broadly.

The huge biker barked commands to his people. He and the men with him climbed back on their motorcycles. The thin blonde woman got behind the huge man on his own motorcycle, leaving the gondola vacant. A biker pulled alongside Thomas and grabbed his shoulder to direct him to climb on.

Majken bundled Alecia in the loose flannel shirt and got into the gondola. Alecia seemed to perk up as the bikers escorted them into the heart of Helena. The little girl turned into the wind as streams of cool night air caressed her face. Majken could not hear the little girl's heartbeat with the roar of motorcycle engine in her ear, but she felt Alecia's blood swishing faster in her tiny body.

Little thrill seeker, she thought.

The rest of the biker gang met and joined the procession.

Majken judged it was well past midnight when the bikers found a saloon somewhere in the heart of Helena. She smiled ruefully as the mass of bikers embarked into the bar. If they were thinking of closing, the bar had just been granted extended hours of operation by the uninvited guests.

The biker leader with long silver hair that had brought her was joined by an equally huge man with long curly reddish-brown hair, the other man at the card game. They spoke for a moment turned away from her. Biker women gathered around Majken and Alecia. Seven women altogether, including the thin blonde that had first tried to touch Alecia. Majken approached the two bikers.

"She needs clothes," she said, glancing at Alecia in her arms, "and we need a place to clean up and sleep."

Already the bikers had loud playing music from inside the bar. Thomas was pushed to Majken's side by the biker that had ridden him. The man with the reddish-brown hair grabbed a biker with long black hair and a pale scar along his throat.

He pointed the man to Alecia.

"You have a daughter her age," he said with a gruff voice. "Find this baby girl some clothes her size." The woman with him whispered in his ear. "And something to sleep in," he added.

The man with black hair was joined by the large bouncer Majken had dumped in the floor of the restaurant. He smiled a toothless grin at her. Majken addressed the biker that had given her the ride. "We need sunscreen, the highest SPF you can find, and dark glasses." She gestured to Thomas, standing beside her. "He, and I, both."

This man said, "Do it," and led Majken with Alecia and Thomas into the bar melee. The party was just getting started as they walked past the crowds inside the bar.

Another biker held an older man by the scruff of his collar and presented him to the biker leaders. "Here's the owner."

The biker with long silver hair placed a meaty arm around the neck of the owner. "I would consider it a personal favor if you'll let these two kids and their little girl stay in your suite at the back." The owner, with thinning white hair, and full moustache and beard, quickly agreed.

They could have whatever they wanted.

Majken took Alecia with her into the suite. The office had full mahogany paneling, a wet bar, and a huge aquarium with tropical fish. The rear of the office had a large circular bed and bathroom. The bedspread was velvet and the ceiling had mirrors.

Thomas looked in the black refrigerator and found nothing but booze. He made a face and grunted with displeasure. Majken knew he wanted water. She directed him to use the crushed ice and chilled water dispenser next to the sink. He drank two glasses of ice water straight away, then ran fingers through his thick ash brown hair. He unzipped Ciecuvich's coat. It was big on him. He plopped on the edge of the circular bed.

Majken set Alecia down for the first time since they left the sacrifice site. Her father's loose flannel shirt hung around her body like a nightshirt. The little girl padded on bare feet to the bed and climbed next to Thomas. Majken took a moment to go to the bathroom and wash the residue of Jeanine's blood from her hands and arms.

When she stepped back into the bedroom suite, Alecia had crawled into the bend of Thomas' arm and they were both laying back staring at their reflections in the mirrored ceiling above them. She climbed on the bed opposite Alecia and lay next to Jeanine's traumatized baby girl. Numb, her body greatly needed sleep after consuming blood hours ago. She had forced herself to remain up out of dire necessity. Alecia seemed to regard her with bright, clear, trusting eyes. Majken looked directly into Alecia's eyes and remembered her promise to Jeanine just before she died.

Jeanine had surely loved Alecia well.

A sudden knock at the door roused Thomas. He got up. The bikers had brought Alecia some clothes and the other items Majken had requested. Majken saw Thomas lay the procured items on the manager's desk and fall back onto the bed. "Are we going to be safe here?" Thomas asked. Majken felt herself going under.

"Thieves' honor," she said, fading from consciousness.

Whatever had happened to her, Alecia would talk when she was ready and only then.

Majken drew Thomas close to her before he awoke. Having passed her comatose sleep after feeding and having rested with natural sleep, she wanted to touch Thomas and feel close to him again. She watched him sleep until she could stand to wait no longer. She kissed him lightly.

His eyes fluttered open, so much like a little boy's. He smiled at her and lay face to face. Thomas gazed into her dark violet eyes. The stubble on his face had grown into the start of a proper beard. She rubbed her fingers across the hair of his chin and decided she liked it. She searched his brown eyes. This was their first real moment together after losing him and finding him again.

She drew his face close to her and kissed him. Lightly at first, then with fervency.

A sob escaped from his lips.

"I thought we were goners," he said. "When I heard the wolves howling, it brought back my recurring nightmare. Then I saw you. My dream finally made sense. The wolves were never hunting me to destroy me. They were hunting me to help you."

Alecia slept soundly on her opposite side cuddled with the toy bear the toothless biker had brought her. The little girl refused to give up the flannel shirt to sleep in. She said Jeanine often wore her dad's shirts around the cabin in the early mornings.

Majken gave a nod of her head and quietly slid to the edge of the circular bed. Thomas slid to the edge with her. Alecia continued to sleep soundly. Standing together, she melted into his arms as he reached for her. The bar was finally silent. Most of the partying bikers had left just before sunrise to find a place to dine. They promised to return soon.

Majken led Thomas into the deserted bar. Evidence of the all-night party was strewn everywhere. Faint morning light filtered from the front of the bar. By all accounts, it was a beautiful sunny first of October morning. They walked to the bar counter together. She told him how she found Jeanine.

Thomas bowed his head and leaned with his body weight on his right arm against the wall. He closed his eyes against the pain. Majken reached for his arm. "Look at the beautiful little girl she raised," Majken said, speaking of Alecia. "Whenever you see her, you will see Jeanine live on." Almost on cue, the roar of motorcycles outside signaled the return of Majken's babysitters.

The thin blonde woman, Esme by name, came in first with an order of biscuits and gravy for the little princess. Only a third of the bikers had returned.

Majken spoke for a few moments to the three biker women who remained. They promised to take good care of Alecia while she was taking Thomas to the bus station. She led Thomas back into the office suite. Alecia woke up.

While Thomas put on sunscreen, Majken knelt before Alecia as she slid to the edge of the bed. The little girl seemed afraid at first. When Majken reached for her, she held her arms wide. Instantly, the little girl flew into her arms. She gave Majken the biggest hug she had ever gotten.

She held Jeanine's baby girl.

Majken remembered the peace in Jeanine's eyes. The only thing she thought about was saving Alecia. Majken smiled at Alecia, but was saddened that she never had the opportunity to know Jeanine herself. Thomas knelt beside Majken.

He lifted the stuffed bear that had fallen onto the thick carpet, and made a voice for the bear, and made the bear dance for Alecia

She giggled and reached for the toy bear.

Majken stood and applied her sunscreen, and found the dark glasses the bikers had found for them. She heard a light knock on the door. Esme appeared with the little girl's breakfast. One of the other biker women, a younger teen with reddish hair, streaked with blue, came in to keep Alecia company.

Majken knelt and promised Alecia she would soon return after she made travel arrangements for Thomas. Two bikers gave them a quick lift to the city transit station. Inside Majken arranged for Thomas' tickets and passage to New Orleans. Thomas leaned nonchalantly at the counter as she paid for his tickets. The bus station had filled up.

He thumbed through his tickets and plotted his journey on the United States map mounted on the wall next to the restrooms.

Majken told him as they waited how Kimberly had come to Charlotte to help her find him. Thomas expressed amazement that Kimberly had figured out the blood drinking part. He kept his face neutral, but Majken sensed from his smile that he loved his baby sister very much. Majken told him to contact Kimberly to let her know he was all right.

Thomas saw a street vendor, an older black man wearing Army green, sit at a little booth. He was selling souvenirs from his suitcase as travelers came by.

He had blank dog tags. He used a little die set to stamp whatever on the tags. Thomas fished into Ciecuvich's trousers and found a wad of hundreds and twenty-dollar bills.

Thomas jammed a hundred-dollar bill and a few twenties back into his pocket and negotiated with the ex-Marine to stamp him a special set of dog tags. He gave the remaining wad of money to the crippled veteran. He held the tinkling dog tags where Majken could read them.

"A gift for Kimberly," he explained.

Majken followed him to the gift shop where he found a mailing envelope to send the gift to his beloved baby sister. He purchased postage and dropped the care package to his sister into a mailbox. Majken smiled at him.

"Who's in New Orleans?" he asked.

"A friend of mine for many years lives there. He's expecting you. I wrote him and told him you will be coming. When I've taken care of Alecia, I will join you."

"How do I find him?" Thomas asked.

"Go to the zoo. He will find you."

Majken went silent for a moment to let two elderly ladies saunter past her to the ladies room. Thomas was looking up. Majken followed his gaze to the big round clock displayed over the bus terminal. A black man came to the bay and announced Thomas' bus was now boarding.

He leaned forward.

Majken kissed him.

When he parted from her, she asked, "How do you feel?" Drifting in a sea of people flowing toward the bus terminal for boarding, Thomas seemed to look all around him. With the many scents, sounds, and colors of life all around him, Majken watched his eyes lighten.

"Alive," he said with certainty.

She kissed him again, then let him board the bus that would take him to Stefan.

Kimberly sauntered barefoot through her parent's house in the late afternoon. Rainfall had made the day especially dreary. She read the mail package she had received that morning over and over again. Addressed to her, it was surely Thomas' handwriting. She slipped the dog tags over her head.

Mom was outside at her garden.

Kimberly found plastic gloves, like what her Mom used to clean the oven, found bright yellow galoshes to cover her feet, and went to the basement. She stepped out of the basement door. The heavy afternoon rain pelted the earth with life-giving water. Sure enough, Mom had a pair of pruning shears in her hand. Patricia was delicately tending to the beautiful English roses that ran up the arbor. Kimberly picked up a second set of pruning shears and came to her Mom. "Show me what to do," she said.

The older woman seemed to regard her daughter with sudden amazement. "Dear, you've never wanted to work the garden before. What made you change your mind?"

Kimberly shrugged. "I figured I have lots of time now that I'm not working."

Patricia smiled at Kimberly. "Oh, dear. You wouldn't have worked that carpentry job much longer anyway. You are able to do so much more and your opportunity will come." Kimberly hugged her Mom.

"Thanks, Mom." She needed her Mom's faith in her. Patricia smiled at her daughter, then patted her hand and seemed to know exactly what she was thinking.

"You'll see him again dear," she said.

Kimberly pulled the dog tag chain from around her neck. One tag had her brother's first name THOMAS; the other had simply the phrase ARMY BRAT stenciled in capital letters. She smiled wistfully. "He always said the one thing an Army brat needed is a set of dog tags." Tears pulled at her eyes. She reached around her Mom. "I really miss him," she confessed.

"I know, dear," Patricia said. "But he's with her now, and they have each other. I believe they will make it. It's all in what people see, and what they choose to see."

Kimberly smiled at her Mom. She believed.

*   *   *

High clouds billowed across the night sky partially hiding the blue-white light of the waning moon. Three days in preparation, Majken carried Alecia on her back up to the site she had prepared for Jeanine's burial. Alecia started crying as soon as she saw Jeanine's body. Majken had washed her hair, cleaned the blood off her, and had dressed her in the prom dress Alecia found in her closet. Majken knelt before the young vampyric girl's body and Alecia climbed off her back. Two days before, she had found and gave to Alecia all of Jeanine's journals. Nine in total.

Farther down, they found a pretty silver crucifix, a rosary, and a prayer book.

Before Majken sealed the body bag to lower into her hidden grave, the air was sweet and gentle under the waning moon. The air itself was peace.

Alecia was sobbing over her Jennie.

Majken touched the silver crucifix placed around Jeanine's lovely neck. She slipped the prayer book in her hands folded over her chest and twined the rosary loosely in her right hand fingertips. The night was broken by the heartfelt tears of a little girl as she trembled and laid the fallen crayon drawing, she made and gave to Jeanine the day before they started running, on her Jennie. The little girl kissed Jeanine on her forehead, sat back, and bowed her head. Majken quietly sealed the bag, lowered it, then covered the grave. She knelt beside Alecia.

Alecia buried her face into Majken's shoulder and begged her to say something. Majken spoke, "Here lies Jeanine Rose Bryer, beloved daughter of Steven Bryer and Roxana Mihnea Bryer."

Her voice cracked and paused.

"God is gracious."

She turned Alecia to face her. "Look at me, sweetie.

Look at me." Alecia looked at her.

"She loved you with all that was within her. She gave her life for yours." Majken tapped her little chest. "All that she is to you will continue to live inside here." She touched the place over Alecia's heart. "You will always have her here."

So much the peace on Jeanine's lovely face.

Majken picked Alecia up and held her on her hip. "Jeanine is at peace, sweetie. Jeanine finally made it home."

Epilogue

Thick low storm clouds obscured the flat Texas expanse, miles upon miles of desert, prairie scrub grass, and sun baked rocky soil. Majken shifted in the back seat of the luxury sedan sandwiched between a young woman expounding the virtues of all natural herbal remedies and a college professor debating the probable long-term effects of the recent rise in international trade with China.

She gazed out the tinted back windshield at the storm clouds and intermittent flashes of lightning.

Hitchhiking from Van Nuys with these people was not her most inspired mode of travel, but she was able to acquire blood easily since these fellow travelers literally passed out when they slept. Their driver, Wild Man Brad, sported curly dreadlocks. He liked the head banging heavy-metal music.

Alecia was safely with her mother and new family.

Sarah Ciecuvich had remarried and moved, but Christopher was finally able to locate her. Majken need offer no explanation to Sarah as to why Alecia's father will not be coming around to reclaim custody. Alecia's new step-father and younger half-brother took up with her instantly.

Majken had high hopes for Alecia. Placing her in a loving family would go far in helping her erase and recover from what her father had tried to do to her. Majken promised herself she would check on Alecia every ten years or so. Their driver was shifting in the road as he fiddled with the radio to find a station he liked.

An oncoming truck swerved into the median.

Headlights flared head on.

A sudden boom, shattering metal, and screaming turned the sedan into scraps of grinding debris shredding apart along the rain-soaked highway.

Majken felt the roof of the sedan collapse as it rolled over and over. A sharp metal spike pierced her left hip.

The girl next to her was instantly killed in the collision.

When the rolling stopped, she was hanging upside down. Through the spider cracked front windshield, she saw red flashing lights approaching before she faded from consciousness.

www.ingramcontent.com/pod-product-compliance
Lightning Source LLC
Chambersburg PA
CBHW051940020726
47501CB00001B/203